An Affair in Mexico

Mexico

A Novel

by

Jack Pausman

DORRANCE
PUBLISHING CO
EST. 1920
PITTSBURGH, PENNSYLVANIA 15238

Dorrance Publishing Co
585 Alpha Drive
Pittsburgh, PA 15238
Visit our website at *www.dorrancebookstore.com*

ISBN: 978-1-6366-1199-0
eISBN: 978-1-6366-1789-3

An Affair in Mexico

Chapter 1

THE LATE AFTERNOON SUN BEAT DOWN the southern Arizona highway. The red 1967 Ford F100 hurriedly moved north bound as it rolled on to North Grand Avenue just south of Tucson. The driver, Arturo Gonzales, left his modest home, which sat just off the corner of Calle Paseo Chula Vista south side of Nogales. Travelling in and out of the United States was common—not so much today.

It was an hour ago, Maria Gonzales was standing in her kitchen preparing breakfast for her husband and two daughters. The knock on her door startled her at first, then she calmly asked her elder daughter to answer the door. Through the kitchen and dimly lit, narrow hallway, Sofia could see the two large figures at the door. She barely opened the door when the men, who did not stop to state their business, burst into the house. The guns pointed at the at the older girl, they then brandished a pistol toward the youngest. The demand to know the whereabouts of Maria's husband was heightened by the continual flailing of their pistols in Maria's face.

Arturo Gonzales stepped from the back room screaming, "What do you want? Get out of my house!"

Marcus Calaban, a lieutenant in the Morales cartel and two thugs moved close to Arturo. Calaban snuffed his cigar on the end-table then knocked it over breaking the small lamp in the process.

"We know you travel to the United States often. You will make another trip today."

The intrusion was a blanket disregard for the safety of Arturo's family and their demeanor was that of an irrational mob. The girls hung on to their mother while the assault took place. Calaban moved closer and jammed an envelope in Arturo's face. Gonzales backed up against the window and Maria's curtains. The white paper envelope contained fifteen $100 bills. Arturo stared at the envelope then back at his wife. Sofia had tears flowing down her eyes; Maria stared at the floor and at her girls. Arturo was shaking so hard, the floors of the house seemed to respond in kind.

"I don't understand," he said. Fifteen-hundred dollars was a lot of money for them, and it was an amount of money that could be enough incentive to do what he was told.

The sun was especially hot today as he remembered the morning events. His truck being without air-conditioning made it even hotter. The straight-line six-cylinder engine was running hot, as usual, but there was no time to stop for water—and no place, even though his engine required it.

Gonzales remembered Calaban's words as he spoke in clear terms. Another envelope—another $1,000.

"This is for customs. Your wife and children will be safe with us."

Sofia was 15 years old and understood her mother's fear. The tears mingled with Sofia's facial sweat, and as it reached her lips, she wiped the salty mixture on her sleeve.

Calaban was a big man, Arturo remembered. The cigar being held in his teeth was black and saliva oozed from his mouth, making the tobacco wrapper wet and limp. The smell permeated throughout the living room. When he smiled, his rotten teeth accentuated his very red gums. He thought of the gash that split his left eye brow and stopped at his eye-lid. It was apparent to Arturo that Calaban was a member of some sort of a gang.

But why me? he thought. He continued his drive north out of Nogales.

Arturo's wrinkled hands, wrapped tightly around the old steering wheel. They bore callouses of a common laborer, and southern Arizona was his workplace. For the last twenty years, Arturo's father migrated from Nogales to northern California to pick the grapes and then south to pick avocados until the day he died. As a child, he remembered his disgust with his father's lack of skills. Now, the nervous twinge in his face was not so much for the border crossing, but more for his family's safety. The process of entering the United States was less complicated with his workers' permit since he crossed the border many times in the last twenty-two years. Arturo conjured up the difficulty in bringing back some kind of contraband. The thought of being arrested and thrown into a Mexican jail was making the veins in his head explode.

He continued his trip regardless of the emotional pain and went through the border gate. He entered the United States without issue. That was an hour ago.

Once on Grand Avenue, he proceeded north, past the Sacred Heart Church to his destination. Throughout the trip, he thought about the instructions and why he was driving to a strange house. The old truck creaked as he rolled over newly repaired highway. More than anything else, Arturo imagined, *How am I going to get back across the border with whatever someone is going to give me? A package that probably contains something illegal.*

He parked in the driveway close to the free-standing, weather-beaten garage. He was greeted by two men; one in farmer's overalls and the other in a torn tee-shirt and jeans. Arturo followed the men into a one-car garage. The double doors barely worked, but they grudgingly swung open after much effort.

The small garage was lit by gaps in the cedar planking across the back wall, allowing narrow spears of light to pass through the openings. Arturo noticed the corner of a wooden box beneath an old farm tool; probably a corn shucker, maybe from the 1920s. The grinder was missing, and most of the tool was completely covered in rust.

One of cartel thugs moved to the tool and lifted it from the equally rusted hook while Arturo watched with interest and concern. A crowbar hung on the adjacent post as he reached to remove it from its resting place. He moved back to the crate.

Arturo leaned forward.

"What's in it?" he asked.

One of the men turned back and scowled at Arturo. The other jammed the crowbar beneath the planks and extracted the nails from the crate.

"This is what you will be taking back into Mexico," one man said. The crate contained 12 Colt AR-15 semi-automatic carbines.

"This is your cargo, and *that* truck you drove will be the way you will take these guns across the border," the second man said as he picked up one of the guns and poked Arturo in the chest with the composite stock.

"This will never work," Arturo responded.

One of the thugs stepped toward him with a pistol aimed at Arturo's head.

"Wait, wait! Let me think about this for a minute…" *His family*.

Another man reached out and lowered the other man's gun, asking, "How do you plan on getting these guns across the border, Gonzales?"

"Ten minutes, just give me 10 minutes to think about this." Arturo walked out the garage and looked at his truck and then back to the rifles.

"Okay, we will remove the wooden slats and rails in the truck-bed. We will then install another set of rails one-half inch deeper than the width of the rifles. Right now, go to Home Depot and buy another complete set of bed rails and 12 six-inch wide oak slats; I'm going to the UPS Store to buy a roll of bubble-wrap."

He placed both arms on the truck's bed rail and nodded.

This could work.

His eyes scanned the garage and saw a blow torch.

"I think we have everything here we need to change the bed of the truck."

The new sub-floor was completed in about two hours, and each gun was wrapped in a protective polymer coat and then bubble wrapped. After that, each piece was strapped down with duct tape, and the old bed rails were re-installed. The old wooden slats were replaced using the same screws and Arturo was then ready for his trip back to Mexico. It was just before 2:15 in the afternoon.

"One more thing," one man said, "We are going to place twenty 10-pound bags of coffee in the bed of your truck and cover it with a tarp. If anything becomes loose, the coffee will muffle the sound, and the dogs can't smell anything through the coffee. Vaya con Dios."

Arturo thanked him.

"What is your name?" he asked anxiously.

"José. José Barrientos."

"Good-bye, José," he said as he jumped in his red Ford's driver's seat.

Arturo was nearing 60 years of age and had owned the truck since he bought it from his father. He was not educated but enjoyed a beyond-average amount of common-sense. His years allowed his nerves to engulf him all the way to the border crossing, and now that he saw the border coming up over the hill, the anxiety was in overdrive. He counted to 10 and then again and again until he finally reached the U.S. side of the border crossing.

The line was always long. He inched up to the guard post.

"Do you have anything to declare?"

The twenty bags of coffee lay strapped down by bungee cords in his truck bed covered with a tarp. Unnoticeable beads of sweat dripped from his thick of mass of graying black hair.

Out of the corner of his eye, he picked up a couple of whining German Shepherds. Some were sniffing around other vehicles, and one was approaching him—handler in tow. The dog knew what he was there for and walked around the vehicle.

The weapons are clean of any oil or gunpowder, Arturo thought.

The agent stood at the tailgate as the dog impatiently waited for the handler's command. The agent glanced at Arturo and stood fast waiting for acknowledgment. Soon Arturo nodded and the command was given.

The two-year old puppy with rather large canines executed a couple of 360-degree turns, sniffed the bags of coffee, and stood at the edge of the bed waiting for his handler's command.

The young Shepherd jumped off the truck bed when given the okay. The border guard came out of his shack with the necessary paperwork and handed it to Arturo.

"Please fill out this form with your name and address; the duty fee will be $125."

Arturo let his nervousness get the best of him, and his hands began to sweat. He finished the document and handed back to the agent with shaking hands. He knew what to expect on the Mexican side. He thought, *Anything short of being shot or hauled off to jail would be a pleasant outcome.*

He rolled up to the guard house and showed his driver's license, work permit, and the duty-fee documents given to him by the U.S. border guard.

"What are you declaring?"

"Twenty bags of coffee for resale." Arturo's head was steadfast and straight forward. His eyes blinked only once.

"Let me see them." Arturo turned off his engine and went to the back of the truck and threw open the tarpaulin that covered the coffee. "Take one from the bottom of the stack and open it up."

"Señor," Arturo calmly protested, "this coffee will be for sale in Nogales. The dogs have already checked it. Please, señor, don't bust the bags."

"This is not duty free. Your cost is…uhm…let me see…$500 American."

"Five hundred American dollars, yes."

For the second time, Arturo pulled money out of his pocket. Arturo hid his sigh of relief, but the smile on his face was immeasurable. He drove the few miles to Nogales at the speed limit of 60 kilometers per hour so as to not draw any attention. When he turned on his street, he noticed two black SUVs parked in front of his house. It was 6:45 in the evening, and up to now, his trip had been without incident. He stopped in his driveway and took another anxious breath, then went inside.

He opened the door to see two men waiting for him. His eyes focused on them, and for an instant, he wasn't sure which would have offered more relief. The men were dressed in jeans and sweatshirts, and each carried a semi-automatic pistol. One was wearing a shoulder holster and asked him a direct question.

Arturo stammered and thought, *Federales or cartel?* He didn't know to whom or which organization's question he would be answering.

"Señor Gonzales, do you have the package?" the man asked.

Immediately, Arturo yelled, "Maria!" There was no reply. "Hija!" There was no reply.

"I brought the coffee," Arturo answered nervously, "I brought twenty 10-pound bags of coffee, and the Mexican border guards took $500 American for the duty fee. I'm supposed to deliver it to the Pietro's Convenience Store in the morning." He turned to the other man, "Where is my family?"

"Later," he said. "Right now, we're going to unload your cargo *with* the coffee. You are going to make a second trip and bring in another load of guns. If you complete this, you will get your family back."

"Señor, the timing is too soon. The guards, they will be suspicious with such short turn-a-round. Please, señor, in a few days. Let me see my family," Arturo begged.

"Your family will be dead in two days," the man said. "If I were you, I would get some sleep if you can, and be on the road in the morning."

It was now that he realized who was screwing with him.

Arturo received the phone call at 7:33 the next day. The guns were unloaded the night before, and now, the pickup was ready for another load. His breathing was heavier now as his heart raced. He buckled his belt and calmly moved to his truck.

Two miles away from his house, he picked up the Parkway north for the second time in as many days. He thought of his wife; he thought of his daughters; he thought of the many times he crossed the border to work in southern Arizona and southern New Mexico for the seasonal work when it was available.

I have my work permit and driver's license… There shouldn't be any problem getting out—just getting back in, Arturo thought. *I'll just tell them I'm framing houses in Tucson.*

A mile from the Mexican border, Arturo was getting into heavy traffic. The wait was long, and the cars were taking what seemed to be forever to clear Mexican Customs. At 1:00 in the afternoon, Arturo and his 1967 Ford pickup entered the check point.

The conversation was short and to the point. Questions were asked about work schedules and length of time out of the country

"In a day or two. We're just about through framing." He knew how to play this game; he'd played it for over 25 years. Arturo felt the stares of the border guard and continued to control his breathing. He was right. "Can I answer any more questions for you, señor?"

The guard shook his head and waved him through.

Arturo started his truck and quickly fell into line behind the other vehicles. He felt the excruciating heat inside the truck. His windows down as the beads of sweat poured down his dark brown face. Like so many others, his life had been hard, and every day was a work in progress. His daydreams would conjure up a new truck, a new house for Maria, or even a formal education for his girls.

A horn blasted in his ear.

"Move it!" Somebody yelled.

Arturo came out of his quasi trance; the vehicles he was in-line with were over 100 feet ahead of him. He waved to the driver while accelerating his truck. He finally crossed into the United States only to be met with the chain-link sliding gate blocking him from his second trip into the United States.

The questions were canned, the same asked—the same answered.

Driving north on N. Grand Avenue, his heart raced again. Maria's face appeared before him and then the faces of his girls—the Cartel. He drove past the Sacred Heart Church and thought, *Stop here. Let me think.*

He pulled off to the side of the road. He stared at the hot, plastic steering wheel for a moment and turned off the engine.

They have me by the cojones. And this will never stop; unless I stop it.

Vehicles drove passed in at high rates of speed, and dust and grime filled the air around him. He turned his head back to the church. His aged, dark eyes squinted at the spire that stood high above cutting a dark ragged edge through the blazing blue sky. The spire cast a long shadow placing the cross at his feet.

Arturo thought for only a moment, *Maybe, they can help me.*

Arturo got out of his truck and approached. As he rounded the corner, he stopped in his tracks. There was the iconic white SUV with the green stripe on the side denoting a Border Patrol vehicle. Arturo thought for a moment and decided to continue to the front door. He heard talking and watched the door open to see the priest of the church being followed by two Border Patrol agents, Jerry Messer and Franco Medellin. The priest was smiling and apparently knew the two.

"Franco, be careful out there," the priest said.

"We will, Father."

The voices faded as the agents got closer to their SUV.

"Agent Messer, take care of yourself, and keep Franco out of trouble. Be careful, there are bad people out there."

The two waved good-bye to the priest as they entered their truck.

"Señores," Arturo called out, "one moment, please."

Jerry answered, "What's up, amigo?"

A nervous tick appeared on Arturo's face as he approached the truck.

"My name is Arturo Gonzales. I live in Nogales. I don't know how to say this. I am in deep trouble. My family is in a lot of trouble, and I don't know what to do."

Franco slid out from the passenger side and walked around the front of their truck.

"Why don't you just start from the beginning," the agent asked.

Arturo told the two federal officers everything; his family; Calaban and who he was, or what he thought he knew.

"Señores, I am only three miles from the house where I will pick up more guns to move into Mexico."

"When are you supposed to be there?" Jerry asked.

"An hour ago."

"Make the trip. Do what they want, and we'll take it from here," Jerry responded by handing him his cellphone number.

Jerry slid into the driver's side and pulled out his cellphone and called his captain. He told him of the chance meeting with the Mexican national and explained his situation.

"Captain, with your permission, we'd like a meeting with the district director. We'd like to be assigned to this case full-time." When the boss asked, why, Franco took the phone and explained that a relationship had started to grow, and the two would like to finish it.

The captain agreed, and the next day, the meeting occurred with the people in San Diego, and all agreed. The district director notified the FBI and the agent in charge located in Phoenix. He assigned Special Agent Jonathan Conroy to the case.

A phone call to the agent was short and to the point. Jonathan was to be assigned to and run with the two agents from the Border Patrol. The gun-running sting was probably the tip of the iceberg, and other agencies would be brought in to assist as needed.

The passing minutes offered up more uncertainty, and now, Arturo's pounding heartbeat was giving him headaches. He spoke with the Border Patrol, and by doing so, he had just signed his and his family's death warrant. A few minutes later, he was in front of the house on West Bilby. The sight of Antonio Morales standing in the doorway, created the thought of scorpions crawling up his arm. Morales was the leader of the northern Mexican Cartel. His cold steel eyes greeted Arturo was one of distain.

"Where in the hell have you been?"

How did he get into the U.S.? There are a dozen warrants out there for this man's arrest.

"The lines were backed up over a mile from the border. It took longer than I expected, señor."

Antonio "King" Morales was wanted by his government for over 100 murders of both civilians and Federales. In 2009, he kidnapped the daughter of the local constabulary and demanded a $50,000 ransom to be paid in three days. The ransom could not be met. The policeman begged and pleaded but went unheeded. His daughter had been a paraplegic since an automobile accident severed her spinal cord seven years previous. Morales removed her head with a chainsaw while she was sitting in her wheelchair; her hands and feet strapped tightly to the frame; she was 15 years old.

Morales was raised by his grandmother after his father, Ricardo, was shot to death by the Federales for robbing a bank in San Luis Potosi. His mother suffered from Gran Mall all of her life and was put to the test when the doctor's told her that having children would be a high-risk event. Ricardo wanted a son, no matter what the risks were, and one night, after drinking with friends at local bar, he came home and raped his wife.

He saw no special need to make periodic visits to his wife's doctor, even though his pregnant wife complained of incessant pains in the abdomen. Ricardo finally succumbed to her painful screams, and at six weeks before the due date, he took her to the emergency room. The resident on duty was horrified. The hospital's director of gynecology was called in to assist. The conclusion from the battery of tests was simple: there was too much amniotic fluid cycling through the fetus' system. The mother was weak and in excruciating pain. The doctors concluded since the fetus was totally viable, they would take it, even though shy of the six weeks normally needed. Two days after Morales' birth, his mother died.

Ricardo Morales now had a son. He would raise the boy the way he wanted to without the interference of sickly woman. He asked the child's abuela to raise the boy during the day, and the grandmother responded that she would if he would keep her in tequila. Morales was on the street when he was six years old. His father was always out of town doing something that never resembled honest work but would always bring Morales a gift when he came home. Morales held a special fondness for the cap pistol his father bought him. When Morales was eight, Ricardo brought home a Daisy "Red Ryder" BB gun and gave to his young son.

The police came to the house one day to question Ricardo about a robbery in Zumpango, a little hamlet north of Mexico City. They entered the house; Morales leveled his BB gun and open-fired at the policeman. The first BB hit him in the chest, but the second took out his right eye. Thus began Morales' odyssey into juvenile jails and onto his self-indulged career path. By the time Morales was 21 years old, two men had fallen dead by his hand; one was 17 years old.

One night in 1992, Morales and one of his rolling buddies decided to rob a convenience store. They walked in the store with guns drawn and a bandito mask on their face. They barged into the store and saw another robbery taking place.

"What the hell are you doin' at my robbery?" screamed Morales.

"What the hell are *you* doin' at *my* robbery?" responded the would-be thief.

With the confrontation going on, the store owner yelled out, "What the hell are both of you doing in my store? He reached below the first shelf and pulled his Smith and Wesson .357 Cobra and screamed at all three of them, "Get the hell out of my store!"

The men ran out the door laughing all the way to the curb. They removed their masks.

"What's your name, amigo?"

"Alejandro Vargas. A-M-I-GO. What's yours?"

"Antonio Morales, and this is Marcus Calaban. We didn't get any money; you didn't get any money, you wanna go back and kill the guy?"

"Nah, I'm gonna get drunk."

"We're with you, A-MI-GO," laughed Morales.

Chapter 2

"*Bring your truck around the back* and then get your ass in here, idiot," Morales said.

Moments later, Arturo entered the house staring at Morales and three of his men. One of them was his lieutenants… *Alejandro Vargas is here – Holy Christ!* There was more reward money standing in the room than he could ever imagine existed. *How do I tell the Border Patrol? How am I going to get out of this alive?*

"You are going to have to do a little more for us this trip," said Morales.

"Come here, old man!" the lieutenant chimed in.

Vargas came out of the shadows looking like an animal that would slice your head off just as soon as look at you. The house was dirtier than before with pizza boxes and cold pizza on the floor. Arturo looked around and said, "Hello" to José. He nodded in response.

Vargas grabbed him by the collar and pushed Arturo into the nearest bedroom. The lighting was meager at best, but Arturo could see the contraband—whatever it might be.

Nervous, he asked, "What's in *those* boxes?" As Arturo looked closer, he realized his fate. "Holy Mother of Jesus, it's dynamite. You want me to take *that* across the border, no way! I can't take that into Mexico!"

"You can, and you will!" exclaimed Morales.

"Señor, I designed the truck to move only 12 rifles; nothing more, señor."

"You will carry this across the border, or you and your family will die." Morales repeated.

"Maybe you will die anyway, punto."

The entire room broke into laughter.

Arturo quelled the laughter.

"Señor Morales, there is no place to hide the explosives in my truck. In my opinion…"

"There is no room for your opinion here." Vargas interrupted him as he leaned into Arturo's face. "You *will* carry the guns and the dynamite, or you *will* die—right here; right now."

Arturo was dying inside. *The heat was bad enough; the bouncing over Mexican roads; the Mexican border guards, you will never live through this, and your family is dead. How do I contact the Border Patrol? That's the problem…*

"Well, cobarde, how are you going to do this? …Are you listening?" the lieutenant jumped in again.

"Si, señor. I'm listening, but it won't work. The sweating alone will make it unstable. A truck like mine—it just will not work. Maybe there is another way. I have a question."

"What is it now?" Vargas asked.

"What are you going to do with it? I mean, how are you going to use the dynamite?"

"I'm about done with you, punto."

Arturo wrangled his way up and out of the chair.

"My grandfather, señor."

"What in the hell does your grandfather have to do with it?" Morales asked.

"He was in a special demolition unit in the Army and caused all kinds of havoc with the German rail system in World War II. He knows how to use what is called white phosphorous. He has told many stories to us. Señor, if you will listen, this can work. So, I ask you again, what do you want to do with it?"

"None of your busin…" interrupted the lieutenant again.

"Shut up, sit down, and learn something, Vargas!" blurted Morales. "Tell me more, Gonzales."

"My grandfather told me about the properties of phosphorous and how it bursts into flames when it comes in contact with the air, so it must be kept in water to maintain stability."

"So?" asked Vargas.

"So, what does water do when it hits the air?" Arturo asked.

The lieutenant could not contain himself, "Nada."

King wheeled his body around, facing his cohort. He yanked his Browning 1911 semi-automatic pistol and shoved the gun barrel up Vargas' left nostril, screaming, "Keep your mouth shut, Vargas!" then turned back to Arturo, "Continue, Señor Gonzales. What does water do when it hits the air?"

"Well…it evaporates, Señor Morales. It evaporates, and the dissolved phosphorous is now in contact with the air as well. When the phosphorous hits the air, it bursts into flames."

King reeled backwards, his eyes widened.

"Where can we get it, and you say it is stable, right?"

"We have to find some, but we can literally hide it in the bed of my truck—in the open. It would only be water, but I wouldn't want to drink it."

"Go get as much as you can, Arturo, and take Vargas with you."

"Señor, please—not Vargas. Look at him. He hasn't had a bath in a month. His face is disfigured from knife cuts, half his teeth are missing, and he doesn't exactly show himself in a way that some would feel comfortable in selling him anything."

The room broke out in laughter again.

Barrientos stepped forward.

"I'll go with him, señor."

Barrientos lived in the house on W. Bilby for over three years and was connected with Morales for all that time. The Mexican government and the U.S. never had a reason to have Barrientos on their radar, but after today, things might be different. Morales agreed and sent both of them on the phosphorous buying mission—together.

—•◊•—

Hours passed. Jerry and Franco, in line with their captain since the meeting with district, maintained their concern about Arturo Gonzales. The wheels were set in motion, and now Jonathan was involved. Within an hour, the two law enforcement agencies were brainstorming strategies. Jonathan listened carefully to Franco. Franco briefed the FBI agent on who Arturo Gonzales appeared to be and what his personal concerns were.

Franco chimed in, "We have the address in Tucson."

The captain proceeded to his communication room and called Agent Mike Thornton. Brought up in Detroit, Mike spent 12 years in the Detroit Police Department. Four of those were undercover. He was very comfortable being around blacks and Latinos alike. He was married to the prettiest girl in high school, and they had two children. On the night of July 15, 1998, a rail of bullets flew through his living room window almost hitting his youngest son. He decided that night he couldn't stop the influx of drugs on a local level, so he was going to do it at national level. He and his family moved to Arizona, and the Border Patrol picked him up as soon as he applied for an open position.

"Mike, get in your car, and go to West Bilby and sit. Keep us updated as much as you can."

"Roger that, Captain."

"How do you intend to play this, Captain?" asked Jonathan.

"We'll help him as long as he helps us. He turned on his own accord, so we'll keep him in play until we get these guys." The Joint Task Force Strategic Planning Board was put up on the wall, and the cast of characters were placed as soon as their names were known. In the dead center of it was the name *ARTURO GONZALES, MULE.*

At that moment, Jerry's cellphone rang.

"Jerry? …Gonzales is on the move, and he has someone in his truck with him."

Jerry responded loud enough for everyone to hear.

"That's strange; he hasn't had the time to load the rifles. Follow him, and don't get too close, Mike."

"Roger that!"

Franco asked Mike to go civilian; no uniform, civilian automobile only, and just follow his movements. The Ford pick-up turned north on Grand.

An hour later, Franco called Mike, "Mike, what's goin' on?"

"They're just driving, Franco."

"Next traffic light, have an accident," Jonathan jumped in. "Be subtle, but find out what you can."

Mike confirmed the instruction and then at the next traffic light turned red, he banged into the rear of Arturo's truck. Mike got out and peered at the damage, he yelled to the driver, "I am really sorry, buddy."

Arturo came out of the driver's side and confronted Mike rather loudly, "You don't pay attention. You hit my truck."

"Yes sir, and I am really sorry. I just wasn't paying much attention. Here's my driver's license and insurance card." Mike pulled out his Border Patrol I.D. Arturo was desperately trying not to have apoplexy.

He whispered to the officer, "*Gracias A Dios*. They are here; all of them, are here."

After regaining his composure, Arturo spoke in a normal voice, "It's okay; let me write down my information."

Arturo took the officer's note book and wrote the words:

King Morales, Alejandro Vargas, want to smuggled dynamite. Suggested moving phosphorous instead.

At that moment, the passenger's side door began to open.

The officer quickly said, "Thank you, Mr…Gon-za-les, my insurance company has offices in Nogales and they *will* be contacting you. Good-bye."

"Damn Gringo, I've had this truck for 46 years, and only the paint job sucked, and…now look at it!"

"Don't worry about it. Let's just find a fertilizer plant," José told him.

Arturo didn't tell him that processed phosphorous is not the same as raw, white phosphorous, but they drove on anyway.

Mike was barely out of ear-shot of the car when he called Jerry.

"Put me on speaker, Jerry." There was pause then, "Guys, we've struck gold. King Morales is here in Tucson, and he's got Vargas with him. They've got the ARs, but now, you can add dynamite to the mix. There is no way, Gonzales is going to get past the border carrying dynamite."

"They are expanding," Jonathan said.

"However," Mike continued, "Gonzales is maneuvering them into a different mindset and is convincing them to change their plans and use phosphorous for whatever they have planned. One more thing, I think that was Barrientos with him." Mike was so excited about the prospects of this bust, he couldn't stop talking,

"I feel he has it pretty well under control. I'd suggest we wait and see where this goes."

"Mike? This is Captain Barnhart," the captain began. "Get back here, change cars, and return to the target house as soon as you can."

"Roger that, sir."

Captain Barnhart called his assistant.

"Marylou, we have three teams running down Coyotes along Ruby Road. Bring 'em in, would you, please."

"Yes, sir, right away."

Jonathan disappeared into another room and pulled out his cell phone. After depressing a hotkey, AIC Dan Rondell quickly picked up.

"What do you have, Jonathan?"

"It's big, Dan. It's bigger than what we originally thought. King Morales is in Tucson with a couple of his lieutenants; one of whom is Vargas." Rondell's experience with Vargas was pretty well known throughout the FBI.

After celebrating his twentieth anniversary with the bureau, Dan Rondell fielded a phone call from the Phoenix police that there was a Mexican national robbing the First National Bank. Rondell headed for the bank on his own and cornered the perpetrator as he was exiting the front door.

Rondell drove his car right up to the door and jumped out. It was Vargas. A half of clip from Vargas' Iuzi riddled the FBI's car, and two of the bullets hit Rondell. Rondell never forgot the robber and had spent the rest of his career chasing him down. There is this old wives' tale that came up during Rondell's initial interview; he said it was his life's dream to catch every "*drug-smugglin' son-of-a-bitch who entered southern Arizona.*"

Chapter 3

ARTURO AND BARRIENTOS LEFT the house in the red Ford, windows down, heading into Tucson.

"What do you think about the drug business, Arturo?" Barrientos asked out of nowhere.

"Huh! What? What did you say?" Arturo was in a daze, thinking about this mess he had gotten himself into and didn't answer. "I think we're gonna have to take this up again tomorrow..." He was looking for a place to turn around. "What did you just ask me, José?"

"What do you think about drugs?"

Arturo thought about his answer and his current predicament.

Almost stammering, Arturo answered, "I don't like it. Why do you do this thing?"

"In a small way, but King is neck deep in it. That is why he's runnin' guns and is gettin' as many as he can; he needs the money to pay for his larger shipments."

"Really? Who are his customers?"

"Over 60 percent of Hollywood and half of San Francisco. He has an organization in Houston and will deliver over twent-five million in Dallas alone. I found out the group in Dallas has connections with the higher-ups in New York, and they want King to expand up there."

"It doesn't seem to me that selling 12 AR-15s at a time is going produce that much money."

"It doesn't. He doesn't sell them. He is going to use them to destroy his competition. He is totally indiscriminate in his killing; women and children are usually the first to go."

"So why does he want the dynamite?"

"That's why you had him reelin' with your phosphorous story. He's going into Sinaloa in two weeks to blow up a train going from Mazatlán to Culiacán. There's an Iranian ship heading for Mazatlán carrying a load of opium poppy from Afghanistan. He's gonna hijack the train."

Arturo was beside himself. Everything was coming at him hard and fast and at 100 miles per hour. Desperately trying to maintain a controlled state, he checked his hands. *Are they shaking?* He brushed his forehead, checking for involuntary sweat. He hadn't peed in his pants yet, but he was darn close.

"I've gotta take a leak."

"Yeah, me too," said José. Arturo stopped at a Shell station, and José jumped out of the car. "Me, first. I'll be right back."

Arturo thought quickly, *If I am going to call somebody, I better do it right now...* He fumbled with his phone and tried to dial the correct numbers the first time. *The three, not the six, damn it—do it again. It's goin' through...* "Hurry!"

Franco picked up the call.

Arturo yelled, "It's bad, it's really bad; worse than we thought—gotta go." He pushed the "end" button just as he saw the door being pushed open.

Jonathan asked, "What did he say, Franco?"

"It's bad, 'worse than we thought.'"

"That's it? What kind of freakin' report is that?" Jonathan responded.

Franco turned to his boss, "He was harried and sounded scared, Captain."

"I don't like this waiting," said the captain. "We are at his mercy. We can't make any money this way. What's your tail up to?"

"Captain, we received a call when he got on station, but nothing since. That was 35 minutes ago."

Chapter 4

JOSÉ LOOKED AT HIS WATCH.

"We need to get back to the house. King is going to be pissed, and you're going have to explain why we didn't buy any containers of that phosphorous stuff."

Arturo turned on West Bilby and drove past a blue 1982 Plymouth. Arturo pointed the car out to José, admiring the classic lines and the probable current cost to own one.

José responded, "Nice, but I don't recognize the guy inside the car."

Arturo's heart skipped a beat—again.

"Maybe he's waiting for the young girl who lives there."

Barrientos agreed, "Yeah, probably."

Mike watched as the red 1967 Ford pulled in the driveway. He continued to watch as the two left the truck and went inside.

Jerry's phone rang again, "They're back and in the house. I did not see anything in the truck bed. Do you guys know any more?"

"Yeah, but not much. We received a rather harried phone call about 20 minutes ago. Gonzales was freakin' out. According to him, it's worse that we thought, but we don't know what it is or how much worse."

AIC Rondell arrived just after an hour. This was Rondell's briar patch, and he was happy to be in it.

"Agent Rondell, these two Border Patrol agents are the ones who had the first contact with the mule. This is Jerry Messer, and the one standing against the wall is Franco Medellin." Introductions offered by Jonathan, they exchanged pleasantries and went directly to Arturo's plight.

"We know where he is, Agent Rondell, and we know what he's working on; at least we did until his last call." Franco gave him the message exactly what was said and exactly how it was written down.

"What do you think it means?' Rondell asked.

"Agent, I wouldn't want to guess."

"I understand he's under surveillance?"

"Yes, sir"

"Agent Messer, get me your guy on the phone. Thornton, is it? Jerry finished dialing and immediately handed the phone to the agent in charge. Mike picked up.

"Agent Thornton, this is AIC Dan Rondell from the Phoenix Office of the FBI. Are you okay to give me an update?"

"Yes, sir. I am two houses down from the target house, and I can hear talking. I am too far away to decipher what they are saying. I did see Gonzales return about 50 minutes ago with, I think, José Barrientos, a local drug dealer with connections to King Morales. There are two men sitting in a black SUV in front of the house, and I believe three inside, not including our mule." Mike paused for a moment. "Agent Rondell, I brought my spook kit with me, maybe I can pick up some conversation from the ones occupied the truck."

"We've got to get them out of the house," Agent Rondell said. "I am going to send a Tucson Electric Power truck over there that will accidently blow out the transformer that serves the entire neighborhood. Agent Thornton, see if you can set something in motion, and I'll do what I can.."

"I may have been made by Barrientos during an encounter earlier on. You may want to send a replacement."

"We will. Thanks." Rondell turned to Captain Barnhart, "Will you take care of that?"

Mike calmly got out of his Plymouth with a pack of cigarettes in his hand and moved down the street and just past the first SUV. He grabbed a cigarette from his pack, then began reaching in and padding his pockets, apparently, looking for matches. He looked on the ground and made a 360-degree turn searching for these imaginary matches (he was quite an actor).

The lead SUV's front window rolled down.

"Whatcha lookin' for, gringo?'

"I swear I had a book of matches in my pocket... Oh, well."

"Here," the driver offered the hot cigarette lighter from the truck. Mike leaned into the front window with both hands propped on the lower edge of the window jam and planted a tiny bug inside the vehicle. His head inside the cabin, he drew in a breath.

"Thanks," he said and walked away.

The micro-bug was placed. Mike and his blue Plymouth were gone, and Officer Dennis Patrick and his 2003 green Mustang with black rally stripes had taken his place.

The Tucson Electric Power truck just turned onto West Bilby. Carl Atkins couldn't believe the instructions that his supervisor gave him:

"Be professional and blow the transformer; do it accidentally, but blow the transformer. Then go to every house on the block and personally apologize to everyone. Tell them that the company is bringing out another transformer, and it should be up in about four to six hours."

Carl had been with the company for over 17 years and always did what he was told.

Inside the house, Arturo explained the problem of returning without the phosphorous. Morales leaned into him.

"Come with me, Arturo, I want to talk to you.

The two went and sat in a corner of the room.

"You are a smart man, and your idea with the phosphorous is incredible. You won't ever have to frame another house, if you don't want to. If you assist me in a particular project of mine, I will release your family.

"You make your choice," Morales said.

Like most Mexicans, all Arturo ever wanted was to provide for his family and be a good husband and father. He was genuinely afraid of this man and the situation in which he had found himself. "You will make plenty of money with me, Arturo."

"Si, I understand. When can I be with my family?"

"Tomorrow," Morales answered.

"Then yes, I will help you." Arturo continued, "Señor, there is a lot to talk about as we will probably need some assistance in acquiring the right kind of phosphorous."

"We can talk about this la—"

At that moment, all the electricity in the house and on the block went out. People were rushing out of their houses yelling at Carl; poor Carl. He then, as he was told, started at the end of the street and began steadily moving from house-to-house, apologizing for his "mistake." When he knocked on the door of Barrientos, he could hear disagreement inside. Carl was already a little apprehensive when the door opened, and Arturo stepped into the doorway.

"What's the problem there…uh…Carl?" Arturo looked at his I.D.

"I'm really sorry, sir. I mistakenly blew out the transformer, and it will be about six hours to get it fixed. Can I do anything for you until the new transformer comes?"

Arturo shook his head, "No," and turned to tell the onlookers standing behind him that it was the transformer that blew up. "We should grab some beer from the icebox and go outside," he suggested to Morales.

"We will sit in the trucks where it's cool, and you and I can talk in private."

The cartel boss took Arturo to the first SUV where the two men were sleeping.

"Get out!" he ordered and told Arturo to sit in the front passenger seat. Closing the door on the driver's side, Morales eased back in the cool armchair of one his five Cadillacs.

"Okay! What do you wish to talk about?"

The two were there alone. Arturo explained, in detail, the methodology behind one's use of a phosphorous device versus using dynamite. It was true, Arturo did not want to move the dynamite across the border, because in reality, this might be a better way.

"Jefe, tell me how you are going to use this incendiary device, so I will know how to design the bomb." Morales said nothing. Arturo then explained that during World War II, the German Rail System was the most advanced in the world, and their trains would move everything across large expanses of terrain. Because, by weight, ammunition was the heaviest and most crucial, it was transported by rail.

"My grandfather and his team urged the Allies to acquire massive amounts of phosphorous and silver nitrate. The Germans always dispatched hundreds of Wehrmacht infantryman to ride atop the cars. When the Resistance attempted to blow up the trains, they used dynamite. Because they had to be in the vicinity when they lit the fuse, they were usually caught and killed. Even if they saw someone throw a bottle of water, they would just laugh it off. My grandfather stayed in enemy territory, and he and his team were responsible for hundreds of thousands of dollars of damage and were never caught.

"King, do you know what a Molotov Cocktail is?"

"No," he replied.

"It is a bottle filled with gasoline with a cloth wick jammed in the bottle-neck. The process is simple; you light the cloth and throw the bottle at a target. The bottle breaks on impact, the gasoline catches fire—*boom!* Here's the difference between the two; you're there when it happens, and if anybody sees you, you're done. By using the phosphorous bomb, you and the target would be miles away from each other when the fire starts. No one will know why it happened or who was responsible."

Morales rolled down the window and rested his arm on the open jam just an inch away from the micro bug. He stared through the window, a Cheshire smile on his face as if he just experienced an internal orgasm.

"What do you need from me?"

"I need to know what the target is."

"We may need your grandfather," Morales smirked.

"He has passed, Jefe, but why would you have needed him?" Arturo asked, being a bit more serious.

"Because, my friend, it *is* a train."

"Will it be moving or stationary? Please give me as much of the details as you know."

King hesitated for a moment, then looked directly into Arturo's eyes.

"The train will be leaving Mazatlán the morning of the fifth at 11:30. It will arrive in Culiacán two hours and 20 minutes later. The beginning of the trip is through open plains; however, the last hour, it will be passing through a mountainous region, so it will move slower. There are grades that slightly exceed five degrees with track winding around mountainous terrain and drops of over 200 feet."

Arturo responded, "Jefe, this is not something impossible to do. The flying time; how long is it?"

"Take-off to landing, a total of two hours."

"Next, Jefe, do you have any connections where we can acquire white phosphorous?"

Now from Morales came the silence; the hesitation; and the hesitation to say anything. He gazed at Arturo at first; then he stared at him. It was quiet as a morgue for a solid two minutes—an eternity. Morales then began to smile, "Yes, I know someone in the chemical business. I have some business in Dallas. He will get me anything I want."

Chapter 5

YOU WOULD THINK THE BORDER PATROL SERVICE and the FBI just found out that Arizona State just won the BCS National Championship over USC. Everyone in the captain's office was laughing, high-fiving each other, and the same time, each one told the other to be quiet. Mike walked in and was immediately asked by Jonathan how he informed Gonzales about the bug being in place.

"He doesn't know. He has no idea he's being bugged."

Franco and Jerry looked awkwardly at each other.

King Morales, without warning, picked up his cellphone and dialed a number. The other end picked up quickly and answered, "Si, El Jefe?"

"Marcus, there has been a change in plans. I want you to release Arturo's family, apologize to them, get them fed, take them home, and guard them with your life, Marcus. If anything happens to them, I will cut you so badly, your own mother won't know who you are.

Ok, my friend?"

The answer was quick: "Si, jefe."

A sigh of immense relief came over Arturo as he smiled and shook his head, laughing, "Thank you, señor."

"I am a man of my word. José will take you to a hotel in Tucson, and we will wait for my friend in Dallas to arrive. I will call him to make the appointment."

Arturo sat there as Morales placed another call.

"Hello, my friend. We have the answer to our problem. I arrived in Tucson…no—wait! It is okay. I came in this morning through the coyotes' trails. No one saw me, and I am here making plans for our trip to Mazatlán. David, send Jack down tomorrow, and I will need you to send a truck here with two; no, three drums of white raw phosphorous."

"How are you going to get it to Mazatlán, Antonio?" the guy on the other side of the phone asked.

"We're going to discuss it tomorrow, David."

King and Arturo spoke for about an hour. Vargas would occasionally walk up to the truck and knock on the window. Morales would blow him off and tell him to go back to the other truck.

After 30 minutes, Morales looked at Arturo.

"I think it's time, my friend. I think your family is home."

Arturo picked up his phone and dialed Maria's cellphone. She answered, and Arturo cried, "Are you okay, Querida?"

"Si," she answered.

"And the girls? Are they alright?"

Sofia was the first to get on the phone. She was hyperventilating, but Arturo knew her fear.

"Papa?"

Arturo calmed her as best he could and after minutes asked to speak with Carmella. She was crying and, according to Maria, had not stopped since the event inside their home.

"In a few days, Maria, in a few days, I am coming home to my beautiful girls. I have to go now. I love you all." The phone went dead.

Chapter 6

"MARYLOU, GET THE DALLAS FBI on the phone. I have a suspicion that Agent Rondell wants to speak with his counterpart."

The call to Dallas was immediately transferred to Agent in Charge Dexter Hayes. Rondell picked up the landline and welcomed his colleague to the fray.

"Dex, we have a situation in southern Arizona that might be right up your alley..." Rondell got to the point. He laid out the back story on Arturo Gonzales and where he was—emotionally; where he was located and with whom. Rondell told him how Border Patrol Agent Thornton had surreptitiously placed a bug inside one of King Morales' trucks, and by some strange but wonderful series of events, they heard his plans, which had facilitated the phone call. Bringing Hayes up to speed, Rondell explained to Hayes the expansive plans that would include people of interest in high places in Dallas.

"Generally speaking, Dex, you got anybody on the radar up there?"

"No specific data-matching, but Culberson Petrochemical has had the I.R.S. interested the last several months. The I.R.S. performed two forensic audits on his books and were very anxious to return. He has let people go but lives high and spends a lot of money on planes and trips to New York. So, who is this Gonzales guy? How come he knows so much about arson?" Hayes asked.

"We don't know, Dex, but we sure aim to find out. Look, Dex, we need your help on this one. Open the books a little harder on this Culberson fellow. Check his account at where keeps these planes, pull his flight plan records, and let us know what you find out, would you? The troops down here are convinced the plans are to do more than just disrupt the normal flow of drugs being moved by the Mexican cartel. They plan to do a lot a killin' in the process."

Chapter 7

VARGAS LOOKED AT HIS WATCH.

"It's been over two hours since that gringo blew out my air conditioner. I'm hungry, and I'm sitting here watching that know-nothin' kissin' up to Antonio."

"Alex, give it a break," José responded to Vargas' anger. "They're talking about the bombing of Mazatlán train."

Vargas stopped talking; he stopped drinking his beer; he stopped breathing and immediately turned to face Barrientos.

"How do you know about the train in Mazatlán?" He grabbed José by the throat. Barrientos' larynx was being crushed and ripped from his body. His windpipe was now void of air. His eyes widened as he desperately tried to release Vargas' grip from his throat. Vargas' thumb and forefinger closed tighter; his eyes went red with rage.

"How do you know this? Who have you told?" His fingers never relaxed, and José had now resolved the end of his life. In less than a minute, Barrientos was dead. Vargas leaped out the truck and quickly paced around in a circle, hands cupped over his head. He stomped with rage to where Morales was speaking with Arturo.

Officer Dennis Patrick sat up in the seat of his Mustang when he saw what was happening. He grabbed his phone and pushed the hotkey.

"I don't know what just happened, but Vargas is visibly upset. He came out of the SUV like a bat outta hell, and he's heading for Morales. There's murder in his eyes. This could be bad; really bad. It took only a minute to get to the truck."

The group in the captain's office began hearing the ravings of a mad man.

"He knows, jefe," screamed Vargas.

"He knows what? What's the matter with you, Alejandro?"

"Barrientos knew about the train and he told *him*, Jefe," Vargas jabbed his finger in Arturo's face, "he told Gonzales."

"*I* told him, Loco. Go back to the truck with Barrientos and cool off."

"I've killed him."

"*WHAT!*" Morales started banging the wheel with his fists over and over. Arturo sat there with his mouth shut and his heart pounding, begging to be released from his chest.

Oh, Christ! Oh, Christ!

Jerry grabbed Franco's shoulder while listening to all of this while it was happening.

"We've got to get him out of there." Franco said.

Jonathan jumped in.

"We can't."

"We are going to lose him, damn it," Jerry yelled back to Jonathan.

The discord continued in the truck and grew louder by the minute.

"Vargas, what have you done? You stupid fool!" Morales was beside himself. "You dumb ass, are *you* going to meet Culberson tomorrow; am I?" Morales was livid. "Other than you and I, punto, the only one Jack knows is Barrientos. Who in the hell else am I going to send, Gonzales here?"

King continued his rage,

JACK PAUSMAN

"You have the strength of a bull and the brain of a gnat, Vargas. Take the SUV to the back of the house and bury him under the garage—do it now!"

King nervously fumbled with his phone. Arturo could see how inflamed he was over Barriento's murder.

"Jefe, we'll talk later. What are you going to do now?"

"This phone call has to made now." Morales looked at his phone and pushed the "1" key. One ring, and David Culberson said, "Yes?"

"David, there's been an incident. Barrientos is dead—Vargas killed him…I know, I know… Tell Jack that Marcus Calaban will meet him tomorrow. He will take him to the hotel, and I will meet him there."

"Listen to me, Antonio, this operation is costing a lot of damn money with results estimated 20- to 30-fold. Neither you nor I need crap like this. You control that freakin' idiot, or I'll be talking to the Sinaloas myself, got it?"

Morales was enraged.

Nobody talks to me that way; not this gringo; not nobody!

Arturo sat next to Morales, watching him being tormented by his own angered frustration. Shaking inside, Arturo sat quietly. King had 120 men dispersed throughout northern Mexico and the most loyal was Vargas. His temper was always the worst part of him, even as a young man.

The night they met during the holdup at the convenience store, Vargas, Morales, and Calaban went out together and got plastered on tequila. Morales was so drunk, he could barely walk. Calaban had to help him get to his front door. Vargas, weaving and unable to maneuver in a straight line, went back to the scene of the attempted robbery, pulled out his Glock 19 pistol, and placed nine bullets in the man's head. If it wasn't for the, *I love you, Lupe* tattoo on the store owner's shoulder, his wife would have never recognized him.

Vargas was a mean and angry man. His father beat him for just about anything; sometimes with a belt; sometimes with his fist. His mother was always drunk, and when his father was at work, she would have other men visiting for most of the afternoon. Vargas' father always thought he knew what was happening and *always* took it out on him.

His meeting up with Morales was like manna in Vargas' eyes. He needed to belong; he needed to be someone's kindred spirit. Morales and Vargas had been friends for twenty-six years.

King snapped out of his steering-wheel gaze when he heard:

"Jefe?" Arturo whispered. "Jefe, can the person coming in tomorrow get us the white phosphorous?"

"What? Oh…si, Arturo, his father owns a large petrochemical plant in Dallas and knows how to get the raw phosphorous and can get us all the product we want."

"What about the ship? Do you know when the ship is coming into port?"

"I am told the Sinaloas will receive the cargo in 10 days"

"Will there be any passengers on board?" Arturo asked.

Jefe answered, "Yes, there are always passengers."

"As soon as I can see a map of the terrain and the track, I feel I can come up with a plan to attack which car and when."

King listened carefully to Arturo's plan for the disruption of the Mazatlán train, but on occasion, he would blurt out, "Damn it, God damn it!" Arturo understood his annoyance with Vargas' actions and somehow his frustration.

It was 4:50 in the afternoon, and the Tucson Electric Power truck rolled up to the busted transformer, and Morales finally cracked a smile. Three vehicles drove down West Bilby. A T.E.P. maintenance truck, a lowboy with a crane carried the new transformer. A Tucson City Police car arrived with both vehicles to maintain traffic flow.

"Holy crap; now what?" Morales said as he slammed his hands on the steering wheel—again.

The innocent patrolman did his job and kept all the traffic moving around the work cones and just after 6:30, all was completed; the crane, the truck, and the cop were gone. That night, everyone was going to sleep in a cool house; all except José Barrientos.

Chapter 8

IT WAS AFTER 6:00 IN DALLAS, and David Culberson was leaving office after long day of wasting time with the I.R.S. They paid a visit unannounced earlier in that afternoon wanting to see the by-product purchasing documents. Everything purchased by Culberson Petrochemical was in the cash market except propane. The first-in; first-out inventory valuation was a cash market system that the I.R.S. agents wish to examine. Taxes were to be paid quarterly on all deliveries to inventory.

"Mr. Culberson, where are your accounts payable records?" One agent asked.

"Look, agents, my accounts payable department has gone home for the day, can you come back here in the morning; say 9:00?"

"We'll be back, Mr. Culberson. Have the last five years of bank statements available when we return," The agent in charge said. The agents packed up their paperwork and walked out the door.

David's issues began when this country's new management was sworn in in 2009. The EPA began its hindrance program against businesses that needed to engage in the mining of raw materials such as natural gas. The letters from the government were arriving about three per week. The new laws would cost petrochemical companies millions of dollars to comply.

The first meeting of the National Association of Petrochemical Plant Managers after the inauguration was in March of 2009. There were already rumors going around that there would be hundreds of new and debilitating laws coming from Washington D.C. and the EPA.

Chapter 9

IN THE SUMMER OF 2011, David and Felicia Culberson took a week off and flew his Gulfstream to Cabo San Lucas. He was working 10 to 11 hours a day, and his company had become his mistress supplanting his wife. Too many days of fighting the I.R.S. and too many nights not being with Felicia had taken its toll. Now, charities and teas had replaced her husband, and neither of the two was happy about the current arrangement.

"So now," Felicia said, sounding pleased, "we lie on beaches of Cabo."

The Mexican winds swirled from every direction, and the taste of salt was sensed with every lick of her tongue to moisten her lips. The thatch-top huts lined the beach for miles, but Felicia would hear none of it. She wanted the sun beating down on her. She wanted the sun to bathe here entire body (the authorities would have none of that as well). The ugly and unfashionable wide-brimmed beach hat covered only her face and she didn't need untanned areas to detract from her classic bronze body.

The beach boy kept her and David supplied with piña coladas for most of the day. The white powdered sands of the Baja found its way everywhere. So at the end of the day, Felicia would trek back to the room, David playfully running after her, gleefully removing the upper half of her suit before she opened the door to their room. Small accumulations of sand would fall from her now empty top. David followed quickly behind her, engaging in the same disregard for mores and disrobing as well until they entered their room lustfully rolling around on the floor.

One evening at the Cabo Wabo Cantina, they danced on the veranda, each feeling the salacious movements of their bodies intertwining. Felicia could feel David moving into her every nape and curve, and she naughtily responded in kind.

"I have to go the rest room," he said. "Hold that thought, I'll be right back."

He worked his way through the crowd of young vacationers and found one stall empty as he entered the rest room. While relieving himself, David was interrupted:

"Your woman is a very sexy dancer," a voice emanated from the adjacent stall.

David turned, "What the hell is it with you, mister?"

"I only offer my congratulations, señor. You are a very lucky man," the voice continued.

David whispered, "Not so much."

Barely hearing David's comment, the man replied, "Señor, I don't think so. I saw you arrive yesterday in that beautiful Gulfstream. You have a beautiful woman, and you must be a very rich man. *I* am a very rich man also."

"Who *are* you?" David abruptly asked.

"Lo ciento mucho, señor. I am very sorry. My name is Antonio Morales, and I still think you have a beautiful woman."

David dried his hands at the water basin.

"Thank you, Mr. Morales, and I'm going back to her now."

"I have but one question, señor, when do you go back to the United States?"

Perturbed, David responded, "What do you want?"

"I would only like to talk with you, señor—nothing more. Please, go back to your woman, and if your schedule permits, I will meet you in the morning at the hotel restaurant."

"What are you selling?"

"Nothing, señor. There are certain classes of raw materials that are of great abundance here, and I feel there is a need for a distribution network. Just a business proposition, that is all."

"Fine!" David responded.

The bathroom door closed behind him leaving Morales at the wash basin.

The subtropical lianas atop the Mexican palm trees swayed with the morning winds that penetrated the veranda door of their room. His eyelids fluttered as the rays of the sun crept in the room, facilitating the morning awakening. He rubbed his eyes, then his face, and finally ran his hands through his salt and pepper hair. His brain demanded more oxygen and forced a big yawn. With foggy vision, he looked at his Rolex Mariner and saw the hands were exactly straight up and down; it was 6:00 in the morning. The black palm tree silhouettes were outlined in daylight, signaling a new day and a promise of breakfast with the man he met the night before.

David glanced to the other side of the bed. Seeing Felicia was sleeping soundly, he rose quietly and moved to the bathroom. The hotel supplied a personal coffee maker: *A little bit to get my blood moving can't hurt.* He emerged from the bathroom and decided to drink his cup of Colombian on the veranda and feel the morning Mexican breeze. The warmth of the Baja had now reached his senses; it was invigorating, and the Pacific breeze so early in the morning gave David a sense of new life.

"What are you thinking about, David?"

He turned in his chair and looked at his wife wearing a slightly opaque sarong. Eyeing her exacting curvature, he said, "You're *up*. Why don't you stay in bed and sleep some more, honey?"

"I smelled the ocean. Lord, I love this place."

"Ms. C, I have been invited to breakfast by a guy that I ran into last night. I won't eat much, so I'll come back after the meeting and pick you up for a full breakfast. Okay?"

Felicia agreed,

"Okay, then, I'm going to take a long and effective bath, and see you in what—an hour?"

"Sure, sweetie, I'm going to get dressed."

Twenty minutes later, David left the room and headed for the restaurant. Morales was already waiting for him in the farthest seat from the entrance over by one of the many windows. He didn't rise to greet him; he just motioned to him bidding his approach. David gave him a recognizing nod.

Great! A man with no manners, he thought.

"Coffee, Mr. Culberson?" Morales was holding a freshly brewed pot above his head.

"Yeah, fine. What do you want to discuss?" Davis asked.

"Señor, I will come to the point. I wish to rent your beautiful airplane."

"That's it. This is why you got me up so early? The answer is unequivocally, NO!" Disgusted, David had barely sat down and was now on his way toward the entrance of the restaurant.

For the first time, Morales followed his lead.

"Señor, wait! Please listen to my proposal."

"You have 10 minutes, Mr. Morales."

"I will give you $2 million up front for the use of this beautiful airplane. I would only like to use it twice per month, and every subsekan, no, subsequan...how do you say...this word...?"

"Subsequent," Morales stammered a little

"Si, subsequent...subsequent years, an additional one million dollars for this rental.

It was obvious that there was surreptitious activity going on, but three, four...maybe even 10 million dollars over time would cure a lot of ills.

"How would you plan on delivering the funds?" David asked.

"Why, señor, I would give it to you in cash, of course."

Chapter 10

THE BORDER PATROL OFFICE was buzzing with its brain-storming session.

"Okay, Jack Culberson will be here tomorrow morning—good. Captain, can you get some mechanic types and some bellman and maid types operational?"

The planning board was filling up quickly like a frat party in co-ed's dorm room.

"I'm on it," Barnhart replied and continued,

"I'll call Dexter Hayes and tell him what we found out. He can get his team in place. And our team? We will start right here."

The morning sun was a classic southern Arizona. Sitting at 2,564 feet above sea level, the ground was cool at Tucson International Airport and McKensey's Fixed Base Operations was open for business. Bob McKensey owned and operated the FBO since his father passed away in 1991. His A&P mechanics were certified and professional in every way. Jonathan walked in his FBO at 8:00 A.M. and showed his FBI identification to McKensey and to him, that's all he *needed* to know.

Jack Culberson's new Beechcraft Bonanza arrived in Tucson precisely at 10:00 A.M. that morning. Jack was that way. *He* didn't like to be kept waiting nor did he want anyone to be waiting for him. He rarely stayed overnight when he had meetings in Tucson, or anywhere else for that matter. Jack once said, "A night spent in a bed is a time not being in the cockpit of my Beech."

Calaban took the SUV to pick him up and brought him to the Four Points Hotel of Tucson. Jack Culberson had no intention of dirtying himself by staying at the house on West Bilby. The ride to the hotel was quiet and Jack only mentioned once the vastness of Saguaro cacti.

The two arrived at the Four Points Hotel, and like a good soldier, Calaban gave Jack the key to his reserved suite as he stopped in front of the entrance door. He thanked Jack for the honor of picking him up and drove away. Jack entered his room as the maid had just finished turning down his bed for later that evening. Agent Cynthia Barlow thanked Jack for his generous tip, left the micro bug on top of bedpost and walked out the door.

It was 11:30 A.M. when Jack called room service for lunch. Morales was due to sneak in the hotel around 1:00. Room service was just a hotkey on the hotel phone.

"Send me one fresh lobster tail, a side of grilled asparagus, and a Vodka Martini."

Agent Samuel Mitchell thanked him for his order and began the preparation.

The idea was to debilitate Jack Culberson to the extent that it would curtail any travelling to Mexico or anywhere else. The pharmacy was just across the street. Sam requested an over-the-counter vial of insulin and a package of needles, figuring that would slow Jack's movement to a crawl. The vial of Eli Lilly insulin would certainly do the trick. A hypoglycemia attack would make him not want to get out of bed. He made the debilitating enhancements to Jack's order that would facilitate his near demise. Sam drew into the syringe 30 units of diabetic lifesaving fluid and injected it into the lobster tail. Another 20 units mixed with the melted butter was spread over the waiting asparagus and in the dipping cup. Sam saw more viscous consistency to the butter, but Jack would never take the time to notice it. The rest was poured in the martini.

The knock on the door came 40 minutes later, and Samuel Mitchell wheeled in Jack's lunch. Later, Jack lay back savoring the sweetness of his favorite Maine seafood, a delicacy that had arrived in Tucson about an hour after he did.

At 1:45, Jack heard a soft knock. He went to the door, and there was Morales wearing a hooded sweatshirt standing in front of him.

"Come in, my friend," Jack motioned without reservation. "Dad told me much of what happened, but I want to hear from you."

"Later…I want you to file a flight plan to Mazatlán, Jack."

"No! I don't think so." Jack replied.

"Listen to me, Jack, I own that fancy plane of yours, so I *want* you to file a flight plan to Mazatlán." Morales insisted. "*Our* Beech can carry an extra 200 pounds of a phosphorous cocktail easy. Remember, this is *our* plane, Jack. According to Gonzales, this has worked many times, and it will work this time."

"Who *is* this guy?" Jack asked.

Morales explained, in detail, as to how his gang had conscripted him to haul guns across the border, and when the dynamite issue came up, he told everyone about the phosphorous.

"You don't think it will work?" he asked.

"No, on the contrary, it's brilliant. It *will* work. After you told Dad and I, we looked it up in some 1st Army and 101st Airborne history. We had troops that reeked some major havoc on the Germans."

"What about the phosphorous, Jack? Is it on its way to Tucson?"

"Tell me about this guy—Gonzales? Do you trust him?"

"Yes, as long as he does what he is supposed to do. Marcus is back watching him and his family." Morales added, "One of the guys is at the store buying long-neck type bottles. We are also buying containers to hold the dissolved phosphorous, and as soon your father's shipment arrives, it will be transferred to the containers, and we will be on our way to Mazatlán."

"Antonio, listen to me, as small beads of sweat appeared on Jack forehead, If I file an international flight plan, I have to state purpose and destination, *and* go through customs when I get there."

"You're stalling, Jack. You're filing a flight plan to vacation in Mazatlán. Period. If you remember, I met David two years ago when he and your mother were vacationing in Cabo, and he flew in on his Gulfstream.

"File the damn flight plan, Jack. We're going to Mazatlán. Just re-member who paid for that fancy Beechcraft of yours. Now call your *daddy* and ask him when the white phosphorous will get here."

Jack confirmed the moving of the special cargo and reported to Morales it was on the way. The question still remained: how would this hellacious cocktail arrive when and where it's supposed to?

The conversation continued with Morales as more beads of sweat rolled down Jack's face. A strong feeling of weakness came over him. The sweat began pouring across his lips; he wanted to collapse. His behavior became irrational. He slurred the words to Morales, "Get me some help."

Jack was feeling mentally and physically disoriented. He moved to the bathroom to grab a towel, stumbling with every step. Jack placed the towel over his head, frantically wiping off the sweat that was now pouring off of him. He was weak, and his body went limp; he wanted to sleep, but more importantly he wanted food; lots of it, and now. His breathing became erratic, and he thought he was going to die.

Morales was not impressed. Jack felt his digested food entering his throat and then the vomiting ensued. By now, Jack's heartbeat was keep-ing time with his breathing. The breathing was shallow as constriction set in across his chest.

"Call a…doctor, Antonio, please." Jack cried out.

"Jack, I am not amused." Morales did not respond to his request. "I want to know when my shipment will be arriving."

"Listen to me, I'm not…faking this…Antonio," Jack slurred his words. As he spoke, the sweat continued to flow from his head like a sieve.

Potassium was drained from his body, and he felt as if he was going into a coma. A metabolic acidic concentration in the body fluids would result either from the accumulation of acids or the abnormal loss of bases from the body (as in diarrhea or renal disease). The vials of insulin lacked the correct amount of clinical testing by the FDA, and the ingestion of the drug had Jack's blood pressure dropping. He could barely stand—he could hardly breathe. He staggered and collapsed again. Now, he could feel the arrhythmia in his heart. A tachycardia was set full upon him.

Morales checked Jack's pulse. Unsure if he was doing it the correct way, he timed his heart rate at over 180 beats per minute.

If this man doesn't get to a doctor, he is going to die, Morales thought. Seeing the pale gaunt look of Jack Culberson's face, Morales had become a believer in his partner's medical problem, but he could not—and would not—become associated with it.

He tried to remember what he touched and where he touched it. So he started wiping everything clean. He missed the bedpost.

Morales grabbed his phone and dialed Calaban.

"Get over here and get me out of this hotel. There's something wrong with Culberson."

"Si, jefe, I am on my way. Shall I call security?" Marcus asked.

"No!" Morales replied.

King Morales looked at Jack lying on the floor, writhing in pain; his clothes soaked with his own vomit.

He exclaimed, "Señor, you better get help soon. You got a plane to fly." He then opened the door, looked both ways, and sneaked down the back exit and out the door into his black SUV being driven by Calaban.

Franco heard the door shut behind Morales. He immediately hot-keyed Sam Mitchell, the agent who delivered the food.

"Sam, get up to Culberson's room, and get him to the hospital. The laced lobster tail had more of a debilitating effect than we wanted."

Once again, Sam Mitchell pretended to be room service and knocked on Jack's door. There was a groan that emanated from inside the room. Sam unlocked the door, entered, and immediately ran to the phone to call an ambulance. He retrieved all the towels from the bathroom, soaked them with cold water and gathered as much ice as he could find and placed it inside the soaking wet towels. He took them to Jack and placed one on the back of Jack's neck, one under his armpit, and one, after removing his pants, between his thighs.

"I've called an ambulance, Mr. Culberson. They're on their way."

Every couple of minutes, Sam would remove a towel and replace it with a fresh cold one.

The EMTs arrived within a six-minute period and proceeded to check Jack's vitals. His blood pressure registered 105/55, and his pulse rate had dropped to 120 bpm. The EMTs placed Jack on a gurney and carried him to University Medical Center. Sam then proceeded to dispose of all plates, silverware, and glasses that were in the room and were touched by Jack. The wet towels were then used to clean up the vomit and other bodily fluids remaining in the carpet. After Sam was satisfied that the carpet was void of all remnants of Jack's mishap, he brought in a container of *Capture* and sprinkled it all over the stained area, brushed it in, and waited.

In the meantime, all the towels were burned, and everything that had any connection with Jack Culberson was erased. It was completed in under 40 minutes. Sam sat back on the sofa and called Franco.

"I'm waiting for the *Capture* to work and then there will nothing left of the stain *or* the underlying residue," Sam said, responding to a question from Jerry. "Yeah, the ambulance took Culberson to University Medical Center about 30 minutes ago; he was in pretty bad shape."

"Sam, when you're through vacuuming, go to the airport, pick up Jonathan and come back here, I have another job for you." the captain said.

"Roger that, Captain."

Chapter 11

ARTURO HELD HIS WIFE, MARIA, and their two daughters. He couldn't stop looking at them with anxious eyes. He would traipse around the room. He felt he was having apoplexy every time he looked at Maria; both had been through so much. Then, out of nowhere, his eyes would glaze over, and the tears would roll down his face. He was but a simple man now engaged in cartel activities and the possible murder of innocent people. His life has been turned upside down, trying to protect his family against these thugs. Arturo was unable to sleep throughout this mess to which he had succumbed.

Now he was being watched by the authorities in the United States and by Morales' cartel. He is about to set fire to a train that could result in sending 100 people over a 200-foot cliff.

Oh, madre mia! Arturo's heart was being attacked from all sides, and his brain was allowing all of it to destroy him. *Maria, the girls, the Border Patrol, Morales, and oh, God, let's not forget Vargas…*

"Arturo, please, don't be upset. It is all over. We are free from their tyranny now, are we not?" Maria asked.

"I know we suffered this together, Querida, but I did not know if I would ever see you and the girls ever again. I am afraid, Chickie, I am very afraid."

Maria rose from the sofa while asking the girls to go to their room. She moved ever so silently toward Arturo and placed her hand on his chest. Both hands were now resting around his neck as she drew herself closer to his body. Her thrusting motion against Arturo's torso quickly brought back memories of sexual release that was coveted by both of them before the girls were born. His body responded quickly as he caressingly moved his hands from the nape of her neck to the small of her back and then on to Maria's more erogenous parts of her body. Both collapsed on the sofa in blinded, sensual expression.

Outside the window, Calaban enjoyed all of what was playing out in front of him. Arturo needed to know that he was loved— what he didn't need was the knowledge that he was being videoed by Calaban.

Arturo was lying on the floor, hoping his children would not walk in. Then his cellphone rang.

"Be here at the house at 9:00 tonight, and don't be late."

Thinking, *Another time across the border. Will this crap ever stop…?* he responded quickly and clicked his "end" button. A moment later, he heard the cellphone outside his front window ring and Calaban answering it.

At 5:40 P.M., Arturo was dressed and walking out the door, saying, "I'll be back, Querida."

He and Calaban arrived within seconds of each other; Calaban had a childish smirk on his face and, rolling his eyes, smiled and shrugged his shoulders at Arturo.

The lights were on, and the air-conditioning was working; that was good. The food in the refrigerator was all spoiled, but Barrientos was not there to care. There was a two-and-a-half ton six-wheel truck sitting outside the house. King peered at them through the passenger side.

Calaban entered through the crew cab door first.

"Qué pasa, Jefe?" Calaban outstretched his arm looking for a fist bump.

"Marcus, sit down and keep your mouth shut! This is the truck from Dallas. We will pull it around to the back, and each of us will guard the contents and truck all night.

"You two," he said, pointing at the two men who were originally sitting the black SUV earlier that day, "take the first watch. You can sit in the truck. If I catch you sleeping, I will gut both of you like a pig. Arturo, you take over at midnight, and Marcus, you spell him at 3:00. Got it? As soon as Vargas gets through with his dirty little project, I'll put him out there around 6:00 in the morning."

Midnight came quickly, and first thug came in the house to wake Arturo.

"Okay! Okay!" he answered, yawning, "I'm up. Give me a minute." Morales stood over him with a cup of coffee.

Arturo asked, "Are we going to Mexico in the morning?"

Morales responded, "Not unless you know how to fly a high-speed airplane."

Arturo rubbed his eyes and then his head.

"What happened to this guy from Dallas?"

"I will call his daddy tomorrow," Morales commented sarcastically.

"Okay! Off to the truck." Arturo rubbed his eyes with his final thought as he stumbled out the door. He moved on to the walkway, his right arm dropped to its side, checking for his cellphone.

Not here—Cripes! Now what?

Two steps later, Arturo tripped on an imaginary crack in the concrete, and he went down on his knees and broke the nicely kilned pottery coffee cup. He remained there for a moment, and while grimacing over his sore knee, he rose up, brushed off his pant leg, and returned to the house...for more coffee.

"Clumsy, oaf," Morales laughed as Arturo came back in the house.

"Whatever it was, I just got the toe of my shoe hung-up. I'm gonna get another cup, and I'll head out there again."

Arturo stepped quickly by his bed and picked up his phone. No one saw anything.

Chapter 12

The back door swung open, and Vargas entered into the kitchen; it was almost one 1:00 in the morning. The lieutenant was filthy and ready for sleep; his task completed, he went directly to the bathroom to get cleaned up. Gonzales was partially right; it was close to a month since Vargas has taken a shower, and tonight, he really needed it. The amount of room available for Barrientos' burial was a bit sparse, so he was compelled to make José's body smaller.

"Where's Gonzales?" Vargas asked as he pulled off his bloody t-shirt.

"He's in the truck, guarding the phosphorous. Did you not see him?"

The blank look on Vargas was compelling. Morales and Vargas flung open the back door while running to the truck. They rounded the far side of the vehicle and saw Arturo on his knees praying; the cup of coffee by his side. Only a minute before, he was speaking with Jerry.

"*We have the phosphorous—yellow six-wheel truck—Vargas killed Barrientos—Culberson in ho…*" End button. He whispered as he crossed himself, "*Gracias a Dios.*"

"You'll have enough to pray about in a couple of weeks," Vargas laughed.

The two went back inside, and the lieutenant was off to his hot shower. Forty minutes later, he stepped into the kitchen with clean clothes; the teeth were still missing, and the knife cuts were still present, but he didn't smell anymore.

Calaban and Morales explained what had transpired at the hotel, with Morales doing most of the talking.

"Do you think he is dead?" Vargas asked.

"Somebody has to go and find out," Morales responded. "We have a three-day window to complete our Mazatlán project."

While the two guards slept, the trio drank, smoked, and talked anarchy until 2:00 in the morning. In the end, they were all drunk. Hours passed, and Arturo stepped inside.

"It's time for you to guard the truck, jefe." He shook the cartel leader. His hangover was so bad, he just rolled over and opened his bloodshot eyes—he could barely focus on Arturo's face.

King Morales pulled himself out of the cushioned chair, staring at Vargas. Unable to stand; unable to speak without slurring every word, he declared, "Vargas, you're a damn fool."

Vargas strolled to the refrigerator and grabbed a half-cold beer.

"Sit down, Gonzales," Morales said. "I have *the* idea that will allow us to succeed in Mazatlán. The bottles will be delivered tomorrow—" He could hardly keep his eyes open. "I want you to start mixing the cocktail and loading the bottles in the truck. Those two nimrods over there will help you. I will call Culberson later on to discuss my plans.

"Vargas, get one of those loco lobos to guard the truck. I'm hungry, and I'll show all of you how we will get that phosphorous to Mazatlán."

The uglier of the two went to the truck while Morales started the black SUV with his two cohorts riding along.

"We are going to get clearance to fly into Buena International Airport with the phosphorous cocktail on board," Morales said.

"How are you going to do that?" Vargas responded.

"I'll let you know as soon as I get off the phone with David Culberson." Morales answered.

At 9:15 that morning, Morales placed a call to Dallas. Expecting David to pick up on the first ring, he was put aback when he heard:

"David Culberson. I'm unavailable at the moment. Please leave your name and number. I will call you back."

Morales called again at 1:00 that afternoon and again at 4:30 later that day. The same response each time: No answer.

Later that evening, after several attempts, Morales finally reached his partner.

"David, I need you to come to Tucson with your Gulfstream. I wish to fly to Sinaloa and speak with that corrupt governor buddy of yours, José Renaldo Reyes, the *honorable* governor of Sinaloa."

"Antonio, I'll call him, but what do you want us to talk about?"

"I want you to convince him that we should be able to land the plane at Buena International Airport without any questioning from customs. I'll send him a gift that will make him happy and convince him he made the right decision. One last thing, David, Jack is in the hospital. He had a horrific attack on his heart, and I think he is dying."

There was dead silence on the phone for what seemed like an eternity.

Finally, David spoke, "I'll be wheels up in an hour. Where is he?"

"He's at University Medical Center, but it's late, so come tomorrow morning."

Shaken, but not deterred, David called the hospital, checked on his son, and felt satisfied with the attending's answer. He filed the flight plan to Tucson for a morning flight. At 9:00 in the morning, he notified Julie, Jack's wife, told Felicia to pack a bag, and the three headed for Addison Airport. In the car, he picked up his cellphone and dialed his friend, the governor of Sinaloa.

"José Renaldo, I am flying to Culiacán tomorrow to take a train ride. I wanted to know if your schedule would permit our meeting together when the train arrives in Mazatlán. I have a couple of urgent items to discuss with you. I should be there by 2:00; can you have someone meet me?"

"No, my friend, I will meet you myself."

The governor's estate sat high on the mountain overlooking the conjoining waters of the Gulf of California and the Pacific Ocean. The house was 6,500 square feet in size, and the fireplace that set at one end of the dining room was over six feet high and built with blocks of hand-cut Texas limestone. A Khyber wool rug concealed the heavy Spanish door that led into a hidden room. There, David and José Renaldo Reyes, gubernador de Sinaloa, would hold their meeting.

David landed his airplane at the Tucson International Airport two hours later. While McKensey's guys serviced the aircraft, David and the two women in his life took a taxi to the hospital. They walked in Jack's room and stared for a moment. His color was a bit peaked, and he looked weak and emaciated.

"What happened?" David asked the attending doctor.

"We don't know just yet," he replied. "We wanted his vitals to return to some semblance of normalcy before we ran any invasive tests. We also sent some hospital employees to the hotel to see if they could find anything that would help us—they didn't; and no one even saw him or had any contact with him.

David asked, "Will he be alright?"

The doctor, with his clipboard in one hand and flipping pages with the other, shrugged his shoulders.

"We'll know more tomorrow or no more than a couple of days."

David looked at his son through the glass facing his room. The single light above his head allowed only a shadowy glimpse of tubes leading to his body and hospital tape holding them in his arm. The bag containing the electrolytes hung just beyond the beam of fluorescent light, and the monitor displaying his vitals and oxygenation levels would occasionally report with short and then longer beeps. Jack was sleeping soundly, and at the moment, it was liken to watching grass grow.

"I'll take you two to the hotel, and we'll get something to eat," David said.

"Julie, would you like to come with us or stay here?"

She looked at the nurse and asked when ICU visiting hours would be over.

"Seven o'clock," was her response.

"I'll come with you," Julie told them. "But I want to come back later."

David and Felicia both nodded in agreement as they walked past the nurse's station, not noticing Jonathan wearing blue jeans and a windbreaker hunched over the counter, talking with a freshly dressed nurse who just came on duty.

In the rental car, David called the Four Points Hotel to reserve two rooms for an indefinite period of time while he had thoughts of other items on his agenda. The desk clerk acknowledged the availability and asked the standard questions before confirming the reservation. Before he could finish, David interrupted and told him they were on their way and would be there in 15 minutes and clicked his "end" key.

It was the second act for Agent Barlow. She waited around until the trio arrived, then quietly moved to her station, which was the room the clerk was going to assign to David and Felicia Culberson. She sat on the sofa until the call came from the front desk. The agent placed the micro-bug directly inside a carving of Texas Blue Bonnets that decorated the foot of the king-size bed. She had just finished vacuuming and was turning down the bed for later when David walked in the door.

"I'm through, sir." Barlow explained.

David offered a subliminal *thank you* with a nod of his head—and no tip. The agent was only slightly disappointed as she closed the door behind her.

During breakfast, David told the girls to get some rest and that he had to go out for a while.

"I'll be back in a few hours and then we'll go back to the hospital."

Felicia never said a word; she just finished her coffee and nodded her head in agreement. Her eyes rolled in his direction as he left the table.

—◆◆◆—

David sat in the driver's seat of the rental car for more than just a moment and thought about his business, his wife; his son. He took a deep breath, started the car, and headed for West Bilby. He had turned off Grand and was heading to Barrientos' house when he noticed two black SUVs in the distance. He drove up and parked behind an old, red Ford pickup. This time, Morales stood from the sofa to greet him as David walked inside.

"Where is this guy, Arturo Gonzales?" David asked.

"I am here, señor," Arturo spoke up while entering from another room.

"I'll come to the point, Mr. Gonzales. You will accompany me tomorrow to Mazatlán to meet with the Governor of Sinaloa, Mexico. You will be neatly dressed and clean shaven. You will exhibit good manners, and you will explain everything to him *when* I ask you to do so. Until then, you will keep your mouth shut. Do you have any of the cocktails ready?"

"Si, señor," Arturo answered.

"Fine. Bring two bottles with you. Make sure they are packed safely; we will leave at seven in the morning. Oh, yeah, we're going to go on a train ride."

"David, do you wish me to go with you?" Morales offered the inclusion.

"Antonio, you have enough problems with all those outstanding warrants. And I don't wish to see *your* ugly face either, Vargas. You guys will stay here and enjoy Tucson's finest pizza. We'll be back around 8:00 or 9:00. Arturo, is it? Here's $200; go get some decent clothes and be at McKensey's at 9:00 in the morning."

The morning brought a new day with Arturo heading to McKensey's FBO. He had stopped at McDonald's for breakfast and was sipping a very hot cup of coffee when David pulled up in his rental car. David stared at the biscuit in Arturo's mouth only for a moment.

"Eat up, Mr. Gonzales, there's no food allowed on the plane." David went to the cockpit and eased himself into the pilot's seat and yelled to Arturo through the open side window. "Are you coming?"

Arturo was aghast. Never in his life had he seen anything so big up close. He hurried to the garbage can and threw the remaining food items away then brushed any crumbs from his new Filipino Barong Tagalog. The embroidered shirt was pure white and made from pineapple fibers. David cracked a relaxing smile and thought, *Yeah, I think he's prepared to meet a governor.*

Through the din of the whirring engines, David yelled instructions back to Arturo, sitting on one of the sofas, on how to attach the seat belt. Satisfied, he moved the twin throttles slightly forward as the Gulfstream's big engines spooled up. He taxied to runway 3-5 Left and lined up on the centerline.

Moments later, David heard the take-off release crack through his headset. The big GEs throttled up quickly, and the plane began to roll. Within minutes, they were wheels up and turning south to Culiacán, Sinaloa, Mexico. The airport rested 593 miles to the south, and David was on his final approach in less than two hours later.

Next to the corporate aircraft side of the terminal waited a large black Mercedes Benz that José Renaldo Reyes had arranged for his friend. David shut down the General Electric engines, and he and Arturo stepped off the plane into the greeting salute of a local limousine driver.

"Take us to the train station," David requested.

The driver nodded and drove the Benz to meet the Culiacàn to Mazatlán train. Arturo took the lined, yellow tablet from his suitcase and doodled until it pulled into the station. Arturo crossed his leg and laid the pad atop his thigh. The process of diagramming the trip began there as he looked southward and drew the track as it disappeared from the station. David came back with the tickets. They waited.

After an hour, the train now stood before them. Steam emanating from the undercarriage beckoned passengers to come aboard. The two men, using the provided step-stool, climbed the steps to enter the assigned passenger car. Arturo got comfortable on the east side with David sitting next to him. The scene appeared a bit strange; two men sitting together in a half empty train—one ostensibly reading a newspaper and the other with a writing pad.

Now moving southward, Arturo took notes on everything; emphasizing location and landmarks. His eyes focused on a slight left curve in the distance and he drew the bend in the track and then watched for details. David noticed how meticulous Arturo was as he laid out the track before him.

The train ramped up to a speed of 60 miles per hour, and David found himself bobbing and weaving his head to view the different possible points of interest that appeared on the way to Mazatlán.

Arturo maintained his concentration and noted every road that crossed the tracks. Every curve was written down, along with estimates of speed and every grade—up or down. When he saw the terrain change, specifically on the right. He notated on his paper the standard and acceptable symbols that indicated a wall of rock. He stared at the right side, determining the height at 600 feet with several crevasses embedded in the ascending side. Constant vigilance translated to constant notetaking. He stopped writing for a moment and turned to David.

"Will there be guns?"

"Of course," David responded.

"Will there be killing?"

"Probably. But, hopefully, only the bad guys," David said.

"They're all bad guys, Mr. Culberson."

"Yeah, but there's a direct correlation between the badness of someone and the amount of money you will make from helping them." David cocked his head and smiled. "Now, I have a question for you. Arturo, where and when do you want the cocktails to be thrown?"

Arturo never hesitated.

"There will be men positioned on the side of a crevasse. There will be men positioned on the high point above the train. They will toss the bottles as the last car passes in front of them."

Arturo looked outside the train and interrupted himself. "Mountains mean we're slowing down," Arturo exclaimed.

The jetting out of precipices were all notated with incredible accuracy. The train approached the rising land mass an hour out of the station. Both men heard the intermittent screeching of the brakes and felt the car rocking as it rolled along the tracks.

"We're slowing down to negotiate a right turn," David said.

"Better than that, Mr. Culberson. Look! The track has disappeared. We're not coming to a curve; we're approaching a very tight right turn."

The two men looked at each other and in unison said, "Perfect!"

David pulled the sleeve of his sport coat to view the time displayed on his watch. He started the count at 2:31 and nine seconds. The train remained at a crawl around the turn, and Arturo looked to the left for strategic position possibilities. At 2:48, the locomotive appeared in front of them, and they witnessed a greater constituency of darker smoke rising from the smoke stack.

"That's 17 minutes." David said. "Perhaps we should wait until we come completely out of the turn. The train will gather momentum, increase speed, and be further down the line when the fire breaks out.

"I agree," said Arturo. "If you look up the track and to the left, you can see the drop-off becomes very steep."

He drew the detail on his pad. After an hour, the train sped up as it had passed the southern edge of the mountainous terrain. Arturo analyzed his drawing and realized the cliff was actually a canyon that the track had followed for over 60 miles. There were four curves, one of which was a very tight 30-degree right turn. This was the place; this was where they would throw the phosphorous cocktails against the top and sides of the Mazatlán-Culiacán train.

"This is perfect." Arturo smiled. David tapped him on the shoulder in agreement.

Chapter 13

THE STATION IN MAZATLÁN WAS BUZZING with visitors when they arrived. Arturo noticed the soldiers of the Mexican Army standing around toting Yugoslavian made AK-47s. He and David moved quickly through the station door and spotted another large black Mercedes, but this one carried two of Sinaloa's flags flapping in the breeze.

"Mr. Culberson, my name is Berin Rodriguez. I work for the governor, and he asked me to escort you and your friend to his hacienda."

David and Arturo entered the rear seat and, after a 20-minute ride, arrived at the estate of José Renaldo Reyes. The Mercedes pulled up to the front door. The governor stepped out from the threshold and moved quickly toward David.

"José Renaldo, this is Arturo Gonzales." David turned and extended his arm to beckon Arturo forward.

"Encantado, Señor Governor."

The governor turned to David, barely acknowledging Arturo's existence. With his arm around David's shoulder, the governor escorted his friend inside the front door. Arturo followed.

José Renaldo asked, "What do you want from me, David?"

"I need to return in a couple of days and not be disturbed by Customs."

"Please tell me that you are not bringing any of Morales' guns down here?"

"No, I am not," David assured the governor.

Through the front door and through the great hall, José Renaldo continued his questioning.

The foyer of the Hacienda was a pure white marble floor and James Earle Frazier's original work, *The End of the Trail*, sat high on one side of the entrance. Arturo stood for a moment, staring at the lone Indian warrior on his very tired horse. After gawking at Frazier's work, Culberson suggested he turn around to view Remington's *Trooper of the Plains* that rested on a five-foot pedestal. Arturo was amazed at the incredible detail of the galloping steed.

Arturo moved steadily behind David as he made his way around the massive dining room table toward the enormous fireplace. The large Persian rug hung next to the massive hearth from the 20-foot ceiling. Culberson only mumbled incoherently to the governor until they reached the fireplace. They passed through the steel door, a guard closed it behind them, and then David turned.

"Now, José Renaldo, no more mumbling, all of your questions will answered. Now what can I tell you?"

"Well, how can I help *you*, my friend?"

David considered his words carefully, "There is a shipment of poppies from Afghanistan arriving on an Iranian ship. It will be in Mazatlán tomorrow. The Sinaloas need it; the Zetas want it. Neither one can have it."

"What do you plan to do about it?" The governor asked.

"You know where the Sinaloas will process the poppies into heroin—*you* know it; *I* know it. The shipment will be loaded on the Mazatlán-Culiacán train on Wednesday. We plan to take it."

The governor's eyes were twitching, and he began to rub his lips with his right hand.

"You can't do this, David."

"Because…because, part of it belongs to you, José Renaldo? No one will ever know who did this, and this is why Señor Gonzales is here.

It will *never* arrive in Culiacán. You, José Renaldo, have to make the decision as to whose side you wish be on: Mine, or theirs."

David felt compelled to approach the governor and placed his mouth an inch from José's ear, "If I see one Customs Agent, Governor, I'll know where you stand, and the next time I see you, it won't be vertical."

David stepped back with a smirk on his face.

"If we are done," David added, "Would you ask your pilot to get us back to Culiacán?"

The governor went to his bar, poured two fingers of José Cuervo *Especial* and picked up his cellphone. There was a knock on the door.

"Berin, take these gentlemen to the airstrip. Carlos is waiting to take them back to Culiacán."

The ride was as quiet as the first, but after 15 minutes, David felt a small punch in his side. He looked at Arturo and saw a very subtle roll of his eyes. David cocked his head, eyes questioning. Arturo's hand gave a rocking motion as his finger movement pointed to the driver. He made numerous attempts to provide David with indications of the driver's disdain seen through the reflection of the rearview mirror; his fidgeting caught Arturo's eye when he saw his right shoulder move forward as if he were reaching for something.

"So, Berin," David asked, "how long have you been with the governor?"

"Only three months, señor."

The road to the governor's air strip was only 10 minutes from his house, and Berin continued to talk about how easy his job was with the governor. David slowly removed his belt from his pants as he joined in the intermittent laugher from the driver. It all came to a head when Berin slowed the car.

David Culberson flipped his belt over Berin's head and yanked him back, so his head and shoulders were over the driver's seatback. Arturo grabbed one arm and pulled. Berin was not a small man, but the leverage favored the passengers. His legs jammed up against the console and tried to reach the wheel to pull himself out from the death grip. His Adam's apple was compressed into his air passage; his left arm flailed helplessly trying to grab the belt—to no avail. Berin slid down into the seat; that didn't work. He felt his eyes coming out of their sockets. He struggled for enough air to fight back, but in the end, he was dead.

The car continued to roll as the two jumped out. David quickly moved to yank the front door open, and Arturo opened the passenger's side door. Both jumped from the car. It continued to roll with the dead man in the driver's seat. Within minutes, the Mercedes rolled off into a ditch. David and Arturo calmly walked until they reached the settled automobile. Both men pulled the dead driver from the car and dragged him to the middle of an adjacent field and proceeded to the airstrip.

David had already gone through the driver's pockets and found a semi-automatic Glock with a silencer attached. One bullet in the chamber and a full clip, he fired one bullet to Berin's head just to make sure then replaced his belt on his pants.

"That one was easy. The next one won't be."

David went to the passenger's side and, on the way, leaned down and grabbed Berin's driver's cap and tossed it out window.

"Look, my friend," David said, "if we want to get out of Mexico alive, this is what I need you to do…"

The governor's twin-engine Beechcraft Baron was all gassed up with the engines running at idle. The pilot, Juan Cordoza, was looking at one of the wings when David and Arturo drove up.

Cordoza approached the duo.

"Where's Berin?" he asked.

"The governor wanted you to drive the car back upon your return," David answered.

He looked concerned, but only for a moment.

"Are you gentlemen ready to go?"

The three entered the aircraft, and Arturo strapped himself in.

"May I sit with you in the cockpit?" David politely asked.

"Sure, no problem."

Cordoza closed and locked the door and moved to the pilot's seat. He got settled in, and his hand eased the twin throttles forward. The two fuel-injected Continentals came alive. The ground speed hit 100 knots; Cordoza eased back on the yoke, and the Baron was airborne.

The avionics and communication fuse box was located in the bulkhead directly behind the pilot's seat. When the airplane reached an altitude of 2,000 feet, David turned and asked Arturo if he was all right—that was his cue to pull the communication fuses. He did.

Cordoza flew the Baron to Culiacán and called for clearance to land with no response from the tower.

"I've been having trouble with this radio off and on," he said. "I will get it fixed while I'm here."

The Baron landed without further incident, and he taxied up to David's Gulfstream. Without shutting off the engines, the governor's pilot said his goodbyes, and David and Arturo disembarked from the Baron and proceeded quickly to get on David's Gulfstream. The sky was clear, and David wanted out of the country as soon as possible.

Within minutes, the two were rolling to the runway, and with little hesitation, David shoved the twin throttles forward, and they were off to Tucson. As the ground passed below them, Arturo noticed the governor's plane and pilot waiting for service on his radio.

At 34 minutes after 8:00 that evening, David called Tucson tower, reported his position, and requested landing instructions.

"Gulfstream 7-4-4 Yankee; make left turn at Sonora marker 1-7-2 degrees. I will call your final."

"Roger, Tucson. Left turn at Sonora 1-7-2 degrees," David responded.

Arturo looked out the window. It was a beautiful night in the southern Arizona skies. The stars were right on top of them, and with no haze, Arturo could see every one of them. The aircraft turned on final at the tower's command, and with a 500-foot-per-minute sink rate, David and Arturo were home safe as the wheels kissed the runway before dark.

To no big surprise, a black SUV sat 20 feet from McKensey's building just off the entrance. The evening crew came forward to chock the wheels and service the plane.

There were two people in the truck. The one sitting on the passenger side struck a match to light a cigarette. The glimmer of light revealed it was Vargas. Without acknowledging his presence, David and Arturo moved to their respective vehicles and headed for West Bilby.

The 1967 Ford pickup pulled up to the house only a minute before David arrived in his rental car. Morales greeted them as both closed the door behind them. Neither David nor Arturo wanted to waste any time debriefing, and neither did Morales. They waited. Morales' eyes pinched together as he stared at the two travelers sitting on the sofa. The menacing, furrowed brow on Morales' forehead accentuated his stare. Arturo was almost compelled to ask if there was a problem; but he didn't.

A minute later, Vargas strolled in carrying a beer.

"Okay, okay, what happened?" Morales was eager to speak.

"With the exception of a couple of events, all-in-all, it went pretty well. We met with

José Renal…"

"Later. What events?" Morales interrupted.

"He is closer to the Sinaloas than we thought. One was working for him and had to be killed."

"Where is he?" Vargas asked.

"Splayed out in an obscure field of high grass—his choice. Can we get to the plan?"

"What do you think they will do when they find him?" Morales asked.

"How many guns do you have, Antonio?" David responded.

Arturo interjected, "Señor King, this plan, it is a good one."

"Before we discuss that, you said there were two events. What was the other one?"

David rested his elbows on his knees and looked directly at Morales, "The pilot of the governor's plane that flew us to Culiacán, we *didn't* kill him." Morales grabbed Vargas' beer and poured the rest of it down his throat. Before Morales could mouth the question, David said, "I didn't think it was necessary, and I'm not into gratuitous killing."

"Jefe," again Arturo spoke out, "the train slows to a crawl at this spot." He placed his finger on his notepad. "This is a very tight curve, and it takes 17 minutes to come completely out of it. We have an advantage in three ways. First, the speed—or lack of it. Second, at that spot and time, the sun is on the southeast side of the track, and the mountain is on the west side. And third, with the track being so close to the mountain, it is very disorienting to the riders atop the train. Right here—" He popped his forefinger on and off the paper as if he were hitting the red button that would set off a bomb—"right here, jefe. This is where we hit them."

"There *are* logistical issues," David told Morales, "One, *you* have to get back into Mexico and get all of your men to that spot." He pointed at Arturo's pad. "How you position them is your business, but we have two days, so tomorrow morning, you need to move it out of here and take these guys with you. Whatever number of guns you have, you need to get to your cache and arm you and your men. This is *not* going to be a cake walk." He sat back in the sofa and crossed his legs.

"There's one more issue," he added. "José Renaldo and his Customs agents."

Morales stood up and not saying a word, went to the refrigerator to grab another beer.

"Can you land your plane on his airstrip at night?" Morales asked.

David Culberson never hesitated with his answer.

"No, and even if we used the Bonanza, that wouldn't work because it's Sinaloa property. The fencing is chain-link and barbed wire. We'd never get your trucks in there to carry off the cases of cocktail."

"I will gather my men and tell them where to be on Wednesday. I will keep my cellphone next to me at all times, so stay available, David." Morales continued, "I don't think he, the governor, will risk it at the airport but *will* try on the way to the train."

"You have your trucks there, and we'll get this done. For now, I'm going back to the hotel."

David stood up and walked out the door.

Chapter 14

FELICIA WELCOMED DAVID with open arms as he entered the hotel room.

"Is everything alright?" she asked

"Everything is fine," he said, "and will be better, honey."

She asked, "Why did you fly into Mexico?"

David took off his jacket and loosened his tie. He turned to face Felicia as her words left her lips.

"Well, did you? Did you fly into Mexico?"

"How's Jack, Felicia?"

"Don't ignore me, damn it. You are screwing around with very dangerous animals." The fire from her cigarette was enough that he could see the disdainful look on her face. She took one more puff and drove the cigarette tip into the glass ashtray.

"David, these are not choirboys. They're murderers and—"

He interrupted, "Felicia, nothing happened today, and nothing is going to happen tomorrow."

"What do you mean, 'Nothing's *going* to happen?' Are you going back there?"

"Felicia, listen to me."

"No, you listen to me. I know about the I.R.S. I know about your connection with the cartel. And I know about New York."

"How do you...?"

"Madeleine called about two weeks ago looking for you. We talked. She likes you; I *love* you."

"Damn it, I *need* the freaking money!" David yelled at her.

Chapter 15

JERRY AND FRANCO WERE DRINKING their fifth cup of coffee together. Culberson's Gulfstream returned from Mexico an hour ago, and there was no word from Arturo.

A few moments later, Jerry's phone rang.

"Hi, Querida," Arturo said. "How are the girls? Are you okay?"

"Yeah, we're fine," Jerry answered. "Anything you can give us?"

"Plenty," he sneaked in a deep breath, "tired, Maria. I'm getting ready to go to bed; I have a busy day tomorrow, and some friends are going to Mexico and asked me to come with them. Maybe you can join us, and you and I can take a train ride; maybe to Culiacán. Let me know if you want to come with us."

Just before Arturo finished his sentence, he heard the screen door slammed shut and saw Vargas coming toward him.

"Say goodnight to the girls—I love you." Arturo clicked his "end" key and looked at Vargas.

"King wants you to call me as soon as the cocktails reach Buelna Airport. He wants you to bring the containers to this farm, pointing at a piece of paper in his hand." Vargas spun around and went back into the house.

Sweet mother of God, Arturo thought as he said, "Thank you, Vargas."

At 6:00 the next morning, Arturo hopped in the yellow, six-wheel truck and headed for McKensey's private terminal, and so did Jonathan.

Arturo stopped at McDonald's for breakfast again. He was alone. He drank his coffee and quickly went through his hash browns and then the Egg McMuffin. Two guys sat down in the booth behind him.

"We saw the truck, Arturo," the voice came from the booth. The man never turned around, always looking straight ahead. "Jerry Messer, Arturo. Where are you going in Mexico?"

Arturo kept his head down and continued to eat his breakfast.

"Mazatlán, but then on to a farm northeast of there," he quietly responded.

"We'll be at Buelna when you get there. No one outside the United States is involved, but you have all the help you need, okay?"

"Gracias, señores."

Arturo rose from his booth, walked to the truck, and took a moment to check the fiberglass tonneau that covered all the containers of phosphorous cocktails. He then continued to the airport. For the first time since this *ordeal* began, he breathed a long and deep sigh of relief—heck, he even noticed that a slight smile spread across his face when he looked in the rear view mirror.

Chapter 16

DAVID CULBERSON WENT TO THE HOSPITAL after an early breakfast with Felicia and Jack's wife, Julie. Jack was still encircled in wires and tubes that monitored his every move and heartbeat. The nurse on duty asked him if there were any messages.

"Just tell him I love him, and I'll see him later." David turned from the nurse and proceeded down the hall to the elevator.

The sun was up, and the early morning coolness had dissipated. The temperature rose at a gradual pace as the morning sun got higher. David parked his rental car and walked around the corner. The yellow truck was sitting next to the Gulfstream's doorway, and he noticed Arturo and Jonathan loading the cases of phosphorous cocktail in the rear storage area.

"Your man here says you're carrying water to Mexico. Is that right, Mr. Culberson?" Jonathan asked.

"That's right. We're building an inventory for the folks down there in case of another eruption in the Gulf of California. The U.S. will be bringing in C-130 transport planes next week to ramp up the process."

"Good for us," Jonathan said. "I'll get the rest of the paperwork ready for you. You'll be able to head out in about 15 minutes."

Jonathan ambled back into the FBO's office.

David settled himself in the cockpit to communicate with ground control when Jonathan returned and handed the papers up through the cockpit window. They both saluted each other in quasi-military fashion and then waited for Jonathan to step down and remove the step ladder. The Gulfstream moved forward on David's throttled command.

An hour before sunrise, Morales and his henchmen left the house on West Bilby and headed for Mexico. Above them, the morning sky was replete with southwestern colors of reds and blues, all outlined in shimmering rays of the morning Arizona sun. Along the southwest Rico region of the Huachuca Mountains, the well-used coyote trails had now been given to Morales and his two lieutenants, Vargas and Calaban. By 2:00 that afternoon, the three were less than an hour away from the border. The mesquite brush was more of an enemy than cover, for every other step, someone was sliced up by an errant thorn or some other kind of underbrush.

A green-striped white SUV of the U.S. Border Patrol was visible on an adjacent road a half a mile away. Morales could barely see the agent who scanned the mountainside with binoculars.

There is no reason to believe that he is for looking us, Morales thought.

A familiar whirring sound was heard overhead as a Predator drone flew directly above and then moved to a different area.

Calaban crouched down on a prickly cactus, and its thorn entered his thigh.

"Holy crap!"

"Keep moving!" Vargas commented.

"Stay down!" Morales said. "Another 1,500 yards, and we will be home, amigos."

"Let me get this thorn out first," Calaban mouthed above a whisper.

"Pull it out while you're moving, punto."

Vargas grabbed Calaban's arm and dragged him screaming down the trail.

A phone call made the night before ensured an old, inconspicuous vehicle would be waiting for them. An old Chevrolet was in position when the trio arrived. Everywhere there was a window, a row of red dingle-balls framed it. The driver was outside the car fixing the low-rider connection when Morales came off the mountain trail.

"Get everyone together. We must leave as soon as we can. We must be in Mazatlán before 3:00 tomorrow morning and in place by 9:00."

The pyramid-calling system soon reached everyone on Morales' gang list. Moments after the phone call, 120 members of the Morales Cartel headed for Mazatlán carrying AR-15s or AK-47s. All carried 10 plastic banana clips with 30 rounds of ammunition, enough to win any argument with the Sinaloas or whoever else decided to participate.

Chapter 17

NINE MEN HAD ALREADY BEEN DISPATCHED to Buelna to carry the cargo to the farm. Each truck at Buelna had three men, an AK-47, and 1,000 rounds of ammunition hidden in a false floor in the bed of their trucks.

At the airport, Morales' men quietly drank coffee in the terminal restaurant, waiting for a white Gulfstream with the number 7-4-4 painted on the tail. Jerry, Franco, and Jonathan sat in the upper observation deck, peering through the glass window waiting for the same aircraft. Franco carried a portable radio tuned to the tower frequency. The Air Force had scrambled three F-16s to get those three agents into Mexico on such short notice, so Franco knew that the Gulfstream was going to touchdown any moment.

Chapter 18

DAVID SENSED THE SWEAT FROM HIS HANDS on the yoke of his airplane as Buelna tower called his final approach. He knew that once this plane landed, a new chapter of his life would begin. He accepted the instructions from the air traffic controller and turned the aircraft to the approach heading. As David bled off speed, he saw runway 3-5 Right rising up to greet him. He knew as he dropped his wheels, it was a precursor to the eminent possibilities of what was about to befall him.

The plane yawed as he neared the ground, but he landed right on the centerline and proceeded to the corporate terminal. Everything was now in motion whether he liked it or not. The agents on the observation deck quietly but methodically rose out of their seats and moved down the stairs. The nine thugs from Morales' cartel paid their bill and headed for their trucks.

The Gulfstream came to a stop at the corporate terminal, and three men approached the plane. They were dressed in the local FBO service coveralls and stood by as David shut down the engines.

They came forward after the engines fell quiet and motioned for David to open his cockpit window.

"Welcome to Mazatlán, señor. Will you be staying long?" one asked.

David yelled back, "For only a couple of days. We have brought water for a hospital in Culiacán."

"We will help you unload, señor, and we can get you a couple of trucks to transport the cargo if you wish."

"That won't be necessary," David yelled from the cockpit window. "We've already hired some men to help us."

David waved to the three trucks sitting by the terminal and motioned them to come closer. He and Arturo left the aircraft, so the three teams of two could board and remove the six trays of the cocktail and place them inside the waiting trucks. Two other men came through the flight line side of the FBO. Arturo did everything he could not to crack a smile and purposely just looked away.

Arturo jumped in the first truck and, in Spanish, told the driver to drive carefully, not to *break* any bottles, not to *spill* any of the bottles. And *don't* drink the water.

Chapter 19

THE SMALL CONVOY HEADED NORTH on Highway 15D. Thirteen miles northwest of Buelna International, the turn-off from the highway was found on a dirt road laden with small rocks and potholes. The eight-mile stretch did not go quickly as the trucks had to slow down to a crawl. Every foot of the last six miles was under the conscious eye of Arturo Gonzales. The last two-miles of the trip took over an hour. The rearview mirror showed the charcoal-colored dust being blown up by the lead truck. The friable granular dirt destroyed most of the visibility of the truck behind him. Finally, Arturo's driver took his foot off the gas pedal and allowed the vehicle to come to a long, rolling stop. They were 50 yards from the farmhouse. It was 9:00 at night.

"We are here, señor," the driver said.

Arturo jumped from the pickup as the southern wind brought the blanket of dust over the top of him. When it dissipated, he turned to David, who moved up next to him.

The moon was high and cast enough light to see donkeys in a corral.

"Look, David, look at the donkeys. How many are here?" Arturo asked the driver.

"Over 50, señor."

"And do we have enough backpacks for all those animals?" David asked the driver.

"Si, enough to carry all of your water," the driver answered.

Arturo produced a well-scripted smile.

David stood next to Arturo and scanned the area between the trucks and the barn. His eyes squinted to peer through the darkness and absorbed every detail. There was only the breeze from the south, but the air smelled of donkey dung. There was no sound; no chickens clucking; no braying in the night.

"Stay with the trucks. I'll be back." David grabbed one of the AR-15s and carefully approached the farmhouse.

The tree line was silhouetted by a half-moon lit sky as David moved slowly against the barely-seen trees. He remained ready with the AR resting catty-corner on his chest. Another few deliberate steps, and David stopped short in his tracks. An old man, slowed down by a definitive limp, stepped out from the shadow of the barn. Everything about him was an anachronism. He wore a high-crowned sombrero with a large bandana that hung loosely around his neck. The truck's headlights revealed the double belts of bandoleers slung over each shoulder holding enough ammunition to protect anything he owned for a long time. He appeared to be the last living member of the Emiliano Zapata gang from the early 1900s.

"What do you want, señor? The old man asked.

"Vargas sent us. I am here with Morales' men," David replied.

The farmer raised his Sharps rifle and motioned for them to come in.

The first truck moved forward carefully and with deliberation. Arturo walked in front of the slow-moving vehicle to guide them through the pitted and rock-infested terrain. Their slow pace, with Arturo's help, gave them a clear path to the barn, staying clear of potholes and rocks—making sure the cocktails remained inert.

Chapter 20

THE INTERNATIONAL MARITIME REGISTRY listed 51 freighters that fly under the flag of the Islamic Republic of Iran Shipping Lines. There were normally four shipping companies that deliver middle east and Asian products to Mexico year-round. The *Hormuz Defender* was one. She neared the end of her voyage that would culminate at the docks of the Port of Mazatlán. Running below the waterline, the freighter could do 17 knots in calm seas, and with an overall length of 760 feet, she had the capability of carrying an excess of 400 steel containers with most of them being of the 20-foot size. The captain and crew totaled over 100 sea-hardened sailors, and she had been on the ocean for over four months.

Seven Mexican automobile dealers brought in Kias from South Korea and Toyotas from Japan. A new hospital in Mexico City purchased a high-priced MRI unit that was manufactured by a division of Siemens in Taiwan. And tomorrow, she would be drop-shipping a 10-foot container of machine parts that will be placed on the Mazatlán-Culiacán train leaving at 10:30 tomorrow morning.

The sea was calm with a three-knot breeze coming from a south-westerly direction, and the *Hormuz Defender* sat five nautical miles off the coast of Mazatlán, Sinaloa, Mexico. The captain, a seaman of 30-plus years, called the port authority to announce their arrival and requested permission to enter the port. At the same time, the captain asked for a pilot to bring them into their assigned slip. Once the process began, the final docking would take three-hours, and off-loading would proceed at 6:30 the next morning.

Fifty-five minutes later, Captain José Huerta arrived by helicopter and immediately went to the bridge. It was a welcome home each time he entered the control area of a ship. The captain stood next to the helmsman as he entered the wheelhouse. Huerta was in his most comfortable position and this vessel welcomed him like a mother seeing her newborn for the first time.

The pilot gazed around his temporary home to get a sense of the layout. It was clean and unsullied. Spotless. Uniforms were immaculate. He acknowledged it all to the captain with a proper salute. He had made this short trip many times, and by regulation, he explained the level of control he would have until the ship was two miles out of port. The tugboats would be in control to finish and escort the freighter to her assigned slip. Each captain signed their part of the maritime document, shook hands, and the landing off the *Hormuz Defender* was under way.

Chapter 21

PORT DIRECTOR JUAN CARLOS ESTABÁN received a phone call from his assistant. It was 4:30 in the afternoon.

"Port Director, the *Hormuz Defender* has received its pilot and will be in port in three hours. We will start off-loading in morning." He hesitated. "Where do want container 1-1-7-4 stored?"

"Place it in warehouse 17, first floor, section 3—up front. And do not let the dogs near it. Tell security to patrol the north sector; start with warehouse 1 through 15 and check every container. I want a full report on their findings."

In the background, Juan Carlos could hear his assistant repeat his orders to security. He placed the receiver back in its cradle and lifted it back to his ear. The dial tone was activated. A three-digit code was entered and was immediately picked up on the other end.

Juan Carlos said four words, "The shipment is here," and hung up the phone. He paused for a moment and took a deep breath. He laid his face in his cupped hands and began rubbing his eyes. It had been a long day. Now, he'd wait.

"Juanita," his head stretched from his chair to the outer office. "Juanita, I'm going home early. Call my wife, and tell her I'm on my way." He stood up, almost in a trance, and walked to the nearby coat hanger; grabbed his jacket, his black lunch pail; and calmly proceeded through the door.

Passing the Port Authority guard house, he stepped through the chain-link gate and continued to his car. His reserved parking spot was not immune to unwanted visitors. There waiting were two men leaning on a truck that they parked directly behind his.

"Where are you going, Juan Carlos?" one asked. He spit a piece of loose tobacco from his lips and then took another puff. Another spit.

"Perhaps, you should not roll your own and buy cigarettes with filter tips," Juan Carlos advised. He backed up against his car and cradled his jacket and lunch box in his arms. "What can I do for you?" Without waiting for answer, Juan Carlos continued, "The ship was three miles offshore 30 minutes ago. A port authority pilot is on board and is bringing the cargo in as we speak. We will have it loaded on the train by 10:00 in the morning."

The second man pushed himself forward and jammed his stiffened forefinger into Juan Carlos' chest. His aberrant smile caught Juan Carlos' attention. Both thugs backed into the waiting truck, never taking their eyes off the director.

He sighed in relief as he leaned back against his car. Still struggling to regain his composure from the incident, he sat in the driver's seat, propped his arms atop the steering wheel, and took a couple of deep breaths.

Chapter 22

IT WAS A SLOW PROCESS ONBOARD the *Hormuz Defender.* The Mexican pilot, Captain José Huerta, had accomplished this final leg many times, and the ship moving at three knots was a tedious endeavor. The first mate brought it to the attention of both the ship's captain and the pilot that four tugboats were heading in their direction, and both men could clearly see the detail of the city of Mazatlán in the distance.

Soon the tugboats set their positions around the large freighter. The cacophony of horn blasts signaled proper thrusts from port to starboard, and the pilot communicated with all the tugs to make sure the speed of the freighter was in sync with their efforts. The freighter was approaching the inlet of the Mazatlán port on schedule. The port side tug began slipping back toward the stern 560 feet away. Captain Huerta turned the wheel four degrees to starboard to counter the propelling force being offered by the tug easing the freighter to the left.

The chief engineer maintained awareness of the ship's delicate maneuvers in this stage of the voyage. He was aware of what was happening and ready to react to any command in a second.

Two bells from the captain's wheelhouse—*all stop.*

A moment later, it was one bell again—*reverse, one-third.* A change in direction; a change in speed.

Every decision was made from experience and feel. After the ship reacted as commanded, she eased up next to her assigned slip, and the two-inch thick lines were attached to their respective cleats, and it was all over.

By 7:30 that evening, all lines were tied down, and the vessel was secure.

Chapter 23

THE FARM DID NOT EXPERIENCE a settling down for the night. Six cases of cocktail were to be moved, and they had three hours to do it. The old man gave orders to bring six bales of hay from the barn and placed them in the adjacent corral. He told David to take two water pails and fill them with corn from the nearby hopper.

"Arturo, por favor, go to the back of the barn and fill this wheelbarrow with alfalfa," the old man asked. "*All* of you, spread the food around the edges of the corral. Don't put too much of one thing in any one area."

Everyone did exactly what the old man asked.

By the time the donkeys finished all that was given to them, halogen lights were turned on. The generator emitted a buzz as the sheer darkness blossomed into daylight. It cast an eerie shadow upon the landscape, and every movement from the trees produced dancing demons in the forest.

The trucks moved up to initiate the transfer. The night wore on as each donkey accepted the backpack and then moved to the next station, where Arturo carefully placed six bottles on each side of the backpack. He grabbed clumps of uneaten straw and dunked them into the unused water. Large amounts of dirt were then mixed in to form a cushioned mixture that protected the bottles.

By the time 4:00 was displayed on David's watch, everyone was exhausted. Most of the donkeys were loaded with the cocktail, and the remainder with banana-clips were loaded with ammunition.

One of the men sat down for a smoke.

"I'm tired. I need a break."

The old man moved close to him and said, "You'll rest later, Puerco. You'll rest when you kiss the ass of the devil, himself—in Hell. Now get up!" He went to the corral adjusting the bandoleers and scarf; then straddled the wooden fence, resting his boot heel on the second rung.

"Señores, we have a three-hour march ahead of us. I know this land very well. We will encounter wolves, snakes, rodent holes, and snake pits. You have no light to guide you other than the moon above and me. I cannot guarantee that either will get you to your destination without mishap. You will take all your piss breaks and do your shitting on the way. Once we arrive at the point of attack, no one leaves his position for any reason. Let's get started, my friends."

The old man came off the fence like a youngster and ran to the front of the column. He grabbed the rein of his lead donkey and without dithering, the rest followed—including the donkeys.

The layered darkness revealed mesquite trees and thorned bushes. The moon showed them as a slight silhouette of a deep thicket that jabbed and scraped the men at every turn.

Three miles through the brush and dried creek beds, one hombre heard the tail of a nearby rattlesnake. The donkey nearest him reacted by shifting to the side and stepped on his foot. He screamed from the pain and slammed his fist against the donkey's hind quarter.

"Stop that!" yelled David.

The bottles shook inside the donkey's side pack, but the man kept walking while he spun around looking for the snake. Unable to soothe the pain in his foot, he rubbed his leg for the rest of the march.

The continuous sound of hooves traipsing through the dense thicket brought the howls of wolves in the distance—closer; ever closer. David pulled the Glock from his pocket and slid a bullet in the chamber.

A rodent hole caught the heel of one of Morales' men, and when he tried to skip out of it, he fell into a patchwork of cactus. The needle-sharp thorns pierced his jeans and shirt, and it dug into his calf and thigh. Pain exploded everywhere as he fell into the thorns of a nearby cactus. The old man stared at him for a moment and then went over to David.

"Give me your gun."

David looked at him, eyes widened.

"What are you going to do?"

The old man extended his arm with his palm facing up.

David renewed his appeal, "You can't do this."

"Give me your gun." The old man said, again. This time David handed it to him and turned away.

The farmer looked down at the wounded man.

"You will shut your mouth. You will stay here until you can catch up or until we return."

He handed the gun back to David.

"He will slow us down. Let's go!"

The moon disappeared behind the recently formed cumulus cloud. Foreboding howls pierced the night; the wolves gathered and drew closer. Their movement could not be heard, but every person and every donkey sensed their presence. Their distance from the group grew smaller by the minute.

The howling stopped. It was replaced by raspish, guttural, lupine utterings. The moon threw just enough light to the old man's right revealed the movement of brush. He stared through the shadowed dark to decipher wolf or wind.

The pack hunted for two days—they were hungry. The guttural snarls were heard through the brush again—no wind this time. The feeding frenzy was about to begin. Closer now and more of them, a big grey showed himself, ears pinned straight back; hackles standing. His muzzle pinched high into his eyes, making them squint He was a 130 pounds of death waiting to happen.

A donkey near the end of the line displayed a level of panic with the smell of a wolf in his nostrils, David grabbed a man with a machete and told him to follow him. Two of the wolves were busy feeding on the man left behind.

A second big grey, with inch-long canines, leaped on last donkey's back. It clawed its way up while struggling to maintain its grip on the backpack. The donkey kicked, landing his hooves on the wolf's testicles. The predator gave a short yelp, then growled and came at it again as he tried to sever the donkey's backbone through the heavy leather straps. The large grey stopped its attack long enough to stare at the man with the machete; eyes like steel daggers. Blood dripped from its mouth. The donkey was down, but his powerful kick wounded the attacking predator. The wolf was undeterred. Its meal was directly in front of him, and tonight, it would eat—man *or* donkey.

David rushed around the donkey's back and grabbed one of the bottles. He moved toward the lupine predator and slammed the bottle against its jaw; the wolf turned to face him. Its mouth filled with cocktail. The wolf's muzzle, up to its eyes, was painted with the phosphorous liquid. It smelled the foul-tasting fluid—it was rancid. Something was wrong.

It backed off.

The burning sensation swelled, and the stricken animal dropped to the ground and raised both paws to his face. A couple of the nearby gang members rushed to see what was happening while David stared. The wolf spun around, quicker now as the water evaporated. The moonlit darkness exposed small patches of smoke that emitted from his fur. An immense heat engulfed him, as the growls turned to whimpers and whining to canine screams. In a matter of seconds, the head of the wolf burst into flames. Every part of its body flailed in the dirt. Most of the men fell to their knees. Some cried at the sight. It was a phenomenon that they've never witnessed before but would soon see again. The wolf's face burned away; it lay dead.

My dear God, thought David as he helped the wounded donkey back to its feet.

While the men crossed themselves, the eight donkeys that were tied to each other by an umbilical cord, were yanked forward by the old farmer. There was no need to give orders to get the hell out of there. Each man grabbed the reins of a lead donkey in their section and ran as fast as they could to clear the area. The wolves were no longer a threat; they now had plenty of food.

Arturo saw traffic moving on the upcoming highway and the flashing red light on the track signaling the exact sharp curve in which they were most interested. Just one more mile.

It was barely sun-up when they had reached the end of their journey when David approached the old man.

"You need to take this caravan into the large crevasse. Over there," he pointed. "We will unload the cocktails, and when that's done, you can lead the donkeys back to the farm. You are out of this, old man. Vaya con Dios."

He argued with David a little, but in the end, he agreed that this was for younger men. David laughed.

Chapter 24

THE MORNING CAME EARLY at the port authority. Six o'clock witnessed; the night give way to a spurt of activity. Clean French-blue uniforms denoting longshoremen and cargo drivers indicated a new day at the docks. Two ships had come into port the previous night, and the off-loading would commence in 30 minutes. The *Maersk* tanker rode low in the water and tanker trucks lined up to receive the transported oil. At the leeward side of the long slip stood the *I.R.I.S. Hormuz Defender*, poised to give up her far-travelled cargo of cars, medical equipment, more cars, and machine parts. Lowboys and auto haulers came in from the west side of the docks all gassed up and ready to receive their cargo. They were prepared to offload up over 500 automobiles and 200 containers.

Juan Carlos was back at his desk peering through his corner window at the cranes moving into position to receive the *Defender's* cargo. By 6:30, the docks were now abuzz with activity. The bevy of halogen lights lit up the darkness and cast a bright light across the early morning dock. He looked at the electronic manifest of the *Defender*. He clicked the *Cargo* tab button, and the monitor filled up with the numbers that were assigned to the containers, crates, and automobiles. The manufacturer, the VIN number, and the location.

1-1-7-4

Enter. The screen went black, and then, seconds later, the entire cargo schematic was displayed on the screen. There, flashing yellow was the exact location of container 1174. Juan Carlos moved the mouse over to *File – Print.* Done.

"Juanita, I'm going down to the docks for a moment. I'll be back soon," the director said as he walked to the door, grabbing the printed page on his way out.

Juan Carlos, with a nonchalant attitude, strolled up to the massive hull of the *Hormuz Defender.* The cranes were hard at work removing Kias and Toyotas. He saw one of the supervisors standing surveying the transfer.

"I am the port director. Can you have your men remove a container for a customer who will be here in a few minutes?"

"Certainly, sir. What is the number and location?" the supervisor responded.

"It's container 1-1-7-4 and its location is Section 12, Row 21, AFT," Juan Carlos answered.

The supervisor agreed, "I'll have it for you on the next pass."

Juan Carlos thanked him and continued his stroll. He moved quickly to the security director's office and entered during the morning detail meeting.

"Team One, proceed to warehouses 1 through 5," the security director said, pointing to the warehouse locations on the wall. Make sure all containers are checked. Teams Two and Three, you complete the same patrol with warehouses 6 through 11 and 12 through 17 respectively."

Juan Carlos' eyes lit up and cleared his throat loud enough to get the security director's attention.

"Wait a minute," said the security supervisor. "Team Three, you make a concentrated effort to locate any contraband in warehouses 12 through 16 and quickly report anything you find." He closed the meeting and walked up to Juan Carlos. "This morning," the sergeant said, "we are short three men, so the patrolling will take much more time than usual."

Chapter 25

THE SUN WAS INCHING ITS WAY INTO Jack's hospital room when the morning nurse came in to change the intravenous solution in his arm. His eyes fluttered as she completed her task and walked out the room. Soon, Jack moaned and was noticed by a visitor of another patient. A casual mention of his movement, and the nurse rushed back to witness his wakening.

With an indistinguishable mouthing of words, Jack asked, "Where's my father?"

"I will call your mother," the nurse responded.

"Fine, but where's my father?" The words were horribly slurred.

She left him twisting and turning in the hospital bed and picked up the nearest phone and he called the hotel. Forty-five minutes passed slowly before Felicia and Julie were standing at his bed; no makeup, but there. The two, in unison, caressed his forehead and fondled over him. Jack grew stronger but wasn't without disdain for this kind of treatment.

"Where's Dad?" he asked for the third time.

"He's in Mexico," Felicia answered.

"This is not good," he said. "I've got to get down there." His speech was unclear and garbled.

"What!" Julie exclaimed. "You're not going anywhere. You've got to be crazy to get out of bed."

The nurse heard the commotion and explained to everyone that the doctor would be there in about an hour. Jack blew out a deep breath and fell back onto his pillow.

"Okay, okay, I'll wait for the doctor," Jack exclaimed as he dropped his head on the pillow. "Go have some breakfast, I'm not going anywhere." Most of his speech remained garbled and made little sense.

Felicia smiled. "Okay."

Jack lay there for a minute, staring at the ceiling.

"*Code Blue! Code Blue!*" The hall speaker exploded with an emergency.

In his stupor, he saw staff-members running down the hall. *Now's the time.*

His hand moved to his left forearm, and he removed the tape that kept the IV in place. It was a little cumbersome with one hand, so he helped it along with his teeth. It was an irrational task, but he was hell-bent on removing it. The tape was obstinate and was not designed to be removed by a patient. In the end, the pulling of the intravenous injection ripped his vein. He hadn't planned on any bloodletting. He wrapped his arm with tissues he found on a nearby table. The oxygen mask was easy to remove as were the EKG pads. Jack saw the roll of tape, so he attached the Kleenex to his arm. The process proved to be exhausting for him.

Although weak, he rose from the bed. His legs buckled at first. He staggered and fell against a chair but made it to the closet. He put on his pants and shirt, picked up his shoes and socks, and stumbled to the elevator. No one saw him.

He was disoriented and hungry, and his words were slurred but not so much that he couldn't ask the standing cab driver to take him to the McDonald's drive-thru and then to the airport. The cab driver obliged. Jack knew his plan was not going to be easy to complete. Flying the Bonanza was tough enough when he was aware, awake, and sober; now, he had not anywhere *near* those faculties.

The airport was just ahead. Jack gathered his thoughts and tried to put himself together. His physical condition was less than adequate, especially to perform what he was about to do. The blood that oozed from his arm had yet to coagulate. He gave the driver a $50 bill and left the cab.

"I'll be leaving now," Jack said to the man behind the counter. He forced lucid syllables from his mouth, but no one really believed his act of competence to fly his airplane.

"Mr. Culberson, are you alright?" The young man behind the counter stared at Jack. "The aircraft mechanic has your keys. I'll go get them for you." He left Jack standing there while he moved to the engine shop. The pilot decided to sit down and tried to regain control.

The shop foreman walked in the lobby

"We need to gas up your plane. Are you all right to fly it?"

"I'm quite capable of flying my own aircraft." He held on tightly to the arms of his chair. His words were barely distinguishable.

When Felicia and Julie returned from breakfast, both saw the blood stains on the sheets, and Felicia fell to the floor; she began hyperventilating. Julie called the Tucson police, and an all-points bulletin was initiated to find Jack. She saw the world as she knew it coming to an end.

Chapter 26

JACK WAS NOT HAVING MUCH SUCCESS in convincing the shop foreman he was well enough to fly. The FBO operator told Jack he was not going to allow him anywhere near his Bonanza. Jack thanked him for his concern and responded with, "Give me my keys!" but the two mechanics were not going to let him take this plane anywhere.

"Would you get my log book?" he asked, leaning against the door jam. His eyelids worked hard to stay open; Jack attempted three times to put his hands in his pockets—he failed.

The foreman shook his head but honored his request. He opened the door and climbed in the front seat. As he leaned forward to open up the glove compartment, Jack climbed up behind him and struck him on the neck with a wrench he had pilfered from the counter. He horse-collared the mechanic and threw him backwards out of the cockpit and on to the tarmac.

No time for pre-flight today… He flipped on the ignition and saw there was three-quarters of a tank of fuel left. *This should be enough*, he thought.

He was in an acrophobic stupor as he turned the key to start the engine. The three blades turned; slowly at first, but within a moment, Jack sensed the aircraft was rolling forward.

This is an escape to a damnable conclusion.

Jack didn't call ground control. He did not call the tower. He didn't wait to see what aircraft were landing or taking off. He quickly made his way to the runway and rammed the throttle through the firewall. The Beechcraft responded with incredible thrust as he gained speed down the runway. The plane veered toward the grass then back to crossing the centerline.

Half way down the runway, Jack settled down and stayed close to center until he reached 80 knots. In a short moment, he was airborne, leaving a Tucson Airport Police car behind him. He knew quite well this act would cost him his license, his plane, and probably his life. He punched in the coordinates for Mazatlán on his Garmin flight deck and headed upward to 8,000 feet cruising altitude, fumbled around to find the autopilot activation—finally.

Now on autopilot, he tried to relax.

Chapter 27

Manuel Cantu worked as a security guard at the Port of Mazatlán for three years. With a new baby in the house, the last three nights had not been conducive for sleeping. The doctors confined Dolores to bed for a week after he brought the two home. Manuel was relegated to the 10:00 P.M., 2:00 and 4:00 A.M. feedings. In the end, they had taken the baby by cesarean, and now. recovery was of prime concern. The last few days, it was relatives in-and-out, and Manuel loved the attention. A conscientious employee *and* father, it was the cause of his being late to work for the last two days. Everyone at the security office knew about the baby and understood his reasons for being late. Today was no different. The clock was nearing 7:30 when he kissed Dolores and the baby and went to the docks to begin his day.

Manuel arrived at 8:15. The dispatch sergeant was on the phone when he arrived for work. The sergeant waved a *hello* and, without thinking, sent him on his way. Manuel went to the ready room and while gathering his equipment, looked at the patrol dispatch board. All of the warehouses were covered, except warehouses 17 and 18. No one was there to assign him or explain otherwise. Taking the initiative, Manual proceeded to warehouse 17 and a date with his destiny.

He hurried to his self-imposed patrol area. The morning was busy with fast-moving forklifts and heavy equipment capable of carrying containers. The forklift approached warehouse 17 with its load—a 10-foot container.

Manuel was walking the northeast side of the warehouse when the sound and smell of the forklift hit him. The forklift disappeared into the warehouse from the south, and Manuel moved swiftly to the sound. The truck stopped in front of section 3, and the operator carefully placed the container between the lines of space number 1. Upon completing the drop, the driver spun the vehicle around and almost caught Manuel in the leg with one of the lifting forks. Manuel jumped back, barely missing the dubious pleasure of winding up in the hospital with a broken leg.

"Hey man, I'm sorry," yelled the operator, "I didn't see you there."

The guard waved his hand in forgiving motion.

"You got a lot of stuff to bring in here today?"

"No, just this container." The operator said, "This is the only one coming here."

"Well, stay busy," Manuel said.

The operator started his forklift and turned to leave when he abruptly turned off the engine.

Two men drove toward them in a large white cargo van. The operator sat in his seat, waiting to see if he could help them remove something.

"Can I help you gentleman?" Manuel asked.

"No thank you, señor, we have it." They were dressed as dockworkers.

"What are you after?" asked Manuel.

"We're here to pick up the contents of a container, looking at a sheet of paper, uh…1-1-7-4."

"May I see your documents?"

"They're coming," the van driver answered.

"Yes, I understand, but I can't let you remove the contents without documentation," Manuel said. "I'll wait here with you until the documents arrive."

The passenger in the truck stepped out of the cab and approached Manuel.

"We can resolve this very quickly, if you allow me to make a phone call," the man said.

"You can make all the phone calls you want, but you're not leaving here with the contents until I see proper documentation." Manuel was firm.

The driver came closer to Manuel with a deliberate agenda; his eyes never blinked.

"Stop right there!" Manuel drew his radio from his belt. "Dispatch! Send a security force to warehouse 17, section 3 immediately—we have a breach."

Oh, crap! Oh, crap!

The dispatch sergeant hung up his phone call. His stomach instantly tightened as he realized his incompetence. He yelled into the two-way, "Got it! Manuel, we're coming." He clicked another radio, "Team Three—warehouse 17—security force—section 3 – Now!" The number 1 button on the sergeant's cell instantly called Juan Carlos., "Señor Director, warehouse 17—now! We have a problem. I'm leaving my office."

The port director stopped meandering around the docks and ran as fast as he could to warehouse 17.

The first guy lunged at Manuel, wielding an eight-inch, folding Karambit. The blade hit its mark across Manuel's throat. The fork-lift driver, shocked at the sight, never felt the 9mm bullet that struck him in the head. The explosive sound sent a reverberating shockwave that permeated every inch of the warehouse. Manuel gurgled at his last attempt to breath—his daughter would never be held by her father again.

The men quickly removed the blowtorch they carried and melted the lock. They swung the door open and unloaded 52-by-two-foot boxes of opium poppy. Now, time was critical.

"Let's get moving," the driver said.

Quickly, they both entered the container and removed two to three boxes at a time. The truck filled up quickly with every minute counted, and two men lay dead on the warehouse floor. Twenty boxes were loaded when the first security guard entered the warehouse. He saw the malaise and yelled for the two to stop. The driver obeyed only long enough to pull his pistol and pump two 9mm bullets in the approaching guard's chest. The first man never skipped a beat. Ten more boxes were now in the truck.

"I'll hold them off," the driver said.

A three-man team entered. The lead yelled at the intruders, "Our sergeant has called the police. They are on the way."

Two shots rang out; the second bullet hit one of the guards. Six more boxes were loaded.

The driver yelled at the man carrying the boxes,

"How many more?"

"Four." He yelled back, "Let's forget 'em. Let's get out of here."

"No!" the driver said. "Get them all!"

Now 50. Both jumped inside the van. The gearshift was thrown into drive, and the accelerator was almost pushed through the floorboard, leaving particles of rubber on the concrete floor. One more shot; one more dead guard as they left the warehouse.

Minutes later, Juan Carlos ran into the warehouse and stood there in shock, his breathing out of control, he stared at the horrific sight of his employees lying on the floor.

The sergeant had arrived only moments before. Both of his hands intertwined behind his neck.

"*Madre mia! Madre mia!*" The van was gone; the container was empty and there was devastation all around him.

The director ran his hands through his gray hair and leaned back against the forklift. *Great Jesus!* Looking into the warehouse and then to the entrance, he murmured to himself, *My God, what have I gotten myself into?* His heart was near apoplexy.

The malaise that lay before him had his hands and his entire body shaking. He could not stop. He saw in front of him the impending investigations. *And* he saw the cartel enraged. *There was no damn reason for this. Worse,* he thought, *who did it and how am I going to explain it?*

"Sergeant, when you have composed yourself, come see me."

Chapter 28

DAVID AND ARTURO WERE METHODICAL in their placement of the men, with David toward the center of the turn, Arturo at back, and Morales at the start. Those positioned on the high ridge brought mesquite brush to hide themselves and the cache of cocktails. Equally as resourceful, were the men in the crevasse.

"The area on the high ridge that is hidden by the sun's glare should have more men," Arturo said. "The Sinaloas will never see them, and they can cut them down like the dogs they are."

David smiled and said,

"You heard him. You!" he added, pointing at one of the men, "Take three of you, and head for that area right there." He yelled up to them when they reached the spot where David wanted them.

It was 10:00 when Arturo spotted a caravan of trucks and cars coming down the highway.

"That's Morales." He stood up and waved his arms and hands. David turned around and saw the extra men driving up to the attacking point.

"We saw the cocktail at work." He told Morales the event with the wolf. His eyes froze on a distant mountain as David finished. Morales blinked to remove the glaze and turned to Arturo nodding his head.

"Good."

Chapter 29

THE LARGE, EIGHT-WHEELED MERCEDES took the boxes filled with poppy to the train station through the streets and morning traffic. They knew the police were never called, so their resolve was only affected by the train schedule. Hundreds of morning commuters on motorcycles zigged and zagged in and out of traffic lanes. A young man with his girlfriend riding on the back of his Yamaha crotch rocket cut in front of the van just as both were going around the traffic circle. She took the initiative to apologize for her friend's bad driving, she gave the van driver the finger; then waved.

The city's circular intersection, housed a traffic pedestal upon which a policeman stood directing the flow of traffic. The van moved to the outside lane in time to take the second exit. The policeman questioned the maneuver, so his whistle signaled the truck to pull over. There were hundreds of automobiles, buses, and motorcycles moving around the circle. The policeman stepped down from his four-foot-high station and, through the traffic, hurried over to the driver in the eight-wheeler. The driver remained calm and held his semi-automatic pistol near the door jam.

"I'm very sorry, officer. I didn't mean to change that lane so fast."

"Where are you going in such a hurry?" the office asked.

"I have this shipment of machine parts that must be on the Culiacán train.

"Let me see your…" A motorcycle came a little too close to him and then noticed the traffic jamming up. "Okay, you can go, but be careful."

Four miles ahead was the entrance gate to the train station.

The cargo car was the car in front of the caboose. The truck turned left on the link-up road and inconspicuously headed to the end of the train. The driver stopped the van next to the large sliding door and opened it with little effort. One of Morales' men met the driver at the opening with the dead train employee lying near the car's window. The boxes of poppy were put on the loading platform and moved to the sliding door. The boxed opium plants were methodically stacked inside.

By 10:15, the job was finished, and the four thugs took a quick breather. One jumped down and drove the van to the parking lot. The Sinaloas climbed aboard the caboose, then to the top of the last car. Everything was in place. The conductor announced the departure—non-stop to Culiacán.

The engineer set the throttle in the forward position, and the steam-diesel hybrid locomotive moved 110 miles up range to Culiacán. No black smoke; no hard-jerking motion, the passengers sensed a smooth, constant increase in speed. The plains that lay ahead held 79 miles of track in her bosom. The conductor glanced at his watch as he went through the five passenger cars welcoming everyone on the journey that he and the engineer worked every day.

The grid called for 55 miles per hour until the train reached Marker 77B, then the engineer began the slowing process for three miles. The target speed then was 10 miles per hour. Fifty yards beyond that point was the crevasse and the sharp left curve. The engineer's job was to maintain the safe speed so as to not overexert the trains stability. When he finally reached the crevasse, it would take 17 minutes to come out the curve.

There was a sudden buffeting from the cars as the locomotive pulled hardily up the grade, and at the same time, the engineer passed Marker 76A.

The warning light flashed yellow. He found no reason to push the envelope up the graded track, as the next mile and a half would demand the intended slow-down. He let the engine settle herself into a calmer slog. Moving up the grade with a small amount of thrust made it easier on the train, rather than having to use the brakes when it hit the other side. He saw *Marker 77B* come at him on the right—he checked his speed while he wiped the sweat from his hands. It was time to throttle back a little more.

—◆◆◆—

Arturo saw the smoke first and motioned to Morales. He reminisced in his mind the stories his grandfather told him about what he did and the subsequent devastation 70 years prior. How they hid in adjacent wooded areas next to the track. How he waited for those German trains carrying munitions and troops to war. In his mind, he brought together the event of today and what his grandfather did during the war, and Arturo's mind played on the difference.

The signal was given to Morales' men hidden on the high ridge with their supply of cocktail next to them. The train was a mile away. Arturo looked down at his shirt; it was soaking wet. He laid the AR-15 down and wiped his hands on his pant leg. Morales slapped him on the back of head; he smiled.

Morales screamed at the top of his voice, "Stay low—stay hidden—don't move until I move first, then hit 'em with everything you got!"

Everyone responded by waving their arms.

David's view was head-on—the visual was the train stopped. There was no discernment of movement from the on-coming train. The locomotive had reached the sharp curve heading into the side of the mountain. Slowly now, she pulled the cars behind her. Bringing the passengers first into the high ground, the train was directly above Arturo. His view of the large steel wheels overcame him. The fear was immense and now he was shaking. The undercarriage was visible in every detail. His mind conjured up the train falling off the track and right on top of him. The wheels rolled less than 10 feet above him.

Twelve minutes passed, and the giant locomotive was more than halfway through the curve, and there remained a stillness in everyone.

The cargo car came into view and then the caboose. Morales, and everyone else, could see the three atop the last car. The constant grating sound of wheels clacking over track kept syncopated to David's heartbeat.

The caboose passed over Morales first. The toss of the first cocktail landed on top of the car and broke beneath the feet of one of the guards. At first, the Sinaloa did not know what to make of the non-threatening action. He laughed at the broken glass as he looked around for the culprit who threw it. The caboose was now entering the turn—it was time. Morales' second toss went inside the window; the broken bottle spewed the cocktail on the floor. Nothing happened; no screaming, no fire, just laughter.

Four snipers 30 feet high open fire on the guards atop the car. The three on top of the caboose returned indiscriminate fire. The first guard to get hit was the man who murdered Manuel. Three shots came simultaneously, and one more of the Sinaloas' gang was dead. The men inside the caboose fired their weapons into the side of the mountain, but could not see to who or at what they were shooting. Arturo's assumption was the sun's glare would mar their vision was correct: The guards had no idea as to the origin of the rifle shots. The guards were sitting ducks. If they jumped, it would be a 200-foot leap to their death. And yet, no fire.

Another bottle was thrown; another; and then another. A bottle was thrown and smashed at one man's feet. Then bottles came in a flurry from the high ridge and landed on top of the guards. Morales' eyes disdainfully stared at Arturo.

"Where's the fucking fire?"

Gonzales responded loudly above the din, "Just wait, jefe, just wait."

In a moment, the Sinaloas inside the caboose were now screaming. Their feet were on fire climbing up their bodies.

Morales' grimacing turned to delight. He stared at the fire. He yelled back to Arturo, "Incredible!"

The caboose was engulfed in flames. The men inside were dead. The one man alive atop the last car was in crisis. The flames were on his pants rising to his torso, He threw his AK-47 away to stop the fire that was engulfing him, but he lost the fight.

Some of the passengers heard what they thought to be gunfire but weren't sure if the sound was wheels thumping over rail ties or something else.

One of Morales' men grabbed two bottles, prepared to throw them, but tripped on the friable ground beneath him. Undeterred and without thinking, he stood up and smashed the cocktails against the car that was directly in front of him. Both bottles broke, and most of the liquid and all of the glass fell directly on top of him. His face was covered in blood and chards from the broken bottles. Everyone was busy with the assault and paid no attention to his cries. Worse, no one paid attention to his screams when the dissolved phosphorous came in contact with the air. The liquid had penetrated his cornea—it was in his hair and all over his face. His hair burst into flames. His hands experienced excruciating heat. Before his eyes were on fire, he saw the smoke arise from his arms, then a ball of fire ensued.

And then it was over.

All the guards on top of the caboose were dead. As the rear of the train came out of the curve, the last car was engulfed in flames. Within minutes of the final turn, the caboose was gone; burned to the wheels. The smoke rose a good 50 feet in the air.

As the train passed the attacker's position, the assailers came off the high-ridge and rushed to gather at their vehicles waiting a few hundred yards back. David stood up to survey the damage. Morales approached him from down the track.

"We did good today," Morales said.

David nodded, but did not join in the revel.

In the first passenger car, a small boy looked out the window.

"Mama! Look at the fire," he said

Reading her book, she turned to her son and asked, "What fire, dear?"

"The train, Mama, the train—see?" the boy yelled.

She looked over shoulder and leaped from her seat, yelling, "Conductor, conductor!"

He calmly walked to her and asked her if he could get her anything.

"The train is on fire," she screamed at him. He called the engineer to stop the train.

The conductor and both porters ran through each car telling the passengers to grab their belongings and get off. Panic ensued. Men trampled over women and children to get off. A pregnant woman going to visit her mother was knocked hard into the railing and would find out later she had suffered a miscarriage.

The train was now empty. They all stood on the side of the track and saw the caboose, 10 cars back, on fire and all wondered why it resulted in a panic.

To Morales, this now was easier than planned. The train was stopped. They proceeded down the track from behind the train. With barely enough room, Morales and his men stepped carefully around what was left of the caboose and moved to the opium-ladened cargo car.

"Listen to me." Morales yelled to the men inside. "We are going to cut this lock off. If you have a weapon in your hands, you will die. A large bolt-cutter was removed from one of the trucks and brought up to the car. In a matter of seconds, the lock was cut, and all the men outside pointed their carbines at the door.

Arturo stepped up to the door and slid it open. There were three men inside guarding the cargo. Their hands rested on top of their heads.

"Good job, boys," said Morales as he turned to his men. "Shoot 'em anyway."

Two men fell to their knees. The third threw his head back and like a slingshot, released his head forward with a timed spit in death, accepting defiance. The bullet split his head apart. The other two were dead seconds later.

"We'll form a line on the track like a bucket brigade. Remove the boxes and take them to the trucks," Arturo said.

Morales agreed.

Arturo got the line started. When it was completed, he returned to Morales.

"The trucks are loaded, and we are headed north. David is going back to Buelna to retrieve his plane; that should take less than an hour."

He had no idea what awaited him.

"Vargas, catch up to the opium," Vargas yelled. "Get to the plant and start the processing immediately. Calaban, you go back with David. I've got a special job for you."

David looked back at the people and the wounded train. The remnants of the phosphorous permeated the entire area as it cast a subtle green fog over the region and came to rest like a blanket covering a purified Gomorrah. The odor of phosphorous replaced the sight of the malaise and was in their nostrils several hundred feet away. The conductor and one of the porters moved the pregnant woman to a safer place, and she was resting comfortably.

David sat in the middle of the vehicle as it rolled southward on South Highway. The job was done. The opium poppies were on their way to Cananéa, just southeast of Nogales, and now, he needed to get his plane back to the U.S. The airport was a few miles away, so he pulled out phone to call the corporate terminal.

"This is David Culberson. Fuel my plane, would you? I'll be leaving soon." He noticed 12 messages, all from Felicia, draped like a curtain on his phone display.

The Gulfstream is ready. I'll see what she wants…

With the push of the "1" key, he began, "Hi, honey, what's up?"

Her answer wasn't exactly what he expected.

"What's up? *What's up?* Where the hell have you been? Jack's gone, and I've been calling for hours. Damn it, David, where are you?"

"I've been in a meeting. What do you mean, Jack's gone? On his own accord? Where did he go?"

"No one knows, but the police are looking for him."

"Did you check his plane?"

"His plane?" Felicia was furious. "He can't fly his plane, hell, he can hardly walk."

"I'll be back in Tucson in a couple of hours. Go! Don't call. Go to the airport to McKensey's office that's on the corporate side. That is where his plane is parked. Maybe they have an idea. Call me when you find out anything."

The "end" key was engaged as they approached the gate to the corporate terminal.

Must be lunch time… he observed.

"No one's at the gate—good. Just drive to the plane, and don't stop," David said.

The sun was in its straight-up position, and it had already been a full day. The truck came to a stop 100 yards from the terminal. The tarmac was filled with Federales.

Christ! He thought.

"They couldn't possibly know about the train—no way—not yet," David said to his driver. "Just keep driving."

"Are you sure, señor?"

David nodded and the driver headed for the Gulfstream.

The truck was now just 30 feet away from David's plane when he ordered the driver to stop. He looked at the man standing in the doorway of the private terminal. David jumped out of the truck and walked to his airplane.

"Just a minute, señor." The voice he heard approached him from the terminal.

He was Federali. "Is this your plane?"

"Yes, it is. Is there a problem with it?"

"No, señor, it is beautiful. Where have you been today?"

"In Culiacán," David continued. "I have to get back to Tucson. My son is ill. Is there anything I can help you with?"

"Only if you spent some time at the Port of Mazatlán this morning?"

He barely noticed his own sigh of relief.

"No, I believe these people can tell you where I went."

The policeman backed away and shrugged his shoulders with outstretched arms. He turned his palms up.

"Okay, señor, have a safe flight."

David opened his door and entered his airplane. His breathing slowed down to a something-less-than-normal rate as he went into the cockpit and sat in his favorite seat. David flipped the avionics switch and waited for them to ramp up. It took a few minutes for this procedure to be completed, so he went outside to complete the pre-flight. The Federali agent watched him move from port to starboard—front to rear.

David re-entered the aircraft and sat down again in the pilot's seat. He flipped the "on" switch for power and cranked up his engines; he called ground control to file his IFR flight plan.

Ground control read his flight plan and acknowledged his flight-path back to Tucson. After receiving approval, he moved quickly to the northbound runway. David's heart was pounding as the picture of today's activities raced through his mind. This was not David Culberson today. This was the work of a madman and a terrorist.

When he reached the entrance to the runway, he contacted the tower and requested take-off instructions. Moments later, the clearance came. David rolled on to Runway 3-6 Right and pushed the plane down the runway.

Get me the hell out of here!

Three minutes-thirty-two seconds later, David was wheels-up and heading for Tucson. He set his course on autopilot and settled back in his seat. He tried to get his breathing under control as he picked up his air phone and pushed a pre-programmed number. A lady answered the call and quietly said.

"New York City Municipal Offices, may I help you?"

"Yes," David said, "Give me the deputy."

Chapter 30

THE MEAGER KNOCK BREACHED JUAN CARLOS' quiet time. One security guard and a new father and a forklift driver were dead. A hapless event that could have been averted.

"Enter," Juan Carlos answered. The door opened slowly. The visitor, not knowing what to expect, sheepishly moved through the portal as the sergeant presented himself. "Don't sit down, Sergeant."

The early afternoon sun barely cast a shadow on the director's face as he sat with his back to the security supervisor. The ships outside the window seemed to give the director solace as his mind pondered the confrontation in warehouse 17.

What might have been an eternity, Juan Carlos stoically asked, "Why did you send that guard to where the container was stored?"

"I...I...was on the..."

"I don't wish to hear it." The swiveling high-back executive chair turned, and he was now facing the sergeant. Juan Carlos picked up his phone for the second time and struck a pre-programmed number. Immediately, the recipient answered.

"God dammit, Estabán. We've been hit."

Juan Carlos sat up in his chair.

The voice on the other end was screaming, "My heroin is gone—stolen. The guards are dead, and *my* heroin is gone?" The port director was beside himself. He looked at the sergeant, then buried his head in the mouthpiece of the phone.

"Who took it?" he asked. The voice was hyper-ventilating so badly, Juan Carlos could not understand a word. "You find those fuckers. You find 'em, and you kill them. You hear me? You kill 'em *real* bad."

"I...I...don't have the wherewithal to do that," Juan Carlos responded.

"Kill 'em, you son-of-a-bitch. Find'em. Rip their hearts out!"

The phone went dead. Juan Carlos' heart stopped—he went white as a ghost.

"Sergeant, we've been hit; hijacked; ripped-off. Find out where the train was attacked. Find out who *hit* he train. Get your ass back here, and tell me what you found out. Find out who did this!"

The sergeant stood still for a moment, waiting for more specific instructions.

"Get out of here!" He tilted his head and leaned toward the door, looking beyond the sergeant, "Juanita, find the phone number for this dead guard, Manuel Cantu, who died today. I need to call his wife."

Chapter 31

CANANÉA IS AN OBSCURE LITTLE TOWN East by southeast of Nogales; nestled in the foothills of the Sierra de Cananéa Mountains. Morales' heroin processing operation lay inside the town. Morales' plant sits just off the town's square hidden by its transparency—a 120-year-old church.

The people of the town saved for two years to install electrical wiring for evening services. When the town attempted the installation on their own, a fire ensued and gutted the ancient building. The state of Sonora built a new church in the same sixteenth century motif as the one that was destroyed. In addition, Morales paid the mayor a half million dollars for the discarded mission.

At midnight, a long, double strand of shimmering beads came out of the bosom of the Sierra de Cananéas. The high-beamed eyes were interspersed with darkness and erratic spacing. The darkness provided a visualization of a fast-moving, luminous reptile slithering into town and coming to rest in front of the church.

Morales was the first to jump out of his black SUV; soon after, Arturo Gonzales stepped from one of the trucks. He stretched his legs and then his arms; he rose them high as if to touch the stars. He gazed at the blackness. The moon was all but gone behind whatever buildings that existed and could barely make out the spire that used to house the church bell. Arturo thought he saw an outline of a fountain made partially visible by the water that surrounded it. The palms of his hands rubbed his face and then his eyes. He could use some sleep.

"Over here, Arturo," Vargas said.

Arturo turned around just as Morales flipped on the newly installed lights. From the street, Arturo could the inside come alive with fluorescent lighting, which exposed the factory. His heart pounded as he passed through the spiritual portal.

My God, he's making heroin in a CHURCH! His hands shook. His whole body was reeling in fear—certainly, fear of what God would do with these people. He then calmly, as if in a trance, moved over to the nearest wall, squatted down, and stayed there with his head resting in his folded arms that he placed on top of his knees.

Morales and Vargas were watching his men bring in the boxes of opium poppies. Another smaller group started up the machinery.

Vargas yelled, "Spread the boxes, and open them up, and let the opium poppies breathe. Check all the flowers and report their condition. If any of the petals have dropped off, let me know immediately."

The next several hours brought the reality of a process that devoured the next two days. The egg-shaped seed pod had to mature on its own, but it had been three months. Once maturity had been reached, the opaque, milky sap was secured by a systematic vertical slicing of the pod. As the sap oozed out, it turned darker and thicker, forming a brownish-black gum.

"When you collect the gum," Morales said, "form it into bricks and wrap them with plastic paper." He then went to another group and gave them different instructions.

"Come here and listen very carefully," Morales spoke to the small group. "When you scrape the pods, take the opium and mix it with two gallons lime juice. Take the mixture and place it in boiling water and wait until it boils down. Remove the film of organic waste from the bottom of the vat. You will then see a white band of morphine formed at the top. Scoop that and reheat it with an ammonia, filter it and reheat again. After that, reheat until it is reduced to a brown paste. Calaban help you." Morales turned away from the group then turned back.

"That, my friends is heroine. Let's go!" He slapped his hands together, "Now!"

Chapter 32

THE GROWTH OF CULBERSON PETROCHEMICAL was a work-in-progress since its beginning. The constant trips to New York and the meetings with the principals of Simons and Simons Brokerage were arduous, at best. The initial public offering was successful out of the gate, but the burn-rate on research and development exceeded their expectations and valuations plummeted.

David got frustrated after the need for a second offering and the fifth time he had to fly into the city. The mayor was celebrating the winning of his second term, and the selling group had been invited. Richard Simons picked up his private line and dialed David's room.

"You need to relax, my man," Simons said, "The mayor's giving a party, and I think you need to come with." David swallowed his last sip of the sweet brandy he held.

"What time are you picking me up?"

"Great! Out front in an hour."

David agreed and hung up the phone. He took a quick shower; grabbed his midnight-blue, silk tuxedo that Felicia packed, and was waiting in the lobby when the limo pulled up.

The Ritz-Carlton was the perfect venue for such an affair. Among the guests were the governor and the senior senator from the state of New York. Richard Simons eyed the deputy mayor, Madeleine Underwood, poking her finger in the chest of the renowned congressman representing Harlem. The conversation was going south when Simons decided to save her.

"Madam Deputy Mayor, excuse me. I wanted to introduce a friend and client, Mr. David Culberson, from Dallas.

"Hello, Deputy Mayor Underwood." David sensed an uncomfortable feeling in her demeanor. It was subtle but apparent.

"Is anything wrong, Madam Deputy Mayor?" David asked.

"No," she smiled and responded politely. "You bear a striking resemblance to my late husband." She stayed in conversation with him, but her memory of Lawrence Underwood came from her subconscious to almost believing he was standing in front of her.

"I am so sorry," she said, "my husband was murdered 10 years ago while traveling in the Middle East."

"I am very sorry," David said. "If I make you uncomfortable, I am happy to leave."

"No, don't be silly. You just made me think of him and how much he liked midnight-blue tuxedos."

David smiled.

The following year and the year after that, David's relationship with Madeleine grew over annual dinners, and a strong friendship ensued. The more time he spent with her, the more he learned about her past. Her husband was a corporate lawyer engaged in international contract negotiations dealing specifically with heads of state. She noted she only cried once over his death and never cried again—she was through with that.

On a trip in November of 2009, she had one more shot of scotch, and her brain put her mouth in gear. Madeleine told the entire story of how Muslim fundamentalists stopped Underwood's car in Croatia. They fired indiscriminately into her husband's car—the police found his mutilated body two weeks later.

Madeleine gazed at the cranberry bean and pumpkin stew on her plate. She began to cry—he never saw that before. She swirled her spoon through and around the French concoction. Tears dropped on her plate; the memory of Lawrence ate at her soul.

She had been deputy mayor for a year and most of New York loved her. She met David for dinner every time he was in town.

David was finding his niche in New York City's highlife. Always the right party at the right time.

Meetings with Simons and Simons for more infusion of funds—the fourth consecutive offering in as many years.

Another party—this time at the International—David wore a white dinner-jacket to celebrate the rights of spring. Madeleine found him ordering a bourbon and water with two ice cubes at the open bar.

"Hi, stranger," she said. "When did you get in?"

He turned to see her smiling face.

"This morning," he said. "Hey, I read the interview you gave to the *Times*. Pretty interesting stuff."

"David, do you have any idea about the amount of drugs that hit our city every year?"

"Not enough?" he said jokingly.

The immediate response to his words were disdainfully displayed on her face, and without hesitating, she turned away and went to converse with someone else. He pushed off his arm resting on the bar and pounced forward. It took three quick steps of chasing before he caught up to her; he softly touched her forearm.

"I'm sorry, Madeleine, I was just kidding."

As if she were reading a cue card, she began, "You guys from Texas are all alike. You carry your guns and have the proximity of the Mexican Border, so you can acquire all the marijuana you want. And don't *even* get me started on the heroin problem."

Madder than a wet hen, she continued, "I asked you a question a minute ago. Do you have any idea as to the amount of illicit drugs that come into my city? Millions of dollars every month, and people, have died from the use. No, David, there's no humor here."

David remained quiet, and he took everything she threw at him, but it sounded a lot like pontificating to him. There were five people who were in ear-shot of her comments. Their hands exploded with applause when she finished lambasting her new friend. The rest of the go-along sheeples joined in with equal exuberance; not having a clue as to why.

Madeleine Underwood was born in Herkimer, New York; a small village about 13 miles south of Utica. Her college days were spent at Bryn Mawr in Pennsylvania, and most of her time was spent learning about the political system from a state up to the national level.

Her career in the political science started as a receptionist for her districts' U.S. Congressman. The first step into a world she was aching for. And now Madeleine Underwood was the Deputy Mayor of New York City with more power than she ever dreamed of having. When she and the newly elected mayor settled in their offices, the mayor's assistant came in to visit with the deputy. She informed Madeleine that her boss would like to have lunch and discuss Madeleine's role his administration. She grabbed her purse and walked back the mayor's office with his assistant.

The lunch was held at Lombardy's and the standard faire was served. Filet mignon and asparagus tips with spicy mash potatoes. The glasses of Merlo were constantly filled while the two leaders of the city laughed and joked about their success and how the city will be run.

"Madeleine," said the mayor, "I want you to concentrate on stopping in influx of illicit drugs in our community. The amount of drugs that enter our city is in the hundreds of millions of dollars each year." He continued, "I want you to work closely with the police commissioner and the DEA. Introduce yourself to these people and get to know them and what they do on a daily basis and *stop* this epidemic.

Madeleine nodded in agreement.

"John, I will make the ceasing of drug flow the foundation of our time in office."

Chapter 33

THE OPIUM WAS ON ITS WAY TO CANANÉA. It was a successful day; if you believed that killing seven men was "successful."

Great! My son is out of his coma, David thought. *Now my son is gone. Taken his airplane somewhere and he can hardly walk.*

David grabbed his radio and switched on Jack's frequency.

"Bonanza 1-3-4-6-Foxtrot. Bonanza 1-3-4-6 Foxtrot. Jack, do you read me?" There was no answer. David tried to reach his son more than just a few times for the next hour to no avail. He picked the airphone again and called Felicia. She answered.

"Have you heard from anyone about Jack?"

"No, but he took his plane after he attacked one of the mechanics."

"I just tried to reach him. I'm 30 minutes out, honey, I'll be home soon."

As promised, David's wheels touched down in less than an hour. He shut the engines down and without saying a word to anyone, locked up the plane and drove to the hotel. He arrived and went into his room. He went right to the bed and fell into oblivion.

Chapter 34

IT WAS 11:00 IN THE MORNING, over three hours after the breech. A short drive to the Cantu's house took him through the barrios of Mazatlán and on to a quiet, lower income housing development. He knew about the birth issues and how even three months after, her recovery had been slow. He got the to the door and knocked. An acknowledgement of the visitor came behind the door.

"The port director, Mrs. Cantu," Juan Carlos answered

"Yes?" Dolores Cantu opened the door

"Mrs. Cantu, I'm Port Director Juan Carlos Estabán. May I come in?"

"Yes. Please." She turned away from the door. Her walking was tenuous, at best, but she continued to stand.

"Where's Manuel?" she asked.

Juan Carlos approached her and eased her over to the sofa.

"Mrs. Cantu, there's been an acci…"

Both of Dolores' palms came up to cover her gaping mouth. Her eyes turned a horrifying red as a lonesome tear rolled down her face.

"Mrs. Cantu, I am here with very bad news." Juan Carlos began. "Manuel is dead; he was killed this morning at the docks."

Stunned by disbelief and anger, she stared at the wall without crying.

"There will be an inquiry," he continued, "and you will be fully informed of the results. He had insurance, and so that has already been put into motion."

"You investigate!" she propped herself up while rising from seat. "I will do what I have to do."

She moved across the sofa and picked up the phone.

"Mama, Manuel is dead. Please come over and take care of the baby. I have to go out.

You can leave, Mr. Port Director, I have a full day ahead of me."

Dolores was dressed when her mother arrived. They hugged and cried—a little.

She drove downtown to see the police. Halfway there, she stopped in the middle of traffic and thought for a moment. People honked at her, yelling to move forward. *No. Wrong choice.* Her stomach was churning by now. Her heart pounded against her ribcage. She would go to the Federales. Their office was two blocks away. Upon arrival, Dolores Cantu left he car in the visitor's area and walked, half stumbling into the local office of the Mexican Federales.

"May I speak to the head of your department?" she asked.

"He's busy now, can I help you?" answered the agent behind a desk.

"My husband was murdered this morning at the docks. I need some help."

Behind the glass door, Colonel José Cruz was finishing telephone call. The three men sitting in his office were patiently waiting for the call to end. For the first time in the history of both Mexico and the United States, federal agents from the north were going to be allowed to work with the Federales inside Mexico.

The three smiled as they walked out of the colonel's office. In broken English, he said, "Welcome to Mexico, agents." A smile appeared on his dark, wrinkle-laden face.

Jonathan thanked him, and the three proceeded out the door. Jerry stopped and turned around, "We'll see you at the docks, Colonel."

Dolores yelled, "Señores, please. You are Federales, yes? My husband, he was murdered this morning, I am waiting to report this to somebody."

"Ma'am, we're Federal agents from the United States," Jerry responded.

"Please help me." Now, Dolores was crying. Whatever mascara she put on earlier ran down her face.

A female assistant came over and helped Dolores into the colonel's office, and the three agents followed her back into the colonel's office. They talked about the director's visit and her conversation with him at her home.

"Mrs. Cantu, there are two Federali agents at the docks investigating the incident right now, and we're on our way out there." Jerry said, "Here's my cell number. We'll stay in touch. I promise."

The colonel gave the FBI agent the keys to his car, and all three headed for the docks.

Protocol requires each security team be comprised of four men—why was Cantu by himself? Why did the dispatch sergeant purposely ignore warehouse 17? What were the killers after? And how did they get into a secured area in the first place? Why was the forklift driver there?

Franco and Jonathan were throwing these questions at each other as they drove to the Mazatlán Port.

"Franco, how do you think the killers got into the secure area in the first place?" Jonathan asked.

"Somebody let them in, I presume, but under what, or *who's* authority?"

"The Federales said the dispatch sergeant was gone. Where did he go?" Jerry asked.

"Why was the forklift driver there?" Franco asked.

"I would think he brought in a crate of some kind." Jonathan responded.

"The two on-scene agents said there's nothing there."

"Okay, they took 'it,' but took what? What was in the crate, and where did they take it?" That was Jonathan's last question as they reached the port security gate.

"May I see your identification, please?" the guard said.

All three agents handed him their respective I.D. folders along with the special invitation from the Federales to be in Mexico.

The guard was surprised, "United States federal agents? This is great. You find out who killed my friend, Manuel."

"How long have you been here?" Jonathan asked.

"I came on at 7:00 this morning."

"And you've been at this gate all along?" asked Franco.

"Except for the time I was called to the security office."

"Who called you, and why did they need you?"

"Manuel is late in the morning because he has a new baby, and his wife is sick from the delivery. One of his morning duties is to help the dispatch sergeant prepare the morning assignments. So, I was called to help him do that."

Jerry gave Franco a smirk as Jonathan nodded his head.

"Thank you."

As he drove off, he heard the faint words from the guard, "You get 'em, you hear!"

The FBI agent drove past warehouses 5, then 9—he stopped.

"What's the matter?" Jerry asked.

"Look at the layout of these warehouses. I can't see 17 yet, but look at the way the entrances don't face the docks. Look at the absence of buildings or anything between them and the guard shack—nothing." He drove on, keeping that picture in his head. He went around more warehouses.

...13...15, there it is: 17.

"There it is!" Franco blurted out.

"See what I mean; 17 is the closest to the open road back to the guard house—farthest from the dock."

"That makes sense," Franco said. "Doesn't it?"

"True, but did you notice warehouses 1 through 8 are all are on the third row. There is no rhyme or reason to the numbers."

"New question. Why'd they do that?" The car rolled closer.

"Why is the entrance of warehouse 17 facing the guard shack we just passed through? This was *planned*."

"Of course, it was, Jonathan." Jerry said.

"No, no, I mean this was *planned*." Jonathan added, "This wasn't the first time a heist has taken place. This is the first time someone has gotten killed, and there are some outside forces that are genuinely concerned. I'm telling you, guys, the shit is going to hit the fan, and we're right in the middle of it."

He pulled the car up to the entrance and the three agents got out. Franco counted six people standing around the three bodies.

"Please stay outside, this is a closed investigation," the Mexican agent barked.

Jerry drew out his I.D. with the Letter of Authority.

"It's okay, we're here to help."

The Mexican was not happy with the palliative attitude, and it showed.

"I don't need any meddling Americans interfering in my investigation," the Federali said with obvious disdain. "Did you agents come here with *anything* or just your Superman cape?"

Jonathan ignored the sarcasm.

"Only a short conversation with the guard's wife." he said. "Have you found anything?"

"There's nothing here to kill someone over. The closest crate is 50 feet away, and it's filled with cases of Bactine, Band-aids, gauze bandages, and two cases of Pepto-Bismol," the Federali said looking at the size of Franco.

"Agent, we think that whatever *was* here has been stolen, but we don't know what was in the container," Jonathan said dropping to his knees.

Jerry stood up from crawling around on the concrete floor.

"Look, Jonathan, see how pronounced the skid marks are to here, then the marks continue, but there's hardly any disruption of dust *or* deep skid-marks after this point. What do you make of that?"

Jonathan and Franco scooted to their hands and knees while the Mexican agent watched them mull around the floor.

"It's obvious the crate was moved a short distance, but removed from the warehouse after it was empty."

"It is clear to me," Jonathan blurted out, "this is an obstruction of justice and a tampering with evidence. Who would do that with two dead bodies lying on the floor?"

"A third party who also got past the guard or…" Jerry concluded.

"Or someone that was already here—a worker, perhaps?" Franco finished Jerry's comment.

"Agent…uh…what was your name again?"

"Mendoza," he said after rolling his eyes.

"Agent Mendoza, would you please begin a suspect board. Any person or job that you think might have a connection here. We'll start writing in their names, okay?"

"Who do I start with?" The Federali asked.

Jonathan looked squarely at Jerry and France.

"I think we'll put the dispatch sergeant at the top for now."

"Jonathan, why don't you go to the dispatch office and see if this guy is there? I'll stay here. Maybe we'll see something in this blood-bath." Franco said.

Jonathan and Jerry left Mendoza and Franco at the warehouse. They ducked under the crime scene tape and walked to the security office. A sign pointed up stairs. Jerry looked at the length of the steps. *Great! An early morning exercise*, he thought.

The steps creaked as they continued upward. A clerk was sitting at her desk when she saw them peering around the corner.

"We're looking for the dispatch sergeant, is he in his office?"

"He's not here right now, he went to see the port director."

At the agent's request, she drew a 'not-to-scale' map of the dock and the port director's office location. The agents got in the golf cart and headed toward the dock. The two passed the Maersk tanker and the *Hormuz Defender* tied in their respective slips.

The port director or the captain of the defender, Jerry thought to himself. At that moment, Jonathan pulled to the edge of the slip and stopped.

"Let's go visit the captain first," Jonathan said. Jerry smiled as he jumped from the golf cart.

The ramp's design meandered left to right and upward as the two humped up the side of the ship's hull to the entrance of this massive vessel. The two displayed their I.D.s to the sailor on deck. He caught his breath, then Jonathan asked, "We would like to speak with the captain, please."

The wait wasn't long. A short, pudgy man approached them wearing a jacket with four stripes on the sleeves signifying he was the captain of the boat.

Franco explained the reasons for their visit.

"I heard," the captain responded, "but why do you wish to speak with me?"

Jonathan explained that the crate had apparently just been removed from the *Defender* and placed in a warehouse that is not supposed to be guarded.

"Please, come to my office and we will check the cargo manifest."

The captain went through the nearest hatchway and the two agents followed.

The computer screen already showed the cargo schematics and the cargo designations.

"You see, agents, 331 cars, 101 20-foot containers, and six 10-foot containers—no crates."

"What was in the six 10-footers?" Franco asked.

"Let's see," said the captain. "Two had cases of medical supplies— verified; two contained dog food—verified; one had Kia bumpers and quarter-panels—verified; and one had machine parts. That container was 1-1-7-4…hmm."

Jonathan peered over the captain's shoulder.

"That one not verified?"

"It arrived just as we were beginning our journey. The manifest was from the company who manufactures machine parts for Toyota. They are 'known-shippers,' so no reason to doubt the contents."

Jonathan asked, "What was the weight."

The captain went to the container's profile—silence.

"What's the matter?" Jerry asked.

"The container's loaded weight was 1,900 pounds."

"What is the empty weight?" Jonathan asked

"Sixteen-hundred pounds." The captain said. "That's 300 pounds of machine parts in a 1-foot shipping container. No one would do that. The cost per pound to ship that amount of weight is prohibitive."

"We need to find that container. Thank you, Captain, we'll show ourselves out."

Jerry opened the door for Jonathan and both walked out of the office.

Jerry turned back to the captain, "I'm sorry, Captain, but you're going to be here awhile."

The captain slammed his hat on his desk.

"I understand. I don't like it, but I understand," the agents could hear through the closed door.

Mendoza was yelling as he was driving as fast as he could up the side dock.

"I'm glad I caught you," he said. "The coroner examined Cantu's throat and found an evenly serrated cut that killed him. It was curved, like a karambit. Some of them are designed to fold, but they're all combat knives used to kill."

"How could he tell if it was curved?" Franco asked.

Mendoza raised his right arm, bent severely at the elbow.

"The killer was right-handed; he swept his hand holding the blade backwards across the guard's throat. The initial cut was the deepest, and that was on left side of his throat. If he would have used a straight blade, like a kitchen knife, the killer would have to move his body around the guard to maintain the depth of the cut. But with a curved blade, you start from one side and with the same pressure, pull the blade across his neck. And we know this one was serrated by the residual tearing of Cantu's throat."

"Find out if anyone in Mazatlán sells such an item—maybe; maybe not. Hopefully, we'll get lucky. We're off to see the port director."

They went through another guard station, but this one was strictly to control traffic to the director's office. Another set of stairs.

"What is it with these people?" Jerry said, looking upward. "They like climbing?"

After puffing half way up the stairs, Jerry was greeted by, "Hola, my name is Juanita, may I help you?"

"We're federal agents from the United States. We'd like to see the port director, please." Jerry tried to take a deep breath.

Jonathan could see the director through the door; the day was already wearing on him. He took it upon himself to walk through the portal and into his office.

The FBI agent flashed his I.D. and began, "We're here about the killing of three of your people this morning."

"Yes, it was terrible," the port director said

"Have you been to the scene?" asked Jonathan. He showed his badge as well as the letter of authorization.

"Oh, yes. It was horrible."

"Who let you know and when?" Jonathan asked.

"The dispatch sergeant. He called me and the same time that Manuel was calling for assistance."

"Manuel? Did you know Manuel well? I mean, you refer to him by his first name." Jerry turned to Juan Carlos after processing the director's office.

"I try to know everyone that works here." Juan Carlos smiled as he answered Jerry's question.

"Really, director? How many people work here?" Jonathan asked.

"I think 300 or so."

Jerry jumped in.

"Now I'm confused. You knew Manuel. You try to know everybody. You don't know how many people work for you. By the way, what was the name of the forklift driver, Mr. Port Director?"

"I don't remember. If there aren't any more questions?"

"One more question, Señor Estabán," Jonathan asked. "What was in the container?"

"I don't know, machine parts, I believe."

"You have quite a memory, Mr. Port Director," Jonathan commented.

The two went downstairs and headed back to the crime scene. The Sinaloa coroner picked up the three bodies and was already heading back to the morgue. The blood and parts of Cantu's throat remained on the warehouse floor.

"Jerry?" Franco said as he saw the cart roll up and stop, "There're a bunch of potholes in this case, and we're not having any success in filling them."

Jonathan walked over to the Federali, Agent Mendoza.

"This port director has a *lot* on his mind, and it's not all about the three killings today. We'd like to do some checking on his financials, his acquaintances, his general activities, and anything else you can come up with. Oh, yeah, I have another name for our suspect board."

The three U.S. federal agents left Mendoza to his analysis and headed for the colonel's car. Jonathan's cell phone rang.

"Agent Conroy? This is the clerk at the Mazatlán Corporate Air Terminal. You asked me to call if anything unusual happened.

"Yes, I did."

"Jack Culberson flew his Bonanza in a couple of minutes ago," the terminal employee reported.

"Is that strange?" Jonathan asked.

"No, not generally, but what was strange is that he could hardly walk or communicate."

"What was his departure point?" Jonathan asked.

"There was no flight plan," the employee answered. "Another thing," the employee continued, "his father flew out of here less than two hours ago."

Chapter 35

THE STENCH FROM THE COOKING OPIUM was all into Arturo's nostrils. The mask didn't help. He stayed in the church, and when not asleep, he witnessed the manufacture of heroin. He meandered out the front door. His eyes didn't deceive him earlier, it *was* a fountain, and it *was* as old as the church—maybe older. The townspeople were up and milling about. Shops opened. Cars and horses were moving throughout the city.

Now, Arturo was hungry. He walked near the fountain and looked in the surprisingly clear water and saw his reflection. It was horrifying. He hadn't shaved, slept, or showered for the last four days. *Jesus Christi! I look like shit.*

The sign said *El Restaurante Calle* was displayed over by the corner. The smell of tortillas reached his nose, and the stench was now a memory.

He grabbed the first table he came to. It was hand-painted green and yellow with some kind of flowers. One leg was uneven, and it was the same with the chair. He looked around the inside—no windows; only large, square openings on three sides of the restaurant. The open sides were held up by a heavy cord tied to cleats.

He looked at what was loosely called a menu. Another chair at the table was pulled back and Morales sat down.

"What do you want to eat?" Morales offered.

"It all looks good. I'm hungry, but I have no appetite," Arturo answered.

"Bring my friend a couple of tacos and cerveza."

"No, King, not at 7:00 in the morning." Arturo looked up at the waiter, "Just tacos, please."

A chair was taken from the next table and swung around—Vargas sat down.

"The bricks are about done. We'll load up in about an hour."

"Where're we going, King?" Arturo asked.

Jonathan and his crew headed for the airport. "How long do you want this sting to last? What are you going to say to him?" Franco asked.

"For damned sure, I want Morales and Vargas," Jonathan said. "I want Culberson and whoever else he's in bed with. I want the son-of-a-bitch that killed the guard and the forklift driver and Manel. *I want* the cargo that somebody thought enough of to kill three people." Jonathan took a deep breath.

They drove through the city on their way to the airport. Traffic was stopped up ahead of them at the circle. Franco could hear the mass of sirens going across town. He noticed a streetlight with a wide base. He ran over and jumped up in the hopes of seeing over the heads of pedestrians.

He yelled back over the din of sirens, "It's an ambulance; no—three. Wait a minute—five ambulances. Bad accident."

A traffic cop looked up at Franco.

"Please get down from there."

"Where's the accident?" Franco asked.

"It wasn't an accident, the Mazatlán-Culiacán train was attacked." Franco was stunned—back to the car.

"We are stupid. We are the dumbest people in the world. We are idio…"

"Stop blabbering, Franco. What's the problem?" Jonathan blurted.

"He told us. Arturo told us that they were going to hit it. They did it. They hit the damned train to Culiacán. People that are hurt; probably some dead. God damn it! Jonathan, one of us needs to be interviewing at the hospital—"

"I'm going!" Franco responded, "I'm on my way."

Jonathan agreed, "Right. Hospital. You do it, Franco. Jerry and I will head for the train. Jack will just have to wait."

It took 30 minutes to walk to the hospital.

"Get out the map, Jerry. Tell me where the track and the main highway are the closest and make a decision."

"This," he said, pointing at the map, "is all rolling hills. No place to hide."

Looking, searching, folding the map to isolate the area, Jerry said, "Wait, Jonathan, here! A crevasse on one side and a high ridge on the other. There's no way this train can maintain the original speed when it hits that curve, so here, Jonathan!" Jerry pointed at the map where Highway 15D, and the tracks were close together and adjacent to the curve. "Just ahead of you. Turn right. That's the entrance to 15D."

Now on the road to Culiacán, there were no lights, and Jonathan had no plans of using the colonel's siren. The speed limit was 90 kilometers per hour. They did every bit of it and more.

Chapter 36

FRANCO HURRIED INTO THE EMERGENCY ROOM AREA. There were no painful screams; rather more dazed people than anything. He had no clue what sort of reaction there would be seeing a U.S. Border patrol agent deep in Mexico, so he did what any self-respecting cop would do, he followed a doctor in to the locker room, found a white jacket, went back to where the passengers were and with a stethoscope around his neck, Franco began questioning the people in the emergency room.

"Excuse me, my name is Franco. If I can be of any service to you, I am here to help." He remained stoic and composed. "Are you hurt? Can you tell me what happened?"

He had small cut just in front of his ear—nothing serious.

"There was a fire." The man said. "In the back of the train. Far from us. I don't know anything else." Franco thanked him and went to the next person. Same response, and then the next person.

"Excuse me, my name is Franco. Can you tell me what happened?" The boy was barely 16.

"Look son," Franco drew close to the kid's ear and whispered, "I'm a federal agent from the United States." The teenager's eyes widened as he stood up being respectful to the agent, he turned around in circles in a voice something akin to singing, "The United States is here! The United States is here!"

People stood from their seats and gathered around Franco.

One said, "They hurt my baby."

Another, "They slammed the brakes of the train and threw us out of our seats."

And yet another, "We saw them rob the train."

"Yeah," said another, "they robbed the train and killed people."

Franco rushed to grab a tablet from the medical station.

"Okay, do you know who they killed?"

The teenager stepped forward.

"They were riding on top of the caboose. I saw them up there when I got on the train."

"I saw them, too," a lady spoke. "They carried guns."

"Was there an explosion?" Franco asked.

"No, we only noticed the fire."

"Then the conductor ran up the aisle," a woman jumped in.

"He threw the brakes," another commented.

"Yeah, the conductor was the one who threw the brakes."

Voices were coming from everywhere and all at the same times. He kept taking notes.

Then Franco raised his hand asking for quiet.

"Did anyone see where the hijackers went?" he asked.

In the silence of the moment, an elder lady stood up.

"They went North on 15D."

Franco calmly approached her.

"Señora, did you see how many of them there were?"

"Yes. I saw 20, maybe 25 cars and trucks heading north."

Franco held her hand and smiled.

"Many thanks, señora."

Chapter 37

"*How fast are you going, Jonathan?*" *Jerry asked.*

"As fast as this seven-year-old car will carry us."

Jerry commented, "I saw the tracks a while back, but they've disappeared on me."

"Got any guess as to what we're going to find?"

Jonathan was experiencing the uselessness of seven-year-old springs.

"I hope the smoke is still around. Any police up here yet?"

"Don't know, don't see any. There're some hills up there. How far do you think they are?"

"About 30 miles, I assume." Jerry said. Twenty minutes later, Jonathan saw the black smoke from the train and poked his partner's shoulder.

"I think we're about five or six minutes out, Jonathan," Jerry offered. "By the way, and no reason to think otherwise, you bring a weapon with you?"

The FBI agent nodded his head.

"You?"

Jerry chuckled, "Oh, yeah. You think our buddy Arturo had anything to do with this?"

"Absolutely!"

Jonathan turned on the dirt road coming off the highway.

"Look at the engine way up there; look at the caboose back here. Who in the hell planned this?"

Jerry searched for any type of clue.

"Arturo. He planned this."

A man in what looked like a conductor's suit approached them. He was 30 feet away, but he still introduced himself as the conductor of the train.

Huffing and puffing, he looked at the Federali.

"Your partner is over there," he said, pointing to the remnants of the boxcar.

Jonathan thanked and looked at Jerry, "What partner?"

"Your buddy has been in the boxcar for the last 40 minutes. They're all dead. I don't know what he's looking for." The conductor was visibly shaken but somehow got the words to come out.

Jonathan parked the colonel's car, and he and Jerry meandered up to the burned-out car.

"Hey, anybody in there?" There was silence, but only for a moment. "Hey!"

"Yes, I'm here," a voice answered. Out from the burned rubble walked the dock's security dispatch sergeant. He looked at the two men in street clothes.

"What do you want?" the sergeant said.

"Sergeant, you need to come down here—now!" asked Jerry.

The man was wearing his dock security uniform; it was covered with soot and ash. He wore his badge, but his pant leg was torn from entering the burned cargo car.

Jonathan pulled his FBI identification, and the sergeant backed up against one of the stringers of the car. It was still hot. He leaped forward with a moan.

"Sergeant, we have a few questions for you. Come *down* here!" Jerry said.

He thought for a moment and made a move to the edge of the car. To his right was track-bed that extended out six feet from the car; to his left, track-bed and a crevasse with a 200-foot drop. The sergeant stared at the crevasse.

"Don't do it, sergeant. You don't need to do this," Jerry said.

The guard backed up to the opposite corner and ran to the burned-out door, then jumped. He hit the edge of the drop-off, spun around, and went over the side. He rolled down the crevasse, hitting stumps and rocks and trees. The creek-bed and the sergeant lay quiet at the bottom.

The conductor stood at the door in disbelief.

"Sir, are there others on the train?" Jerry said.

"Yes. Two porters and the engineer."

"Go get them, please," Jonathan asked. He looked at the caboose, at the cargo car, and peered downwards. "Wait! Wait a second." Jonathan dropped down to one knee.

"What do you have there?" Jerry responded.

"Got something growing on a track-bed."

"Nothing grows on a track-bed." The conductor looked on.

"Exactly, so what is this?"

Jerry moved closer to the plant. He smiled.

"Two of your questions just got answered, Jonathan. The *what* and the *why*. This is an opium poppy plant." Jerry pulled his cellphone from his pocket.

Franco's dialing code was the number 1. Pressed.

He answered, "What did you find out down there?"

"The conductor caused the injuries, but there *was* a robbery after the fire started. Approximately 25 vehicles went north carrying the cargo. What do you have?"

"You're right about the fire," Franco began as Jonathan moved closer to Jerry's phone. "But it was the last two cars on the train. There was no need to panic-brake the train."

Jonathan stared at the conductor.

"The burned car was filled with opium, and it's gone—apparently north, but where?"

"Anyone still up there?" Franco asked.

"The conductor, two porters, and the engineer." Jonathan continued, "We found the dispatch sergeant. He went paws-up over a cliff.

We'll bring the opium plant back with the crew. One more thing, there are six bodies on the train, you're going to have to facilitate their removal. We're going to search the high-ridge and the crevasse, just in case there are others. I'll call you.

"Jerry, you take one porter and the conductor to the edge of the crevasse, I'll take a porter and the engineer and head up the mountain."

The teams split up and went their separate ways. The high-ridge team encountered mesquite brush and cactus six feet up the hill. The team spread out and found shell-casings and more shell-casings.

"Pick up everything you find," yelled Jonathan. The shell-casings were all over the ground. One of the porters grabbed some plastic bags from storage, and they filled them up. There were hundreds of shells left on the ground.

"Agent?" yelled one of the porters, "over here. A man—he's alive." Jonathan climbed up the hill to wounded man. He was hit in the chest and bleeding out. Writhing in pain, he was moaning, "Chistos! Madre mia!"

"We'll get you down," Jonathan attempted to comfort him. "We have water, just hang in there."

He groaned and complained about his legs. His breathing was shallow, it was difficult to speak. Jonathan helped him down the hill and that the same time asked him about the robbery. He could only talk in short broken sentences and words, like "fire," "Sinaloa," "bottles," "fire." Not surprising, Jonathan understood all of it. The next question was simple: "Where did they go?"

The man had lost too much blood; his eyes rolled back into his head—he was dying, and he knew it. As best as he good, he raised his head and murmured, "North," and he died.

Agent Conway lowered his head from his arms and whispered, "Thank you," and walked down the hill.

"Agent," the engineer cried out from across the ridge, "here's a bottle of water."

"Don't drink it!" Jonathan yelled and loud enough for Jerry to hear. The scream reverberated throughout the mountain side down to the crevasse.

Jerry screamed up to the ridge, "Don't drink it!"

"Okay, okay!" the engineer yelled back.

"Bring it to me, carefully," Jonathan called out.

The top 15 feet of the crevasse told part of the story. Jerry and the engineer found the area trampled and burned out. The attack came from above *and* below. The guards atop the caboose never knew what hit them, and other than the three men inside, the guards were dead in a matter of minutes. The conductor gathered the empty shells while the second porter carefully acquired the bottles of cocktail and met at the base of the car.

The FBI agent looked at the conductor and the two porters.

"Tell me who stopped the train?" he finally asked.

"I didn't mean to hurt anybody." The conductor stepped forward. "But the man, he was there at the door. He had guns—big ones."

"What man are you talking about?" Jerry asked.

"He was there at the door—alone," said the porter.

"When the train stopped, did he go into the cargo car?" Jerry asked

"No, Agent, he jumped from the train."

"There was gunfire and gang members throwing cocktails of . . ." Jerry stopped short.

"Do you know what he looks like?" Jonathan chimed in.

"I'll never forget him," the conductor said.

"Me too," the porter chimed in.

"Where'd he go?" Jonathan asked.

The three men looked at each other.

"He jumped in the crevasse," the second porter jumped in.

"What did this guy look like?" Jerry asked.

"Agent, I don't have to tell what he looked like," the conductor said, "I know who he was. His picture is all over Mexico. It was Alejandro Vargas."

Both agents now knew exactly what happened. They were told days ago. Now, it was critical to know where the hijackers went. Jerry looked at the conductor,

"Taking this road north, where does it go? Is there a town on village North of here?"

The conductor scratched his head. One of the porters standing near them, shouted out, "Cananéa."

"Where's Cananéa?" Jonathan asked the conductor.

"Jerry, call Franco. Tell him to get back to the colonel's office and wait for us. Tell him to get a chopper ready. Call your captain in Tucson; tell him to put together a S.W.A.T. team. Tell them we are on our way. Hold back on everything until we get there. I'll bet my life on this."

The government provided a nice transition from southern Sinaloa to the north sector of the country, which headed directly into the mountain town of Cananéa, Sinaloa, Mexico. The highway was well paved with four lanes to move the consistent flow of traffic. Conway called Franco and told they were headed back to pick him up.

"Franco, we'll be at the hospital in 30 minutes," Jerry took the phone from Jonathan,

"Yes. One more thing, Franco," Jerry said. "We found an opium poppy plant by the train. Jonathan thinks they're headed for Cananéa."

"The factory is *there*?" Franco asked.

Chapter 38

JACK LEFT THE RESTAURANT WITH A FULL STOMACH and blood flowing once again in his left arm. He went down to the private terminal, his face feeling flush and breathing steady. He walked inside the terminal.

"You had a Gulfstream here today. The tail number was 7-4-4-Y. How long has it been gone?"

The man behind the counter looked at the day's service logbook.

"It left here an hour ago."

"Thanks," Jack said. "Top me off, would you, please, and I'll be on my way."

The counter man looked at his watch again. He called the FBI over two hours ago, and there was no reason to detain him.

"Yes sir, right away."

Jack knew it all. He knew of Cananéa. He knew about the church; and he knew where the finished heroin was going once the process was completed. And no word about the episode in Tucson—*Good*.

Jack climbed in his seat, received his instructions from ground control, and headed for the runway. Without delay, the tower gave him the permission he required, and he was wheels-up moments later.

Just north of Cananéa, there's a small municipal airport. Jack dialed in the co-ordinates to his destination, and five hours and 10 minutes later, the Bonanza rolled to a stop in Cananéa, Sonora. One lone flight-line worker approached him. Jack asked to be taken into town. It was only a mile away and some from the airport. He obliged.

The worker's truck was old, but it got him to the center of town. The fountain—still there.

"Let me off here. Thank you," Jack said.

He walked to the church, expecting the inside to be full production. There was one man sitting on the steps. The church doors were closed and locked. The man, unshaven and dirty just sat there alone.

"Hello. Where is everybody?" he asked.

"They are gone; all gone," the man answered.

"Do you know when they left?"

The man rubbed his parched lips with the back of his dried wrinkled hand, "They left about four hours ago. I fell asleep, and they left me here."

"Who are you?" Jack asked.

"My name is Arturo Gonzales. What is a gringo doing in Cananéa?"

"Looking for the man who owns this church."

Arturo saw the man's face go pale. He staggered and tottered before he collapsed to a sitting position.

Arturo stood up and hurried to him. The sweat poured down Jack's face and gathered around the collar of his soiled white Ralph Lauren silk shirt.

"Can someone get a doctor?" Arturo yelled to anyone who would listen. He gathered some water with cupped hands from the fountain and laid the cool water over Jack's face.

A nurse arrived from the local medico and took over.

"What is your name?" she asked Jack. There was incoherent mumbling, but Arturo heard something like Cabesen. But wasn't sure. "Where are you from?" The nurse asked. More mumbling.

Arturo leaned into the man's face, "Are you Jack Culberson?" There was an agreeing nod. "Let's take him to the hospital and care for him there."

The nurse agreed.

The doctor on call built up his potassium levels and replenished his electrolytes in the emergency room. A couple of hours passed, and the redness in his eyes diminished and were clearer. His heart rate slowed to some level of normalcy.

After a while, Jack was lucid.

"You're the guy who helped me."

Arturo nodded.

"Who were you looking for?" Arturo asked.

"The man who owns the church. You wouldn't know him."

"Morales?" Arturo answered. "He is well known around here."

"I need to find him." Jack said.

Jack laid in his hospital bed with the pitcher of water next to him. The morning sun blanketed his face. It was warm, and it felt enticing.

A nurse entered his room. Her English was less than perfect, but he understood when she asked what he wanted for breakfast.

He smiled and replied, "Not lobster tails." She had a questioning look on her face. "Just kidding." Jack answered, "Anything."

"We have eggs and bacon." She was polite, and Jack noticed the immaculate, starched white uniform she was wearing, not like the multi-colored scrubs he saw in Tucson.

"Yes, that is fine. Thank you. Would you please get my phone?" he asked.

It was not necessary for Jack to search for the number. He touched the '3' button, and it rang once. He could hear road noise and felt a breeze through the open windows. It was Morales on other end.

"Jack, where are you?" Static. Signal in-and-out. "Jack, can you hear me?"

"I'm in Cananéa, Antonio," Jack answered.

"Can you hear me?" No response. It made no sense to yell, so he called him back.

He pushed the "3" again. A single ring, and Morales picked up.

"Jack, where are you?" This time it was clearer—no yelling.

Morales stopped the caravan and climbed up an adjacent hill.

"I'm in Cananéa. Where are *you*?" Jack responded.

"We are four hours out of Cananéa, on Highway 2, five miles west of Highway 14, just south of Aquamondo."

"Alright, stay there. Enjoy the sights. I'll be there in four or five hours. Be patient, I'm coming."

Jack laid back in his bed and waited for his breakfast.

Arturo came to visit again. He remained disheveled in his appearance, but he shaved and taken a bath in a local hotel, paid for by Jack.

"I'll be leaving soon, Arturo. I'd like to help you get back home, but I need to get out of here first."

"Where are you going, señor?" Arturo asked.

"I have to meet a friend east of here."

"Thank you. I will have breakfast and wait for you to come back."

Arturo's cellphone had been dead for two days with no communication with the outside world—not Maria; not the Border Patrol.

"Excuse me," he interrupted a nurse, "I need to put a charge on my phone, do you have this kind of connection?"

She looked.

"No, but I think the other nurse has that phone."

It was a short walk to the next nursing station, and he asked the same question. She peered at his phone and said, "Yes."

After plugging his phone to her charger, Arturo looked at the status bar; it showed nothing. He waited. Finally, a red bar appeared; he waited a little longer. *Come on!* It finally turned green and he pushed the "on" key. Now ramping up. He ran the 'Contacts' screen; Jerry. *It's been two days—he probably thinks I'm dead.*

"Jerry? Arturo. My phon…"

"Where the hell are you?" Jerry interrupted.

"In a minute. Sixty-five bricks on the way to Dallas. Right now, being hauled by a caravan led by King Morales. Jack Culberson is here in Cananéa. He'll be flying to meet the caravan and move the stuff across the border. I know he's heading east. Highway 2 is the only way out of here. They left here about 2:00, so they're about four hours out. I don't know where his father is. I left him when we hit the train."

"Who's he delivering the stuff to?" Jerry asked.

"I don't know that either."

"One thing, Arturo, do you know where Morales is manufacturing the stuff?"

There was an involuntary silence. He formed the words, but like blood-clots in his throat, he stopped. A tap on his shoulder—it was Jack. His thumb touched the case next to the 'END' button. The idea was desperate.

"Can I ride with you? Morales knows me."

This was the first time Arturo saw suspicion on Jack's face.

"Why were you sitting on the church steps?" Jack asked.

Chapter 39

MAZATLÁN HOSPITAL EMERGENCY WAS CRAWLING with victims from the train stopping om the hillside. The pregnant woman lay still on her gurney, staring into the ceiling. The tears had not stopped.

Jerry walked into the hospital with Jonathan. He grabbed Franco by the arm and pulled him into a small alcove.

"Franco, we need to update the captain and the district office. There is a war coming, and ground zero is Cananéa. It is time to pay another visit to the port director."

"Jonathan?" Franco poked his head through the door. "We're going back to the docks, want to come?" With all three in agreement—the docks, for sure—the agents jumped in the colonel's car, and the three headed for the Port of Mazatlán docks.

The three arrived at the stairwell outside the port director's office.

"Up those stairs, again?" Jerry said.

The others just looked at each other and laughed.

The conversation in the car was more about the port director than anything else. Franco suggested 'person of interest' status, and Jerry disagreed. There were too many holes everywhere, and Jerry believed the director was right in the middle of it.

"He an accessory and I know it!"

Jonathan listened and occasionally, nodded in agreement. Jonathan joined in. "His foreknowledge of the heist makes him an accomplice and an accessory to murder; if…"

"If you can prove it," Jerry said. He looked at the stairs that confronted him, "Okay." He took a deep breath and took them on. Another deep breath at the top.

"Hello, Juanita, the port director, please."

"He has someone in his office. His assistant."

"Good. We'll talk to the two of them," Franco responded.

"How's the investigation going?" Jonathan asked.

The assistant looked at his boss and back to the three agents.

"Who are you?" The assistant scanned the federal agents

"What are you looking at?" he asked as he pulled his badge from his pocket.

Jerry was still speaking with Juanita.

"Does your phone keep track of every incoming and outgoing call to and from this office?" Jerry didn't expect the answer he received, but he was happy that he got it.

"Yes, Agent Messer. We installed the PhonePad Electronic System last year. It will take a couple of minutes to print out the last two days."

"No worries, Juanita." Jerry smiled and thanked her.

In the office, Franco asked, "You sir, what do *you* do as an assistant?"

"I help the director in his day-to-day activities," quipped the assistant.

"That's a good place to start. Tell me about the activities yesterday afternoon, say, when the *Hormuz Defender* entered port. What were you doing for the director?"

"I…I…was…informing him of the arrival of the Maersk tanker."

"And?" asked Jonathan.

"And what?" asked the assistant.

"Did you not inform him of the *Hormuz Defender's* arrival?" Jonathan asked.

"Yes, I suppose I did."

"What time was that?" Jonathan again.

"I don't know, maybe 3:00 or 4:00." The assistant looked at the director.

"Franco, go ask Jerry if he's come up with anything yet."

"Sure, Jonathan." Franco stood from his seat and moved quickly to the anteroom. Jonathon turned backed to Juan Carlos. "The dispatching sergeant is dead. He jumped into a 200-foot ravine earlier today. When we found him, every bone in his body was broken from hitting rocks and trees as he fell. Oh, yeah, stumps and boulders, and…"

"Okay, okay, I got it!" Juan Carlos said.

"What was a port security official doing at a train hijacking an hour and a half away from here?"

Jerry walked in with the phone-call report in his hand.

"I've got a phone number here. It's not from yesterday, it's from today—about four hours ago." Jerry leaned in to the director's face.

"Where's it from?" asked Jonathan.

Jerry responded, "New York City. And—here, too—yesterday afternoon. Same number."

"Who were you calling, Mr. Estabán?" Franco could not contain himself and leaped into the fray.

"A cousin, but those were wrong numbers." There was anxiety in the director's voice, and he was apparently getting quite nervous.

"Jerry, download the assistant's phone number." Jonathan asked, "When and how many calls came in from him?"

Jerry searched the Excel sheet and found, "One, Jonathan, at 3:47 yesterday afternoon."

Jonathan pulled up a straight-back chair and spun it around; threw his leg over the seat and folded both arms across the back of the chair.

Then Jonathan, sitting in front of the assistant, asked, "You didn't see fit to call your boss when the Maersk arrived?"

"I didn't think it was necessary."

"You didn't think it was necessary to inform the port director when an oil tanker arrived, but a freighter with cars and machine parts was a different story, right?"

"Well, I did..." the assistant stuttered. Sweat dripped down his face. His skin tightened and began to throb and itch. He started to scratch his legs and arms as if he suffered from the hives.

"Did you know Manuel Cantu?" Jonathan pressed harder and placed his hands on the assistant's hand to make him stop.

"Who? I don't believe so." The veins on the assistant's head were now showing major distress.

"How many security people do you know, Mr. Assistant?" Jonathan asked again.

"I don't know any of those people," he said, trying to placate the federal agent

"Are you married?" Jerry jumped into the fray.

"Yes, I am."

"What's your wife's name?" Jerry asked.

"Rosa," the assistant answered. The port director sat quietly. Profuse sweat clung to his hands as he wiped his face.

Jonathan turned his attention to the port director.

"Mr. Estabán, who do you know in New York City?"

"My aunt," he responded.

"You mean your cousin," Jonathan reminded him.

"Well, it's her son." Beads of sweat appeared on Estabán's forehead. A glass of water sat on his desk for more than an hour. The constant sipping provided little cooling effect, and the incessant clicking of the overhead fan did little to soothe his state of mind. Juan Carlos knew he was trouble. He reached for the glass and gulped in down.

"Who were the people who picked up the machine parts?" Jerry asked.

"I don't know," Juan Carlos responded.

"Who were the people who picked up the machine parts, Mr. Estabán? Think before you answer." Jonathan leaned in close to Juan Carlos' face.

"Oh, yes…uh…I remember the meeting. I'll have to find the paperwork and get back to you."

"This is crap." Jonathan stood up from the straight-back, and it slid into the left knee of the assistant. Jonathan ignored the grimace. The agent walked around Juan Carlos' desk and positioned his butt on the window edge, looking down at the director.

"Port Director, who removed the 10-foot container from warehouse 17?" Jonathan's face was now within an inch of the port director's ear.

"I don't know." The director answered.

"Franco, call the Federali Colonel and ask him to send a couple of interrogators over to the port director's office. Then call the Federali Agent Mendoza and tell him to come up. Jerry, would you get Juanita and bring her in here and sit her in this chair. I think we're going to be here for a while."

Chapter 40

THE 2020 NATIONAL MAYOR'S CONFERENCE was held in Dallas, Texas. The parties were outrageous in the money spent with lobsters flown in from New England; the steaks were from Kansas City. Madeleine Underwood, with her graciousness and poise, did all she could to represent New York City. She jokingly told her assistant one day that she would sleep with the mayor just to come to this conference. He gave her the chance—no strings attached. The Anatole was the official headquarters for the meeting and parties, but most were spread throughout the city.

Madeleine called David when she arrived and asked if he had time for dinner.

"Yes," he responded. He would pick her up at 7:00 for an 8:00 reservation at Ruth Chris' Steak House north of the city. They exchanged pleasantries, and he kissed her on the cheek.

"Welcome to Dallas," he said. He started his Mabak and headed for the restaurant. Most of the conversation was irrelevant—mainly small talk. The valet took the keys, and the two walked inside.

At the table, the waiter brought two glasses of a slightly chilled pinot noir. Little was said and then out of nowhere, Madeleine spoke.

"I know about the I.R.S. probe." She touched his arm. "I'm concerned about you."

"I'll get through it; don't worry about it."

A small team of wait-staff surrounded the table. Some scraped the breadcrumbs, while another one refilled the water glasses.

David ordered château briand, the only way it is served in Texas—medium rare.

Finally, he asked, "How do you know about the probe?"

She dodged the question but implied certain friends in certain places.

Dinner was almost over. The waiter approached with a carafe of hot Colombian coffee. They both nodded.

"I have people, David, who are interested in you," she said.

"What kind of people?"

"The kind that are able to get you out of this mess," she answered.

"We need to go. I'll take you back." David signed the check and rose from the table. No words were spoken for the entire ride to the hotel. He pulled into the circular drive and stopped. Madeleine opened her door. She turned to David.

"Think about it, and let me know."

"I have." He put the car in park and offered the key to the valet. She smiled.

They entered her room.

"You won't mind if I get out of this dress, would you?"

He flippantly raised his arm and waved his wrist in approval. The night was clear; the view of Renaissance Tower framed in green argon appeared in double image through the thick plate glass window.

"David."

He turned from the view. Madeleine looked more comfortable. She was wearing a t-shirt with the New York City Marathon logo and a pair of walking shorts.

"Sit down?" she asked.

"What's this all about?" he questioned.

"I have come to the conclusion that the press and their fantasies are directly opposite to reality," Madeleine said.

"I agree. If they can't find a story, they just make it up. However, mine is not made up." David nodded his head.

"I know, David, but mine is."

"In what way? You aren't as brilliant and witty as people think you are?" He laughed at his own question.

"Don't be silly. I mean, the election. I didn't earn it; it was bought and paid for."

"With whose money?" He brought his body to the edge of the sofa and leaned forward. "Are you in trouble?" he asked.

"Not hardly." She said, "But I do owe a lot of people. The money came from different sources. Some by the illicit means in New York, and some from Mexico." She sat next to him.

"That speech you gave a couple of years ago?" he asked.

"Bullshit." The words flowed from her tongue.

"Apparently," he said in response.

"There are people who wish to expand the market in the northeast, and they're deadly serious about it. They want to have some conversation with you about your Gulfstream."

"It's already in use." David looked at her as he spoke the words,

"You don't understand, David," she placed her hand on his knee. "I told them you would speak with them."

"You don't understand, Madeleine; it's already being used." David's response threw Madeleine back in her chair, and David continued, "Are *you* in with the cartel, Madeleine?"

"One of them," she answered.

"Which one; the Sinaloas or Zetas?"

"Neither. A separatist group." Madeleine expelled a deep breath.

"What kind of separatist group?" David leaned into Madeleine's face.

"They're out of Nogales," she replied.

"I'll say. You're dealing with Antonio Morales?"

"You know of him?"

David's face went white as a sheet.

"Madeleine, what in the hell have you gotten yourself involved in? These guys will cut your tits off and feed them to the sharks on a whim." His breathing was rushed and shallow, "Are you crazy? He's a fucking psychopath." He stood and moved to the window and stared at the Dallas skyline.

"David, I think you're overreacting."

He turned to face her, his voice much louder now.

"Madeleine, he took a chainsaw to the head of a 15-year-old girl in a wheelchair for God's sake." He took a long, deep breath and asked, "Okay, how much have you bought from him?"

"Three million, so far. He wants to boost it, and my people agree." Madeleine stood and drew herself in close to his body. "Will you help me?"

David looked down and stared at the horrible, soft, blue and pink-flowered carpet laid out in front of him. She moved around the table lamp and faced him. Madeleine Underwood was 50 years old and was in sensational shape. Maneuvering him back into a chair, she sat on his lap and felt the pressure from David's pants on the inside of her thigh. She smiled. She slid her hand through her bare legs to the obvious rise of sexual attraction.

David responded by moving his hand up the front her t-shirt. She arched her back as his hand explored every inch of her firm breasts. David looked up to witness the pleasure, then stood up.

"I'll call you."

"You sycophantic dick-head," Madeleine said, dissatisfied with his response.

"Maybe so, Madeleine, maybe so."

Chapter 41

TWO WEEKS HAD PASSED SINCE THE ENCOUNTER with Madeleine, and the meetings with the I.R.S. offered no solution. He was sitting in office on a Friday afternoon, his head resting in his cupped hands. He lifted his eyes to look out the window of his corner office.

Piss on it, he thought.

"Who shall I say is calling?" said the special operator.

"David Culberson," he answered, "I would like speak with the deputy mayor."

"Yes, sir."

David waited for less than three minutes—then...

"David? Where are you?" Madeleine's voice sounded pleased about the call.

"Hello, Madeleine. Nice talking to you, too. I'm sitting at my desk in Dallas looking at the skyline and the clouds above it." His words—rambling, and his tone—anxious. He was speaking like he was under extreme pressure. His demeanor was like seeing a 22-year-old boy picking up his 14-year-old daughter to go on a date. He knew the culmination of what was about to happen won't end well.

"Are you alright?" She asked.

"Never mind that, Madeleine. It's been a very long day. Let us skip the bull shit; I need the $8 million in two days."

"I'll call my people tomorrow," she answered above a whisper.

"I don't care if you *screw* your people. You have two days—$8 million. No excuses. No grace period, Madeleine."

"Okay, David, I understand. No problem."

"Madeleine, 3:00 Monday and no money—you're done, I'm history. Got it?"

"What do you mean, I'm done?" she asked.

"Morales will leave Mexico tomorrow with your stuff. You will be flush with 265 bricks of heroin in two days. You have that money in Dallas."

"Okay, okay. Where will he deliver it?" she asked. The thought of having that much product in two days excited her.

"Dallas. Sunday morning. My office. You bring the New York City jet. No one will question you."

He slammed the "end" key and slumped back in his chair.

Chapter 42

"Jerry, Captain Barnhart here. I've been on the phone with the district director's office for the last hour. We want to have an update meeting with you guys A.S.A.P. The Federales want these folks, and so do we. We're sending a Lear down there this afternoon to pick up you, Franco, and that FBI agent."

"Captain, the timing isn't good right now. We're in the middle of questioning a key witness. Could we meet tomorrow?"

"I'll pick you up late this afternoon," Barnhart interrupted.

"Fine." Jerry closed his cellphone.

The sound of Mendoza's squeaky shoes was Juan Carlos' hint the party was about to begin. Agent Mendoza was a little rough around the edges but seemed to be committed to his job. He served on the Mexico City Police Force for six years. Three years ago, he was the second in command during a drug raid. A man and wife team were selling cocaine out of their house with a two-year-old asleep in the bedroom.

The plan was simple. An undercover cop knocked on the door asking to buy some dope. The wife asked him a slew of questions before she opened the door. Convinced he was sent by another customer, she decided to make the transaction. The door was barely unlatched. The undercover and the six policemen behind him burst in with guns blazing. Mendoza yelled at them to stop—no one listened. The man, his wife, and the two-year-old lay dead.

The inquiry brought little closure to Mendoza's vivid memory of the event. People were dead; drugs were missing. An attempt was made to move some of the money into his bank account; when that didn't work, his captain honored his request for transfer to the Federales.

"Agents?" Mendoza said. "What do we have here?"

"Some sloppy planning," said Jonathan.

Jerry walked up to Mendoza and quietly asked him to, "Contact the captain of the *Hormuz Defender* and ask him to turn over his cargo records to you."

Mendoza agreed and walked back down the stairs.

Jonathan pulled the straight-back underneath him and held the back of the chair with his two out-stretched arms like a little kid on a swing.

"Tell me about container 1-1-7-4, Juan Carlos?" Jonathan asked. "We know what was in it. What I want to know is who took it."

"I don't know." Juan Carlos' nerves were shot. He wanted to go home. He knew he wasn't going anywhere.

"You keep saying that." Jerry chimed in. "The container had no verification; was not certified; and yet the recipient knew where to go to pick up his cargo. Once again, who removed the container after it was emptied?"

"I don't know. I don't know anything about it," Juan Carlos said in near tears.

Jonathan's face was not an inch from Juan Carlos' ear.

"You are lying." It was a loud whisper. He turned the assistant.

"Where are the poppies, Assistant?" Jonathan asked.

"I don't know." The assistant stopped mid-sentence when he heard the sound of cowboy boots coming up the stairs. Stomping almost, both men wore suits and each presented his Federali I.D. Both were over six-foot-three. Both wore guns the size of a small cannon.

Jonathan pulled away from the chair and introduced himself and the Border Patrol agents.

JACK PAUSMAN

"Watch these guys, all of them. Agent Mendoza will be back in a moment. We like them as accessories to the murder this morning. We'll call you," Franco commented as the three U.S. agents walked out the director's office, and Jerry looked back at Juan Carlos. He pursed his lips and produced a kissing sound. Jerry shook his head and proceeded down the stairs.

The trio drove to the airport and waited in the terminal restaurant. They completed a long lunch with more than just a couple of beers. A Lear 35 pulled up to the corporate terminal. *IGS Energy Corporation* was printed on the side.

"Nice plane," Jerry said. They continued to drink. Jonathan's cellphone rang.

"You guys coming or not?" said the pilot. "I'm in the Lear."

"We're coming," Jonathan replied.

Three hours later, their plane touched down at San Diego International Airport. A black, tinted-glass GMC SUV was there to meet them. The southwest district director and Phoenix FBI Agent Rondell were waiting for them in the stretch limousine. Each of the three gave their respective bosses an account of the events surrounding the last three days.

"We have not heard from Arturo Gonzales in two days," Jonathan said. "We don't know his status."

"We don't know if he's alive or dead," Franco chimed in.

"What do you know about Cananéa?" Rondell asked.

"Only that we believe it is where they processed the opium." Jerry offered.

They passed through a yellow traffic light and entered the parking garage leased by the Border Patrol. Up the elevator to the third floor, the operational status questions continued to flow. They were greeted by Captain Barnhart and a man who introduced himself as Austin Willingham, United States Department of Justice.

Great! A freaking lawyer, Franco thought.

Jonathan shook his hand; the other two flicked their wrists, acknowledging his presence.

"Three murders; eight cartel members dead; two suspects; a train car filled with raw opium poppies—stolen, and one lost Mexican national." Jonathan put it in a nutshell.

Rondell added,

"And one petrochemical CEO."

"How'd they get the train to stop and steal all that opium?" asked Willingham.

"With a phosphorous cocktail," answered Franco.

"What the hell is that?" The director of the Border Patrol stood and looked at Franco.

Jonathan pulled out his cell phone and flipped through a half a dozen snapshots of what was left of the caboose.

"Let's get to it," offered the district director. "Break this down, Jerry. Segment the issues."

Jerry moved to the director's whiteboard and flowcharted the event. He drew the current *Suspect Board* on one side, the known cartel participants on the other. In the middle, he wrote the words, *Hormuz Defender* and a not-to-scale layout of the warehouses at the Poet of Mazatlán.

"What we know per segment, Director, is what you see before you. What we need is an evaluation on how to reconcile all of this. Capture those who are involved and find the heroin."

Jerry turned back to the director and expelled a deep breath.

"Director, if I may," Jonathan started, "We're going to need a viable force to take Morales down. We believe the Opium is in Cananéa. We do not know if it has been processed yet; we can only assume it has. We hope Arturo Gonzales is still alive; we do not know if he is."

"If the Sinaloas find out who stole their opium, there will be an all-out war; worse than we've witnessed in the past," Franco chimed in. "The FBI has had their sights on this guy, David Culberson, but there is no evidence that he is selling the dope; we *do feel*, however, he is assisting the cartel in bringing the product across the border. He was in Mazatlán the day before the attack."

Franco continued, "We also have three murders at the Mazatlán docks. We think the two, maybe three, persons of interest know more than what they're saying."

"Where do you think your contact is at this moment?" asked Rondell. "I mean, if you had to guess, Jonathan?"

"We know he designed the cocktail. So, if that is true, then he was probably at the train when it was attacked. And if *that is* true, he probably went with Morales to Cananéa– just a guess you understand."

"I have a question?" asked Willingham, "If Culberson is marketing the heroin for Morales, who are his customers? That is, who is going to buy a carload of heroin? That's got to have a street price of over $50 million."

"I have a question as well," interjected Rondell, "how do we let the Sinaloas know where their stuff is without telling them where their stuff is?"

"I think I can answer that one, Agent Rondell," Franco said.

"What do you have, Franco?" The director asked.

"Director, the governor of Sinaloa is purported to have ties with the cartel." Jonathan interjected. "He turns his head away, and they throw him a couple of bones. If true, there are ways to funnel information to him and watch how it plays out."

"I know who will get to him," Jerry said. "When we return, we'll make it happen."

"Right now, Director, our problem is the heroin and the means by which the product will be brought into the United States," Jonathan said.

Chapter 43

THE GOVERNOR'S MANSION SAT IN A DESOLATED spot atop the cliffs overlooking the Gulf of California. The veranda jetted out only far enough to hear the waves crashing over the rocky embankment below. The soothing sound was directly below the governor's bedroom.

The approach to the mansion was a winding two-lane asphalt road which offered little room for vehicles travelling in opposite directions. With no moon, the stars provided little guidance for the man walking to the governor's hacienda. Each step was methodically plotted up the dark road. There were no streetlights or neighbors with house lights to assist him. Motte and thicket lined his right side, and crashing waves were on his left. The darkened evening brought sounds from nocturnal animals scurrying through trees. He stopped to watch a momma coati and her babies quietly moving up the road. Calaban was only nervous about what he could not see.

His legs ached from the climb as he reached his target's home. His heart raced as he viewed the iron fence that surrounded the mansion. The long, iron vanguards were embedded into the concrete. The gate was designed in the same manner, electronically controlled, and all over eight feet high. There were no lights from the house.

Calaban peered at his watch. It was 8:30. He found a large bush; he went behind it and sat.

After an hour, his eyes slowly closed and fell asleep, but was awakened two hours later by the grumbling sound of an Italian sports car—a Ferrari, or perhaps a Lamborghini—speeding toward him. The special halogen headlights cast a giant blanket of light as the vehicle made its way up the road. He flipped his hoody over his head to cover his face.

The car slowed down only to give the driver enough time to depress the 'Open' button on his remote control. The gates swung open, and the intruder followed the car through the entrance. The two people got out of the automobile, laughing and stumbling as the man fumbled for the house key. The headlights stayed on long enough for Calaban to see the silhouette of the governor of Sinaloa's short, pudgy, little body.

Once inside, he reached behind his companion and unzipped her dress. Calaban watched them from the shadows as he moved slowly to the door. The man inside was so drunk, he barely closed the door— *Good enough*, Calaban thought.

The giggling went softer as they moved deeper into the house— then the lights went out.

Calaban slowly opened the front door. The darkness gave him plenty of cover as he proceeded directly to the dining room The massively sized drapes that hid the 'silent' room adjacent to the fireplace were just like he remembered them.

He entered the room and waited.

Two hours…? How long does it take to get laid?

He removed his penlight from his pocket and used it find the bedroom. Each step was performed with all the stealth his soft, leather shoes would allow. He neared the bed, his left arm extended; the green light helped him find his mark.

The crashing waves helped mask any extraneous sound he might make. It threw a soft blanket of light across the beard of Governor José Renaldo Reyes. In quick response, he dispatched the serrated blade swiftly and deep across his throat—barely a moan was heard.

He moved the light across the bed. She was sound asleep. He painted her entire body with the light before he moved back to the governor. The sheets were drenched in blood.

Morales will be pleased, he thought.

Calaban moved back to the foyer. He remembered the gate control and the alarm was on the wall by the door. He pressed the gate control and left the house as quietly as he entered.

He continued his walk down the winding road, and then, he was gone.

Chapter 44

THE PHOENIX FBI AGENT IN CHARGE RONDELL returned to the conference room. The private meeting with the Border Patrol director, the director of the FBI, the national security advisor, and the president of the United States was short but effective.

"We've come to some preliminary conclusions. I want to run them past you."

Franco put his coffee down and leaned back against the high-backed chair. Jerry turned from looking out the window.

Rondell continued, "We've had conversations with the Mexican government *and* the president of the United States. We have contacted a Colonel William J. Beauchamp, 1ˢᵗ Cavalry at Fort Hood."

"What in the world?" Jonathan interjected.

"Here me out, Jonathan. The three of you have made quite a name for yourselves—a good one, I might add. So, Jonathan, *you* are going to Cananéa and meet up with this mule of yours—I hope he is still alive. Jerry, Franco, you guys are going back to Mazatlán. The first thing you are going to do is get to the governor of Sinaloa, by whatever means you had in mind, and let him know where the opium is located, if it's still in that state. The Federales are going to interrogate the port director and his assistant. You're going to have to find out who else is involved; like who took the missing container."

"Don, who is this Beauchamp fellow, and what does he have to do with our investigation?" Jonathan asked.

"I'm getting to that. The Mexican government is allowing us to get our feet wet with this Morales fellow. They want to end the cartel forever and everything associated with it."

"Getting our feet wet?" Jonathan asked.

"As we speak, orders are being cut to import 20 gunships from the 1st Cavalry out of Fort Hood, Texas. Colonel Beauchamp is the Division Commander of the 1st AirCav, Iron Horse Division. He will be submitting an overt attack strategy against the Morales cartel. Once more, the Mexicans have approved his entry into the fray. Four companies of Apache helicopters will arrive in Tucson tomorrow morning. Along with them, 120 combat-ready soldiers from the 3rd Infantry Division will arrive simultaneously by a C-130. Their mission is the surgical removal of the cartel; capture or kill, it does not matter. Troop carriers will take the troops south; the staging area is the north side of Cananéa. Beauchamp's mission is to seek out the enemy and destroy them or turn them over to the Federales if still alive."

The Lear was waiting for the agents when they arrived at the San Diego Airport. Jonathan's bothersome look worried Jerry.

"What's up, Jonathan?"

"Surgical capture, my ass; this is going to be a blood-bath, and you know it, Jerry."

Jonathan and his team landed in Tucson two hours and 22 minutes later. They rolled up to the corporate terminal, and the three left the elaborately equipped government airplane. Jerry noticed the two identical Beech Barons being pre-flighted on the tarmac but thought little about it. They entered the terminal office. The girl standing behind the counter was a young lady about 19. Jerry thought, *A little young to be in the aviation business.*

"May I help you?" she asked.

Franco explained that they had booked two airplanes for the day and asked, "Those two Barons belong to us?" She looked at their I.D.s and nodded.

"When will you be ready to go?" she asked.

"Anytime, I'll be right back." Jerry looked at the "Men" sign—*Ah, the restroom.*

She smiled, then looked at Franco.

"Your package is on board," she added,

"Which one of you is going to Cananéa?" The three-striped epaulets on the guy's shoulder indicated he was one the pilots.

"I am, and who are you?" Jonathan asked. The pilot moved into the restroom.

"Marc Simpson, DEA. Here's my I.D."

"Okay, DEA, you are flying me to Cananéa?" Jonathan responded anxiously.

"Better than that." Marc added, "We know where Jack Culberson is and where he's going."

Franco jumped in, "You going to tell us, or do we have to play 20 questions?"

"Earlier today, Jack took his Bonanza and another guy and headed east flying visual over Highway 2. Morales has held up his caravan, expecting Jack to move the heroin across the border to, we believe, Dallas. Are you ram-rodding this operation, Agent?"

Jonathan nodded, then said, "Here's our biggest problem. The Apache's ETA is in the morning. Jack now has nine hours on us, and tomorrow, the stuff will over the border. Simpson, do you have access to any weaponry, now?"

"We can get what we need," the DEA answered.

"Then grab what you can and as many men that will fit in the Baron, and let's intercept them."

The local DEA office sent over three men, six AR-15s, and 30 banana clips to the waiting Baron. The preflight was completed, but this was blacktops; there would be no flight plan.

The twin engine Baron left Tucson heading for Highway 2 east out of Cananéa.

Through his headset, Marc said, "We have a couple of items going for us. In the time it takes for us to get to where they are, they'll be using lots of that time loading 265 bricks of heroin on Jack's plane."

"What's the second thing?" Jerry asked.

"The three men sitting behind you are DEA snipers," Marc smiled.

Thirty minutes out of Nogales, a blue haze settled in the pass that split the two peaks through the Sierra de Cananéa Mountains. The west side of Highway 2 ran through it. Marc eased the yoke forward and dissected the mountain tops for a speedier arrival at the rendezvous point.

"Jonathan, what's your plan, since this is *not* a gunship," Marc asked.

Jonathan grabbed his cellphone and pushed calculator icon.

"If the caravan is three hours out of Cananéa, we will intercept in less than an hour and a half at our present speed. It will take them longer to load all that heroin in that amount of time.

"We'll climb to 7,000 feet; circle in from the north just above Aquamondo. If the loading is still going on, we'll take them from the east. If Jack's airborne, we'll either shoot him down, and I don't have a clue how that will happen, or come over the top of them and let our propellers clip off his rudder. That will knock him out of the sky. Period."

"You want me to land this plane on the highway?" Marc asked.

"I do," Jonathan answered.

The mountain range gave way to the foothills as they approached Cananéa. The road leaving the town was plainly seen from the air, and they followed it easily from a cloudless sky.

"I don't think this has been done before," Jonathan said, looking at the three DEA snipers. "So, upon egress, spread out, keep low, and disable Jack's plane. Kill anybody you have to."

Chapter 45

THE CROWDED PARKING LOT SHOWED a busy day at Buelna International Airport. The second Baron was held in pattern due to the many aircraft arriving—few leaving. Through Franco's window, he saw many more corporate jets than commercial. The Baron's pilot called the tower and requested instructions to land, and it was given. The landing was smooth, and the Baron took the first available exit. They received a call from ground control.

"Stay on the tarmac past corporate terminal and park in front of Building 12; transportation to the terminal will be provided."

"Roger, Ground Control."

The Baron taxied to and parked at the assigned area. The two government agents, plus their pilot, waited. An elongated airport golf cart finally arrived, picked up its passengers, and headed back to the terminal.

"Why so crowded?" Franco asked the driver.

"The governor of Sinaloa was murdered," he said.

Cripes! Franco thought. "What happened?"

"The maid found him in the morning lying in bed with his throat slit."

"Do they have any suspects?" Jerry asked.

"They have only rumors," said the driver.

The trio pulled up to the terminal and checked in the Baron's tail number. They grabbed a standing taxi, and the three climbed aboard. Franco asked to be taken to the docks; Jerry scanned his messages. The taxi stopped at the gate leading to the poet complex; the two would relieve the Federali agents guarding the port director. The same guard was on duty.

"Anything unusual happening here?" Franco asked.

The guard shook his head.

"No, Agents. Except—"

"Except, what?"

"The port director has never passed through this gate while I have been on duty, and he has never signed out."

The two Border Patrol agents thanked him and drove to the director's office.

Once again, Jerry looked upward to the top of the stairs—he took a deep breath. He listened for conversations; or music; something—any sound—but he heard nothing.

He and Franco walked up slowly. Almost at the top, they encountered an eerie stillness. Jerry drew his M9 and released the de-cock mechanism. Franco followed suit. Jerry reached the top first and quickly side-stepped to allow room for Franco to get into position.

The two men proceeded to the director's office. Passed the copier, the open door revealed Juanita, lying on the floor with her throat cut. Moving cautiously around the drinking fountain, the second body was discovered in a pool of blood oozing from his neck. The assistant and then Agent Mendoza in similar condition. Mendoza's gun remained in its holster—the man never knew what hit him.

As they completed their discovery, more pools of blood were seen everywhere. Juan Carlos was hanging by his wrists and by his genitals, his throat sliced from ear to ear. The two large Federali agents were gone.

Jerry and Franco ran down the stairs and jumped in the colonel's car. They headed downtown to pay a visit to the Federali office. Within 20 minutes, they were standing in front of the receptionist's desk.

"We need to see the colonel." Jerry's demeanor was harried.

"He's busy at the moment."

"He's gonna be a lot busier." Franco leaned into her face. "Now, *please*, get him—now!"

"I'll call his office…"

"Lady, if you can read this badge, then you will get off your ass and go get him. If you don't remember who we are, let us explain it to you, we are United States federal agents working under the auspices of the president of Mexico, so get off your ass and go get him—now!"

She returned and sheepishly told the two agents, "You may see him now."

Franco entered first and held the door for Jerry, then closed it behind him.

"Mendoza has been murdered, Estabán, his assistant, and his secretary have been murdered. The two Federali agents we left in charge are gone. Do you know their whereabouts, Colonel?"

Franco left his pleasant disposition at the port director's office.

"At this moment, no," the colonel answered. "Neither of the two called in, let alone reported for work. We have been looking for them for two days. We all knew about the hijacking," the colonel continued.

Franco jumped in, interrupting the colonel, "Telephone records show that Juan Carlos received a call from a security sergeant that he sent to the crippled train. The witnesses said that a caravan with the opium were heading north. The conclusion was either Nogales or Cananéa. We have gone after them."

Franco excused himself and went into a room adjacent to the colonel's. He dialed his captain.

"Captain, call this Colonel Beauchamp and make sure he deviates his battalion to an area 200 miles east of Cananéa on Highway 2 where it intersects with Highway 14. Any and all action will culminate at that spot, I'm sure of it. If he flies into Tucson, he will be wasting precious time." Franco took a deep breath.

The captain reported, "Conroy is in sight of them now, but he brings a total of six men; they have over 80—with firepower."

Chapter 46

MARC PULLED THE YOKE BACK, added power as he put the Beech Baron in a climbing right turn. Jonathan glanced out over the right wing to view what looked like a colony of ants swarming in protection of what looked like the queen. At 6,000 feet, the pilot dropped the starboard wing and pulled back the power. Nose down, he dropped to 1,000 feet heading directly west on the eastbound highway. Morales saw the subsequent landing about to occur. Traffic was light, but the plane landed anyway. He and his goons went for their guns with 120 bricks left to load. Marc landed hot and engaged full right brake that almost ground-looped the Baron. The two starboard doors flung open, and Jonathan and the DEA snipers went for the ground.

"Blow out a tire!" yelled Jonathan.

The attack on Morales and Jack's plane was job one—they needed to be stopped.

Morales' men were ready. One of his lieutenants started firing as soon as he saw the agents leave the airplane—he missed. The number two sniper saw him and placed a two-shot group in his heart. Number three went for the powerful Continental that drove the Bonanza and fired two rounds into the cowling.

Another shot from Morales' gang and then another. The left tire was blown out, and the Baron sank to one side. Number three saw two of the thugs running to a nearby tree—two shots—two dead. The 3-9X40 Red Dot Magnifier and the MP5s were a perfect combination.

Bullet holes were all over the Baron, and the engine of the Bonanza was on fire. Neither aircraft was going anywhere.

The five-man team broke away from the damaged Baron and moved up the adjacent hillside, using the local mesquite tree as cover. Number one sniper found a nearby arroyo. Two small boulders conveniently placed provided excellent cover for him. Few trees were there to give them satisfactory cover, but each one was used.

Number three rolled to his side to grab another 30-round magazine. Jonathan heard the crack behind him as he ran to flank the cartel thugs—he turned briefly. A lucky bullet struck the agent on the top of his head and moved through his jaw and into his heart. Jonathan stopped only for a second of regret and then continued to run to cover. He slid behind a fallen tree trunk and aimed his AR-15 into the group of cartel members. He gravely wounded three and killed one.

Vargas ordered five men to flank the agents. Marc saw Vargas' mini-summit and took aim at the group. One stood to leave; the .223 cal bullet left Marc's weapon at 1,700 feet per second, it quickly met its mark in the man's left temple. His brains spewed and blanketed Vargas and two of the other men. Another was hit in the neck and another was hit in the left side. Marc's carbine did its job and ripped out the thug's upper left torso. A number of men fired indiscriminately—hitting no one.

Thirty or more of Morales' men lay dead at his feet. The sweat poured down his squalid, brown face. His movements were erratic. He kneeled, protected by the collapsed fuselage, then to the back of his SUV—then back to the plane. Number two sniper saw the apparent frustration, and so did everyone else. Five of his men quietly moved back to their trucks. Vargas saw them run and shot two of them in the back. *Cowards.*

Morales ordered his men to rush the four remaining agents. A group of 10 stood, yelling as they rushed the spread-out DEA. It was suicide of the first order. Most were hit as they left the cover of what was left of Jack's Bonanza. One ran wildly, firing his AK, hitting no one.

The remaining fired until their clips were empty and found themselves in no man's land without ammo; they died within seconds.

Through the smoke and the ongoing dust-up, Jonathan's eyes picked up a man hiding. It was Jack, hiding underneath one of the SUVs with another man. Their heads down with eyes closed, it was apparent they wanted no part of this fight.

Morales and Vargas' personas were well-known, so in the midst of this fire-fight, Jonathan called Marc on his cellphone,

"We've got to finish this. We have a man in there." Jonathan said. "Do you see Morales?"

"The one in the red shirt?" Marc asked.

"Yes, and the guy crouched next to him is Alejandro Vargas. Call your guys and see if they can take those two out?"

Jack's Bonanza was totally in flames, and 200 bricks of heroin lay burned to a crisp. At that moment, one of Morales' men crawled up to him and yelled in his ear.

"Jefe, we have no more ammo."

Morales flailed his arms in anger and looked back at his men— most had run away. He raised his U.S. made AR-15 rifle and stood up. Number three sniper's rifle responded quick and deadly. The bullet hit at just below the chin; the anterior tubercle was in 100 pieces, and his head flopped backward, attached to his body only by his intact esophagus.

Vargas, seeing his long-time comrade dead at his feet, grabbed his machete and took up Morales' position. Jonathan had crawled closer to the two leaders. Seeing Morales dead, he stood to his feet, standing squarely, facing Vargas His right hand fit comfortably on his M9 Beretta as he pointed it at the rushing Vargas. The bullet cleared the six-inch barrel, and Vargas fell helplessly, feeling the pain of a surgically removed knee cap.

Thirty men stood in unison and raised their empty arms. Some were wounded; some not. They got in their vehicles and headed west.

One agent walked up to Vargas and handcuffed him. Jonathan moved slowly to the two men hiding under the truck.

"Get out of there!" he said. The two crawled out from underneath the vehicle. He spun Jack around and slammed him against him against the body of the SUV, then he smiled at Arturo.

"Marc!" Jonathan yelled, "Take this Mexican fella and put him in the SUV. I'm taking *this* one with me." He yelled back at the two remaining snipers, "Put those bricks in one of these trucks, and we'll take them to Tucson."

"Who's going to clean up this mess?" Marc asked.

"Let the Mexicans do it," Jonathan answered. He turned back to the cartel lieutenant. "Mr. Vargas, my name is Special Agent Jonathan Conroy with the FBI. First, let me inform you that you are under arrest, and I will read you your rights later. I know you're hurting, and I'm going to see to it you are taken care of. The faster you answer some of my questions, the faster you will headed to the hospital, got it?"

"Fuck you!" Vargas responded.

"Great! This is not a good start for you," Jonathan responded. "I do not have any aspirin with me, so you're *really* going to need a doctor. We have two accessories to this crime sitting in the car; one American, one Mexican. The Federales are on their way, and they will pick up the stragglers. Each one of those men knows as much as you do."

Vargas remained silent.

Jonathan grabbed his phone.

"Jerry, we stopped the plane. Morales is dead, and I am sitting here with Alejandro Vargas. He lost his kneecap. What's left of it is east of here—somewhere."

Jerry interrupted, "Listen to me! Mendoza, the port director, and his two assistants are dead. The two Federali agents went rogue, and they are on their way to you. They are being chased, but by whom, we do not know. I have called the captain, and they are re-routing the choppers from Fort Hood. They should hopefullybe there before the rogue cops get to you."

"We've got Arturo and Jack," Jonathan said. "Jack's scared, and Arturo's fine—shaken, but fine. We are *all* going back to Cananéa to run forensics on the plant. The issue now is where the bricks were being delivered." Jonathan then rested his voice.

The four agents jumped in the four trucks with the dead Morales covered by a sheet in the back. The rearview mirror was a blazed with death and destruction of burning airplanes. Somebody was going to have to clean up that mess.

Jonathan remembered Dolores Cantu's phone call. He returned it. She answered.

"Hello?"

"Mrs. Cantu, Agent Conroy. I've been delayed; how can I help you?"

"Agent, a man came to see me. He gave me $250,000. He told me to get out of Mazatlán."

"Mrs. Cantu, call this number. It belongs to Agent Franco Medellin. Tell him I told you to call and that he needs to get you and your daughter out of Mexico—my treat. He will take care of it. He should be leaving pretty quick, so don't pack anything. Get to him as soon as you can."

The drive back to Cananéa was long, arduous, and painful for Vargas. It offered plenty of time for him to think about the burned heroin and where it was headed. A street value of over $50 million of product would never reach the streets.

The Sinaloas possession was an $8 million short-fall, and they are pissed— they have to be. The buyer is looking for his stuff and will never see it, Jonathan thought.

He looked over to Arturo.

"You've been through a lot."

The old man just stared out the window.

His eyes moved to the outside mirror, "My heart pounds with remorse. I have crossed the line; my heart will never see the light again." Tears began to flow from Arturo's eyes; he did not touch them; he did not wipe them from his face.

"You are a brave and an intelligent man, Arturo; there will be rewards for what you've done."

"No, Agent. What I have done has hurt, killed, and destroyed lives, and I will burn in hell for it." The words barely came out of Arturo's mouth.

The town of Cananéa lay ahead. Jack Culberson, with handcuffs wrapped around his wrists, stared upward at the greenish-gray headliner of the late model SUV that once belonged to Morales. He felt a coldness surround him and yet sweat dripped down his forehead; he tried to blow it away—to no avail. The quarter-million-dollar airplane was in rubble, but that was the least of his worries.

Madeleine Underwood was bringing $8 million to Dallas tomorrow morning. My father will be waiting for her. There will be no heroine. That thought rolled over and over in Jack's head. He and his father were in deep shit, and he knew it.

Two and a half hours later, the caravan drove into town. On the corner sat *El Restaurante Calle*, and just beyond the large wooden awnings, there was the city's fountain. Arturo told the driver to stop.

The driver acknowledged the request. Arturo thought for a moment; Jack was in the car behind him. The car stopped, and he stared out the window. The vision of the cool, dancing spray of water responding to the southern breeze put a melancholy smile on his face. He opened the door and leaned closely to the trough and grabbed a moist bouquet of water to wet his lips. He watched the children playing soccer on- and off-street just beyond the square.

"Stop the car!" Arturo ordered again. His eyes glazed over.

"We *have* stopped," said the driver.

Just above a whisper, he said, "The church." Arturo slid out the vehicle and proceeded with deliberate resolve to the front door of the old mission.

Jack looked at him with shock.

"Is he crazy? What the hell is he doing?"

Vargas sat in the first car and found it difficult to sit up and view what was happening, but he saw just enough.

"God damn you!" he screamed, "I will cut your nuts off and make you eat them, you son-of-a-bitch." He fell back into the seat writhing in pain. The windows were closed; his ranting was muffled and only heard by the driver.

At the top of the steps Arturo turned and pointed to Jonathan and then back to the door. The agent got out of the car, leaving the DEA agent to supervise Jack. He ran up to Arturo and rested both hands on his shoulders.

"You know they will kill you for this, my friend."

"I know."

He turned away from Jonathan and methodically proceeded down the steps. He pulled Morales' Browning 1911 that he stole from his body. The gun behind him, he moved up to Vargas sitting in the back seat. He asked the driver to drop the rear window—he wished to face Vargas. The power window dropped only two-thirds of the way. Arturo raised the barrel—without saying a word; without listening to Vargas scream for his life, he aimed and pulled the trigger. A single .45cal slug drove deep into Vargas' head. Brain matter and shards of skull blanketed the rear of the SUV. The rear window turned crimson red with blotches of gray. Arturo's heart raced, his eyes focused, but now his breathing was controlled—there were no feelings of anything—least of all, regret.

Jonathan looked down the steps to the car and then to the doors of the church. Vargas' death was done, so he turned his attention to the church and what he was about to find behind the mission doors. His inclination was to break it down, but Arturo walked up the steps and placed his hand on the agent's shoulder while handing him the Browning.

Arturo's eyes never blinked, "Jonathan, please do not break the door. These are from Vargas' pocket."

Jonathan took the key ring and began trying each key.

The large iron locks gave way to the fourth try. The 120-year-old doors swung open as Arturo and Jonathan pushed the great rings forward against the patina backplates. Inside, the pews were replaced with tables and vats with propane tanks beneath them. A burned-out Madonna stood watchful as she saw evil spread from her grace time after time. Water spots remained below her eyes as if she had been crying over what was her burdened to survey. Jonathan wept.

Chapter 47

JONATHAN CAME DOWN THE STAIRS and sat next to Marc.

"What now, FBI? You have quite a mess here, *and* out there," he said, pointing east.

The FBI agent did not say anything, he just nodded his head.

"The local police will be here any second—and will want answers," Marc said as he wiped his face.

"They all want answers, Marc. Your boss is going to want to know what happened to his plane and his dead agent. Mine will want to know if I've gone totally crazy."

"How do you plan to play the locals?" Marc asked.

"I'll tell them the Federales are on their way. Let them clean up the mess to the east."

Jonathan stood up and walked back to Arturo. "You know where the dope was going?"

"No," Arturo said, "but I know who does." His eyes followed a visual path to the third car. Jack Culberson.

Jack pulled himself into a comfortable position in the back seat. Jonathan opened the back car door and scooted next to him.

"So Jack, where's your father?" Jonathan began.

"How would I know?" A couple of strands from his charcoal hair fell onto his eye and with a quick movement, he protruded his lower lip under his nose and blew the strands away from his face.

"Jack, we know he's involved in this heist. Who's buying the dope?"

"You'll have to ask *him*." Jack looked away from the agent.

A small contingent of Apaches arrived and landed in a field just beyond the square. Colonel Beauchamp was not among them. A Captain Miller egressed from one of the attack choppers and approached the lead black SUV.

"We saw the mess out east of here," said the captain. "Where would one Jonathan Conway be found?"

"Right here, Captain," he yelled down from the church steps.

"Agent, you got some bad shit back yonder. Who's going to clean that mess up?"

"Yeah, it *is* kind of a mess; we'll get someone to work on it," Jonathan responded. "Hey, where's the colonel?"

"Intercepting an incoming *Jet Ranger* that belongs to them Federali folks."

"They may be the two rogue agents we were told about," Jonathan said as he turned back to Jack.

"Here's the issue, Mr. Culberson. The FBI has staked out your father's petrochemical plant, and they are not leaving. Your dad's Gulfstream is fully displayed on our radar. The Sinaloas attack squad is after him, and the state of Arizona wants both of you. I will get to the United States Attorney's office in a minute. One more thing, Jack, these fellas landing now in that Ranger are rogue Federali, and when they find out who you are, they are going to kill you," Jonathan spoke and stood there looking at Jack.

Jack sat motionless, listening to the Jonathan speak to him as he thought, *They don't know about New York, and they don't know about what was not going to take place in his father's office.* For all Jack knew, David already banked the $8 million. If he spent *any* of it, he was a dead man. *Today is Friday*, he thought. *Sunday afternoon, the shit hits the fan.*

"...Are you listening to me?" Jonathan's squinted eyes peered into Jack's face.

Culberson's heart was racing so fast, he thought it was about to explode. He wished he was back in his hospital bed. The handcuffs that hobbled his wrists were physically affecting his bandaged arm. The torn vein was not healed. He needed a doctor.

"I hear you," Jack said. "Take me back to Tucson; you got nothing on me. Get me out of Mexico—now!" He grimaced at the oozing blood from his arm.

"Does that Bonanza back there, belong to you?" Jonathan asked, but he was interrupted.

"Excuse me!' The approaching voice was heard from around the corner of the restaurant. Jonathan and his team looked up to see the local chief of police coming toward them.

"What are you doing in my city?" the policeman asked. A pudgy little man, short and bald. His butt shifted from side to side like a duck waddling to a pond. His enlarged stomach hung over his gun belt, bringing the holster hanging below his crotch. When he finished blurting out his question, he belched. Jonathan looked at the caricature and laughed.

"Why is the church door open?" the chief asked.

Jonathan presented his credentials and his Letter of Appointment. His eyes squinted as to filter out the glare from Vargas' back window. As the chief walked around to the side, he saw the blood, the brain matter, and brains, and…

"Vargas. Too bad." Cananéa's top cop moved to where Jack Culberson was sitting. He leaned in the window and smirked, "How's your arm, young man?"

He turned back to the town square, his hand rubbing his round face in a circular motion.

"How can I help you?" the chief said.

"You can start with that mess east of here," Marc blurted. The chief looked to where the DEA agent was pointing.

"I don't see anything."

Chapter 48

THE FIRST BEECHCRAFT BARON TOUCHED DOWN at Tucson International long enough to turn Dolores Cantu, her mother, and her baby over to a United States attorney who was ordered to find refuge for the three-some. The aircraft was refueled, and Franco and Jerry re-boarded. The turnaround for Culiacán happened in less than 15 minutes.

The DEA pilot of the Baron received his first radio transmission; it was from Jonathan.

"Most of the heroin was destroyed," Jonathan reported. "What was left, we've taken as evidence against the Culbersons. The attempt to move it into the U.S. failed," he said.

Franco edged his way to the cockpit and tapped the pilot's shoulder. The pilot gave him his headset.

"The dead pool was long and painful; especially for the innocent," Franco told Jonathan.

"Now, two more pieces to the puzzle, at least, were in place," Jonathan responded through the pilot's headset. "Me and four DEA in-tercepted a transfer of 265 bricks of heroin east of Cananéa. We had a fire fight, and two planes were destroyed—one Bonanza and one gov-ernment Baron. Morales was killed during the confrontation, and Var-gas was shot in Cananéa. We lost a DEA agent. Our mule was with them, and he is fine."

"Jonathan," Jerry placed the headset close to his mouth. "One more thing; there are two rogue Federali agents who are looking for the stolen stuff. They headed for Nogales as we speak. We don't think it will be long before they go to Plan B."

"Which is?" Jonathan asked.

"Cananéa." Jerry answered. "They are looking for the dope, and they intend to find it."

"Okay!" said Jonathan, "but we need to find out who the buyer is and where the stuff was going."

Chapter 49

MADELEINE UNDERWOOD ROSE EARLY. Actually, she did not sleep much that night. She made her three phone calls, and the needed $8 million was on its way to her. She sat on the edge of her bed, rubbed her eyes and fussed with her hair, then scratched the back and the top of her scalp.

She moved to the kitchen to pour herself a cup of coffee. The first special courier was due in an hour and a half; plenty of time for a soothing, hot shower.

She stepped into the sensuous pleasure that only hot beads of water from seven shower heads can give. The warm sun was already depositing its rays through her large picture window. There were no drapes, but she was on the twelfth floor—no reason to have them. She threw on a pair of Neiman's slacks and a silk blouse and went back to brush her teeth. The speaker buzzed.

"Madam Deputy Mayor? There is a lawyer from Wilcox, Smith, and Wilcox to see you. Shall I send her up?"

"That will be fine, George. Thank you."

The elevator ride was quick for 12 floors, so it was not long before there was a knock on the door.

"Madam Deputy Mayor, I have this suitcase, and I was told to deliver it directly into your hands."

"Thank you." Madeleine said as she opened the door—short and sweet. The toe of a woman's leather shoe was resting in the door jam. She returned it to the open position.

"Yes?" she said.

"Ms. Underwood…a moment, please. May I come in?"

Madeleine extended the invitation by widening the door opening and backing up, reaching for the suitcase.

"What's on your mind, Ms…"

"Haywood, Christina Haywood. Madam Deputy Mayor, I will be brief. I am paid $80,000 a year as a new associate, not a delivery person—especially a suitcase filled with—whatever." The young lawyer continued, "I do not wish to be disbarred, nor do I wish to go to jail. I *do*, however, want to know what I delivered to you."

Madeleine thought for a moment—*Don't react…respond!*

"Come in, Ms. Haywood, and please sit down. Just to establish a point here; Michael Wilcox is my attorney; therefore, you and I will be speaking under attorney/client privilege, right?"

Christina Haywood acknowledged the comment by nodding her head. The young lawyer sat in the chair adjacent to Madeleine. Her long legs showed off her age—maybe late twenties. The black pinstriped suit was all she needed to understand what kind of lawyer she was dealing with. Strong-willed, sensible, and smart.

"The city is embarking on a project of enormous importance," Madeleine started. "People of all races and background will benefit. However, the area where the improvements will be concentrated is going to require the tearing down of slums in the area and a subsequent city bond issue. The Chinese wall must be in effect and must be kept from greedy investors. We do not want those bastards coming out of the woodwork." Madeine was thinking very fast. "If the minutes from prior meetings, the regulatory publications, and preliminary discussions with the Selling Groups are divulged, there would be a run on the property values. I cannot allow all of that to be brought here in banker's boxes. I…we would have the *Times* banging down my door before you reached to the elevator. I will be meeting with your boss on Monday, and I'll discuss your sincere concerns about this."

"Thank you very much, Madam Deputy Mayor." She stood and extended her right hand. Madeleine smiled at the obvious success of her bullshit story. She escorted the young lawyer to the door and thanked her for bringing the *documents* to her. She closed and locked the door and went to sit in the nearest chair. Madeleine splayed out her legs and took a deep breath.

I wonder if it's too early for a glass of wine....?

The next knock was much heavier.

That would be Carmine, she thought. She pushed her butt back to stand and lifted herself out of the seat. She sauntered to the door—not hurrying. The concierge knew Madeleine's next guest he sent directly to the elevator.

"Hello, Carmine, won't you come in?" She looked at the suitcase, "Um...leather; nice touch."

"Hello, Madeleine." The middle-aged man let himself in the apartment. "When will your friend have the stuff?" Carmine's $2,000 suit and his fast talking codified his lack of patience and need for pleasantries.

"We're meeting at his office on Sunday afternoon. Want to come?" she asked.

"No, thank you. Granddaughter's sixteenth birthday. Look, Madeleine, in that suitcase, sits $3.5 million in unmarked $100 dollar—it's not exactly insured. My people are counting on you. Don't fuck this up!"

She turned and moved to the high-backed chair. She sat and gracefully crossed her legs.

"They are on the way, Carmine. Don't worry."

"Fine." He turned to the door. "I'll speak with you on Monday."

He was gone and Madeleine released a deep sigh of relief. Two matching large suitcases lay in front of her. She stared at them for a moment and headed for the kitchen.

Time for breakfast.

She picked up her cellphone and pushed David's hotkey.

"I'm leaving for Dallas tomorrow."

The buzzer rang again.

"Yes, George?"

"Madam Deputy Mayor, a gentleman to see you."

"Send him up—thank you, George. David, got to go, bye!"

Madeleine's Keurig topped off the fresh cup of coffee as the doorbell rang. It was followed by a knock on the door. She was in no hurry. The cream was stirred and just a dab of sugar—another knock.

She reached for her French grandeur doorknob and dropped the handle enough for the locking device to be drawn into the door. It flung open at that instant; a man burst into her room, both arms extended and pushing up against her shoulders.

"Where the fuck is my dope?" His strength dropped her to the floor; his left arm flew backward, caught the door and slammed it shut.

"I…" Madeleine's heart rate went into overdrive. The man was Mexican, but she didn't know him.

"Don't fuck with me, bitch. Where IS it? Where's my shit? They will find your stinking body in 50 pieces next spring if you don't tell me." The man was clean shaven and wore decent looking suit.

"It got hit." The words could hardly come out of her mouth.

"Dammit, I know it got hit," he screamed. "Who took it? Where the fuck is it?"

She was shaking.

"It'll be in Dallas on Sunday afternoon." Her head hurt from hitting the floor; the silk top drenched with coffee. He pulled out his semi-automatic and attached the silencer.

"No! It isn't, bitch." The buzzer erupted again. "Get up! Wipe all that shit from your face; change shirts and answer the fucking door." She stood up; he shoved his hand against her back, pushing her closer to the buzzer.

A couple of deep breaths, "Y…yes, George?"

"Another visitor, Madam Deputy Mayor."

"Tell them, I..." His gun pressed heavy to her temple. He moved the barrel in an upward motion, then back against her head.

"Tell them, I would like for them to come up; thank you, George."

"That's your third delivery, right?" He looked in the corner. "That's the $5.5 million?"

She stuttered, "Y...yes."

Her legs were like jelly. They shook so hard, she had to hold on to the wall as she moved to her bedroom to change. He looked at her as she removed the coffee drenched top. He moved close to her and placed his hand on her breast. She let him.

"Nice." Madeleine cringed at his touch. He reached inside her bra and toyed with her nipple.

"Maybe later."

The shaking had not stopped when the doorbell sounded. She opened the second drawer and yanked the first top she came to—it was cotton; a red cotton t-shirt. Her legs were shaking; her heart was pounding. She stood from the bed and reluctantly went to open the door.

She greeted Francisco as he wheeled in the large paisley suitcase. Her body covered the entrance to her apartment.

"Are you going to let me in?" He asked.

"Uh...it's kind of a turmoil around here this morning, I'll just take..."

The Mexican stepped out from behind the door, with the gun pointed at Madeleine.

"Why don't you join the party?" he demanded.

Francisco Parizzi entered Madeleine's apartment willingly, "There's no need for guns, we're all friends here." Parizzi looked at Madeleine. He saw the fear in her eyes; he could feel a slight shaking of the floor emanating from her body. Francisco was well aware of what the brain can do to the nervous system under fear conditions—he wasn't a doctor; he was a made-man in the New York syndicate who oversaw the drug trafficking in Queens and Brooklyn. He had five of his men sitting in the car waiting for him.

Madeleine met him at a party 10 years ago. She did not know who he was until he fell in love with her right away; everybody falls in love with Madeine. His name was mentioned one day in a meeting of borough chiefs of the New York Police Department. She knew this friendship was not going anywhere—so did he.

Francisco understood Madeleine's phone call telling him any relationship more than just knowing him would never go any higher. He knew the *acquaintance* label would never be more than that. The second party was a little different. New York City is liberal. The bosses did not want another chief attorney like the one there had been 20 years ago to come in and be pro-active in cleaning up crime. They needed someone smart and witty to beat the Republican challenger. Madeleine Underwood popped up on the radar screen a couple of years earlier. She was invited to a fundraiser to give a speech. Everyone fell in love with her.

After campaigning a few months, her poll numbers weren't showing a lot of progress. One evening, she arrived at her small apartment in Sheepshead Bay and proceeded up the walkway. Out of the dark, stepped a figure of a man—it scared the crap out of her until she heard:

"Madeleine, it's Francisco. Don't be alarmed! Can we talk?"

For whatever reason, the next poll taken showed her besting her numbers by double-digit and closing in on her Primary opponents. The meetings with Francisco Parizzi were always in secret; and always profitable. Millions of dollars were infused into her campaign coffer. The Primary was easily won. Four months later, the Republican challenger didn't have a chance—Madeleine Underwood was bought and paid for.

Now, Parizzi was in Madeleine's apartment for over an hour. A New York City Police car cruised the entrance three times. The mob boss of the Bronx sat patiently in his limousine, which spewed a steady stream of fumes from the exhaust. The fourth time, the police car stopped. The officer dropped the window and motioned to the limo driver to move on.

A wise guy slid out from the front seat and headed into the building.

George sat behind his welcome-desk and stood to activate the guest buzzer—a moment went by. Madeleine finally answered.

He said, "Madam Deputy Mayor, another gentleman calling. He says he's here to pick up Mr. Parizzi. He's quite insistent that he come up, Madam Deputy Mayor."

—◆◆◆—

Parizzi jumped close to the speaker, "Tell him to get the hell outta here." The blow from the Sinaloa's gun came hard against his head. It drove him to the ground and left him unconscious.

"You dumb son-of-a-bitch, do you know what you've just done?" Madeleine said.

The struggle was heard through the speaker, "Boss! Hey, boss!" He yelled at George, "Get me up there—now!"

The doorman held the elevator as the wise guy ran to the street to wave down the limo coming down the street.

"We have a problem!" Three men jumped from the moving car and ran into the building. The foursome attached silencers to their semi-automatics as they rode up to the twelfth floor.

The Sinaloa's arm reached around Madeleine's neck. Her heart was beating so fast, her body shook. She could not stand; she couldn't speak. Her last attempt to scream came out as a guttural moan. The Mexican turned his back to Francisco as he threw her on one the chairs. Parizzi awoke with just enough strength to drop the doorhandle. The door remained slightly open for a few moments.

The sound of an elevator opening was barely heard through the melee inside Madeleine's apartment. In an instant, it burst open, and the men rushed into the apartment—two low; one high with one holding back in reserve. The Sinaloan fired, and two men responded in kind—one bullet hit the Mexican in the face. He collapsed, writhing in pain—it was over in just a few seconds. Two of the men kneeled to help Parizzi to a chair; he was dead. Shot in the back.

Madeleine raised her hand across her mouth. She could not emit a sound. Her breathing was heavy, but she managed to cross over the room to the wounded Mexican—he was still alive with the left side of his cheek and half his jaw lying beside him on the carpet.

"You stupid son-of-bitch," Madeleine screamed at the Mexican.

He screamed in pain as Parizzi's men moved to the side of the apartment and stood against the wall staring at the Mexican.

"Call the fixer!" she ordered one of the wise guys, "And you; you son-of-a-bitch, don't fucking move!" She drove the tip of her three-inch heel into the man's sprawled right palm. One of the bodyguards closed his flip-phone and told Madeleine that the people were on their way.

She nodded as she grabbed the cell from her purse and dialed the head of the Herrera cartel. One of cartel leader's goons answered the phone. She checked her emotions—her stoicism embodied Madeleine's every word.

"I have your $8 million. I want the product delivered Sunday morning to Culberson Petrochemical in Dallas." She paused. "I don't know the address; look it up! By the way, we have your man—if you want him back, bring a shoe box."

Madeleine took a deep breath and looked from Francisco's dead body.

"Tell your new boss I owe him, and tell him I want to see him—alone."

The four members of Parizzi's mob family sat quietly until the buzzer rang. By now, Madeleine had calmed down. She went to the speaker and told George to allow her new guests to come up.

She wanted a glass of wine while she waited for the elevator to reach her floor. She paced back and forth, occasionally glancing at Francisco. The urge to smoke was strong; the urge to slam her heels into the Mexican's jaw was even greater. She resolved herself to the wait. She really did not know what to expect when she opened the door. Madeleine never thought of any scenario such as the one she was experiencing.

The sound of the elevator door got her attention, and she moved towards the door.

She dropped the latch and saw three men; all calm and neatly dressed. The four bodyguards left their wall position and moved to the center of the room, standing quietly as Madeleine's newest friends entered the apartment.

The family's consigliere, Marco Davino, removed his hat and placed it across his heart. He moved past Madeleine without saying a word and knelt next to his mentor, who lay dead. He ran his cupped fingers through Parizzi's hair, and tears fell upon the blood stains on the carpet. Madeleine watched as he moved next to the four men.

He looked at the injured Sinaloan then fixed his stare upon his face. The consigliere drew closer as if he were interested in the details of the wound.

"Which one of you shot him in the face?"

The second man through the door, stepped forward.

"I did, Consigliere." The lawyer glanced at the Deputy Mayor, then gave a soft, loving slap across the shooter's face, "Thank you for not killing him," he responded.

The fixer removed his coat. He took special care in folding it and laying across the back of the nearest chair. He stepped forward and opened his briefcase and lifted two large plastic sheets. He spread one sheet under Francisco and removed his hands and head. He placed everything neatly in a box and placed it near the picture window. He then went to work cleaning the $100-a-yard Edward Fields carpet. The cleansing process was over in less than an hour. One man remained; the rest followed the fixer out the door. No indications of Francisco Parizzi's visiting Madeleine Underwood ever existed.

Madeleine turned and walked to the door of her bedroom, motioning to the consigliere to follow.

"Drag this piece of dog-shit away from the mayor's bedroom," the lawyer said before closing and locking the door behind him. The three men moved forward and lifted the Mexican from the floor and placed him in a chair. They washed his wound and bandaged the face—weapons held against his cracked jaw.

Madeleine was already in her bedroom sitting in the chair by the window. The lawyer sat on the bed.

"It's a beautiful view you have here, Madam Deputy Mayor." Madeleine nodded. Her eyes never left the skyline of her city. There was silence for a while; Madeleine had a very powerful individual sitting on her bed, so best not screw this up. After a minute, she turned her chair around and spoke to the consigliere.

"May I assume Francisco shared this plan with you." She asked.

The lawyer nodded, but sat quietly. Madeleine, waiting for a response, continued, "The original plan was to move fifty boxes of Opium from Mazatlán to Culiacán—process the lot and bring it over the border by plane." Her demeanor was calm as she explained the plan to her visitor.

"I found out from a friend the shipment would be hijacked by an offshoot cartel organization—the cost to us would then be $8 million; not $20." The mob lawyer sat on the bed and listened while Madeleine outlined the plans as she explained her concern that no one had contacted her to facilitate the exchange—as yet.

"The bricks were to be picked up on Sunday afternoon while I was in Dallas for the International Conference of Mayors. A plane from Mexico would land at Love Field, and trucks would take the product to the gathering point. The problem is, Consigliere, I have $8 million in the living room, and I don't know where the fucking dope is. And now, Francisco Parizzi is dead."

Her voice took on a hard edge as she said, "That piece of dog-shit, as you called him, is our key. He's a Sinaloan, and I want to use him as our conduit to the cartel."

"What do you want from me, signora?"

"I owe you, Consigliere. I know that. We get him to call the cartel. I have already spoken with one of Herrera's lieutenants. We then cut a deal with them. There will be a need more money, but we *need* is to get the shit up here as soon as we can," she responded.

"And what has convinced you that after you fucked over them one time, they will lick your feet now?" The lawyer was quick to posit a reality check.

"Consigliere, I believe I can give them $8 *million* reasons to move forward with us." She lifted herself from the swivel chair and walked across her bedroom.

Madeleine unlocked the door, and the lawyer followed her. He smiled as she gasped at her living room. Except for the chair where the Mexican was sitting, the room was perfect.

"I assume you've spoken with Herrera, right?" the lawyer asked the Mexican as he approached. The Mexican nodded. "Get him back on the phone! I'm not talking to one of his lieutenants this time—I want to speak to Herrera."

The Mexican only nodded—answering was impossible. He gently touched his missing jaw.

Chapter 50

Federales and the 1st Cavalry from Fort Hood blanketed the streets of Cananéa. Federal agents from both countries set up headquarter tents on the city square and were like bees buzzing around their respective hives. Jonathan ordered food from the *El Restaunte Calle* and charged it to the United States as always.

He finished his taco and walked to the company commander.

"Captain, I need some people taken back to Tucson."

"The colonel's chopper will get you there; how many?" the captain answered.

"Two."

Jonathan shifted his attention to Arturo.

"We're going to get you out of here—back to Tucson, and you can take Jack with you. It's getting a little too busy around here," Jonathan told him. Arturo nodded with a thankful smile as Jonathan walked away.

"Excuse me, Agent." Jonathan turned around. "We are here to confiscate the heroin taken in the attack."

Jonathan recognized them as the two Federali agents in Mazatlán.

"Who are you?" Jonathan asked.

Both men pulled their I.D.s.

"We're Federali. The heroin needs to be placed in our custody."

"Right," Jonathan answered with a smirk. "I'll get it for you." He looked around for Marc; he was just finishing his breakfast. "Hey, Marc," he yelled, "Give me a hand here, would you?"

The two Federali drew closer to each other.

Jonathan spoke softly, "The port director's murder?" Marc nodded as looked back to the two Federalis. "These are the guys that did it; they want the dope."

Marc tried an inconspicuous nod as he turned to speak with the Mexican agents.

"I'm really sorry, guys, all the drugs have been confiscated and sent to Tucson as evidence. We have an American in custody, and he's leaving soon—sorry."

The slight grimace on one of the agents told the story. Marc could see how pissed off they were as he removed himself from the conversation. Jonathan moved quickly and grabbed Marc's arm. He drew close to Marc's ear, whispering. He then motioned to the captain, who, in turn, waved his arm at three of 1st CAV troopers, motioning for them to come forward.

"We don't want any issues here," Jonathan yelled back to the two Federali agents. "The dope is gone. If you want to assist in cleaning up the problem back east of here, maybe you can find some remnants back there." Jonathan turned to walk away. "We're done here."

One of the Federali yelled back to Jonathan in response, "Call your helicopter back!"

"No!" blurted Marc.

A confrontation was seemingly eminent. The captain ordered the three troopers to unsling their ARs. They gathered around the two Mexican agents, hands on the forward-assists. Jonathan came closer to the pair; his heart beating a little faster, anticipating a physical confrontation and a deadly serious look came upon his face.

"You have no authority here," one of the Federales said.

"We have all the authority we need. Captain, please relieve these men of their weapons and take them to jail for their own safety. I'll get with them later." Jonathan's request to the army captain was apathetically stoic. The police chief, watching from the wings, moved cautiously toward the escorted Mexican agents and took charge of the two. A physical protest was an option, but three loaded AR-15s pointed at the Federali agents diminished their bravado.

The confrontation averted, Jonathan and Marc headed for the restaurant for some Mexican coffee. The local food, edible as it was, did not come near to that served in Tucson. The captain joined the two to discuss upcoming operations with his Apaches. He explained the company and squad concept to the FBI and DEA.

"Jonathan, we have 12 Apaches for this operation," the captain explained. "Each squad in this operation will contain three AH-64 Apache helicopters loaded with stinger missiles, one gatling gun and two .30 cal machine guns mounted port and starboard on each aircraft. We are ready."

Both Jonathan and Marc were at the edge of their seats as the young captain went through his explanation. He stopped as the sound of a twin engine aircraft caught their attention. All three men went to the nearest SUV and headed to the airstrip.

. Their truck pulled up to the terminal just as the Baron landed. It taxied to the private terminal, and before shutting down, the pilot spun the plane around to allow a more direct access to the terminal office. The plane, painted simply white, had only one mark on its tail—that of an American flag. The engines now quiet, Marc approached the door and waited for it drop

"Can I help you?" he asked.

The two passengers extended their arms holding the identification of a United States Border Patrol agent.

"Messer and Medellin. You got quite a party going on, Agent," Franco retorted.

"C'mon, I'll take you to it," Marc answered.

The SUV entered the square and came to a stop at the fountain. Arturo was sitting on the ornate bulkhead moving his hand the clear, cool water. Franco walked up to him and rested his arm on his shoulder.

Arturo looked up to see his friends. Franco saw the eyes of a beaten man. His face was dirty; his demeanor was that of a man engulfed in crime.

Franco knew Arturo was hurting through all of this. Jonathan walked up behind them.

"He put a bullet through Vargas' head; he's been that way ever since," he told Franco.

"Where's Morales?" Franco asked.

"*I* killed him. He's in that mess east of here."

"So, is it over? Can I go home now?" Arturo said.

Franco looked at a despondent Jack Culberson in the car—then at Arturo, "I'm afraid not—we have a couple more hurdles to go over."

A crowd soon gathered at the fountain to watch the American soldiers rip out the inside of the old church. The propane tanks and vats were taken to the edge of Cananéa and blown apart. The tables where the processing of the heroin was processed were brought into the square and destroyed. The people watched as their steady influx of money disappeared into smoke and ash.

Jerry and Franco walked over to the third SUV. Jack saw them coming. His shackled wrists were now swollen behind him.

Franco swung open the door and dragged Jack from the back seat.

"It's time for us to have a talk, Jack," he said.

"I have rights; you can't..." was his interrupted response.

"Shut up, Jack! You forget where you are." Jerry and Franco took him around the corner of the church and flung him up against the mission wall.

"You have three choices, Jack; we take you back to Tucson, where you will face all kinds of trafficking charges..." Franco's mouth was less than inch from Jack's face. "We turn your ass over to the Federales, and you can deal with them; or you can save your ass and help us finish this—your choice." There was no yelling or screaming; just a quiet explanation of Jack's options.

Jack's heart and head were pounding—the headache started near him temples was already causing pain in his jaw; it was difficult to determine which felt worse, and his left arm was still bleeding. His beloved plane was gone; his life was over. The food he devoured only minutes before was climbing up to his throat.

A local policeman entered the square and whispered in the police chief's ear. It was hard to shield the smile as he pompously proceeded back to the jail. Franco caught the pleasurable look out of the corner of his eye and followed him

The duo moved quietly down the street to the jail and where the two rogue Federali cops were held. The two, each smiling at each other, moved closer to their office. The chief motioned to another to join them. The activity in the square warranted a police presence, but not enough to keep three policemen with a watchful eye. Franco threw the coffee cup in a nearby trash can and excused himself. He stayed a comfortable distance behind the three laughing policemen as they entered the jail. Franco never claimed to be fluent in Spanish, but it was not difficult to figure out "cartel," "Culiacán," "Culberson," and especially—"New York City."

He left his position by the door and scurried back to the square. He called to Jonathan as he got close.

"Get Jack out of here—now! And get Arturo in the back of that Blackhawk and keep him there."

"What's the matter?" Jonathan asked.

"Something's going down." Franco's heart pumped a little faster from running (mostly). "The two rogue agents received a phone call; I think everything has turned south."

The captain grabbed Jack and moved quickly. They hopped aboard a waiting UH-1 Huey helicopter. Jack needed help. He was still shackled; harnesses were attached in the government chopper—it was gone. The dust-up shrouded the streets as the large blades lifted the two men from eminent danger.

"David Culberson's contact is in New York City," Franco turned to Jonathan and whispered. He turned back from Jonathan's ear to see the chief of police standing in front of him amidst the settling dust.

"Captain?" Jonathan walked to him. "Can you release two of your troopers to stand guard over those rogue cops? I have called the Federales in Culiacán, and they are sending a team to take these two into custody."

Chapter 51

THE CONSIGLIERE WAITED PATIENTLY. Parizzi was taken away by the fixer while the Mexican sat in the chair by the window with half his jaw missing. Thick plastic was beneath and all around him.

The phone rang; the lawyer walked across the room to answer it; his tolerance for waiting was shorter than the walk, but Madeleine got to the phone first.

"Hello, this is Underwood." The dialect on the other end of the call was almost unrecognizable. She turned to the lawyer, "I...I think it's Spanish, but it is so strong, I can't tell."

He moved forward from his position, "Hello!" The voice rattled off a Spanish accent the lawyer had never encountered.

"Wait a minute," the consigliere began, but the voice kept on speaking, ignoring all rebuttal. *"Wait a minute, dammit!"* the consigliere repeated. He looked at his soldier, "Bring that piece of dog shit over here!"

Madeleine said, "He can't talk!"

"He can talk better with half a jaw than that ass-hole on the phone with shit in his mouth." The soldier grabbed his arm as the killer stood up on the plastic. He had a pounding headache from his jaw. He took one step, and his foot slipped out from under him; he fell on his back and head. He screamed in pain, again.

"Get up, asshole, and talk to your boss." The lawyer's patience was gone.

The lawyer's lone soldier reached down and lifted the cartel lieutenant to his feet. He was handed the phone.

"Hola!" The word barely recognizable as he cringed at the attempt to move his tongue. He groaned. His ability to speak clearly was non-existent. The consigliere's proposal was simple, he would turn over the $8 million, pick up the original cache of dope, and bring it back to the United States. Halfway through the translation, the cartel leader interrupted and answered in Spanish.

"No! This is the way it will work. *You* will bring me $11 million dollars and the heads of Jack and David Culberson, and you will take back the heroin we have. *You* will bring that bitch, Madeleine Underwood, with you and she will, by her own hand, turn over the $11 million—in two days."

The line went dead.

The lieutenant turned to the lawyer and repeated it word for word. Davino had been the consigliere for the Parizzi family for 35 years. Even as a young lawyer, a year out of Harvard Law, no one had ever spoken to him that way—not even his mentor, Francisco Parizzi. Madeleine was visibly shaken as she sat down on the nearest chair, her elbows rested on each thigh. She stared at the consigliere.

"What do we do now?" she asked.

The lawyer looked at his soldier.

"Take him to the hospital, then call me." Davino then pulled a chair next to Madeleine. Looking directly into her eyes, he said, "This will only work one way—my way. Call your friend, tell him to meet us here in four hours."

The consigliere pulled his cell from his coat pocket.

"Call the family heads," he said to the man at the other end, "Tonight—at the place. Ask Don Carlo to have everybody there—got it? Get back to me!"

"Is your man going to kill that cartel lieutenant?" she asked.

"Don't worry about it; the Mexican will be in a happier place. Now, Madam Deputy Mayor, tell me how this war between you and the cartel got started."

Madeleine explained the relationship with David Culberson and Morales' plans to hijack the Mazatlán train before it reached the Sinaloa's plant.

"I broke the agreement with the cartel to work with this Morales guy. David was already doing business with him. I made the move on my own."

"Where's the stuff?"

Madeleine looked at the floor; she wrapped both arms around her waist.

"I don't know—I haven't heard from anybody." It was obvious the Madeleine was worn out from the day's ordeal, so an afternoon nap was in order.

"Get some rest, Madam Deputy Ma…"

"I'm going," she finished his sentence waving to everyone.

"I'll be back in four hours. He better be here."

She agreed; Davino let himself out.

THE DOWN PILLOW OFFERED LITTLE RELIEF to the knot on the back of her head. She rolled on her stomach and tried to sleep faced down; that did not work either. She maneuvered her body with the goal of achieving the least amount of pressure on her back and her head. Her exhaustion won out, and soon, she was asleep.

The buzzer woke her up in what seemed to be only minutes, butshe looked at the nightstand clock. It was 4:00 in the afternoon. She rose slowly. Her sea-legs returned, but her head still ached.

"Yes, George?"

"A Mr. Culberson, Madam Deputy Mayor."

"You may send him up, George." She released the button.

Look at me, I'm a mess. Wash your face, and for God's sake, put on some lipstick—first, a glass of wine. The doorbell rang.

She moved to the door and dropped the doorlatch.

"Hi, David." She backed away offering entrance.

He looked at her for a moment and cocked his head.

"Are you alright? What happened?"

"It's a long story," she said, "I'll tell you while you're here, but now, we have more immediate issues to deal with." Madeleine went over to the corner of the room and showed him the suitcases. "Here's the $8 million."

"Great, but we planned for you to bring it with you on Sunday."

"The cartel was the fourth visitor this morning."

"What?" David answered with surprise.

"There's more—Francisco Parizzi was killed in this apartment today." Madeleine continued, "A mob 'fixer' cleaned up the mess. They probably killed the Mexican that was here, and we now found out, the cartel wants another three million."

"This morning." She nodded to his comment. "What did you do in the afternoon—kill the president?"

Madeleine smirked.

"We'll see how much of a smart ass you are while you're sitting with the four mob families in New York later on today."

"Really? When is *that* supposed to happen?"

"The consigliere of the Parizzi family is picking you up in two hours. Try not to say, 'I don't know' to any question they ask you."

Madeleine walked to the kitchen for a glass of wine.

Chapter 52

Davino's car arrived promptly at 6:00. No more soiling his hands

"A couple of you guys go inside and call the Deputy Mayor." Davino turned his head to the guys in the back seat. "Ask her to send down this guy, Culberson—I don't want to be late."

The two soldiers left the limousine, and five minutes later, David was sitting between two mob soldiers.

The Texan received shallow pleasantries as he sat down across from the consigliere. The silence was deafening—then…

"How was your flight up, Mr. Culberson?" Davino asked. "I understand you fly your own plane."

"It was quiet and comfortable, and yes, I do."

"Do you read *The New York Times*, Mr. Culberson?" Another politically correct question from Davino.

"No, I do not, Mr. Davino," David answered as the fly to the spider.

"Well," said the consigliere, "you might want to read today."

He handed David the second page—above the fold.

An Offshoot Cartel Massacre

Cananéa, Mexico

The cartel was attacked by a special task force made of FBI and Border Patrol agents today. The attack was the culmination of planning by U.S. federal agents and American soldiers from Ft. Hood, Texas. Both cartel leaders, Antonio

*Morales and his lieutenant, Alejandro Vargas, were killed in
the process. An American, Jack Culberson has been taken
into custody for drug smuggling, and all of the heroin in his
procession was destroyed.*

*Two Federali agents were arrested by the task force for
conspiracy and murder of the Mazatlán port director, his assistant, and his secretary. The government of Mexico is ap-
palled at the amount of killing substances that move across
the friendly borders.*

*"We always appreciate the assistance from north, but we
think the U.S. should clean up their own messes first," a government official said.*

David was beside himself. Pictures of burned-out airplanes—one Bonanza—and his son in handcuffs being led off to an army helicopter;
two body bags laying side by side.

"What do want from me?" David asked.

The spider was about to pounce on the trapped fly.

"The cartel knows about the heist; they know about the train. You
made an agreement with them on the heroin from Culiacán. You
changed your..."

"No!" David interrupted.

"Be quiet, Mr. Culberson. You broke your agreement with the cartel. You don't do that," Davino answered.

"I did not make the agreement with the cartel," David said. "Ask
Madeleine."

His stomach morphed into the knot not unlike a hangman's noose.
He knew this trip was his last as he glanced at the East River.

The limousine crossed the Washington bridge into New Jersey—
Maybe Orange or Jersey City.

A mile into the state, the limo made an abrupt left turn. The long,
winding driveway was lined with black poplar trees with their leaves

swirling in a light wind, leaving the road with a bed of pearls for the guests to ride upon. The trees, lined up and set 10 feet apart, provided a perfect canopy for the ride to the front door. The diamond-shaped leaves were thick and threw clusters of different shadows across the driveway. The white mansion that lay ahead was something out of the antebellum south. The Appalachian-style, split-rail fencing offered little defense against escape by the grazing thoroughbreds in the paddock on the right.

The limousine stopped at the large, solid-wood doors, and a prim and proper yet aged butler stepped through the open door. David, Davino, and the lieutenants of the late Francisco Parizzi, stepped from the car. The driver pulled away and drove to the garage patio, where four other limos were already lay in waiting.

The butler escorted the quartet inside and to a meeting with the five crime bosses of New York. David was out of his element.

"Sit down, Mr. Culberson." The woman who spoke was beautifully Italian—black hair, dark eyes, and olive skin. "You are welcome in this house. What can we get you?"

"Nothing, thank you," David answered.

The man sitting in the center chair stood up and approached David. He stopped mid-way and looked back at the other three men sitting; then back to facing David.

"What are we going to do about this, Mr. Culberson?" the man asked.

"The devil's in the details," David answered. "I don't know. What are your levels of commitment?"

A second man stood.

"We want our fucking dope! Is that clear enough?"

The first man looked back and motioned for him to calm down. He spoke.

"Mr. Culberson, we want our dope, and we need to know how you intend to get it—simple enough?" David looked over at Parizzis' consigliere.

"I *have* played around with a plan, but if it's going to work, I will need some men and other assets—I don't know what, just yet—I *am* working on it."

"Take all the time you need; but you've got three days," the man said. "You will stay here and have the run of the house—anything in or outside. My name is Carlo—that's all you need to know."

The bosses took a vote—right then and there, and they all agreed, but for one thing: If it does not work, they hand the cartel Culberson's head.

"May I ask one favor, Carlo?" David asked. "May I have a confidant and partner? Don Parizzi's consigliere."

Carlo looked toward Davino and cocked his head in a questioning motion.

The consigliere nodded, "Yes."

Carlo's wife showed the men to their respective rooms. She asked for their clothes sizes and the kind of toiletries they liked.

"They will be ordered today." She closed David's door and left.

The brain-storming session started an hour later. The met in a small conference room located just off the veranda, which overlooked the long line of black poplar trees. Four thoroughbred colts pranced about just beneath them. David chuckled.

Marco entered and closed the door behind him. Before he could say anything, David took charge and brought the meeting to order.

"First off, we're going to need an airplane—not mine; the Federales have seen my Gulfstream too many times. Secondly, we need to find a guy—his name is Arturo Gonzales. He will be of great help."

"What is your ultimate goal here—besides the dope?" Carlo asked, apparently for the other mob bosses.

The consigliere remained stoic. He looked out the window and followed the movements of a young colt trying to get under his mom's shadow.

"You're going to start a war—a war in Mexico," said one of the men sitting on a folding chair.

David pulled a writing tablet from the desk drawer. He tilted the leather high-back chair back to clear his mind. He formulated the strategy he and Davino would need to take care of the cartel—and grab the $50 million street value in heroin.

"We've got to find Arturo Gonzales," David insisted, "then on to Dallas to change the white phosphorous into his special cocktail."

"What's that for?" one boss asked.

"You'll see, my friend—you'll see."

Chapter 53

THE CHIEF OF POLICE MOVED ACROSS THE SQUARE toward the two Border Patrol agents.

"Who was that man who left with the gringo?"

Franco turned to face the police chief and saw the two rogue Federali agents following behind. The chief wore his arrogance hat as he shifted his weight on the balls of his feet—hands on his hips—chin high and to the right. Franco smiled and placed an arm over the chief's left shoulder. He looked at the two rogue Federali cops.

"Why don't you two go help those people clean up that mess east of here?" Franco offered advice to the Federali agents. The bigger of the two yelled out something in Spanish. Franco did not understand a lot of Spanish, but *that* he knew. He also knew how to answer it, but discretion got the best of him.

"Jonathan," Franco said. "You told me this wasn't over. You come with me and bring Gonzales with you. We're heading south."

Jonathan grabbed what little gear he had, and he and Franco headed for the warmed-up Blackhawk. On the way, Franco slapped the captain on his back, smiled, and asked, "Captain, can you get us back to Culiacán?"

As the pilot confirmed the request,

Jonathan glanced at Franco fiddling with his headset. He set the mic in front of his mouth and repeated, "Culiacán, it is."

The rotors came alive at the captain's circular arm movement.

Thump…thump…thump, thump, thump…

The large jet-helicopter engines grew loud as the big UH-60 lifted off the ground, Jonathan yelled back the troopers from the 1ˢᵗ AirCav: "KEEP AN EYE ON THOSE TWO—DON'T LET THEM LEAVE!"

The armed trooper dropped his hand from his ear and nodded while he covered his eyes. The pilot turned the cyclic to the left. As he moved the throttle forward, he added more cyclic; slowly, the chopper went to the flight mode. At 150 feet, he spun the chopper around to a heading of 1-8-5 degrees south.

The noise cancelling headsets were new, so the communication was clear. The din of the engines above them could hardly be heard.

"What do we do when we get there?" Arturo asked. No one spoke.

"You and Franco are going to have to find the heroin plant," Jonathan responded, "or the Sinaloas' headquarters."

"The colonel has plans; we're just doing the front work," Jerry interjected.

"We are going to start a war, aren't we?" Arturo asked.

"I'm afraid so," Jerry responded.

"Yeah," Jonathan repeated

Another voice, "Yeah."

They sat back in their seat and contemplated the next few days. Arturo pushed the mic away from his face, cupped his hands over his eyes, and cried, "My home; my Mexico."

Dusk was long upon them. The sky eased to a blackness from the east, and they were 10 miles out of Culiacán. Jonathan poked the pilot on the shoulder.

"We'll land two miles north of town." He turned to Franco and Arturo, "You guys walk the two miles. If you catch a ride, all the better—speak only Spanish."

Franco smiled, "Yeah, right!"

Moments later, the chopper landed a few yards off the highway. The walk into town started as soon as the chopper left for another location. The duo hiked through the field of cactus and mesquite until they stood on the main road into Culiacán.

The first step, and it began to rain. Nocturnal animals scurried around them. The giggling sound of a coati startled Franco at first. Arturo looked at Franco, "He's harmless—just a part of Mexico."

The rain came at a drizzle at first, but minutes later, the rain turned into a torrential thunderstorm. Soaked, the two continued to walk; there was nothing to hide under anyway. Three-quarters of a mile into the short journey, a truck drove by and stopped just ahead of them. The obvious invitation was compelling, and the two men jumped in the back and under a loose tarp. Less than a mile to go, the driver slid open the rear cab window.

"Where do you want to go?" he asked.

"A hotel would be good," Arturo answered.

The only hotel the driver was aware of was the *El Camino Real*.

"I am sorry, señor, I know it is run-down and in a bad part of town, but it is the only one I know."

It was seedy. Franco entered the hotel and saw part of the stain-glass entrance was missing. The hotel was built in the fifties and rented its rooms four or five times a day.

"We're out of the rain," Arturo said happily.

The night clerk reeked with equal parts of Mezcal, sweat and the wet cigarette that dangled from his toothless mouth and filled the stale ashtray next to the room keys. The same smells that infused the lobby, brightly lit but dingy with years of neglect and hanging smoke.

"You queers?" he asked. "I can move a larger bed into the room."

"No," Arturo said. "We only want two rooms to spend the night."

"I ain't got no two rooms. You can have *one*—you want it?"

"We'll take it." Arturo responded, "By the way, where can we get some clean clothes?"

"The Mercado closes in an hour—the rain should last for another two."

"How 'bout a restaurant—one nearby?" Franco asked.

"Around the corner—two doors—bring me back some tacos, willya, huh?"

"Bueno," said Franco.

That was the worst dialect I have ever heard, Arturo smiled.

The two opened the creaking front door and proceeded around the corner. The Mercado was open.

She used to be pretty, I bet. Franco eyed the woman smiling at him in the doorway. He went to talk to her, but Arturo jumped in.

"We need some clothes. Can you help us?"

Her big round eyes were shaded like deep St. Augustine grass; her hair was red—not natural red, but a dyed red. The stained, oversized sweatshirt covered her from her shoulders down to the middle of her thighs. The cigarette that hung from the left side of her mouth carried an inch of ash hanging precariously from the tip. She was bare-footed and proudly displayed the scars of torture. She spoke only Spanish.

"I'll show you," she said as she showed a slight limp when she escorted them to the men's clothing section. "We only have work clothes; no dressy stuff," she reported.

"Bueno," Franco showed off his Spanish—again.

"You work around here?" she asked.

"Looking," Arturo answered.

"Where you from?" She grabbed a pair of Levi's from the table, "You like? These are good jeans."

Franco took the pants from her and tossed them over his shoulder.

"Mexico City," he said.

She walked back down the aisle and looked at Franco—first, shot him the finger, then threw the back of her hand under her chin in a whipping motion—chenga!

The clothes seem to fit alright. The multi-colored, tie-dyed t-shirt was the perfect choice, especially with *Che Guevara's* head printed on the front. Franco's was a little less obtrusive; *Viva la Mexico* was air-brushed on the front, and the Mexican flag was printed on the back.

They put on the new clothes and moved to the checkout counter. She could not contain herself.

Arturo blurted out, "We were in pris…"

Franco suddenly wielded his left hand across Arturo's face.

"Alto! stop it!" The agent turned back to the girl. "Nada, nothing!"

It was time to eat. The two were starving, and the restaurant was next door. With the bag of wet clothes at their side, the duo entered the half-empty place and sat down at the first table they saw. Arturo was still rubbing his face as he yelled out the waiter cleaning shot-glasses behind the bar.

"Enchiladas y cervezas por dos personas, por favor."

The man scowled at the two. Franco did not like the glaring but saw his head was only a couple of inches from the deer rack chandelier above him. Only the arms of his red, plaid shirt were not covered by the dirty and blood-stained white apron that covered the rest of him. The avocado and melted cheese stains covered most of the apron. Franco had no idea about the origin of the blood. He only hoped it came a slaughtered cow and not a slaughtered human-being. Arturo could almost see the e-coli crawling up into his unshaven face.

"Do you *really* want to eat here?" Arturo asked.

"We could take the limo to the Ritz Carlton, if you'd like." Franco said, addressing his concerns.

The hard rain stopped, but a drizzle lingered; it was not enough to keep the rise in humidity in check.

"Could we have our beers, please?" Arturo asked—again.

Franco stood up and marched to the man behind the counter. He stuck his forefinger in the large man's face, then flicked the middle digit.

"Dos cervezas, por favor—ahora!"

Arturo just planted his face in his hands.

Jesus, are we lookin' for a fight…? He wondered.

Two guys sitting at a table across the restaurant saw Franco's action and came over to the table.

Franco was Special Forces attached to Wolverine 1, 2nd Infantry Division that captured Saddam Hussein in December 2003. He spent 11 years in the Army and was awarded of the Purple Heart with two clusters and the Silver Star—he was an expert in hand-to-hand combat.

Arturo looked up.

"Can I help you?"

The larger man wheel-housed him across the face with the back of his hand.

"Whoa! Whoa! Whoa!" Franco rushed back to the table. The second blow commenced with the man's hand, held high ready to strike downward.

It was like a 300-pound defensive end coveting a 170-pound quarterback. Franco blocked the forward thrust of the blow and, at the same time, wrapped his arm around the man's neck. He threw him across the restaurant where he came to a stop at the base of bar. The other drew his knife out of instinct but quickly backed away from the fray.

Franco looked at Arturo's face; little blood, so he wiped it away with a paper towel. He walked back over to the injured man and extended his arm to help him up. Franco figured he and Arturo might have struck gold. He saw no harm in pursuing it.

"My name is Franco Medellin. My friend and I are looking for work."

"They call me, Tortuga," the big man answered while rubbing his throat. He stammered a little; Franco patted his shoulder. The man was solid and stood six-foot-two—maybe -three. His unshaven face formed a hairy frame around his mouth which lacked a proper number of teeth.

"Bueno," Franco answered, "Why don't you and your friend join us?"

The night went longer than expected.

The rays of the morning sun slipped through the rips in the dark green curtains. At 8:00, the spears of light crept up the bed hit Arturo square in the face; he blinked and rolled back in his head as he thought something was moving across his sheets…

It wasn't a dream—a large Mexican roach was passing from one side of his bed to the other. He leaped from the sheet, looking for his shoe. The roach scrambled in circles, then off the bed. He looked at the adjacent bed and screamed, "Get up, Franco! Get the hell up! We are sleeping someplace else tonight."

"Okay, okay." Franco yawned, "I'm going to the bathroom."

Arturo was dressed when he returned to the room, and they exchanged places. The toilet flushed, and Arturo came out to a man standing at the door; last night's guy with the knife.

"Where's your friend?" he asked.

Arturo motioned to the hotel room. The two moved down the hallway. The dim light showing the stairwell flickered just bright enough for Arturo to see another figure standing three steps down—it was Tortuga.

"We want to talk to you and your friend," he said.

"You couldn't wait until breakfast?" Arturo reached the door and knocked. All was quiet; he knocked again. With no response, he opened the door. The big man shoved Arturo to the side and entered the room. The last man to come in was the man with the knife. The door slammed hard behind him, and all three spun around. Franco brought the barrel of his 9mm pistol to the big man's head.

"Sit down—both of you." Franco said, "What are you doing here at 8:30 in the morning?"

Tortuga looked up at Franco.

"We have guys waiting in the car. They want to talk to you."

"About what?" Arturo said.

"Just talk," was the response.

"Franco, I'm not sitting in no car at this time of the morning with people I don't or who I'm talking to." Arturo was quite explicit.

"We've opened the restaurant," Tortuga said.

Franco and Arturo told the two to stand and move out. They passed through the door, and Arturo turned to check the room for the last time. Just as he flipped the light switch, he saw the roach surrey underneath a chair. He nodded his head and smiled.

Chapter 54

WITH DAVINO'S HELP, IT TOOK JUST OVER SIX HOURS to process the raw phosphorous into a highly flammable liquid. The taxi-limo arrived at David's office right on time. The elongated Hummer had a rear door, which made it easy to load the containers of cocktail. The consigliere knew what it was but had never seen it work. The four large containers each held 24 gently-packed bottles of dissolved phosphorous on its way to Culiacán.

Carlo's jet arrived at Addison Airport the night before. Six of the rear seats were removed to handle the containers. The Hummer pulled up next to the Learjet, and four of Carlo's men loaded the cargo. The Cessna Citation belonging to the Staten Island boss arrived from Richmond County minutes before the process started. Twelve gangsters stepped out onto the Addison tarmac. Hawaiian shirts covered their over-hanging, spaghetti-stuffed bellies—and their guns.

"Welcome to Texas," Davino said.

"We're going for some coffee, we'll be back in a few minutes," one of the mobsters remarked as he stretched his arms and legs, nearly displaying his weapon. It was early, but Millionaire Private Air terminal was open for business and serving breakfast. Twenty-two guys from the New York mob packed into the restaurant while the Learjet and Carlo's Citation were being topped off with Jet-A fuel and pre-flighted. An hour later, all were settled into their seats, the cocktails safely loaded, and the two aircraft were heading for Mexico.

The Lear and the Citation slid through the air with ease. David, riding in the Learjet, radioed the Citation, telling the pilot to ease back on the throttle.

"We're landing together," David said in his transmission.

At 20,000 feet, David noticed on the Lear's GPS they passed Cananéa a few minutes prior.

The time had ticked off to 30 minutes. The Citation pilot's mic squawked. It was David.

"We're 40 minutes out from Culiacán; we'll be starting our descent in three minutes."

Davino used the pilot's head-set to call the Lear.

"You got transportation, right, David?"

"What's left of Morales' gang have agreed to help us," David replied. "They have trucks and cars to get us to where we're going.."

"Okay," Davino answered. The lights of Culiacán appeared in the distance. The consigliere began to sweat. He was not a soldier, but a lawyer by trade, but he *was* prepared for any happenstance. Seven miles out, both planes picked up the airport radio signal. They dialed in the airport frequency, clicked their respective mics twice, and the runway lights turned on. The Lear made the first move and entered the pattern for a proper landing. Five minutes later, the Citation made the same maneuver. The two aircraft passed the runway on their left and flew five more miles before making a wide U-turn for a centerline landing. Both aircraft were on the ground in less than 30 minutes, and it was barely sunrise.

The vehicles approached both planes quickly. The Citation's cargo door was thrown open and the containers off-loaded and carried to the waiting trucks. No one talked; they took their luggage and went to a waiting vehicle. Once full, it drove to the pre-determined gathering spot—the farm. The slow and steady ride took over two hours.

The gate opened, and the caravan was greeted by two men. Calaban saw David and rushed to greet him. His arm was in a sling, and he walked with a definite limp. The other was the old man from the farm just north of Mazatlán. He wore his sombrero and bandoleers and held his Sharps rifle.

"You get around, old man," David yelled out.

"So do you," he said while he eyed the 70-some-odd Mexican. "Who are your friends, David?"

"These guys are from New York. This is Marco Davino, Consigliere to the Parizzi family." The old man looked him up and down.

"I understand," he said, "A mob lawyer—no offense intended."

"None taken, old man," Davino answered laughingly.

"Okay—business." David chimed in, "The 'take' from the train is gone. Morales and Vargas are dead—my son is in handcuffs—I want... we want the Sinaloas' cache of heroin..." David stepped toward the injured Calaban. "Marcus, you've done well, my friend. I'm sorry about the loss of your friends."

Calaban nodded in response.

"And we want the Sinaloa's leader." Davino made his voice heard again. "Do you know where they do the cooking?"

The old man saw in the lawyer's eyes more than just an inquisitive nature; he saw hate and revenge. He saw the resolve in why he was there.

"I will take you to the Sinaloa's place where they make their heroin." Davino smiled, but it was interrupted by the old man, "Did you bring guns?"

"Plenty," was the response.

"Did you bring any of that cocktail?" David nodded. "Then I have an idea. And this will work."

"How long will it take for the water to evaporate inside an air-conditioned room?" the old man asked.

"I really don't know," David answered.

"I think it would take longer than being outside in the air with the wind blowing," Davino offered.

"Then we let the cleaning crew do all the work for us," The old man said.

Davino asked, "How do we get the cleaning crew to use our stuff?"

"They're standing right behind you. Why don't you ask them?" the old man laughed.

David looked behind him to see four seedy individuals standing behind the gangsters from New York.

"This solution needs to be slopped on the floor; not mopped," David addressed the cleaning crew. "You start from the farthest part of the building—move quickly and don't get this on your shoes. *Don't* get this stuff on your shoes!"

The old man confirmed David's words, for he had witnessed the anguish of one poor wolf being wrapped up in a phosphorous cocktail.

"When you are through, calmly walk out of the factory—don't run. There is no reason to run, but *don't* watch it dry—just leave," The old man added.

The men picked up one the resting containers and carried it outside. The empty buckets stood ready to receive the deadly payload.

Davino was curious. He was not aware of this kind of a destructive cocktail. His interest piqued as he listened to the plan. The 22 mobsters wanted to see it work as well—if only once.

"Leave that crew alone," David remarked coldly. "There will plenty of time to see the cocktail complete its work."

David then turned to the old man, "Where's the factory?" he asked, ignoring their request for a demonstration?"

The old man replied, "It is two blocks away. Everybody knows it: The police know about it; the Federales know about it…nobody does nothing about it."

David moved from the door and sat in a nearby chair.

"What are we going to do with 22 guys with guns?" the old man asked.

"You said this cocktail will burn the factory to the ground," Davino commented. "When the Sinaloas enter the building to put out the fire, we will keep them in there."

The old man stepped in, "Because the back will be mopped first, it will burst into flames first. With them on the floor trying to extinguish the fire, their shoes will soaking up the cocktail; they'll never know hit them."

David smiled at Calaban.

"The old man has a grip on the concept. This should work fine."

The consigliere went to the front door. He watched the four cleanup crew roll the buckets down the uneven and cracked sidewalk.

"You and you," Davino pointed to two of the gangsters, "follow them. Make sure they get there with no problems—go! Go!"

No streetlights, only shadows lined the broken sidewalk. A prostitute leaned against one of the failed street lamp. Her shoulder and left hip pressed the lower quarter of the pole. The heel of her shoe rested on the electric plate that covered the missing wires.

"Want a date?" she asked.

The two continued on their mission, just shaking their head.

Just ahead, a small portion of the street lit up as the door to the factory revealed the entrance, and the four were let in—buckets in tow. The quick appearance of light disappeared as the door closed. A slight breeze moved the cirrus clouds above them, and stars became visible again. The duo turned around and proceeded back to where everyone was waiting. The prostitute was still leaning against the voided streetlight.

"You sure you don't want to…" She attempted to force an answer.

The bigger of the two stopped and shoved his finger in her face.

"Go home—no interestado."

They continued on—then stopped. The big guy looked back her.

"You want a party? Come on, I'll give you a party."

She smiled, not knowing what was about to happen.

The three entered the building. David jumped out of his chair, Marco right behind him.

"What the hell are you doing?" David yelled.

"She saw us. She will see all of us in the street in a few hours, boss. We need to keep her here."

David looked at Davino and shrugged his shoulders in agreement. "Okay, sit her down and don't touch her—don't even look at her." David's face showed his disgust.

Chapter 55

THE DIMLY LIT STAIRS CREAKED WITH EVERY STEP. Tortuga took the lead in the short trip to the restaurant. He moved past the desk clerk and pushed the cut-glass door to the dark street. The restaurant was next door, lights on and side-panels pulled up tight. The four men sat at a table and waited for the two new guests. Tortuga pulled up two more chairs, and the new arrivals sat facing Franco and Arturo.

"Sit down, amigos!" the seemingly head of the group said. "Who the hell are you?"

"Who the hell are *you?*" Franco asked.

"Never mind, who he is," the girl from the Mercado's voice sounded in the doorway. The shoulder-length hair and her sweatshirt still draped to her thighs. It was still stained from who knows what.

"Good morning, señorita, nice to see you again." Arturo smiled at her.

"Shut up! Who are you? What are you doing here?" she asked, snapping at Arturo.

"I told you last night, we are looking for a job," Arturo answered.

"What kind of a job? Shoveling horse shit? Give me your hands!" she demanded. Arturo's hands were coarse and callous-ridden. Franco's were of another species. They were strong like his partner's, but hard like a fighter's. His sensory and motor skills worked as one; his hands were fast—very fast. She leaned back against the wall.

A dark shadow stepped out from behind the counter, Panama hat pulled low across his eyes with a toothpick floating between the left side of his mouth and the right. His blouse was full sleeved, crimson red with micro dots embedded though out the cotton fabric. His boots were smothered in a combo of cow-shit and mud. He spoke to the woman; even Arturo did not understand him. His dialect was thick and indistinguishable. She appeared to listen, though Arturo did not believe it was anything but jibberish. .

Franco knew his Spanish was weak at best, and he would never get away with trying to pull this hat off. In English, he said,

"I am Mexican-American and former Special Forces. We just got out of jail in Mexico City. We are seriously looking for a job."

She chimed in, "He is Chicano... and *dead*."

Tortuga stood and the first to put his hands on his silver-bladed karambit.

"No, we have a use for this gringo, this *Mexican American*."

Franco was right—dead right. The two wanted into this pride, and the Alpha-male stood in front of them.

The interrogation began.

"Who are you? Who is your mother? Who is your father? How many have you killed? ...Where are your body marks?" The questions came hard and fast—face against face.

Arturo knew he was about to die. His heart pounded so loud; he could feel the need to soil his pants...and yet, he was able to smile and remained calm.

Tortuga led the questioning of Franco. His was a different tact. They went into the street. The bright clear morning was getting hotter as the sun continued to creep higher from the east.

"What do you want, Tortuga?" Franco asked.

"You took me once; you will never take me again. You will have to kill me this time." He lunged with his special blade in his hand—curved and serrated. Franco stepped into it and just to the side. Tortuga's thrust went between Franco's torso and arm. Only inches from the attacker, he jerked the knife-held arm at the elbow and lifted the man a foot off the ground. The knife fell from Tortuga's hand as he felt the pain of his arm hanging down backwards. Franco's left hand struck quickly against his nose, thrusting the cartilage up into his brain. Tortuga's head fell backward, resting on the nape of his neck. His eyes rolled back into the skull then recessed into the sockets of his head. The doors to his soul shrunk back into his brain. He was dead. Two of Tortuga's friends jumped up from the table and moved toward Franco guns drawn.

"No!" the man from the shadows said. "Tortuga was a fool. Let him be. I wanted to know this man's skills, and I have found out what I wanted."

"Take them to the hotel!" the woman ordered. "Get them cleaned up; this one over here looks like shit."

Arturo laughed as he nodded his head.

These trucks are nicer, Arturo thought as he slid in the front passenger seat. *Nothing like those beat-up pieces of crap that belonged to Morales' gang.*

The lead Escalade had leather trim with the back of an alligator to compliment the gator's belly that was wrapped around the steering wheel. The ridges dug into Arturo's back in the most uncomfortable way. *Who would install this kind of leather seat? You would have to be crazy!* Arturo readjusted his butt and back to get comfortable.

The Caddy moved down the street with five SUVs in line. The vehicles had little regard for traffic signals, and the police did not care.

Culiacán was a fair-sized city in the state of Sinaloa. The town flourished in many ways; specifically—tourism. Unlike Mazatlán, Culiacán rested peacefully in a valley surrounded by two mountain ranges and sat 190 miles from the Gulf of California. Steeped in agriculture, many farmers carried on traditions of their forefathers, planting corn and avocados. In the city of over 900,000 people, churches and wide streets abound. Motorcycles outnumber automobiles, and bicycles outnumber the motor bikes that move in and out of traffic lanes disrupting traffic in the city.

Just as shopping centers are overrun with shops that offer finery of all shapes, the dark side of Culiacán offers a different world. Arturo and

Franco drove through the heart of downtown, searching and looking; neither knowing for what. Both knew when they saw it, they would know it. Beautiful hotels and beautiful women; nightclubs and shops; and then drug addicts sleeping on the streets without regard. The sun cast its light into the shadowy entrance of an alley. They saw her on her knees, bobbing back and forth; he turned to look at Franco.

The mayor of the city made ovations one time of building shelters for the homeless and getting help for addicts. He once met with Vincente Herrera, the head of the Sinaloa cartel. The meeting took place in a field 10 miles out of town under a canopy, the hillside filled with grazing donkeys. That was late September. The cartel brought 200 men to protect Herrera from the 300 policemen who protected the mayor. No one knew how many cartel soldiers were undercover and how many were there to protect the mayor. Furthermore, no one knew how many of the policemen were corrupt and working for Herrera.

The wheat had been taken from the land, and the stubs waved briskly in the fall breeze. The mayor's assistant set up the meeting and brought a picnic basket with wine-coolers. No photographers were allowed, and the entourage from both sides could not be any closer than 100 feet from each party.

The two toasted the first wine-cooler with, "To a peaceful understanding!" in their city.

"No more killing and raping of young girls, Vincente," The mayor stated codifying this new contract with the Herrera cartel. "You can maintain your operation without censure." The mayor offered a Cuban cigar to Herrera.

"Sure," Herrera replied. The mayor's assistant beamed with the completion of a successful negotiation. She saw her career soaring in the next election.

"I will no longer allow my drugs to be sold to the people on the street at a price higher than the national average," Herrera responded.

The mayor could not understand Herrera's comment due to his very thick dialect and looked at him strangely. It had to be re-translated in Spanish. Once he understood, the mayor's smile faltered.

"I want the killing to stop, Mr. Herrera. Your drug business has put the tourism trade in the dumpster." The mayor threw the document on the table. "With no tourists, you suffer losses every year and so do we. Stop the killing, Mr. Herrera."

Herrera stood from the leather chair.

"You run your government without interference from me; I run my government without interference from you. This meeting is over."

Herrera turned his back to the mayor and placed both arms ladened with old knife wounds around two of his lieutenants.

The sun was now high in the sky as Arturo passed a sixteenth century Catholic Church. They approached the Boulevard Diego Valadez Rios, and the Hotel Lucerna stood majestically in front of them.

"How will it take for this water to evaporate?"

David looked at his Rolex and answered the consigliere, "Indoors? Air-conditioned? Another two hours."

"Then it is time to meet this drug lord. Old man, make the call!" It was tantamount to sounding a bugle-call.

Twelve-plus mob soldiers pulled their small arms from their holsters while others removed the AR-15s from their scabbards. The Hoppe's kits came out; lint-free rags and lubricating oil were passed around to everyone. Banana-clips were duct-taped in opposite directions designed for quick change. The Hawaiian shirts were doffed and replaced with over-sized black t-shirts. Black knit caps were donned and pulled low across their faces.

"The crew has finished slopping the cocktail in Herrera's factory." The old man entered the room while flipping his phone to the 'off' position.

"David, you stay here," Davino said. "Old man, you three come with me." Pointing to the other men after they finished their gun-cleaning, he added, "Grab one suitcase!"

The old man climbed into the back seat of the rental. The consigliere maneuvered the limo through the streets of Culiacán at the old man's directions. They passed the factory and drove down through the living decadence of the city. The lawyer's face remained stoic and resolved as the old man proffered directions. Davino never needed to ask.

The streets widen into a buzzing metropolis. The old man mused at the bars which were open so early in the morning. The lawyer finally spoke.

"Where is this 'Hotel Lucerna'?"

"Three blocks from here, consigliere," responded the old man.

He pressed the accelerator and the digital speedometer quickly as the old man's head hit the back of the seat. The classic, majestic edifice bore the hotel's name on the marquee; he made the quick turn to the left. The attendant at the valet stand opened the door on the driver's side. Davino slid out and gave attendant a $10 bill. The old man jumped out the back seat.

They proceeded through the large, thick sliding-glass entrance with the three soldiers in tow. The old man rushed to a house phone. The lawyer bought a red rose from the lobby flower shop and placed it in his lapel.

"He has the entire fifth floor," the old man said. "There is an escort waiting for us."

The consigliere looked at the soldier. Davino had his friend Parizzi's paisley suitcase in hand. The elevator was an anachronism to the high-tech design of the hotel. The manned elevator with a mechanical handle was quite a departure from the heavy, glass entrance with automatic sliding doors.

"Fifth floor, please." Davino looked straight ahead.

The elevator operator stood there in silence, then faced the consigliere. His steel eyes never moved. The operator moved the elevator handle a quarter turn to the right. The whirring of the motors took the lax position of the cables to tight, and the elevator rose to the fifth floor. The lawyer took a quick reconnoiter of his men—then looked back straight, smiling at the elevator operator. The door slid open—the five faced three men—all in red bandanas and sunglasses, and carrying Israeli-made Uzis. The three mob soldiers were searched and their weapons removed.

The woman from the Mercado met them at the door, complete with her over-sized, stained sweatshirt. Her pleasantries were short.

"That the $11 million?" she asked. Davino said nothing. The old man stepped in front of him. "We're here to see Herrera." She and her three gorillas stepped against the wall and let the five enter the room. The paisley suitcase rode heavy on the plush carpet. One of the New York thugs commented to Davino how much bigger the wheels needed to be; Davino ignored him.

The non-smoking suite had three bedrooms, two baths, and a hot tub. Herrera sat sweating in the water, smoking a Cuban cigar.

"Is that my money?" he asked.

The lawyer was not amused.

"Not all of it," Davino answered. "Where are my drugs?"

"All in good time, señor, all in good time." Herrera spoke with complete indifference.

Davino processed the room quickly, as he was taught in earlier days with Francisco. The eye movements were the best tell. They would stare or blink before a gun was drawn. Davino's eyes traversed the room efficiently—a back room, door open an inch, maybe two. Another man stood behind the bar, turned at a 45-degree angle mixing a non-drink—too much bourbon and vodka in a brandy glass.

"In the suitcase, $3 million." Davino reported. "The rest is here—in Culiacán. I don't wish to spend the rest of the day here. I want my dope—now."

"You Americans…way too impatient," Herrera said while spitting out a wet piece of tobacco. "Franco, get my robe!"

The backroom door opened, and Herrera's bathrobe was brought into the room by Franco.

"Where's David Culberson?" Herrera asked.

"You can have him when we conclude our business," the lawyer answered as he turned away, motioning to the old man to follow.

Herrera told them to wait. His arms, draped around two women, slid down to their backs as he pushed them out of the hot tub. The hookers climbed out of the tub and looked at the old man who was staring at them. One covered her crotch with one hand and beckoned him with the other. He turned away.

"Enough of this nonsense," the lawyer said. "Cover up that hideous body of yours, and let us do some business."

Herrera moved to the bedroom. He yelled out to Franco to get another driver and bring two Escalades to the front of the hotel. Franco understood only two words; *dos* and *Escalade*. He grabbed the one behind the bar, and the two went to the garage.

Herrera's entourage entered the hotel's circular driveway only moments later, and all slid into the two waiting SUVs and headed for places unknown. The police knew Herrera's putrid yellow Cadillac. They did little to interfere with its movements as the two SUVs passed through the traffic light on to Francisco Madera Boulevard, Highway 15. Three miles to the south, Highway 280, De Los Insurgentes presented the intersection at which they would turn.

The roads are smooth and surprisingly well maintained, Franco thought as he kept both hands on the wheels and did little sight-seeing. The John Deere *did* catch his eye in the field to the right.

"Turn here, Franco," Herrera said. The road narrowed down to two asphalt lanes, and concertina wire lay on both sides. The countryside they entered was expansive with soft, rolling hills and cattle—Santa

Gertrudis. The Mexican sun showed their hides a brighter red than they actually were.

The Cadillac slowed down. Davino had never seen anything so beautiful, except for Carlo's thoroughbreds. They moved past the herd and sped up to get to the warehouse.

And still, David waited on the dark side of town. The prostitute waited; the mob soldiers waited.

The gate at the warehouse was nothing fancy; 15 feet long made from eight-foot slats of cedar. A long strand of twisted wire attached to the top of gate post held it balanced for easy opening. The guards stood silent but presented a sloppy salute as the two vehicles passed through the entrance. As they drove further, more guards came to a position on the road, standing at quasi-attention and presenting a sloppy salute. All Davino was thinking about was all these Mexican thugs *dead*.

The warehouse was a gray stucco. Yellow water stains marked the side beneath the toilets. Apparently, they leaked for years. A one-story building set amidst the edge of a mesquite brush line, thorny and thick.

The first SUV pulled up to the door, and the lights were turned on and blinked twice, a three second pause, and then a third blink. Through the window, Davino could barely see the stacks of bricks they would be taking home. The large corrugated steel doors slid open. Franco and the other driver turned in unison to the large opening and drove inside.

"Two hundred and sixty bricks," Herrera said.

Davino repeated it.

Four thugs walked from the other side of the warehouse looked for permission from their leader. He waved his arm in a high circular motion, and the loading process began. Wheelbarrows were brought into the warehouse, and 30 bricks rolled out of the shadowy darkness. Two of Davino's soldiers neatly stacked the bricks in the back of the Caddy. Thirty more trips, and 30 more loads of heroin bricks.

Davino stopped the wheelbarrows intermittently and pulled a brick—stabbed it with a pen-knife and tasted the dope. Satisfied it was real, he would let it continue. The process took just over two hours.

The old man grabbed the standing suitcase and rolled it over to one of Herrera's lieutenants.

"Eight million more," said the chieftain. "And I want David Culberson's head. And one more thing, lawyer. You send for that bitch."

The consigliere circumvented the answer about the deputy mayor as the sounds of whirring of a helicopter motor were heard in the distance. Herrera was constantly anxious about unwanted noises.

Franco looked up.

Nice, Jonathan.

Chapter 56

THE PILOT OF THE HELICOPTER made sure of his height and distance. Jonathan made the call to Colonel Beauchamp during 'stand-down' at Cananéa. The colonel yelled from his make-shift office to the captain to start all engines—Apaches and Blackhawks. The monstrous and odious sounds from the choppers shook the ground. Within minutes, a grayish dust blanketed the square. The colonel raised his arm and swung it in a circular motion. He climbed into the lead Apache and called for an immediate confirmation of engine and weapon status. Within minutes, all 30 attack helicopters responded—all system-go.

The dust grew thicker as First Platoon lifted into the air, then Second Platoon, then Third. Once airborne, the personnel carrier moved into position. Twenty infantrymen loaded up, and soon it was in hot pursuit of the attacking choppers.

The day was hotter and the air thinner around the cartel warehouse. Jonathan's chopper moved innocently off to an unnoticeable distance from what was to become a not-so-pleasant sight for the cartel. Herrera's senses realized the diminished sound of helicopter blades and took it as a police chopper and put the incident out of his mind. The SUVs with neatly-stacked bricks of heroin left the compound on the way to retrieve the remaining $8 million.

Herrera's cellphone rang; he did not answer it. He was discussing his New York contact and did not want to get off subject.

"That bitch made the deal with me. Morales gave her a better deal, but with my dope. She will not get away with this," said the translator. "I'm going to give her the thrill of a lifetime, and then I'm going to remove her head."

Franco drove the Caddy as his knuckles grew tighter, not knowing the contact about who he was referring. The phone rang again.

"Culberson set up the attack on the train with Morales. I don't know how he set fire to the last two cars without harming the opium. I will find out before I slice off his head."

Franco squinted, giving his facial muscles something else to do except smile.

They came to the intersection at the De Los Insurgentes Highway and turned back toward the city. A break in the conversation allowed Herrera to view the last four unanswered phone calls—it was the same number. He tapped the display and pushed the 'call' button.

"Jefe! Jefe! The factory is on fire! I called the director of the fire department 10 minutes ago—they have not arrived." The man's voice was one of terror.

"What! Are you crazy! How did this happen?" Herrera yelled into the phone.

The man on the other end didn't know how to respond.

"The building just went up in flames, jefe."

Herrera was beside himself. There was no plan B. The old man thought about a possibility but blew them off as nonsense.

Chapter 57

ARTURO LAID IN BED, occasionally struggling to get to the bathroom to vomit and rehydrate himself. The food from that Mexican e-coli breeding farm made for a sleepless night. His head ached from the pounding in his temples; his stomach constantly churned and gurgled, and his upper esophagus was the on-deck resident of this horror they called "Mexican food."

The hotel doctor finally arrived and gave him a shot of antibiotics. Jonathan's plan did not cover being sick in bed. He threw his head back on the pillow as he listened to Tejano music permeating through the tin walls. His life was turned upside-down, and he was in the middle of more than he knew how to handle. The combination of physical and emotional stress caused more anxiety, more sweating, and more concern from the doctor. He reached the point where he was tired of playing this dangerous game.

The doctor placed the samples of antibiotics on the nightstand; he told Arturo to rest for the day and left. Arturo could see a hot shower beckoning his name, so slowly he rose out of the bed and staggered to the bathroom. He was right—the stinging hot water massaged and kneaded his blood vessels *and* arteries. It was like a mongoose attacking a cobra, but it soon felt invigorating.

He could hear the accordion back-up to the first song that Emilio Navaira recorded in 1991 as the music migrated through the wall. Arturo thought he used to like Tejano music, but now, it all sounded the same. He felt better as he whistled what he could hear as he threw a shirt over his head and buttoned the lower half of the shirt.

He grabbed his boots and saw they had been cleaned. He would have to tip the cleaning lady for her kindness. He left the room and followed the hallway to the elevator that would take him to the lobby. He had no desire to eat, but fresh air would do him good.

The elevator operator looked at Arturo and asked, "Lobby?"

Arturo gave the man a quick look and nodded.

The operator went through seven floors, and the doors opened at the main floor. Arturo slowly left the elevator and headed for the main entrance of the hotel. The sun was high in the sky, and it was a bright, hot day. He stopped at the hotel convenience shop and tried on six or seven styles of sunglasses. He noticed the wrap-around; they looked good, and he felt good. He gave the girl his room number and walked out into the sun. A walk down the street would do him good.

The polarized lenses did a real good job of filtering out the glare, so when the yellow Escalade came into view a block away, he saw it make a left turn and head for the factory.

The Escalade stood out like snow on a field of corn. The four black SUVs that followed him were not any less obvious. The lead, and those which closely shadowed behind it, darted through intersections with no regard for traffic lights.

The smoke was seen three blocks away; the sight of the fire came soon after.

By now, the Culiacán Fire Department *and* the police were on-scene. Herrera's heartbeat grew faster, and his anger showed on his face: It was flush, and the fire in his eyes told his feelings of disgust. When he pulled to what remained of his factory, his slammed on his brakes and, like a petulant child, jumped from his vehicle, slammed the door, and stomped to the fire-infested front door.

His dialect was strong and totally incoherent. He shouted obscenities to everyone as the consigliere sat quietly in the lead car. The old man pushed back even a slight smile, although he really did not know what chemicals existed inside prior to the fire.

Down the street, a thug leaned against a streetlamp watching all the activity. Occasionally, he strolled back inside to where David was now cleaning his Glock.

"How many?" David asked.

The mob soldier turned, "Too many, but I saw Davino."

The sun shifted to the 2:00 position in the cloudless sky as a farmer climbed up on his brand-new John Deere tractor. The air-conditioned cabin sure helped in this heat. His lunch was over, and the last 200 acres needed to be plowed. He placed his sunglasses on his face as he thought of the four or five hours of plowing ahead of him.

The alfalfa is next, and I'll finish with the summer wheat, he thought to himself.

The big diesel engine was loud but powerful, and the Mexican clay was deeply embedded in the dirt. His headphones were attached to the CD his daughter gave him for his birthday, and he had it turned up to cover up the din offered by the diesel engine.

The cabin, which sat above the big engine, protected him from the bright sun as he moved to his daily grind. The sun's rays beat down on the open field, and the diesel engine just hummed along. Later, the glare started to fade, and the sunglasses were no longer needed.

What a change, he thought, *must be clouding up.*

A large shadow appeared in front of him, moving at slow but steady pace. He stopped and turned off the tractor. It was like a syncopated *thump* at first, so he figured it was coming from his CD player.

It got louder. The farmer turned off the Tejano music—the *thump, thump* continued and grew louder. The noise remained, and now, darkness fell directly above him. He got out of the cabin and looked skyward. He did not have to look far.

Madre mia! The sky was amassed with hovering Apache helicopters. Colonel Beauchamp was careful not to be discovered. Now he was and could not afford having a witness. His Apache moved forward of the tractor, spun 180 degrees, and landed in front of the farmer's tractor. He called the rear chopper and ordered his advance to the area.

"Señor, I'm afraid today's plowing is over," the colonel said. "You'll be taken to a place where it is safe." The sergeant led him to the troop carrier that just landed next to the colonel's Apache. The farmer locked his cabin, they continued on their mission.

"We'll stay on plan—no higher than 50 feet, and everyone in tandem—let's go!"

Three miles from the warehouse, Herrera's men were either sleeping, drinking, or eating—definitely *not* paying attention. Hovering high at 6,000 feet and five miles from the warehouse, the two OH-68 Kiowas sat quietly, monitoring activity at the warehouse and the upcoming onslaught.

Their highly sensitive, onboard computers displayed in an extreme detail, all movement and all that was static, it was all viewed in Washington, D.C., as well. Alpha and Bravo companies remained in single-file; they were two miles from the target. The bellies of each Apache carried a .50 cal Gatling gun capable of swiveling 360 degrees. The triggers were attached to a slave unit connected to the pilot's eye-piece. Charlie Company hovered to the south and Delta to the west. Their armament consisted of two pods, each carrying eight Hellfire missiles. The eyes in the sky reported no prepatory action.

The colonel's watch struck "go-time." His battalion responded in unison. The tactic had been practiced many months ago, and so now, it was time to change practice into reality.

Alpha rose to 100 feet and attacked from the east. Charlie climbed to 75 feet and started to attack one minute later. The maneuvering was deliberate and at high speed. Delta flew in at 40 feet above the ground with .30 cal machine guns coughing up 300 rounds per minute.

Caught totally be surprise, the men grabbed anything they could get their hands on. Five of Herrera's men scampered for an equal number of RPGs. Two headed for the roof, two out the back door, one crouched in the kitchen, thinking the refrigerator would protect him.

As the last of Delta cleared the building, the five thinly-spread choppers of Charlie Company laid a blanket of stinger missiles from their pods. Charlie Two's second pass caught the visual of an RPG. The pilot looked back at him, and the Gatling gun followed his visual instructions. As his Apache made his turn, he maintained visual contact, and the Gatling responded in kind. He fired. The building lit up like the Fourth of July.

Bravo Company, which was held in reserve, never fired a shot.

The five choppers from Delta Company proceeded one-half mile north of the target and reversed course simultaneously, hovering side-by-side like Regimental Pikemen. On command, the five increased throttle pressure as the noses dipped in a striking position. The Apaches moved steadily and with resolve toward their target to complete the day's mission.

Bravo One's Gatling guns were ready to enter the fray with 1,000-round belts layered in adjacent metal cans. At 50 yards from the burning building, the guns exploded.

The head of security ducked behind the cement wall and fumbled with his cellphone to call Herrera. The first chopper of Delta Company fired through the wall, separating the man's hand from his arm, then his arm from his shoulder. The remaining burst severed his head. Delta Three dropped to 10 feet and hovered facing the wrath of two men aiming pistols. The pilot's eye-controlled aiming device zeroed in and a short burst from the Gatling gun tore through their bodies.

Delta Four moved to his beam. The forward-looking Infrared (F.L.I.R.) system picked up five more cartel members peering around the corner of the yet untouched burning building. The attacker saw the fear in their eyes. He also was aware that two had AK-47s, and one held a shoulder-fired rocket launcher. Two Hellfire missiles were released and struck just above them. The wall of the building and the east side of the rood crumbled down upon them.

Alpha Three spotted four men heading for a truck. Their panic attempt to escape was met with catching the wrath of one Hellfire in the cabin of the vehicle. Desperate, despicable lives lay dead.

The last man carrying an RPG crawled out from the kitchen and peered through the window. Charlie Two was hovering showing his starboard beam. The rocket was fired and caught the Apache just in front of the tail rotor. The chopper spun violently and bobbed up then headed for the ground. It tipped slightly upon reaching the ground and one of the giant blades slammed hard against a large rock. The Apache broke into and both aviators were thrown from the cockpit. The reciprocating blade slashed through the ground until it snapped just missing one of the pilots. The broken piece of the rotor flew into the building like a projectile in a tornado, hitting the shooter and severing his head. The fray over and medics from the Blackhawk rushed in; cared for the two combat aviators. They were hauled away with little injury.

Chapter 58

ARTURO BOUGHT THE FIRST WHITE SHIRT he saw on the rack in the downtown Culiacán Mercado. He was wearing it when he checked out. His stomach was better, and most of his color had returned. He told the clerk he was going to change back into the shirt he wore when he entered the store, and she nodded. He turned to face the sweatshirted woman once again. This time, there were two of Herrera's men standing with her.

"When are you going to change that shirt?" he said. "It's full of stains." His heart beat faster at the sight of Herrera's girl; she wasn't amused.

"You are feeling better, I see." Her eyes were like cold steel. She stood in the middle of two men, both with light windbreakers, in the middle of summer.

Arturo tried to smile; he tried to joke; he tried to lick his dry lips with his saliva, but he had none. He saw worse being around Morales.

"How can I help you?" he asked.

"There was a fire," she said. "Herrera wants you to come to the factory."

That's it? "What kind of fire—an explosion?" he asked.

"I don't know. He told me to bring you—come on!"

The four walked to the black SUV and climbed in. The traffic was light until they came within a couple of blocks of the fire. The black smoke rose high into the sky, and white fire trucks surrounded what was left. The immediate area was like a parking lot filled with Herrera's SUVs.

Arturo slid out the front door and froze—the old man.

Christ! What the fuck is he doing here? His pulse raced as he gazed at the smoldering ashes and then back at the old man. *What now?*

The old man's tilted sombrero covered the back of his head as he stared at the mesmerizing sight. The white fire engines continued the onslaught on Herrera's factory as on-lookers grew.

The woman yelled to Arturo, "Hey! Herrera wants to see you. Get out of there!"

After seeing the old man, Arturo could not move; it was as if he was frozen in time. His legs would not move. Everything came back to him: The trek through the mesquite brush, the wolf attack, and now, the old man.

Arturo gathered his strength and slid out of the vehicle. He pulled his cap down to where it covered the frames of his sunglasses. He moved directly to Franco. Herrera was just ahead.

"Get me out of here! We have a problem," he whispered. Franco turned to see the fear in Arturo's eyes. Arturo grabbed his arm and collapsed.

Franco called out to Herrera, "He's sick again. I'll get him to the doctor."

He lifted Arturo from his curled position and dragged him to an empty SUV. He moaned in pain until Franco put the vehicle in reverse and backed out of the area.

Arturo kept his head low and covered.

"The old man with the bandoleers, did you see him?"

"I did. Who is he?"

"He is one of Morales' men. His donkeys helped us carry the cocktail to the train. He knows me. He knows Morales is dead, and he knows that I killed Vargas."

"He brought the mobster from New York down here.

That means David Culberson is here with him," Franco said.

"I believe this is true." Arturo nodded his head.

Franco thought for a moment and began to display a slight smile.

"They're here to kill Herrera. We're here to destroy the Sinaloas cache and their operation; they're here to take over the operation and kill the cartel leader. You're right, Arturo. David Culberson *is* here. What they don't know is that the warehouse was destroyed and most of his men are dead."

"*The* warehouse?" Arturo asked.

Franco looked at his partner with a raised eye-brow.

"What do you mean, '*the* warehouse,' how many do you think there are?"

The SUV rounded the corner to the local hospital. Arturo dropped the sun-visor to see if he could make himself look sick. The visor mirror popped open and immediately, he flipped it closed.

"We're being followed." he said. "Franco, pull up to the emergency room entrance. And yes, there is more than one warehouse—maybe many. We've got to find them." He opened the door and fell to the ground and staggered through the door. His acting skills were getting better.

Franco looked in the rearview mirror. The SUV pulled over to the side and parked.

Green scrub-adorned nurses moved in and out of the entrance. Most left due to shift-change while others assisted ambulance-drivers that were bringing in new patients. One nurse noticed Arturo lying on the concrete driveway. She ran to assist and performed preliminary triage n him. Deciding his level of illness was important enough for immediate check-in, a gurney was called, for and Arturo entered the hospital as a patient.. Franco parked the vehicle and went in the hospital after him. While sitting in the waiting room, he pulled his cell phone from his pocket and pushed his favorite hotkey.

"Jerry, contact Colonel Beauchamp. Tell him there are more warehouses. We'll find out as much as we can."

Arturo sat next to the admitting nurse and listened to her questions. Franco moved down the halls to the main entrance. The black SUV was parked 30 feet in front of him. He pulled his semi-automatic

Beretta, opened the passenger-side door, and slid into the vehicle. The barrel was pointed at the driver's face.

"Who are you?" Franco asked. The man, startled, remained motionless.

He answered, "David Culberson."

"Why are you following me?"

"I know the man who is with you."

"And who might that be?"

"I knew him as Arturo Gonzales." Across the hospital entrance, Franco saw another SUV parked just cattycorner on Fuentes del Valle—a black one.

"Get out of the car and come with me, *and* cover your face." Franco said.

The two opened their respective doors, and Franco slid back out with his Beretta in hand. David followed suit and moved to the front of the Escalade. Once inside the hospital, David looked at Franco.

"You work for Herrera." He waited for an answer—none came. "You're going to kill me." Franco didn't respond. "I got involved in this transaction because of Madeleine Underwood—she needed the dope." Franco continued to allow David to keep talking. "Listen, we're here to buy the dope and…"

A blurred figure masked by a darkened hallway appeared over Franco's shoulder. His face hidden by the dark hallway; his voice echoed hollow as it bounced off the plastered walls.

"David?"

He tried to stand amidst the threat of Franco's semi-automatic pistol, but the barrel kept him pinned against the wall. The man came closer; the voice became clearer.

"David?" Arturo seemed anxious to renew the murderous kinship. "What are you doing in Culiacán?" The instant smile quickly disappeared as the steel barrel tapped his temple. Not knowing Franco's true association, Dave continued with his story of buying drugs from Herrera.

"Why is the old man here, David? He was related to Morales." Arturo asked.

Franco leaned into David's face.

"You're here to kill Herrera, aren't you?"

David tried to maintain silence, but the sweat rolling down his face did all the talking for him.

Franco continued, "Who's the Italian? David remained silent.

David was reticent with his response, so Franco's M9 shoved in his mouth unlocked his silence.

"One of Herrera's men killed a mob boss—his boss. The New York mob wants Herrera dead. But before, we want the $11 million dollars of heroin originally purchased from Morales."

Knowing exactly what happened to the shipment, Franco asked, "Where's the shit now?"

"Gone—burned up in my son's plane."

An ambulance rolled by with a siren; another fireman was hurt.

Arturo raised up from his leaning position and looked at the passing emergency vehicle. He saw the black SUV parked at the corner.

A slight tap on Franco's shoulder brought his attention to Arturo.

"Don't look! That SUV has been parked at the corner for as long as David has been here."

Viewing the vehicle from inside the corridor gave them ample cover. Franco then blurted out,

"Move into the hospital and out of this hallway alcove."

Arturo replaced his hoody; Franco placed his gun inside his belt and drew his shirt over to cover it. The main area was bright with flower shops and a pharmacy. It had two restaurants and a large information desk. The three entered the area and walked over to the emergency room. The three walked to the emergency room and noticed the fireman as he was being wheeled into the back. Arturo saw his blackened Air Pack; it was cracked. Arturo pulled Franco aside.

"The fireman's face mask is split. That is hard plastic—only incredibly high heat could cause such damage."

"Like phosphorous?" Franco asked.

Arturo looked at David and then back to Franco. He blinked once and never said a word.

Franco moved forward and grabbed David, "Come with me—now!"

They went into the hall, trying knobs every 10 feet.

Finally, one that's unlocked!

David opened the door and stepped inside an x-ray room. He slammed David against a plate holder; it came crashing to the ground.

"Alright, fuck-head, where'd you get the phosphorous, and how did you get it down here?"

David was shaking, partly because his head was being bounced against the wall.

"You and the Italians aren't planning to rid the world of Herrera all by yourselves. How many men did you bring, and where in the fuck are they?"

Arturo stepped outside the x-ray room and dialed Jonathan. On the ground, somewhere east of Culiacán, the waiting FBI agent answered. Arturo spoke immediately when he heard Jonathan's voice:

"We have Culberson. Some big guy from the New York mob is here, and they're planning to kill Herrera. He brought some men—Franco is with him now, finding out how many; and David used my formula to burn Herrera's factory."

"We destroyed a warehouse south of here, but we think there may be more," Jonathan said. "Who's doing the buying, Arturo?"

He answered, "The Italian guy, and I don't think Herrera knows that David is here."

"Why do you think that?"

"Because, Herrera has *got* to know what happened on that train. He's *got* to know that both Morales and Vargas are dead and that the shipment never got to wherever it was going; although everyone thinks it was Dallas. But why the New York mob? What do *they* have to do with this?"

"Do you think Culberson knows?" Jonathan asked.

Arturo saw a gurney being rolled down the aisle. He maintained his stance outside the x-ray room. The orderly looked at him and rolled the patient to the next room. Arturo went back inside, keeping the line open.

David's face had formed a couple of bruises; no blood yet. Arturo lifted the phone to his mouth, "I'll find out." He tapped Franco on the shoulder and motioned for him to step away. He whispered to him, "I have Jonathan," and he handed the phone to Franco.

"Find out why the mob is involved with this." Franco heard Jonathan's question; he then turned to David.

"Mr. Culberson, where's you plane?

David hesitated for a moment.

"It's in New York," he said while rubbing his cheekbone, trying to soothe the bruises. He tried to stand, but his legs were weak.

Franco leaned over him.

"How did you get down here?"

His jaw was now aching.

"Friends," he said.

"We're done playing games, asshole. Is it the Italian the mob?" Franco asked.

David stuttered, coughed, and sucked in the mucous from his runny nose, "Yes. And—

Franco waited, "…And?"

"And they're going to pick-up another 300 bricks of cocaine tonight and then there's going to be a blood bath. One of Herrera's men killed a made-man, and the mob does not forget that. I promise you: Herrera will pay for it."

David settled back sitting on the floor.

Franco stood over Culberson; staring at first. Then…

"Look, you stupid piece of work, I'm United States federal agent, and you are going tell me which of the other factories are they heading to."

David looked at Franco. One eye was swollen and almost shut; it was turning a blackish blue.

"The one in the office park just southeast of the city."

Arturo left the room again and called Jonathan.

"We guessed right," Jonathan said, "I'm calling the Army now. They will be on their way. Franco, keep the civilians out of sight."

Chapter 59

SCOTT WHITFIELD, PRESIDENT OF THE UNITED STATES, jocularly bounced down the semi-circular staircase from the residential floor of the White House. Congress was in recess, and the only meeting he had was with the Majority Leader, who flew back from Minneapolis. He was greeted by a not-so-happy National Security Advisor Barbara Petersen, a graduate of the University of Texas with a Masters in Economics. She was a brilliant black woman, who everyone adored on *both* sides of the aisle.

"A word, Mr. President?" she asked.

"Have you had your morning coffee, Director?"

"No, sir. It's too early for me. Sir, we have an event." There was calm and purpose in her demeanor.

"Come with me." The president escorted her into the Oval Office and shut the concave door behind him, "Sit, please, Barbara, what's the event?"

Director Petersen carefully placed the aerial photographs of Culiacán, Sinaloa, Mexico on the coffee table in the order of their importance for POTUS to view.

"This one is a picture of the city at 10:00 in the morning. This one..." she slid a more detailed photograph in front of the president, "was taken on the satellite's second pass. This is Herrera's factory, burning to the ground."

President Whitfield moved to the edge of high-back chair. His eyes widened as a slight smile came across his face. Barbara placed a third photograph in front of him. He turned and offered a stoic gaze. The president asked her sit down for a moment,

"Barbara, I know," he said.

Initially, her eyes widened with surprised, then narrowed in disbelief. He tabled her response until a more suitable time in the conversation.

"What happened to the lens?" he asked, "What are all these spots across this section?" He pointed to a southwest section of the picture.

Scowling a little, she replied, "That's the event, Mr. President. Those are not spots; they are a company of Apache attack helicopters, and this spot here," she moved her forefinger to the area around the north west corner, "this is an OH-68 Kiowa Warrior calling the real-time attack module to the Apaches."

The president stood up and walked to the door. He quietly moved over to Margaret Whitcomb's desk, his private secretary for over 20 years.

"Maggie, ask General Caldwell to come over. I need to talk with him."

She obeyed immediately and called the Army's Commanding Officer.

He apologized to his NSA director for leaving the briefing and returned to his seat. He stared at the next photo.

"Holy Christ! What was the target?"

"The RTAM was at the cartel's warehouse in southwest Culiacán. The building held upwards of 1,000 bricks of pure heroine and any movements of inventory were monitored minute by minute. The scratchy lines you see are the actual strike from the Hellfire missiles." She showed him the last set of pictures. They told the complete story of devastation—the destroyed building—the dead bodies and the melted monitoring system.

"Were there any casualties on our side?" His face went solemn and he looked at his NSA director.

"One down, but no injuries," she responded

"What's the current status?"

"Right now, Mr. President, Colonel Beauchamp has ordered a S.E.A.D. He believes there are more warehouses, so the search is on to seek them out and destroy them.

"Barbara, let's call President Ruiz. We should talk."

"First, Mr. President, with respect, I need to know my role here; and why keep this attack from the NSA?"

They walked around the Seal of the United States and leaned against his desk.

"Barbara, you are the best in everything you do around here. I know you love this job, and I know you love this country. There is one more thing I know about you: You do not like the sight of blood. Sometimes, that's a problem. Here. Today, that was a problem. These are thugs in every respect, and they don't understand anything but violence. This guy, Herrera, produces and smuggles into this country over $50 million of cocaine and heroin every year. You cannot negotiate with these thugs. Now that you are aware, you're in it—just like the rest of us—the general, the president of Mexico, me, and now you."

"Oh, I see."

"Coffee's here, Barbara, is it late enough, now?"

It was tough for to smile, but she did—and quipped, "I think now is the time for Scotch."

Thirty-two minutes later, Margaret Whitcomb knocked on the Oval Office door and announced the arrival General Michael Caldwell, U.S. Army. Mike Caldwell celebrated his thirty-first year as a soldier last November. A 1983 graduate of the Citadel, he spent all of his tenure with the 101st Airborne Rangers and adorned enough medals to sink a medium-sized tank. Atop his seven rows of ribbons sat a Command Air Assault Badge and a Command Combat Infantryman's Badge. Just below, a Silver Star with three clusters, the Ghazi Mir Bacha Khan Medal (Afghanistan), the Order of the Golden Lily (Bosnia), and the Purple Heart. Sitting atop all that told the story of his commitment to service was the one ribbon that was wrapped in blue and blanketed with stars—the Congressional Medal of Honor.

"Explain to the NSA, how familiar are you with this mission in Culiacán?"

"Very familiar, Mr. President. After you codified the presence of the FBI and the Border Patrol in country, we set all contingencies in motion. The on-site OH-68 Kiowa Warrior is equipped with a Remote Combat Management System. We are in real-time with every movement that the Apaches made in-country, and we can see the effects of their efforts here in Washington."

Mike Caldwell opened his Panasonic laptop and turned it on. Within seconds, Colonel Beauchamp and the general were on screen and in communication with the president and the NSA director listening. The turned the laptop around so it faced the president.

"Colonel Beauchamp, where will you start your search for the other warehouses?" the president asked.

"Good evening, Mr. President. It is our contention that Herrera would not want to travel out of his comfort zone and too far from a distribution point if he needed to ship the goods out quickly. In that regard, sir, we have formed a 75-mile perimeter and arbitrarily eliminated any mountainous or plains regions." Beauchamp held up his area map to the embedded computer camera. The cockpit overhead light flickered as he continued, "Here, Mr. President," he pointed at a group of industrial parks just east of the city, "are some strong possibilities."

All three looked at the topography of General Caldwell's map.

"Mr. President, see these topo lines that are close together? They represent hills close to a mile farther east that the industrial park. There's just enough height to hide the OH-58 Kiowa's and three companies of Apaches. Alpha Company is enroute and will approach from the northwest. Bravo Company has a full contingency of Hellfire missiles and will be approaching from the southeast. Delta will hover two klicks to the northeast with the Kiowas. Echo Company infantry will reconnoiter on foot. The 30 infantrymen will be brought in by UH-64 Troop Carriers. This S.E.A.D. mission will be accomplished in this manner until all the cocaine is found and destroyed. There are no civilian targets at this time."

The president turned to General Caldwell, "Will we be able to see all of this?"

The general responded, "Just like driving down US-1, sir."

The general stood up and thanked the president and the NSA director for their time and exited the Oval Office.

Just outside the White House, the general's car was waiting. The young staff sergeant came out the driver's seat and ran to open the rear door. The general's phone rang.

"General Caldwell? This is Dan Rondell, Agent in Charge, FBI, Phoenix. Our man, Agent Conroy, just called. His team found out there will be a pickup of 300 bricks of heroin at the second warehouse tonight. The warehouse is a mile east of the city.

"We guessed it right, Agent Rondell. We're on our way there now. I know where to hide them and will facilitate that action within 30 minutes. Thanks."

The general asked his sergeant to wait and walked back into the White House.

"Mrs. Whitcomb, would you please ask the president if he could give me five very important minutes?"

Margaret rose from her chair and knocked on the door of the Oval Office and entered. A minute later, General Caldwell was sitting again with the president of the United States.

"Mr. President, thank you for allowing my return. It has recently come to my attention that the raid will, in fact, be tonight. If it is your wish, we will have the video set to go in the Situation Room in less than an hour."

The president nodded in approval.

Chapter 60

HERRERA STOOD WATCHING THE FIRE ENVELOP his building and those adjacent to it. His face, red from the heat. He was unable to breathe normally, but he would not budge from his spot. The consigliere tried to convince him to move back; the fire chief tried to convince him to move back, but he would hear none of it. The aquifer beneath the city supplied the water; the new white fire engine delivered it, but neither had any success. The fire chief approached Herrera again.

"This is not a normal fire," he said. "Water has little effect on the outcome. We need to smother it," he yelled into Herrera's ear. "The flames near the center of the fire are white, not red. I need to know the source," he added as he turned and walked away.

It took six hours for the abundant amount of water to evaporate; it took less than three hours for the brick building to be gutted by fire.

Davino approached Herrera and was sickened by his gesture of placing his arm around Herrera's neck and consoling him.

"I have decided to buy another $8 million dollars of product from you. Can you handle it?"

Herrera's cell phone rang again. The noise from the high-pressure water hoses and the building crumbling muffled the sound from the other end. Screaming at Davino, Herrera listened to both Davino and his caller. Finally, he hung up his cellphone and faced the consigliere,

"We are down only to 100 bricks at the south warehouse," Herrera screamed into Davino's ear. The sound of the building crashing to the ground was so immense, no one could hear himself think. "I will take you to another warehouse just east of here—do you have the money?"

Davino replied affirmatively, "It's all in my plane."

"Go get it, and take a couple of my men with you."

"I'll go get my keys. I'll be back in a moment." The consigliere stayed in the middle of the street, out of the way of the hoses and the trucks. The lawyer reached the corner and quickly glanced back—then walked into the building where David and the mob were waiting. He entered the front door to see one of his soldiers zipping up his pants and the prostitute on her knees with another goon.

Davino screamed, "Get the fuck outta here! Where's Culberson? You guys get ready; we're going to the other warehouse. Where the fuck is Culberson?"

"He left, boss," one of the goons offered.

"Well, go find him!" Davino stepped to the corner of the large room. He picked up his phone. It rang—and rang—and rang.

Madeleine, what the fuck are you doing? Answer the phone when I call!

Finally, after several rings, the deputy mayor finally picked up the phone.

"Madeleine, where in the hell have you been? I want you to get another $5 million and get down here. I've got an extra $3 million with me, and I'm buying another $8 million tonight. I can stall him, but not after tomorrow." Davino closed his flip phone and turned to the remaining goons.

"You, wait 'til we're gone! Grab the rentals and follow us—but keep your distance." He grabbed the keys from the pilot of his Learjet and stormed out the door and back to the square. He rounded the corner and headed back to Herrera. "Let's go!"

The yellow SUV was covered with caked dust and foam while inside the Escalade, Herrera talked about the transaction. Every so often, he would mention David Culberson's head and how he was going to personally remove it. The guitar music sounded again from his phone—and again, he ignored it.

The sun was creeping down over the western slope, and the vehicle stopped for gas. The soldier sitting in the passenger seat slid out to see if a car wash was available. The answer was, "Yes, but only an automatic one."

Herrera ordered everyone out, except Davino.

"We will ride through the carwash." Steam and water began oozing through the washer-heads. Ultra-hot water pounded the SUV; the vehicle moved slowly forward. Herrera turned to the lawyer and spoke, "Consigliere, you come to my country with two jet planes—why?" Herrera's demeanor changed; his unrecognizable dialect disappeared. He was not formally educated, but his English was as good as anybody's. Davino knew he couldn't have hidden the second Learjet. He started to give him his canned answer, but it was interrupted.

"Don't bullshit me, lawyer."

Special soap was now being applied to the SUV. It possessed a formula that was used to remove the hard, caked clay from the region. Davino was too smart to stutter or to have a nervous cough, but he did think for a moment.

"I brought David Culberson in the other plane," he said, looking directly into Herrera's eyes. His phone rang again, and he saw his wife's name displayed. Whatever she wanted, it would wait; this was too important to talk to her now.

"You deliver him to me after you get the heroin," Herrera said. The drying process began as the hot air from the blowers shook the Escalade. Herrera raised his voice, "Call him. Tell him to meet you at the entrance to the industrial park on the corner of Boulevard Universitano and Carretera a Imala east of the city. Tell him to bring his head," Herrera laughed at his joke.

Davino smiled.

The washing process was over, and the putrid-yellow Escalade drove out into the sun.

"You bring Culberson with you tonight. We'll have a surprise waiting for him. I'll pick you up at 7:00," Herrera said.

Chapter 61

"WHAT ARE WE GOING TO DO WITH HIM?" Arturo asked. "What are we going to do with the guy in the SUV?" Franco peered out the door; he was still sitting there. The trio walked out the x-ray room and saw an empty gurney.

"Climb aboard, Mr. Culberson, and shut up." Franco was encouraging. The available sheet covered his body, but not Franco's handy work. The ambulance driver and his partner were at the coffee bar on a break before leaving.

Arturo approached them and said, "Could you help me with this patient? I have to get him to x-rays. The two followed him around the corner. Franco's left hand came down hard on the last man's neck. When he fell against a standing steel tray, his partner turned. His eyes never saw Franco's right hand. Both were sent to sleep for a while.

The jackets were pulled off the drivers, and Arturo put one on. Franco peered around the corner, looking for unwanted visitors. Franco moved quickly to the second driver and had to turn him over twice just to get the coat off. He slipped his arms into the sleeves; his massive shoulders gave little acceptance to the fit. Arturo and Franco rolled David to the waiting ambulance. Arturo opened the back door and looked back at Franco. Arturo's experience with gurneys was something less than effectual. He had no idea how to get the legs to fold under the gurney. A quick instruction from Franco, and they rolled the gurney into the truck.

Franco slammed the rear doors and hurried to the driver's seat. The red-light flasher and siren switches were activated as they sped around the parked SUV and proceeded back to the dark side of the city.

—◦◦◦—

Two more engines arrived to save the adjacent buildings, but to no avail. The amount of devastation was enormous, and as Herrera stood there, he knew exactly what it meant. His processing plant was destroyed. His remaining inventory of heroin lay safely intact on the northeast side of town.

—◦◦◦—

Franco's ambulance blended in with the chaotic scene as they rolled up to and past the fire. At David's request, Franco drove around the corner and came to a stop in front of a seemingly empty building.

"Get out!" Franco said, "Get out of Culiacán—get out of Mexico!" David slid out the back and waved at Arturo without saying a word. Arturo drove the ambulance around the far side of the block and let Franco off to walk back to the square.

Now Arturo was alone—again. He pulled his cellphone from his pocket and saw his bars were low and the battery near drained. Maybe he had enough juice to call Jonathan and let him know what was happening.

"Can you take a taxi to the east side of the city?" Jonathan asked. "There's an industrial park just beyond the Boulevard Universitano—can you find it?"

Arturo answered, "I can find it.

"We will meet you there." Jonathan pushed the "end" key.

Chapter 62

IT WAS NEARING DUSK. The four Apache companies stood in readiness one and a half miles east of Culiacán hidden by a shallow mountainous range of rolling hills and mesas. The OH-58's MMS (mass mounted sight) broke the horizontal plane of the closest hilltop and began receiving data. The area was quiet, and as it grew darker, more attack choppers moved into position, settling behind the hill. Beauchamp made the decision to remain at rest and send out scouts on foot to reconnoiter the industrial park. A couple of Rangers changed clothes to jeans and t-shirt and left for a coffee shop with M9s tucked in behind them. Others with same attire strolled lazily around the park. Earpieces active with wrist microphones. The Latino troopers carried on innate conversations with the locals, being ever mindful of their mission.

Young First Lieutenant Rutledge Sheehan from Buford, South Carolina sat on a bench reading *Lonesome Dove*. He had been reading the book through all of his flight training since he received his commission; it'd taken him a year and a half. This was a good opportunity for him complete another couple of chapters—or maybe three. The streetlamp cast a soft halogen halo around the bench and he as he read. He kept moving around to keep the M9 barrel from jabbing in his side.

The specialist fourth-class sitting in the coffee shop was the first to notice a stream of headlights approaching. To signal the lieutenant, he removed the red bandana from his head.

The first vehicle got through the traffic light over a mile away while the others were held up. The lieutenant radioed Colonel Beauchamp; his orders transmitted back to him. He slowly stood, tucked his book under his arm, and moved to the back of the park. The embarkation point was just over a mile away. A jeep waited for the five-man party to whisk them back to the foothills over raw, winding terrain. Lieutenant Sheehan tried to change into his flight suit with the jeep traveling at speeds in excess of 40 miles per hour and barely made it before arrived at his now warmed-up Apache.

Sheehan graduated from Fort Rucker's Advanced Attack Helicopter School seven months ago. He had prepared himself for a stint in Afghanistan before he met Colonel William Beauchamp at the Officer's Club one Sunday morning. The restaurant section was full, save one seat at the Battalion Commander's table. Sheehan saw the empty chair, but he hesitated. He asked if he might sit down. Sheehan stood at attention and never moved until the colonel looked up.

"Lieutenant, sit down. Your breakfast is getting cold."

Sheehan acknowledged his permission and relaxed.

It was small talk at first, then the colonel got serious.

"Where did you graduate in your class?"

"First, sir," the lieutenant answered.

"So, you like choppers, do you?" Beauchamp asked.

"My stepfather was a Med-Evac at the Ia Drang Valley, 7th Cavalry in 1964—he flew…"

"I know what he flew, lieutenant," the colonel responded. "Is he still alive?"

"Yes, sir, retired Chief Warrant Officer 04. My mom and he live in Florida—they play golf every day and…" He tried to continue, but was cut short.

"Why don't you come see me at Range Four tomorrow at 0730 hours. Come dressed to work."

The colonel stood, and Sheehan followed suit.

"Thank y—"

The colonel just raised his waving good-bye.

Sheehan's alarm went off at 0500 the following morning. He showered, ate breakfast, and was at Range Four at 0715. Colonel Beauchamp stood facing five AH-64D Apache attack helicopters, each carrying a drop-down 7.62mm Gatling gun and six Hellfire missiles. The lieutenant walked up behind him and reported.

"Locked; cocked; and ready to rock, Lieutenant?"

"U-Rah, Sir!" the lieutenant responded.

"Lieutenant, do the pre-flight, then climb aboard. Take the front seat; I'll take the radio. We are going to hunt some bad guys. Rucker tower, Apache 0-1-4-5 Foxtrot, ready for training mission 0-0-1-5."

"Roger, 0-1-4-5 Foxtrot; take-off when ready. Proceed on heading 0-9-0 degrees, and good hunting."

"Roger that, tower." The colonel switched on the intercom. "Lieutenant, put the coals to it. Let's get out of here."

The twin 1,900 horsepower turbo-shaft engines brought the four-bladed rotors alive and eager to lift the attack helicopter into the air. Within seconds, the Apache was proceeding on a heading of 0-9-0 at a speed of over 170 knots.

Sheehan's technique was smooth and effortless. It was cool that morning as the Apache's blades cut through the air with amazing ease. The lieutenant dropped his F.L.I.R. slave aiming device over his eye and waited for any command from the back seat.

It came quicker than he expected.

"0-8-2 degrees; enemy tank—kill it!" the colonel ordered.

As soon as his last words left his lips, Lieutenant Sheehan brought the nose up 10 degrees to bleed off some speed and looked directly at the target. Within seconds, the laser-guided system locked onto the tank. Sheehan fired Hellfire-1—direct hit. The 20 plywood men that surrounded the tank were dispatched as the Gatling gun split all the wood in half. Sheehan displayed his prowess as a helicopter attack pilot went on for an hour dispatching target after target.

"Let's go back. We're done here," the colonel said.

Sheehan brought the nose up 30 degrees; the Apache stopped. He leveled the nose to the horizon and initiated full left rudder. The chopper responded immediately, and the colonel found himself facing the exact reciprocal of the heading held seconds before. Communication with Fort Rucker tower was clear and concise as they received permission to land. Sheehan descended out of his assigned altitude. The Apache touched the ground with the ease of cutting butter.

—◆◆◆—

The foothills east of Culiacán hid Sheehan's Apache as well as the other 19. On the south end of the line, the first Kiowa's MMS peered above the hilltop. The mass mounted sight displayed nine SUVs approaching the industrial park. The sighting was reported to the colonel seated in Bravo Two with the rest of the attack force. The second Kiowa picked up a woman walking a baby in a stroller in front of the coffee shop. She then sat on the same bench that Lieutenant Sheehan parked himself moments before.

The green F.L.I.R. display caused halo effects as the headlights came closer, so the contrast was turned down, and now, the woman and her baby were no longer in sight.

The Kiowa relayed live data to the colonel as it happened. Everyone in the White House Situation room saw the cars parking in one small area in the industrial park and the occupants walking from their cars to the door of one property.

"Nine cartel; one civilian," reported the OH-58 pilot. "This is funny, Colonel," the pilot from the Kiowa reported, "we have an old guy wearing two bandoleers carrying a long rifle walking with them."

The colonel transmitted, "Roger. Alpha One, on my command, take your company, proceed to 180 degrees at 50 feet. Form up on the south side of the warehouses. Delta One, on my command, take your company and move north to 360 degrees and form up on the north end; same altitude."

—◆◆◆—

A taxi arrived at the entrance. Arturo Gonzales climbed out of the back seat. In the distance, he saw a woman sitting on a bench rocking a stroller; everything else was quiet. Darkness now covered the park, but behind him, the remnants of late dusk was moving to the west. He looked for Jonathan, but saw nothing but the woman, so he turned north and started to walk. Fifty feet ahead of him, a man stood underneath the only streetlight in the area. Arturo continued to walk toward the light while the man continued to stare at him. He drew closer to the light. The man was dressed jeans and a t-shirt. His face was shadowed by the hoodie that he wore, but he maintained his position under the streetlight. Arturo could barely see a two, maybe three-day growth on his face—he kept walking.

"Where are you going?" the man said in Spanish.

"I'm looking for my dog." Arturo responded.

"How much money do you have?" the man asked.

Arturo's heart started to race; a nervous lump formed in the pit of his stomach. Only the man noticed the nine SUVs entering the parking area in front of the row of warehouses. Only a moment later, Arturo saw the man's eyes. They were a welcome sight.

Jonathan said, "Pretty awesome, huh? Only took me three days to grow this."

"What's happening?" Arturo smiled and asked.

"The army, our Army is going to destroy everything in that warehouse and everybody in it who doesn't surrender. Just stand here and watch."

The five Apaches of Bravo Company hovered at 50 feet above the ground just 100 feet in front of the warehouse. Colonel Beauchamp turned on his megaphone.

"Herrera, you have five minutes for you and your men to remove yourselves from the warehouse. One second after that, the wrath of these five Apache attack helicopters will be turned loose, and they will the cause of your and everyone else's *muerta*."

There was no movement, and three minutes elapsed.

Bravo Two flipped the release that exposed the 7.62mm Gatling gun. An off-centered window opened, and an RPG was shown sitting on someone's shoulder. The colonel aimed the Gatling gun at him and pulled the trigger—too late.

Before the man's head was torn off by the colonel, the RPG left the window and scored a direct hit in Bravo Two's cockpit. The grenade broke the cockpit glass and killed both pilots immediately. The grenade entered from the left side, blowing the Apache apart and to the right. Shrapnel hit Bravo One, sending it into a tailspin. One of the 48-foot rotors slammed into a tree, and the turbo-shafted engines exploded.

Bravo Three released 1,000 rounds in 50-shot bursts from their Gatling gun. The Kiowa relayed the event to Charlie Company, and five Apaches popped up from behind the foothill and headed toward the park. Bravo One ordered his company to move into position. On Sheehan's command, all Apaches backed away so as *not* to be damaged by the results of the Hellfire missile that was about to be fired. Alpha Company, in unison, moved from the south and to the front, facing the building as they finished their attack with the two remaining Apaches from Bravo Company. Twelve cartel goons escaped to the rear of the warehouse and were greeted by Gatling gun fire from Charlie Company.

The sky lit up like a Christmas tree with yellow and red flames reaching upwards of 50 feet in the air. Arturo and Jonathan looked with amazement as they heard the sirens racing up the Boulevard—mostly police, but some fire trucks.

The woman sitting on the bench ran past Arturo 15 minutes ago, screaming. Windows blew out 30 feet from the building; smoke and flames rose 56 feet in the air. The wrath of God and the 1ˢᵗ Cavalry lit up the skies in east Culiacán, and they were not through. Gatling guns from each Apache exploded at the same time, and each pointed in one direction.

There was no way anyone was left alive.

Chapter 63

THE SITUATION ROOM IN THE BASEMENT of the White House was quiet. President Whitfield sat motionless, his elbows resting on his thighs and his hands clasped in front of his eyes. He heard about the remote coverage technology when SEAL Team Six took down Osama Ben Laden. If he hadn't seen this with his own eyes, he would have never believed it. General Michael Caldwell stood behind him, one hand cupped around his chin. No one uttered a word.

The first transmission came from Alpha One 30 minutes after the melee.

"Ranger One, commence clean-up. Alpha Four, Bravo Four: Move to staging area two and hold."

The Apache, call-sign Bravo Four turned to 275 degrees and moved 75 yards to his west; Alpha Four followed as Ranger One, a UH-60 Black-hawk, approached through the billowing smoke and ash. Eleven fully-equipped infantrymen from the Third Infantry Division egressed as it hovered before touching down. Weapons drawn, the infantry company proceeded into what was left of the destroyed building. The top of the warehouse was partially gone; multiple beams of light crisscrossing steel showed as each company member turned his head looking for anyone who remained alive. A transmission back to the Kiowa Warriors reported, "Still a lot of heat, but no sign of life at this moment. We continue to search."

Jonathan slowly approached the burned-out warehouse, his FBI identification in hand. The police chief arrived with city officials to examine what was left of the lives *and* the structure.

Five infantrymen walked from the building, suffering from minor smoke-inhalation and needed medical attention.

The lieutenant's bars could be barely seen in the moon lit night as the mayor approached him.

"Lieutenant, my name is Jesus Montaña, I am the Mayor of Culiacán."

The officer switched off his helmet-mounted flashlight.

"Tell me what you found inside?"

The lieutenant was diplomatic, but honest.

"A large number of bodies were strewn throughout the warehouse. Most were burned beyond recognition. The smell of cocaine was prevalent from one side of the building. We found a large inventory of heroin on the other side; most of it burned."

He turned and pointed at all the destruction.

The last three rangers turned to leave—one heard a weak cough from inside.

"Did you hear that?" one said. It sounded again. "Go find out who it might be, and let me know!"

The two remaining soldiers follow the sound, stepping over burned bodies.

"That door—look!" one said.

They moved quickly to a room in the corner. One soldier tested the heat from the doorknob—it was still hot. Another weak cough, then a cry for help—in English. Through the Nomex gloves, the other soldiers tested the knob again; still hot. He pulled out his girlfriend's protection scarf and wrapped it around his hand. The two twisted and pushed until the men's bathroom door gave way.

His face blackened by the fire and smoke, coughing when he could, wheezing most of the time, the two soldiers carried the man out with his arms around their shoulders. The firemen placed an oxygen mask on his face and a cold compress around his eyes. No fire had touched him, but ash and smoke inhalation caused most of the pain. A couple of Mexican EMTs checked his vitals and looked for signs of second- or third-degree burns.

"Whoever he is, he is very lucky," the medic said.

"Take him to the hospital—we'll find out who he is later," the mayor said.

The second fire in as many days drew a larger crowd than the first. The manicured park was blanketed with parts of Apache helicopters. Business-owners of the adjacent buildings were aghast at the damage of their own businesses.

One man stood in the crowd, his heart near apoplexy. The tears rolled down his face as he gaped at the horrific sight of death and destruction. The Sinaloas' business was gone.

Morales and Vargas were dead; Jack Culberson was in jail; Herrera—no one knew—yet.

Arturo turned away and proceeded to wait for Jonathan by the streetlight just down the walkway.

Who is going to clean up this mess? he thought. *I suppose the United States will.*

The night crept on as the crowd dissipated. Colonel Beauchamp's body and that of his gunner were removed and placed on the waiting Blackhawk. What was left of his face was draped by a small six-by-eight-inch American Flag; his gunner, a tarpaulin to protect his remains. The remaining squadron dispatched behind the foothills and bivouacked for the night. First Lieutenant Rutledge Sheehan sat near the campfire and wrote his report of the event.

The inside of the warehouse smoldered with a blanket of ash and destroyed cocaine and heroin covering the floor. The modernized tilt-wall construction had blown out, covering what used to be greenery and tropical plants with a flagstone walkway. The windows had all melted along with the surrounding frames that supported them. The metal shelves that held the heroin were nothing more than half-melted, twisted metal lying on the floor.

A lone fire inspector strolled inside, methodically examining the damage. Close to 100 burned bodies lay on the floor. He examined the dead in a cursory manner; the coroner would be more precise in the morning. His flashlight brought the reflection of shiny objects around one of the bodies. He drew closer and saw it was a couple of bandoleers straddled across one of the dead; his burned-out Sharps rifle lay clasped in his blackened hands. He slowly moved to the back corner and thought he heard a moaning noise.

The fire inspector moved cautiously in the darkness. He tripped over another body; this one, a young woman. He stared for a moment at the unfortunate demise of a poor innocent bystander.

Poor thing, he thought. The only clothes she owned was the over-sized sweatshirt she was wearing. He continued to the moaning. Against the back corner, a weak knock emanated from the other bathroom. He yelled, "I'm coming; stay with me; I'm coming to help you!"

He touched the doorknob. It was warm to the touch. He went back to where the metal shelving lay and grabbed a small section.

He pounded at the doorknob until it broke loose. The door flung open. Another man lay in pain; his face wrapped in a wet cloth towel he took from the dispenser above him. He had soaked it in the toilet and covered his face with it.

The inspector helped the man to his feet and walked him outside into the night air and laid him on the ground. The fire inspector removed his coat; he folded it and placed it beneath the man's head.

"I'll get you some water; I'll be right back."

The man weakly nodded.

He ran back from his truck with the bottled water.

"Are you burned?" he asked. The man shook his head. "Are you in pain anywhere?" He shook his head again.

"I'll call an ambulance."

The man touched his arm, trying to pull it toward him.

With a raspish voice, he said, "No."

The fire inspector stared at the man's soiled and ash-covered clothes. His face was partially blistered, his eye-lids half-closed and swollen. He checked his arms and legs for searing. He looked for first- and second-degree burns, which appeared on his legs.

"Sir, I have to take you to the hospital."

The man resisted again and tried to stand up. His breathing was clearer as his conversation became curt with the inspector.

"Look, dammit, I'll be fine, so back the fuck off."

The man's strength regained enough for him to roll over and prop himself up on his hands and knees. He coughed incessantly and then vomited. The inspector watched his stubborn attempt to recover from near death. A moment later, the inspector's truck radio startled him.

"Inspector 21, do you read? Come in, please."

He proceeded to his truck to answer the call.

As he walked away, the man murmured to the inspector, "Don't say anything."

He could hardly speak anyway. Moving away from the injured man, he just shrugged his shoulders.

"Inspector!" the man yelled one more time.

The inspector stopped and turned around. The man pulled a semi-automatic pistol from inside his pants and pointed it at him. With two shaking hands, he pulled the hammer back to cock it.

"Say anything, Inspector and you're a dead man." The man could barely see out of his swollen eyes.

The radio called again.

"I have to answer it!" he said.

The inspector reached inside the truck and grabbed the micro-phone. He lifted it to his face; his eyes were suddenly blinded by a series of headlights coming up the boulevard.

"Inspector 21!" The radio exploded again. He addressed the call as he watched the caravan of SUVs pass him to the parking area, "I'll get back to you in a moment," he said.

The headlights stopped, and the people inside quickly surveyed the park and the front of the burned-out warehouse. The vehicles moved swerving back and forth, looking at the downed helicopters, the blown-out building, and a man sitting with his back against a tree. His hand held a pistol, and his arms wrapped around his folded-up legs. The SUV stopped. Franco jumped out; he looked at the inspector as he ran to the wounded man.

Approaching the survivor, he dropped to his knees to closely examine him—more than anything, wanting to know who he was. He calmly removed the gun from his grip and placed it in his belt. Franco moved the survivor's head to the light—it was Herrera.

"Take me to Aristoterios!" his voice was weak, debilitating, but with resolve. Franco looked back at the EMT, "I'll take care of him."

"What is he talking about?" The EMT asked.

"A doctor takes care of him," he said. "He will recover there."

Franco and the cartel soldier lifted him up walked him to a waiting SUV, the yellow one. The back seat was laid flat, and Herrera was placed in the back. One last look at the horrific scene, Franco shook his head and smiled.

That was one hellava cocktail.

Julio Moreno was Vincente Herrera's doctor of choice. A man of questionable background, Moreno set up practice in Culiacán in the shadows after being thrown out of Mexico City. The only place to go was to the largest cartel in Sinaloa; they did not much care if he was licensed or not. Back-street abortions and gunshot wounds were his mainline business in today's world. In addition, Herrera paid him a little extra when he helped his men get free of the cocaine and heroin habit. He sat next to Franco and while he barked out orders to call Moreno.

The cartel leader was lucky *and* smart. At the sight of the eminent strike, he quietly moved to the rear of his warehouse and into the safest place he could find; the bathtub. The destruction all around him, he stayed where he was throughout the melee. His burns, although superficial, hurt, and Herrera was in need of his doctor.

Moreno's so-called clinic was in a garage in the back of an old, deserted house. There were no visits from the health department or other medical associations. Generally speaking, it was filthy, and to look after a burn victim, it had to be cleaned up, scrubbed down, and sanitized.

The call was made to Moreno and information about Herrera's condition was given to the doctor.

"The garage has to be cleaned up," he said. "Herrera was caught in a fire; he can hardly breathe. Clean out the scorpions, the rat shit, and the insects."

"I have no ointment for his burns, but I can give him morphine," was Moreno's response.

Herrera's phone rang again. The man reached back over the seat and extracted it from the cartel leader's pocket; it was his wife. The display screen listed phone messages from seven hours ago. He decided one more message wouldn't lessen Herrera's problems.

Aristoterios was only three miles away, and Moreno would have little time to make his garage operating-room sterile.

The doctor met the SUV at his front door and escorted them to the back. With Herrera's arms slung over Franco and the other guy, the doctor cleared a path through dog shit and potholes. Two fluorescent lights hung overhead as they crossed the portal. Rats already left their mark on the hardwood wooden table. The doctor quickly brushed the droppings off with his hands and scrubbed the table with soap and water. Herrera hung on Franco's shoulder in pain, but most of it was the remnants of the heat. There was redness all over his body, but little to no blistering. There were slight wounds from the metal cabinet that he placed on top of him during the attack. The dried bloodstains made Franco sick in his stomach. He held up just long enough to lay Herrera on the table, then he left the garage and puked.

Herrera's issue was mainly smoke inhalation. Part of his clothing stuck as the blisters popped along his arms. The oxygen he was given gave a little clarity to his lungs, and the raspish voice dissipated. His wife, the doctor, and Franco could listen to him without the incessant hacking.

"Find the consigliere!" Herrera said. His voice was weak; the words came intermittently with coughs, "Bring him to me!" The frog caught his throat again. "He has $8 million of my money."

"I'll find him." Franco said, "I'll bring him to you, jefe."

He left the makeshift operating room and stopped on the other side of the large double doors and leaned back against the jam. The conversation inside was more about Herrera than anything else. Then he spewed out:

"When that gringo shows his face, get him on this table and make damn sure he tells you where my $8 million is located, then kill him."

Franco eased away from the door and ran to the waiting SUV. He was alone for the first time since he moved into the Herrera cartel.

David Culberson stepped out of the corner warehouse. The streets were dark except for the glowing, flickering shadows cast by the smoldering fire. The explosion east of the city grabbed everyone's attention, but there was no way he was leaving his comfort zone again. The prostitute moved to more lucrative territory, and the 22 goons had grown tired of waiting and were ready to go—anywhere.

Around the corner, one fire truck remained with a two-man team to make sure there was no residual fire. The brick spall was swept from the streets and a few sports cars were again cruising the area.

David heard the sound of an ambulance coming from the east side, and he thought of his ordeal with Herrera's man earlier that day. He thought of Arturo.

The ambulance screeched to a halt in from of the emergency room entrance. A trauma nurse and three orderlies ran to the vehicle and threw open the back door. The partially burned figure inside was lying still and breathing better with the help of oxygen; his oxygenation levels were at 85 percent. The orderlies pulled the gurney to the street and rolled him into the hospital. The nurse moved him to the ER with them, checking his vitals every inch of the way. Blisters formed on his face and arms. Silver sulfadiazine cream was gently placed everywhere there were a signs of second- or third-degree burns or blistered flesh.

Davino moaned in pain as the gurney was pushed into the emergency room. The fluorescent lights passed above him, his eyes barely distinguished the low light. He fought to hear the muffled sounds of voices speaking to him as they oscillated in his hearing canal. The blisters grew on his face around his eyes, and on his arms and chest. The attack was devastating, all were dead; burned alive and…and there was Davino in excruciating pain, wishing he amongst those left behind.

Behind the curtain, Davino's clothes were gently cut and removed from his body. The orderly brought in a container of silver sulfadiazine, and the attending team applied the salve over his entire body. The consigliere was moved to the first floor intensive care unit for recovery.

The first gas station appeared a couple of miles outside of the doctor's neighborhood. Franco pulled in to add gasoline to the near full tank. He slid out the front seat and placed the nozzle in the gas tank. A quick move to the side of the filling station, a push of a button on his cellphone, and Jonathan answered.

His voice was drowned out by a large semi-trailer carrying hogs to the Culiacán auction. The squealing forced Franco to yell—something he did not want to do.

"Herrera escaped the attack!" Franco screamed into the phone. "Did anyone else leave the building alive?" he cupped his hand over the microphone and his mouth to filter the sound of the hogs.

The clacking diesel engine added to the noise that drowned out Franco's voice. The call was fruitless, so he hung up and decided he would call back later.

After waiting 30 minutes, Franco called again; the porcine motorhome was gone.

"Jonathan?" Franco asked, "Did you hear me before? Did anyone else manage to escape the attack?"

"Yes, he was taken to the General Hospital of Culiacán. We found out he is with the Parizzi family in New York."

"See if you can get to him," Franco said. "I think I know where Culberson is—I'll call you back."

Franco jumped in the SUV and headed for the empty warehouse where he dropped off David Culberson the day before. It started raining again. It was slow at first, but as Franco moved through the streets, the rain plummeted the windshield that soon became quarter-sized hail. The wipers of the Escalade were not fast enough to keep off the shower of large pellets, and he could hardly see through them. He knew Herrera's truck was getting a pounding.

He's just going to have to deal with it.

It was difficult to see anyone or anything in front or to the side. No one was dumb enough to walk on the streets in this downpour, and Franco could barely make out the color of the traffic lights, so he plowed through the intersections. A pair of twin red taillights grew large in front of him, and he slammed on his brakes. No accident today.

Franco finally reached the other side of the city and passed the burned-out plant.

The warehouse is around the corner, he remembered.

The hail turned to rain, and it began to let up. The cumulus clouds churned in the sky, and Franco looked up. The clouds were intertwined with multiple shades of gray and black, and as he continued to watch, the formations changed from ghost-riders to unicorns. Franco shook his head and ran to get under the precipice. He knocked on the door with no answer.

He knocked one more time and then banged on the door.

"Culberson, open the door. Your buddy from New York is in a burn unit in the hospital."

Moments later, the door swung open. A large guerilla-type Neanderthal stuck the barrel of an IDF .50 cal Desert Eagle semi-automatic in Franco's face. Franco leaned forward and placed his forefinger inside the barrel.

"Back up!" he said to the goon in the door. "Pull that trigger and you'll blow my hand off. Pull the trigger, and you will lose your head, so back up."

The wise guy retreated back to where the rest of the crew were sitting. Franco rubbed his finger while thinking a sigh of relief.

"It's over!" he yelled out to the small band of New York goons. "Your boss is in the hospital; a burn unit—he may or may not make it. Herrera was injured and is holed-up in a make-shift care facility in a doctor's garage. The heroin is gone, burned to a crisp. You boys need to hop on that plane and fly back to the States—I would do it as soon as possible." Franco was quite succinct in his suggestion.

The front two legs of a straight-back chair resting in the corner hit the old wooden floor as the two feet muffled the sound.

"Boys, this guy is a United States Federal officer." David Culberson stood and walked from the corner of the building.

"I want no part of any of you wise guys—except you, Mr. Culberson, *you* are under arrest."

Franco's head turned to the band of Neanderthals.

"Don't do anything stupid! No one wants you down here; leave it that way." Franco looked at David. "I *do* have one question, though. Where's the $8 million?"

Dead silence.

"That is *your* ticket for leaving here." Franco added, "You're *not* leaving here with that money."

"Who's gonna stop us?" the goon with the Desert Eagle cradled in his arms asked.

Franco finished shoving Culberson back in his straight-back chair.

"The warehouse that was blown to shit? It was done by two companies of Apache helicopters from Texas. Right now, they are resting quietly in a circle surrounding two American corporate jets."

The tin precipice outside indicated the storm was passing. The clamor of thousands of rain pellets pounding on tin gave way to the sounds of soft rain.

Chapter 64

PRESIDENT WHITFIELD SAT IN SILENCE staring at the remote telecast as if he were in a trance. A glass of tea was brought to him and his DOD placed it in his hand; he was startled by the coldness.

"Maggie, get President Ruiz on the phone, would you, please?"

She gave the president a smile and a "Right away, sir,' response. A moment later, she returned.

"The president of Mexico, sir," Maggie said.

"Mr. President," POTUS began. "The entire event was transmitted to us here in Washington. It was a horrific display of how two neighboring countries, working jointly and with a common cause, can facilitate the demise of an unwanted insect. The world, Mr. President, is better off today knowing our war on the cartel is over. Drugs will no longer be a part of our society and the children of the world will be better for it."

There was laughter heard at the other end of the phone-line as POTUS' pontificating was translated. The president of Mexico took a moment to contain himself.

"Mr. President, do you *really* think this is over? I agreed to allow you and your army to come into my country and assist us rooting out this cartel—to arrest them. I did not tell you that burning one of my cities to the ground was an acceptable solution. We have four civilians dead and 10 injured. What do I tell their families, Mr. President?" The Mexican president continued, "I expect to see the commanding officer in my office in two days to give himself up to our authorities."

Silence fell over the Situation Room in the White House basement—then the president spoke.

"President Ruiz, let me clarify a couple of issues for you. This was our war—yours and mine. It is being prosecuted in both countries—every day. Last year, Phoenix, Arizona, held the dubious honor of being the number one kidnapping city in the western hemisphere. Southern Arizona and New Mexico hold the distinction of being the second highest concentration of drugs crossing *our* border in the world. Today, Mr. President, the war was taken to Culiacán and two cartel buildings belonging to the cartel were destroyed—the head of the organization was killed. Both of us signed the Status of Forces Agreement before all of this started, so the commanding officer *will not* be turning himself in two days from now."

"Three!"

"Three, what, Mr. President?" POTUS asked.

"Three cartel buildings were destroyed by your people with hundreds of thousands of dollars in damage to our downtown area along with three injured firemen."

"What are you talking about?" The U.S. President was not aware.

"I thought we were being honest with each other, Mr. President?" Ruiz asked.

"President Ruiz, my entire battle staff, my DOD, and the director of the NSA are all standing behind me. No one has a clue of what you speak. What and *where* was the third attack?"

"Herrera's plant in the city was set afire with a delayed bomb of some sort. It destroyed two businesses on each side. Mr. President, two firefighters were injured in your feeble attempt to eliminate the Herrera cartel. I expect that you will send a team of contractors and engineers to rebuild what you destroyed."

"President Ruiz, we scanned a fire on the satellite, but we were unaware of the site about which you speak." POTUS continued, "I will have my people establish a team of contractors and engineers to assist your people in the rebuild, but I can assure you, we had nothing to do with that fire. In fact, Mr. President, with your permission, I would like to send a team of arson investigators who will give us the origin of this fire and then help you catch the perpetrators."

"That will be fine, Mr. President. They can work closely with the Culiacán fire inspectors as well."

"Was there a fire in Culiacán as well?" President Whitfield asked.

"The mess on the highway east of the town is a small battleground strewn with dead bodies and broken airplanes. Traffic is at a standstill."

Whitfield turned to his NSA director.

"Barbara, we need to get those planes back here. Can you get me some help on this?"

She quietly nodded yes to the president's request. He turned his attention back to the Mexican president.

"We will help you in the cleanup, Mr. President," he said.

Pleasantries completed, POTUS rose from his chair and approached his assistant.

"Maggie, call the mayor's office in New York City. Ask him to have the New York fire department commissioner contact us as soon as he is able."

"First thing in the morning, Mr. President."

Margret Whitcomb, the president's private assistant, thanked him and walked out the door.

Chapter 65

NINE O'CLOCK ON THE POTOMAC was cool and a little breezy. The dog-woods hadn't been seen for months. The sky was clear as the few cumulus clouds blew north into Maryland. President Whitfield passed Maggie as his entered the Oval Office.

"The mayor is out of town," She told him before he could ask. "The deputy mayor is on her way to speak with you. I told her of your request."

Within minutes, POTUS was sitting behind the *HMS Resolute* desk that served so many presidents in the past.

"Deputy Mayor Underwood, thank you for taking my call," the president said stoically. "There's an issue we are compelled to resolve in Mexico, and Homeland Security has been thrown into it. Will you be in your office this afternoon?"

In the seconds that followed the president's question, Madeleine Underwood's mind conjured up 50 reasons why this call was being made. The face of a dead Francisco Parizzi appeared in front of her; her connection with Morales and the Herrera cartel whispered in her ear.

"...Madeleine?" POTUS asked.

"Yes, I'm sorry, Mr. President. What did you say?"

"I asked you if you were going to be in your office this afternoon."

"Yes. I will be here if you need me to be." Madeleine tried to control her breathing.

"I'm sending a couple of FBI agents from the New York City office to speak with you about mid-afternoon. Would you schedule them in."

"I'll be expecting them," she answered. "Goodbye, sir."

Director Petersen stood up and walked across the infamous rug that bore the Seal of the United States and drew closer to the presidential desk. She placed the knuckles on what was the bulkhead leading to the captain's stateroom on the *Resolute*.

"Mr. President, how deep in the weeds are you looking for us to be involved in this third fire?"

"Barbara, we are going to give this to the city of New York; a few hundred thousand dollars out of your budget and call it a day."

The NSA director acknowledged the president's decision and excused herself from his presence. As she walked out of the Oval Office, Petersen heard POTUS tell Maggie to call the New York office of the FBI.

Chapter 66

THAT AFTERNOON, TWO AGENTS FROM the New York FBI office drove up to the municipal building on Broadway and Chambers. The rows of *Government Vehicles Only* signs allowed the black Chevrolet SUVs to park close to the main entrance. Both agents wore charcoal-gray suits, button-down, white dress shirts, and rep-striped ties. As they approached the security-ladened revolving door, the duo draped their badge-holders outside the breast pocket of their jackets. The on-duty security guard asked for their I.D.s, and both opened their coats to display their M9 Beretta pistols.

One agent asked, "The deputy mayor's office, please." The guard lifted his hand and pointed three fingers to the executive bank of elevators. The agent replied, "Thanks."

The elevator stopped on the seventh floor. A large oak door, gilded in gold lettering displaying the *Office of the Deputy Mayor* stood in front of them. The molding was of Roman design and embedded with brass rosettes; the door was eight feet high.

The first agent entered and walked through the foyer to the receptionist's desk. Without showing his credentials asked, "The deputy mayor, please." The question as to who was calling, barely came out of the receptionist's mouth when Madeleine's assistant came out of her office.

"How can we assist the FBI?" she asked.

The agent responded, "The deputy mayor, please." The two moved to the anteroom to wait for the deputy mayor. One of the agents found a comfortable straight-back antique chair and was about to sit down when Madeleine walked in from her private powder room.

One of the agents noticed how dramatically stoic she was as she walked in the room with no smile, no greeting; she sat in front of the two agents peering out of the window. She only turned to face them when one the agents began to speak.

"Madam Deputy Mayor, we have an issue in Culiacán, Sinaloa. Homeland Security and the White House have asked us to visit with you concerning our investigating the goings-on in this city in Mexico." Madeleine looked straight at the agent, rarely blinking. She grabbed a tissue and patted a bead of sweat from her brow. *The ambiguity of his comments are killing me*, she thought. *Why doesn't he just come out and accuse me?* Madeleine patted her forehead again.

The mayor's assistant took the World News section of *The New York Times* from her alligator-skin briefcase and handed it to Madeleine. The deputy mayor stood and walked to the window with the news article in her hand. She did not have to search for long. Above the fold and dead center, she read the headlines. Her throat tightened as the knot in her stomach grew to a large ball. Moving to the floor-to-ceiling window, she proceeded reading the article.

On the street, Madeleine saw two policemen. One was playing with his baton as the other finished off his lunch—a hotdog from a street vendor; she licked her lips as if she was enjoying the meal along with him. She looked down to the paper and read *The New York Times* story dated September 21.

United States Brings War to Small
Mexican Town

Culiacán, Sinaloa, Mexico
United States Army Helicopters attack two major strongholds of the Herrera cartel south and east of Culiacán, Sinaloa. Eighty members of the Sinaloa cartel were

killed by U.S. Army forces from Fort Hood, Texas. Three civilians died in the willful attack. Sources tell this writer that the suspected members of the cartel were hiding in two separate warehouses, each housing over 500 processed bricks of heroin. A third fire was started in an area just east of downtown.

The Mexican government is concerned about the long-standing friendship with the United States, and some fear, this will cause undue strain on U.S./Mexican relationships. President Ruiz is in constant communication with President Whitfield. To date, the United States Army has not removed its forces from this peaceful country.

The deputy mayor fell against a nearby chair.

Mother fuck, she thought. The assistant ran to the wall bar and grabbed a container of water.

"Madam Deputy Mayor," one agent jumped to his feet, "are you alright?"

Madeleine regained her composure.

"Were there any Americans killed?"

"Ma'am?" one agent asked.

The other agent joined in, "Why would you ask such a question, Madam Deputy Mayor?"

"I'm always concerned about American citizens in another county," she responded while taking a sip of water and wiping the excess drips from the side of her mouth.

"In fact, there were two, but we don't know who they were as yet," one agent responded.

The second one chimed in, "Madam Deputy Mayor, this is obviously upsetting; we can visit later."

The two stood and without saying another word and moved quickly out the door. One of the agents turned and smiled.

"Madam Deputy Mayor, we should meet again. We *do* have an issue to discuss."

Madeleine, obviously shaken, moved from the guest chair to her thickly padded, high-backed, leather chair that waited for her.

"Yes, yes we will meet again." She turned to her assistant.

"Give me a moment," she said.

"Certainly."

As she watched her boss sit down behind her desk, the assistant reached in and closed the deputy mayor's door.

Madeleine took a deep reconciling breath and leaned down to her purse underneath her desk. She pulled the cellphone from the external pocket and pushed the "5" button.

"Yes?" the voice answered.

Another breath, "He's in Culiacán—in Mexico."

A quick tap on the "end" key, and she splayed her legs in front of her, draped her arms over both armrests, and stared at the nineteenth century, five-bladed fan that gently spun above her.

One more settling deep breath of air, and she flipped her feet underneath her knees and stood. A short stroll to her wall bar—three rocks, two fingers of Chivas Regal, and a splash of water. She sat back at her desk, placed the cellphone on her desktop, and waited for the phone call.

Chapter 67

THE PELLETS OF RAIN POUNDED ON Consigliere Davino's hospital room before dawn. By 9:00 in the morning, it had turned to a torrential rain. Lights flickered in the hallway and buzzers were going off throughout the hospital. Monitors would go black, then boot up again. Davino's heartbeat and vitals were steady and showed his oxygenation levels at 92 percent. His breathing was steady but shallow. The constant and steady blips on the monitor displayed a good, solid heart function.

Davino sensed the rain as it fell against his window, and his mind continued to drift. The explosive muzzle fire appeared in front of him. The chattering of the Gatling guns pounding and piercing through solid walls came in view of his mind's eye. Davino's head rolled back against the pillow as he felt waves of helicopter blades thrashing in the night air. Each pellet of rain was a cacophony of bullets smashing against the window.

Drifting further into total retreat, he heard in his head a muffled yell coming from the corner of the building—it was Herrera.

He was calling me... The boisterous din of a thousand helicopter blades beating outside; men frantically running around him; the muffled yell—again. It oscillated amidst the noise outside—*It called for me to come. In the dark, amongst the screaming and the crying, I felt disoriented—my mind would not; could not distinguish the direction from where Herrera was yelling Through the darkness, a hand reached out and grabbed me—I was being dragged out of the fray. For a moment, I sensed a silence...*

"RUN!" I heard, "RUN FASTER." My legs refused to work. The walls ahead of me reflected the bright flash behind me; now another blast; another flash. Then fire and more screaming. Walls caved in; the roof collapsed—fire, smoke and immense heat permeated what was left of the warehouse.

"I was locked in the bathroom. I remember now."

Davino pushed off his right elbow to change positions. His burned flesh, exacerbated by the movement, experienced a palpitating sensation. He wanted to scratch—his brain told him to scratch, but his body would not allow it. Each attempt moved a part of his skin that aggravated an open wound.

The rain continued to strike the window at a fierce pace. He fought to keep his swollen eye-lids open. The window shook from the hurricane-like wind and water pounding against it. The wind brushed the rain back and forth like a metronome, and it almost hypnotized him. The itching bothered him less. Color returned in his chest and crept up beyond his neck. His breathing became shallow. His heart went into a tachycardia—the arrhythmia was too much for his broken body. He dropped his head deep into the cheap hospital pillow—a clear expulsion of air left his lungs. It was his last.

Chapter 68

THE BLACK GOVERNMENT SUV WAITED just outside the deputy mayor's office for its two FBI occupants. Robert Assiani was a nine-year veteran who recently transferred from the San Diego office. He spent four years in the Army, two of which were spent on a short tour in Kuwait. He entered the University of Texas at El Paso at 22 years old and graduated at 25. Three years at Southern Methodist University Law School, and Quantico was the next stop.

Donald Miller graduated from Miami University and was a seven-year veteran of the FBI—they had never worked together until today.

Robert sat behind the wheel for a moment and then looked at his new partner.

"What'd you sense up there with the deputy mayor?"

"I wouldn't commit to anything, but she was certainly on edge by our presence," Miller answered.

"I'll call it in." Robert looked to his left and entered traffic. Talking to their supervisor, Assiani summarized the conversation with the deputy mayor. Donnie asked for the phone.

"Look," Donnie said, "we went there to engage the city's head fire inspector—a simple task. We walked to her office, and everything went south from there. I don't like hearing about dead Americans either, but that woman was visibly upset."

Robert quickly pulled the car to the curb and threw it in park.

"We need to go back," he said.

"And ask her what?" Donnie asked.

"I don't know, but I'm thinking about it," Robert responded.

Robert gazed out the window for a moment. "Maybe, she knew someone down there."

"Who? A cop, a fireman, a member of the cartel? Somebody in the army?" Donnie said, "What's *your* theory?"

"I don't have one just yet, but I don't want to table this either." Robert pushed the "1" key while placing his cellphone to his ear.

"Boss, we need a meeting. We are a block away from Municipal Park. Can you meet us at the south entrance?"

"What's going on? I sent you on a simple mission to talk to the mayor and ask him a sim—"

"Boss," Assiani interrupted, "a half-hour. We do not want to leave the area. Meet us in a half-hour—south entrance."

The phone went dead.

Even from a block away, it was like watching roaches scurrying for doughnuts as the two looked at the people climbing that massive set of steps that greeted you when you entered Municipal One and its giant, revolving, glass entrance. Some leaned against the large concrete lions that guarded the main portal smoking or reading *The New York Times*.

Assiani watched the people. Donnie Miller looked at his watch—22 minutes since they called their boss. A government-issued, black Chevrolet SUV pulled up to the south entrance to the park. He was right across the street. Robert Assiani moved his vehicle quickly across six lanes of bi-directional traffic and stopped in front of two of New York's finest; they recognized the Capital Building on the license plate and waved.

The New York Agent in Charge of the FBI sat on a bench facing Municipal One.

"Boss, we've got a story to tell you," Donnie Miller, walking up to him, started first.

And as the two agents finished the story, Miller added, "We want to pursue this."

"You don't have anything," the Agent in Charge said, "except a hysterical woman—what else is new?" He continued, "Here's your problem: one, you can't search her financial records—yet; two—you cannot bring her in and question her about those responses you experienced.

"But you *can* watch her discreetly—and I *mean* discreetly. I'll give you the authority do to that."

He stood and walked to his Chevrolet, then stopped and turned.

"Be careful, boys—don't screw this up."

Assiani and Miller sat on the bench and gave each other a low voltage high-five.

It was getting near 5:00; closing time for city government. The surveilling duo parked beneath the building, two rows from the deputy mayor's assigned parking space by the elevator. It was empty. Madeleine Underwood didn't own a car, so the city provided her with a limousine service to bring her to and from work. They waited.

Six-thirty came and went; no limo; no deputy mayor; no food. The visual to the elevator doors was a clean view. By 8:00, the underground lighting went to 25 percent. At 8:15, the glass door entrance to the bank of elevators was pushed open by two women. They wore no smiles and were dead serious as they proceeded to their rental car. Still no Madeleine.

As the two drove up the ramp, Miller took notice of their license plate and put the piece of paper in his shirt pocket.

"Enough for the night. I'm hungry, and tomorrow's another day."

Robert started the SUV and proceeded to the exit ramp.

Robert's alarm clock almost vibrated its way off his nightstand at 6:30 the next morning. He did not like that soothing music bullshit to wake him. When he wanted to get up, he wanted to be damn-well told to get up. The screeching buzzer was the only way.

His morning piss took an excruciatingly long time, and while he stood relieving himself, he kept thinking about the "whys" as to the mayor response; nothing he knew or read about this woman would warrant that kind of attitude. He ate a quick breakfast, all the while wondering what was in her head. He put on his charcoal gray suit, white button-down dress shirt, and rep-striped tie—the FBI uniform. Donnie was waiting for him in front of his apartment door. He and Robert both carried Beretta M9s, and his specially styled jacket hid it well.

"We've been cleared to rent a civilian car," Donnie said. "We can dress that way as well, if you wish."

"We'll see. Right now, back to the parking lot—hopefully before she gets there," Robert responded. An egg and cheese biscuit for Donnie, and it was back to the visitor's section for more waiting.

The underground parking lot was dark and had a dank smell to it. Something like the boy's high school locker room. Only two of the six lights were on, and it was difficult to see much of anything, let alone recognizing anyone of interest. The visitor section filled up quickly with people with city business.

At 8:15, a gray Lexus pulled up to the elevator entrance, and the deputy mayor slid out of the back seat. She waved to the driver and walked through the glass doors. She stood there for a moment, contemplating something. She didn't respond to the constant opening of the elevator doors and people going into work. Donnie thought it curious that she was walking around and not going up her office. By 10:00, the comings and goings calmed down, and the deputy mayor remained, now pacing with anger.

"Hey, Robert!" Donnie poked him in his side as two women approached the glass door. The lack of lighting made it difficult to see, but Donnie blurred out: "Those two women—aren't those two the ones we saw last night?"

Robert stared for a moment, "Maybe."

"They're standing next to the deputy mayor, but I don't see any interaction." Donnie sat up and tried to change to binoculars. "Hell, man, I don't even know who the other two are and if there is a connection in the first place."

The three moved to the elevator door. The light was better, and now the agents could see that one was Mexican. All three were dressed for the city, but Donnie could see by her stride and demeanor, her upbringing was more of a low-income status. The three stood in front of the elevator bank and waited. The door behind them opened and—

"Holy shit!" Robert jumped up in his seat. "The deputy mayor and those two."

The elevator started to close, and Madeleine swung her arm to stop it. She looked into the parking lot and got back inside. The door closed in front of her, and the three were now in the building. The agents sat there and did not move.

The day was going to drag on, and the heat started to get to Donnie *and* Robert—but not too long. Less than an hour, all three women exited the elevator, and within minutes the gray Lexus arrived as the mayor and the woman entered the back of the car and drove off.

"We'll follow these three." Robert said. They started the car and began the surveillance; following, but not too close. He held a $10 bill in hand, hopefully, for a speedy transaction when they hit tunnel. The exit demanded only a right-hand turn.

Good, no cross traffic.

The Lexus sped southward on Broadway, heading for the FDR. They were steady at 45 miles per hour, but zig-zagged around traffic to make every light. The end of Manhattan was two blocks away. She would turn north on the FDR.

Robert was used to handling a Humvee, so keeping up was not difficult. Spooking her was not a problem; she was too busy "racing the

Baja" to notice. A yellow light appeared at the intersection of Broadway and FDR. She ran it; it caught Robert.

"Crap!"

The chase was over. Wherever Madeleine was going, it would have to be picked up again—in the morning.

"Let's run over to the Sunglass Store on Grand, we're going to change our look," Donnie said.

The next morning, Donnie picked up Robert again. Robert came down the stairs with a one-day growth on his face, a t-shirt and a light jacket to hide his piece. Donnie did not look much different, but a baseball cap pulled down covered his new sunglasses, and he'd arrived in a 1981 Trans-Am.

"Cool, Donnie, where'd you get the ride?"

"My next-door neighbor's boy," Donnie said, trying to look like a teenager. "Here, throw these on your face."

The wrap-around Maui Jim's fit Robert's head perfectly. He smiled as he slid into the bucket seat of the 1972 muscle car; the T-top had been removed. The extremely black Trans-Am with the iconic firebird on the hood was the perfect hiding place for these two 40-year-old agents.

Donnie slammed the pedal to the floor, and the 455 high output engine did everything except leaving them sitting on the street. Street residue and dust spewed upward from the rear as Donnie tried to calm the fish-tailing effect. Robert's knuckles were white holding on as he looked over at him.

"We going back to the Muni One?" Donnie yelled through the open cabin.

Donnie slipped the hurst, synchromesh, seven-speed shifter into second gear and popped the clutch again as the two rear tires left city dust and rubber on Delancy Street, then on to flowing traffic. Robert couldn't help it. He had to say it:

"You're having *way* too much fun."

Donnie laughed and slowed down.

They arrived at Municipal Park just before 8:00, crossed over in front of southbound cars, and down the ramp to park the Trans-Am in their regular parking spot. At 8:30, the deputy mayor's limo stopped at the glass door entrance. Within minutes, she disappeared and was on the seventh floor. Another day of waiting...

Underground parking filled up quickly as New York began the day. By 9:00, cars were cruising the parking lot in the hopes of finding a place to lite. It was a long and boring wait for the clock to strike 5:00. The agents were whipped from doing nothing.

The night security guard's shift had ended, and he was walking through the parking lot on the way home. Donnie saw him approach the second row behind them and decided he was not in the mood to explain anything. He started the engine, and the pipes threw out a thunderous noise that reverberated off the concrete walls. The security looked and kept walking.

Robert's cellphone rang. The New York City division chief was on the other end.

"Robert, we sent out an 'Active Bulletin' and we got a hit from Dallas AIC Hayes. Culberson Petrochemical has I.R.S. issues, and he's been seen with your friend, the deputy mayor, on several occasions. There is an active investigation out of the Phoenix office. AIC Dan Rondell and Hayes are the only two that have responded. The lead is an Agent Jonathan Conroy, assisted by two Border Patrol agents—a Messer and Medellin—all are in Mexico in the town of Culiacán in Sinaloa. Sound familiar? Looks like you two fell into some slick shit without knowing it."

"What's her role in this, boss?" Donnie yelled out.

"That's the shit part of the slick, boys. We don't know, but drop what you're doin' and be in the office in the morning with bags packed. You're going to Mexico. See you in the morning."

The division chief abruptly hung up the phone.

Chapter 69

Robert and Donnie sat in the two visitor's chairs in their boss' office when he arrived at 7:30 in the morning. Both were in their FBI uniforms and clean-shaven.

The division director was in his long-weekend fishing shorts and a t-shirt that had *War and Peace* printed across the front.

The director's instructions were to the point.

"Your team consists of three FBI agents, two Border Patrol, one DEA, and two Apache attack companies from Fort Hood. I am sending a forensic fire inspector with you. He is *not* an agent, so take care of him. I'll be out of pocket for the weekend, but call if you need me. Be careful!"

Later that day, a Lear 35 with international registration landed at Culiacán International Airport. Robert and Donnie were greeted by Jonathan, the agent in charge of the operation. They casually moved to one of the two waiting SUVs. Franco and Jerry slid out of the second car to introduce themselves.

"We brought spook stuff," Donnie said. "Where's the rest of the crew?"

Local ground crew moved about chocking the airplane and retrieving the luggage.

"They're about," Jonathan responded flippantly, in case of any eavesdroppers. The luggage loaded up, the pilot moved into the airport for lunch. The two black SUVs headed northeast to their destination. Bachigualato Federal International Airport was just under 10 miles from the city of Culiacán. The two vehicles moved swiftly down the highway to their destination. The sky turned dark; clouds formed in the east, but it did not subdue the heat. They entered the city with a few lights from the local discotheques.

"I don't think Madeleine is going to be out running around," Robert spurted out. "Why not have dinner and call it a night?"

Franco immediately turned to Robert and told him about conversations regarding a Madeleine Underwood.

"The same," Robert responded. "It still doesn't prove anything yet."

"Where are we?" asked Jonathan as he noticed the sign, *Boulevard Enrique Sanchez Alonso*.

"There," he blurted out, "El Palamar del Rio—that'll work." The restaurant was not crowded, and the people on the patio seemed to being enjoying themselves. The five stayed for over an hour, paid their bill, and left.

The morning came early for the two border patrol agents. The rest of the group rose a little later—around 9:30 and too late for breakfast. Robert handed out photos of Madeleine and the only shot of her Mexican companions—poor lighting and an unclear image.

They left the hotel in five separate directions, looking for Madeleine and her companions. The day passed slowly and the sun got hotter.

"Have you seen this woman?" Jonathan asked a street vendor.

"Have you seen this woman?" Franco asked a bartender.

"No, sé, señor."

The five were getting nowhere. The sun was casting a massive shadow over the town and into the Culiacán desert.

The night the nightlife and colorful bulbs hung from all the shops. You heard the cacophony of music escaping each bar along the avenue. People were milling around shops and bars. The smell of jalapeño juice permeated the air along with a slight residual of cannabis extract.

"Looks like a pretty decent place, guys," Miller said. "I think it's time for a few beers."

The four followed the FBI Agent into the number one bar in the city. The República de Culiacán Restaurant and Bar was fancy and dark. Thin beaded streams of light fired above and hit directly on one of every six or seven tables. You could barely see anything until your eyes got use to the partial darkness.

Franco made his way to the bar, and after a while, finally broke through the crowd and asked the bartender for five beers. Fifteen minutes to find his group, and the five federal agents finally had time to relax and recuperate from the day.

After Jonathan finished his first beer, he and Robert decided to mosey around the club. An hour or so later, they returned with little to report.

One of the waitresses mentioned a tall, blond, classy American woman was in the bar three days ago, but she had not seen her since. Before she left, she had some conversation with another patron who came in here often.

"He is not here tonight," she said, "but usually comes in twice a week."

Last night—she thought—and probably this coming Friday night.

"That's two days, guys," Robert screamed over the incessant loud Tejano music.

The five slept in and woke up around 10:30 in the morning. Putting on street clothes, they hit local tamales vendor working on the boulevard for an early lunch. The sun showed high noon; they split up again and started asking questions about Madeleine. Two days passed with some yeses, some maybes, but mostly no's. It was exhausting business; more Mexican food, more nightclubs; more of nothing.

Jonathan commented, "I'm thinking we may be barking up the wronge tree. We don't even know if she's here."

Some agreed. Donnie suggested they continue to look for her.

The fourth day was more of the same; walking the downtown area asking questions.

A Zapatero, Miller thought, *women love shoes, why not?*

He casually walked over and into the shop. He looked around for a bit 'til the shop was void of shoppers.

"Señorita, escúse me! Have you seen this woman?"

The girl looked at the picture and immediately responded with a nod. Then, "Si! She was here yesterday. She bought these beautiful lambskin, custom-made dress shoes. They were orde…"

Miller thanked her while cutting off.

"Did she leave any kind of an address?"

"No," she said, but she had a little dog with her and wanted to know where she could get the dog bathed and brushed." The young girl pointed to a pet salon four stores down the street. "She thanked me and quickly left the store with her puppy"

"When will her shoes be ready, señorita?" Donnie Miller asked. After the clerk answered, he thanked her again and ran out the store.

The cellphone worked; minimally, at best.

His signal was weak as he said, "We got her, boys. I'll meet you at the fountain at the square right now and explain everything."

Miller called the remaining three and the message was the same.

Together at the fountain, with tourists throwing pennies into the fountain for luck, the agents mulled around, waiting for the last one. Robert arrived, and the strategy session began.

"Okay, she purchased custom-made shoes two days ago from that shoe store and took her dog to be groomed at that pet salon," he said, pointing, "yesterday." Miller was excited.

Jonathan chimed in, "We don't know if the dog is ready. Donnie, stay and watch the salon, but I'm thinking those shoes are for something special, and I think Friday night at the República is going to be a good bet."

Donnie Miller reported to the team after the pet salon closed that Madeleine had not shown up.

"No problem," Jonathan said. "We'll wait for Friday night and look for her then. I'm betting we're going to have good night."

Chapter 70

THURSDAY, 0945. THE FIVE AGENTS ALMOST woke up together thinking this was going to be a day of rest and relaxation. Jonathan, with a bit of a hangover, suggested a trip down to Dulique a Primavera Lake, a little fun in the sun and come back to Culiacán the following day. The 22-minute drive lasted over an hour due to a farmer driving his tractor on the south highway.

The hot summer day invited many patrons to the resort. The checked-in was no problems and mimosas were waiting in each of their rooms. The array of soft billowing clouds allowed spears of piercing light to pass through and a soft breeze from the mountains made the afternoon bearable.

The small sailboat kept Jonathan's interest as it meandered around the lake, sometimes coming too close to the shoreline. The guys rested on the man-made beach, drinking piña coladas. The wind changed, and the sailboat tacked and returned to sail in front of the resting agents.

That boats' getting a little too close to shore, Jonathan thought as he looked for the waiter. *That sailor is going to break that dagger board.*

"I'm going to find a concierge. You guys want anything?" Jonathan asked.

"A beer!" shouted Donnie.

Jonathan walked along the so-called beach toward the bar where the bartender stood wiping a freshly-cleaned shot glasses. From the corner of his eye, the rider on the sailboat, a tall, white-skinned blond egressed from her resting position from the boat. Jonathan did every-thing he could not to stop dead in his tracks at look at her. She was coming toward him, heading in the same direction.

No, I couldn't be this lucky.

He patted the pocket in his bathing suit as if he were looking for something, turned around, and headed back to the large beach towel.

"Donnie, look past me 'bout 30 feet. Is that who I think it is?"

Donnie squinted, then rubbed his eyes and squinted again. Donnie cocked his head slightly at Jonathan.

"Yes, that' s her, that's Madeleine Underwood."

"Okay! I've got it. I'll be back, Oh, yeah, give me your cigarettes."

"You don't smoke," Donnie said. The other agents lifted their heads.

"What's going on?" Robert asked.

Donnie answered, "He found the mayor."

"No shit," Franco grunted.

"She's here?" said another.

They sat up except Robert and Donnie, who buried their heads back in the towel.

There was a small space next to the deputy mayor at the bar, so Jonathan took it. After two or three minutes, Jonathan turned his and said, "Hello."

"Hello back," she responded.

"I couldn't help but notice your sailing prowess." She immediately burst with laughter, "Have you been sailing long?" Jonathan asked.

In her up-state New York accent, she replied, "No, that was my first time. Why do you ask?"

"The way you handled the daggerboard."

"What's that?" she asked.

"Well, it's board that penetrates the hull to mainta…never mind. My name is Jonathan, what's yours?"

"Madeleine. Are you a sailor, Jonathan?"

"No, just an employee of a garment factory down here on vacation."

"Where are you from?" she asked.

"Arizona. Look! Please do not think me forward, but would have dinner with me tonight?" Jonathan asked noninvasively.

"No! I can't," she answered quickly. "I have to be in Culiacán tonight. Maybe we'll see each other again sometime?"

You can bet on it, he thought.

"Enjoy your Pina Coláda and take care," Jonathan said as he got up and walked away.

Madeleine looked at him as he walked back to the towel and four friends—he never looked back.

Franco and Jerry jumped up.

"What happened, Jonathan?"

"Well, guys, we've met," he answered. "She's going back to Culiacán tonight, and *we* are going to follow her. So get ready to check out after she does."

Robert and Donnie entered the hotel through the beachside back door and scooted up to their rooms. Jonathan went back to the bar and sat where he had a good view of people checking out. He was there for two hours and was startled by a feminine whisper in his ear, saying, "Come to Culiacán."

He leaped to his feet and spun around as his chair rocked backed on its two hind legs There she was; tall, blond with that beautiful ivory skin. *Just gorgeous.*

"What?" he asked.

She repeated the offer, "Come to Culiacán. Tomorrow night. There is a party for some important people—República a Culiacán. Bring a suit, *and* your friends.

"Uh! Sure," Jonathan was startled; not only by her surprise appearance, but also by her glowing beauty. Her hips swayed as she walked to the check-out desk.

Somehow, he could not help but notice. Jonathan walked back to his crew, trying to imitate her movements; he was not as good as she was. Not even close.

"Guys, we've caught the marlin of the year. A party tomorrow tonight—maybe *the* party. Miss Deputy Mayor has invited all of us—that is, except you two." Robert and Donnie just cocked their heads and smiled. "However," Jonathan continued, "get a car and settle in outside of the club. We'll have our micro-radios, so if you see anything strange, let us know. So, we need to get a move-on and make plans. The three of us will need suits. I'll meet you guys in the lobby in an hour."

Within two hours, the crew was headed back up north.

Chapter 71

BRIGHT LIGHTS AND LOUD TEJANO MUSIC continued to fill the Culiacán sky. There were thousands of people walking the street. You couldn't whisper anything to anybody; you'd had to yell if you wanted anyone to hear you.

The club was not too far from their hotel, and besides, there were no cars allowed on the streets anyway. Robert and Donnie drove almost a mile outside of town before doubling back past the burned-out industrial park in order to park in a spot viewing the front door of the club. They found a spot across the park with a view directly across the street and between two palm trees. The hot summer day transformed into a cool night with a soft northern breeze that actually felt good.

"That will 50 pesos—each," the maître d' proclaimed as the three entered the dark República a Culiacán. The crew meandered around the bar, the semi-private rooms, the dance floor, and back past the private area. They saw no one they recognized. They danced their way to the bar and were interrupted by, "Señores, beer?"

"Sure," screamed Franco. "Three, por favor," he said as he held up three fingers.

They found an empty wall and stood against it. It was now 11:37 P.M. Something needed to happen quickly.

The soft touch of a woman's lips hit Jonathan's ear. It startled him, but this time, he smiled. In a voice akin to Mae West, the words came smooth and inviting: "You boys been here a long time?"

"Just waiting for you," Johnathan answered back.

Madeleine, in between Johnathan and Franco, took both of their arms and asked, "What are *your* names?" Jerry and Franco smiled, then answered her.

"Well, come with me Johnathan, Franco, and Jerry, we have a party to go to."

They weaved in and out of fast-moving people dancing on the floor with sparkling giant ball circling above them. Across the dance floor and past the semi-private rooms, they were momentarily stopped when they found themselves in front of a private room having a very private party. The bouncer who greeted them was not too big—maybe six-foot-four and 320 pounds, but the tuxedo fit him great.

"These are my friends," she looked up at him, and he opened the giant two-piece door, and it all went quiet, except for the conversation and soft jazz playing in the background; it was quite a change.

Madeleine walked toward the main sofa to introduce the three to her friend. As they got closer, Franco stumbled and fell on his left knee writhing in pain.

"Boy, you okay?" asked Jerry

"That's...Herrera, you know the head of the cartel. I thought he was *dead*. I was his driver, remember? Holy crap."

People gathered around to help him up. Franco thanked them as he hobbled out of the room, back across the dance floor, hobbling all the way to the entrance. His party time over, he quickly found Robert and Donnie across the street. When he got to the car, he told the agents who the guest of honor was. They knew they struck gold back in New York, and now the culmination of their efforts were right across the street.

"Now what?" blurted Donnie. "Jonathan and Jerry are in there with Vincente Herrera, what the hell."

Inside, Herrera was drunk by this time and never saw Franco fall. Madeleine continued to walk to the sofa. Her demeanor was gracious as it is always.

"Señor Herrera, this is Jonathan and Jerry. I asked them to join us for this evening's festivities."

"Welcome my friends." The words could barely come out of the cartel leader's mouth. "Sit down and enjoy." It didn't take long after the first Cuba Libre when Herrera started asking questions.

"Where are you guys from? What do you do? Why would you pick Culialán to vacation?" Herrera's slurred words hardly came out.

Jerry took the lead, "I have a friend who is from Sinaloa, and my buddy here has never experienced the beauty of this country—he's from Tucson and has not a clue.

Emilio Escarda sat at the end of the sofa, an obvious bodyguard to Herrera. He was packing a rather large .357 cal pistol. *A diamondback perhaps*, Jonathan thought, but the bulge in his jacket told him this could be trouble. Jerry's broad frame reeked of former military; his massive broad shoulders, 35-inch waist, and short, tight haircut invited looks from more than just women. The girls around Herrera noticed him right away, and flirty eyes converged upon him.

Jonathan was better looking. His tall six-foot, two-inch frame drew swift attention to his Hollywood face and wavy, blackish hair. One of Herrera's whores went to sit next to him, and Madeleine moved swiftly to shoo her away.

Drinks and girls kept coming; it was 3:30 in the morning, and nothing had slowed down. Finally, almost in unison Madeleine rose from the high-backed leather chair, and Herrera jumped up from the sofa.

"Gentlemen," Herrera said with definite slur, "it is time for this lady and I to talk. If you will excuse us."

When Emilio got up, his jacket flung open. Jonathan was wrong; the bulge turned out to be a Colt Anaconda, .45 cal. The spears of light from the main ballroom helped the two federal agents watch the three walk through the club.

"We can't lose them," Jerry whispered to Jonathan as they moved cautiously through the thinning crowd. They reached a set of stairs with the friendly giant standing in front.

"Well, what do we do now?" Jonathan turning to Jerry's direction.

"We could take a couple of drinks up to them," Jerry responded.

"You think he's *that stupid?*" Jonathan asked quietly.

"Well, you got any other ideas?" Jerry questioned.

"This couldn't possibly work." Jonathan went to the bar and ordered three margaritas on a tray.

The guard's eyes were drawn to the two agents as they got closer. Both agents were weaving, pretending to be drunk as they approached the stairs.

"Madeleine called, she said to bring a few drinks for her and Señor Herrera."

The half-man, half-mountain looked at the agents, looked at the tray of margaritas, and stepped aside.

"*Holy shit*, Jerry!"

They found themselves with an opening to the top of the stairs. Careful not to spill the drinks, the two walked up the stairs listening for something at every step—only mumbling now. They continued the climb. Three steps to go, and they could see the room open up with Herrera, Emilio, Madeleine, and two others sitting at large conference table.

Oh, shit, Jerry thought as they were noticed immediately.

Emilio jumped up from his chair and ran to the two agents.

"What the fuck are you doing up here? Are you fucking crazy? Who the fuck are you?" Emilio was raving mad as approached the two standing at the entrance to the meeting.

Jonathan answered innocently, "We thought Madeleine and *Señor* Herrera would like some refreshment at their extended party. We didn't know it was a meeting."

Emilio drew his Anaconda and stuck the .45 cal barrel in Jerry's face. Jerry's former Black Ops training got the best of him, his swift right arm flew across his body with such speed, Emilio never saw it. Smashing into Emilio'a forearm, instinct told him to fire; he did. The sound was deafening, going off in those close quarters. The wall reverberated with the explosion, and it bounced off the walls in the meeting room. Jonathan dropped the tray as Jerry bent the gunman's hand backward. Jonathan grabbed his gun. Emilio screamed in pain from the broken forefinger as Jerry continued the flipping maneuver; tossing him over his shoulder and down the flight of stairs. There were 22 concrete steps. He landed on the first riser at the base of the stairwell with a broken neck, dead.

Jonathan could barely hear anything; his ears were still ringing as he tried to explain they were just bringing up some drinks. The five still had their hands cupped over their ears, when Herrera ran to the two grabbed their collars and dragged them to the base of the table and dropped them to the floor.

"Who the fuck are you!" Herrera screamed.

"You might want to get your money back on that Colt Anaconda. It's a little big to use inside," Jerry replied sarcastically. A swift kick from Herrera's size 13 Luchese boot into Jonathan's rib squelched Jerry's humor.

"Who the fuck are you, and I'm not to ask you again."

Madeleine sat quietly as the other two rose from their chairs and picked up Jonathan and placed him in Herrera's high-back chair.

"He works for garment manufacturer in Tucson," Madeleine chimed in. "Please leave him alone."

"Hey, gringo, you work for garment manufacturer in Tucson, gringo?" The grimace on Jonathan's face showed the pain; nothing came out of his mouth. The multi-colored carpet gave him something to stare at, so he stared at the carpet. He felt a hand lifting his chin, he knew this was going to hurt. He was not disappointed. Blood spewed from Jonathan's mouth; his cheekbone was black with bluish hue.

"Why are you here, gringo?" One of the two men asked. Another blow to Jonathan's face; this time into his temple. He reeled back, taking the high-back to the floor.

"Get both of these puntos out of here. Take them to the house in Carrizolejo; we'll deal with them there," Herrera jumped in.

"Stop this! Stop this, now! I won't put up with this shit," Madeleine shouted. The three men looked at her with immediate disdain. "I move a lot of your shit for you; millions of it, and I'm not going to allow you to do this—not to two Americans. So put away those guns and stop acting like stupid people."

Herrera acted quickly.

"Stupid people? Is that how you fucking whites think of us? You fucking bitch. I made you and that fuck-head Culberson rich, and you call me stupid?"

It was like they forgot who was in the room with them. One was yelling at the other and no one realized, or cared, that they were in an open room over a bar with a dead man at the base of the stairwell. Jerry and Jonathan kept their mouths shut and just listened to the confessions. Jonathan's face was all bruised and bleeding, his lip was swollen, and his left eye was half shut. Onlookers formed at the top of the stairs. Some shouted names, like "Herrera" and "Jesus Montaña," "Mr. Mayor." Someone downstairs called the Federales and five Mexican cops were on their way.

"Son-of-a-bitch, I'm going to kill you mother fuckers," Herrera screamed at the two agents. "We need to get the hell out of here, now—before we're fighting the Federales.

There were five windows on the second floor, the mayor ran through all of escape possibilities. The mayor turned to his secretary and told him stand by the bar downstairs and then said,

"Señor Herrera, we have stairs at this window."

Madeleine helped Jonathan took his feet, and Herrera grabbed Jerry; the four headed for the window for an immediate escape.

"I'll take the thin one," Herrera said. "He'll be easier to handle."

Jonathan was smarter than that and laid quietly and forced them to drag him to the window. He was lighter than Jerry, but wasn't easier to pull. Jonathan twisted and turned to make it tougher to pull across the room. The Federales just entered the building, and Madeleine grabbed Jerry to pulled him down the stairs. It all went unnoticed when the Mexican investigators approached the base of the stairwell. They had no idea who was in the room above the club and what possibly confronted them.

Thrown in the back of his yellow Escalade, Herrera's gun on them, Madeleine drove off into the darkness down the dirt road backstreet from the club. Robert saw the four as they drove off heading east.

The yellow SUV was not hard to follow, and so it began. They drove for 37 miles into the night without a word. More than just a few lights appeared in the black horizon. She picked out a couple of headlights parked on the side of the road. As the lights grew larger and brighter, Herrera told Madeleine to flick the lights three times.

The fluorescent lights of the República a Culiacán brightened the dancefloor and the set of stairs going to the second-floor meeting room. Every light in the private party rooms were turned on and music stopped. The inspector went to at the bottom of the stairs to view the body lying there. His head was splayed backward; his eyes wide open and dead—the .357 magnum by his side. The federal officer mentioned how lucky it was that no one had stolen such a big and valuable weapon. At the top of the stairs, two men stood waiting for the Mexican police to arrive. José Ramirez was the first to extend his hand to the chief investigator with an extreme apology for having the gun of the mayor's bodyguard accidently discharge in such a crowded area.

"He mis-stepped on the stairway while confronting drunk patron wanting an autograph—a horrible accident," he said.

"Sorry, Mr. Mayor." The cop replied, "May I speak with the patron?"

"Absolutely," the mayor's assistant responded. "I'll go downstairs and bring him up."

"No need, I'll send someone down," the investigator replied, pointing to one of his officers.

"I told him to stay at the near side of the bar."

"Thank you, Mr. Ramirez," the chief inspector responded. It didn't take long before the autograph seeker reappeared upstairs, escorted by a policeman frightened and obviously shaken by the gunshot experience.

"What happened?" the investigator asked.

"It was my fault. I am very sorry. I thought I could get the mayor's autograph. I am very sorry."

"Yes, yes," responded the investigator, "Were you here all night?"

"Yes," was his answer.

"Where you sitting and who were you with?" The inspector wrote every answer in his notebook.

"I can show you," he replied.

As they walked to the stairwell, the investigator stopped in his tracks.

"Please provide me with list of the people you partied with?"

"Okay," the man answered, looking at the dead bodyguard. "So, you were saying, you came up the stairs to get an autograph. Go on, continue," prompted the inspector.

"I saw the mayor when I reached the top of the stairs, Emi...the man with the gun approached me and asked me my business. I stated my reason, and he got mad, and I felt like he was trying to push me down the stairs. Yeah...that's right. He tried to push me down the stairs. Then he pulled this pistol and aimed it at me. I...I moved his arm to the side and it went off—the gun, I mean, and he fell. I...I mean he fell down the stairs. I am very sorry."

The investigator listened and placed his hand on his shoulder.

"Son, it was an accident. As soon as your story is confirmed, we will be able to shut it down. Please, have that list on my desk in the morning—before noontime would be good."

"What?" the young man looked at the inspector with eyes widened.

"The list, son, the list. Have it on my desk tomorrow—before noon," the investigator repeated as he walked down the stairs to examine the body again. The back of his head presented a soft cast of blue and when the investigator turned his body over, the back of his neck displayed black and blue marks down the first five cervical vertebrae. It did not appear the deceased had fallen down the stairs; it appeared he was in the air most of the time. He looked up the narrow stairwell and at the 175-pound patron stood staring at the policeman from the top of the stairs.

"Tomorrow morning," the investigator said looking up to the top of the stairs.

It was not a big house. The structure looked like tilt wall with stucco finish and some that laid on the ground. There were two windows of equidistance on every wall. The lights were turned on as the four entered the house, and both agents processed the room as soon they arrived. Inside the main room of the house, there were half-empty bottles of tequila and Wild Turkey sitting atop three very heavy wood tables—*Maybe, six inches thick*, Jerry thought. Dried tamales were left on the tables with four or five baskets of old fruit. The smell of liquor permeated the entire main room. Madeleine was familiar with the smell, the liquor, and the room—she'd been here many times and dealt with this slug in this house before.

"You've done it this time, Herrera," Madeleine said, yelling at their host. "These are stupid civilians. They are Americans and probably have families! What are we going to do with these two guys?"

Jerry rose from seated position. His new, light gray suit was a mess, torn at the left sleeve and ripped at the right knee.

"Look, I don't who they are, and I don't..." Herrera interrupted her.

Jonathan quit his unconscious act, stood up, and walked to Jerry. They both took a deep breath.

Jonathan hobbled over to the cartel leader:

"You are both under arrest. This man's name is Jerry Messer, United States Border Patrol, and I'm Jonathan Conroy, Federal Bureau of Investigation."

Herrera leaped to his feet. The remnant of second-degree burns turned red—his rage maddening.

"Goddamn you, Madeleine. This is who you bring into my house? I'm going to kill all of you!"

Herrera pulled his Colt 1911 from his belt. He drew thew slide back pointed it at Jonathan.

"Put the gun down!" the voice from just outside the window was familiar and welcome. Another figure stood at the front door.

"Agent Assiani," Jerry said. "Let me introduce you to the head of the Sinaloa Cartel, Señor Vincente Herrera; and I guess you know the deputy mayor of New York City?"

Jonathan brushed himself off.

"How many guns did you bring?" Jerry asked.

"We didn't bring any for you. What we have is what we got," Franco responded, showing his face to Herrera. Herrera's face white as a sheet as he scolded Franco for being a traitor. He pointed his Colt at Franco, but Donnie fired his Beretta, and the cartel leader caught the 9mm bullet on his left side. The sound of an expelled firearm was an invitation for the other cartel thugs to rush the house.

"We are in deep shit. We're right in the middle cartel country with five pistols between us!" Jonathan exclaimed. "There were no reserves. We were all here; the five of us, with maybe enough ammunition not to get us all killed."

The three agents jumped through the windows and surrounded the wooden tables. They knocked them over to facilitate some semblance of a protective barrier. Not two minutes passed, before the first voice came from an outside window.

"You have one minute to come out with your hands empty of your guns."

A bleak streak of gold appeared on the Eastern horizon; dawn would show its face soon. Herrera saw the shadows of his men approaching the house. He tried to rise from his present position. Jerry went for his gun the same way he retrieved Emilio's. The 1911 was now in Jerry's hand, and the butt of the pistol came down heavy on Herrera's head, knocking him out. Four of his thugs now showed their faces in four windows. Jonathan grabbed the liquor bottles and with torn clothing made as many Molotov cocktails as he could make with what he had.

Madeleine crawled to a corner to be safe. The Mexican showed his face at the window—Jerry fired and the Mexican fell.

The line in the sand had been drawn. The five were in a mess with 10 to 15 members of the Herrera cartel with no place no go; with one possible caveat—they *did* have Herrera, and they *did* have Madeleine. The outside walls were covered with cartel members, and the inside; the inside had six bottles of liquor, a seemingly bulletproof wooden table, and 60 rounds of ammunition. While Madeleine remained in the corner, the table barricades sufficed in protecting the agents from out-side harm.

A shot came from another window, and Madeleine screamed as a piece of the fireplace flew in front of her. The bottle of tequila lay next to Jerry. He looked at the bottle of tequila and ripped a piece of his shirt and twisting the fabric, plunged it into the bottle, and set a fire. The flames took quickly to the cotton; Jerry picked a target and threw the bottle of tequila. It broke against the head of one of the attackers, splitting his head open and spilling flammable booze on his clothing. Before he could extinguish it, the fire engulfed the man's shirt. He screamed as it covered his body in flames.

The other agents looked at Jerry and went to grab bottles of their own. Jonathan found a bottle of Wild Turkey, and amidst bullets flying everywhere, he managed to fling the bottle toward another group. They started to back off, the entrance impenetrable, but only for a mo-ment. Behind the barricade, Jonathan saw another room. *Another room, more bottles of booze,* a good thought, and crawling on his stomach, he got to the room only find cases of tequila. He grabbed one case and scrambled back to the main room.

The sun had cleared the horizon and sent blades of piercing light through the windows. The firing went on without recess and the armed agents were running low on ammo. The kept firing their pistols until it was over.

"Here," Jonathan yelled out, handing a bottle to Franco and tossing one to Donnie. "Tear some cloth and make more Molotov cocktails."

One of the cartel entered through the window, and before Donnie could light his bottle, the guy was upon him, so Donnie blocked him by throwing the bottle at him. It broke against the guy, and he stopped—he just stopped—he couldn't move; he wouldn't move.. The firing stopped and all looked at him—waiting—waiting for something—waiting for what?

Herrera woke, saw his man, and tried again to jump to his feet screaming, "Help him!"

"Help him?" Jonathan yelled. "Help him do what?"

Franco grabbed a bottle and thew it at another cartel members. Everyone scattered. The sun brought much wanted light into the room with every eye on the drenched man just standing quietly. Suddenly, smoke emanated from man's body; the heat was immeasurable on human skin.

He screamed, "Help me!"

His arm burst into flames; his hair and his head. Soon, the screams stopped as a burned skeleton lay on the floor. Still behind the barricades, Jonathan tossed the bottles to the other agents. Still, their eyes rested upon the lone thug. Little blotches of phosphorous painted the floor. The man was burned to a crisp in less than three minutes.

"What the hell?" Donnie yelled.

They all screamed for their cohort in crime. They began firing indiscriminately; bullets were flying everywhere. The heavy tables splayed in front of them were full of bullet holes, none of which penetrated the dense wood. The agents threw bottles everywhere a thug showed his face. Bottles of the phosphorous cocktail broke on every attacker. People were screaming, ripping off their clothes, throwing down their weapons and running helter-skelter.

Running from the cocktail that already soaked their clothing was futile. The faster they ran to escape the infernal menace, the quicker the water evaporated. The cold inimical eyes of Vincente Herrera lay steadfast on the dead bodies that were strewn in and of his house. Jonathan crawled over to Madeleine; he grabbed her and threw her out of the nearest window. Robert caught a view of Herrera through the fire and turned to pull the trigger. Herrera managed enough strength to grab a fallen AK-47 and fire it at nearest person. It caught Robert in the neck just as he fired his 9mm. He struck Herrera again on the left side just above his third rib. He went down as did the agent. Franco kept firing and was mindful of his ammo inventory—it was not good. Three, maybe four bullets left.

The call came from local resident to the volunteer fire station. Two volunteer trucks were on the way as a crowd gathered after the fracas but disbursed quickly. The local police drove their 1980 Pontiacs through the main part of town. It was the fire chief who removed the remaining four from the fire and immediately had someone attend to Robert's wound. Herrera kept screaming hysterically to the policeman: Where was his money!

You could hardly understand him as he lay there marred from second degree burns and two gunshot wounds.

"What was that?' Robert asked.

Franco chimed in, "That, my friend, was phosphoric dihydrate, or more commonly said, white phosphorous. I'll tell you about it on the way back to New York." He nodded to Donnie, then to Madeleine, "Why don't you do the honors?"

"Madeleine Underwood, you are under arrest and you have the right the right to remain silent, anything you say will be held against you in a court of law. If you cannot afford an attorney, one will be appointed for you. You are free to hire your own attorney. Do you understand these right as I have said them to you?"

Donnie then broke from the group to look for Herrera. His men were dead or gone and so was he. He asked the closest policeman, "Where's Herrera?"

The officer just shook his head; he had no idea.

Robert went to the hospital in an ambulance, and the four remaining agents hopped into a yellow Chevrolet SUV and headed back to Culiacán along with the deputy mayor of New York City in handcuffs.

The interview room at the Culiacán Police Station was conscripted with little permission from the constabularies. Jonathan introduced himself to local desk sergeant and told him they needed a room—that was it. The deputy mayor sat across from Jonathan and his team. He asked her about her tenure as one of the leaders of the largest city in the U.S., and that was just for starters. She spoke about her growing-up years in Herkimer in upstate New York and about her father and how hard he worked building his data processing company. Her demeanor radically changed when she was asked how her father would feel about her being arrested. She started to cry.

"His whole life," she said, "he concentrated on building; constantly building. He rarely had time for me or my mother." She continued, "I met Antonio Morales while vacationing in Mexico three years ago and, by some strange coincidence, met David Culberson six weeks later." He was in bed with Morales, and he mentioned he found this Mexican fella to help them steal $50 million of street value heroin. His plan was foolproof; some kind of bomb or something…" she said.

Jonathan confirmed her statement, "Yeah, just like you saw this morning."

She nodded.

"It was horrible, I never could imagine anything like that. Who would do such a thing?"

Franco jumped in, "How did you plan on getting $50 million in street value to New York?" Her demeanor hardened and became stoic. Franco moved closer to her and bent over, looking at Madeleine a foot away from her face; she smiled at him—nothing.

Franco asked again, only this time with codifying information.

"Miss Underwood, David Culberson was meeting with you in Dallas this coming Sunday morning, how did you plan to get $50 million of heroin to him, so that he could load up his Gulfstream and deliver the stuff to you?"

She stared at Franco.

He knows about Jack; he knows about Morales, he must have an inkling of this was going to work… She blinked a couple of times.

"I don't know, I really don't know."

Franco drew away and Jonathan took his place. He asked, "How well did you know Jack Culberson and how much did you trust him to complete his part?" She dropped her eyes in contemplation. Jonathan backed off and asked her "Madeleine, what's the matter?"

She responded, "I never met him, and I never trusted him to get all of the product to Dallas." The deputy mayor stopped for a moment, then continued, "He could never put 250 bricks of heroin on that plane of his."

At this time, Donnie stepped into the fray.

"Where's the $8 million?"

Madeleine flopped back in her chair, releasing a lung full of air. She looked directly at Jonathan and said, "I have it."

The agents looked at her as she answered.

Finally Donnie asked,

"Well, Madeleine…?"

"Well, what? You do not expect me to tell you. Seriously, do you?"

"Where did you get it, and yes, *seriously*, we want to know where you have it hidden," Jonathan said, looking into her eyes.

Madeleine stood tall in her chair now.

"That's mob…"

"Mob money," Jonathan finished the sentence and placed his bruised face directly in front of hers. "I don't give a shit, Madeleine, you *will* give us that money; the mob can suck it. I don't care. But you, my dear, will spend the next 30 years in federal prison, got it?"

Franco, with a slight punch in Donnie and Jerry's sides, excused themselves for a moment. Down the hall and in another room, they closed the door, Franco began, "The money is not in New York, and I'm sure it's not in Dallas. She was in a meeting with Herrera and the local mayor, so it has to be here, and there are only two places."

Donnie quickly answered, "Her hotel room."

There was silence for a brief moment and then Jerry blurted out just as Franco pointed his finger at Jerry, "The plane!"

They went back into the interview room. Franco leaned into Jonathan's ear.

"We know where it is, and we're going after it."

They stepped out of the room and asked one of the sergeants where they could replenish their ammo. The policeman pointed them down the hall to the weapons room and said, "The officer there will help you."

The mob's Learjet sat in the number two hanger at Bachigualado Federal Airport north of Culiacán. It was nine miles from the police station. Still in the rental car, the three agents headed for the airport.

"You know these guys are not going to give up $8 million dollars, don't you?"

Donnie and Jerry looked at Franco after he asked the question. It was a genuine concern as to how this was going to go down.

"What's the plan to have these goons turn over the eight million?" Jerry asked.

Fifteen minutes into the trip, they arrived at the airport and proceeded to the private hangers. Hanger Two lay dead ahead. Mechanics from the base operator hovered over a Continental engine on which they were working. The engines from the Lear were off, but the lights and air conditioner were working from the internal battery. Franco turned off the headlights and rolled up to the plane. The three got out of the car, but only Donnie went to the door of the Learjet. By design, Learjets do not have an abundance of headroom, so swift movement is restrictive at best. Donnie knocked on the door and waited for it to open.

A muffled voice was heard from inside; Donnie repeated the knock and again the muffled voice was questioning the uninvited visit. Finally, the door dropped revealing the steps leading into the aircraft. A big guy, hunched over, stood at the doorway.

"Can I help you," he asked.

Donnie pulled his badge as the others came to a stop next to him.

"We're federal agents from the United States, and we need to come aboard."

Surprised, the guy stuttered a bit; not knowing what to say, he muttered the first thing that came to mind, "You got a warrant?"

Franco could hardly contain himself.

"We're in Mexico, you dumb ass, we don't need a warrant, so step back."

The three boarded the plane with their I.D.s in one hand and their Beretta M9s in the other. One guy got up from the plush seat, bent over, and went for his gun. Donnie rushed over to him yelling, "Don't even think about it, motherfucker—sit down!"

Jerry looked about the plane. He meandered to the front, and inside the "garment bag" section sat a large paisley suitcase. He rolled it out into the aisle. The big guy stepped forward, "You can't have that. That's…"

"We know what 'that' is, and that's why we're taking it off your hands," Franco said.

Donnie stepped in, "You can stay here until we get back, and we'll help you guys the best we can, or you can go back to New York without $8 million and explain it to the mob; the choice is yours. So, if we get back and the plane is gone, we'll understand."

They left the plane, and Franco looked at Donnie.

"Well, that was easy."

They arrived back at the police station in a little better than 11 minutes from the airport. The three agents rolled the paisley suitcase into the interview room and stood it in front of Madeleine; she slid down in her chair and started crying all over again. Moments later, she took a deep breath.

"Morales stole this money by robbing the Mazatlán/Cauliacán train. As far I know…"

Jonathan stopped her and handed her a tablet of paper, "Start over, Madeleine."

She did.

As far I know…

Five pages later, handwritten and signed, almost on cue, the Mexican investigator walked into the murder room. He asked three officers if a young man came in and left a list of names and addresses on his desk. No one knew; no one answered. He described the man; no one saw the young man.

The investigator spoke in a loud voice addressing the entire station.

"You know; about the shots at The República last night!"

No one said anything. Disgusted, he barged into the room that held Deputy Mayor Madeleine Underwood.

"Who are *you*, Madam?" the inspector asked. His eyes immediately caught the presence of four other individuals, "and who the hell are you and what are you doing in my police station?" he asked with little patience.

Jonathan moved forward to introduce himself.

"Yes. Well, I am Jonathan Conroy with the Federal Bureau of Investigation, and I'll let my colleagues introduce themselves, but before they do that, this is Ms. Madeleine Underwood, Deputy Mayor of New York, and she's been arrested for felonious drug trafficking, felonious drug possession, the RICO Act, consorting with Vincente Herrera, and obstruction of justice. We were all the Republicá a Culiacán last and witnessed a meeting with Herrera, Ms. Underwood, the Mayor of Culiacán, his assistant, and his secretary. One made the mistake of attacking my big friend over there and was immediately dispatched the base of a long narrow stairwell."

He drew a breath. "Now, would you like to introduce yourself?"

As the investigator responded, he then took a deep breath.

"Do you think, Agent Conroy, you have…uh, wrapped up this case? I fear not." The investigator continued, "There are more strings out there. Ms. Underwood," the Mexican investigator said, looking at Madeleine, "were you conspiring with the Mayor of Culiacán to export drugs to the United States?"

She nodded. The policeman walked to the door and asked someone to come in to witness the interview with the deputy mayor. He turned and asked Donnie and Jonathan to join him while he arrested the mayor of his city.

They arrived at the square in minutes and parked in front of the city municipal building. The three walked up the stairs and moved quickly down the hall. The door was marked clearly "The Mayor," and the three walked in. Two members of the city council were meeting with him. The plans they were discussing were the expansion of the west side of the city.

"How can I help you?" the mayor asked.

"Stand up, you son-of-a-bitch! You know these guys, Mayor? Huh? You son-of-a-bitch." The Mexican investigator grabbed both his arms and turned him to the wall. The handcuffs were securely placed on the mayor's wrists as securely as his blood flow would allow. With some shortness of breath, he asked, "You know who these two guys are? huh! Mr. Mayor, they're with the FBI, and I don't like them doin' my job."

The investigator was visibly aggravated.

"You lied to me, you punk-ass, and so did that creep from last night, and you're going tell me where his little punk-ass is *and* your assistant. I want his ass, too."

While the two agents introduced themselves, the Mexican investigator finally got his breath back. The two seated council members sat quietly, only staring at each other and wondering what was happening to the of the city...

They would soon find out.

As the three lawmen left the mayor's office, his assistant passed through the entry portal into Jonathan's arms. His face went stone-cold for a moment and remembered the person from the previous night. He reversed his direction only long enough for Jonathan to wrap his hands around his shoulders; slam him against the door jam, and place handcuffs on his wrists.

"That'll be two being turned over to the police," Donnie blurted as he turned his head back to the investigator.

Chapter 72

FRANCO AND JERRY ARRIVED at the Culiacán airport just before Jonathan arrived with Madeleine in tow. They walked to the hanger that housed the mob's Learjet—it was gone. Franco glanced over at Jerry; he did not have to say a word. Jerry responded to the look, "What do you think the New York family is going to do with those guys when they come back without the $8 million and no heroin?"

Franco smiled once again.

"Either we will never see them again; or they will wind up in the East River, and we'll never see them again."

Jerry smiled as they walked to the G-5. Being the first ones aboard, they were greeted with a scotch and water and a very comfortable seat. The rest of the crew showed up 20 minutes later all with the same greeting; with one exception—Madeleine. Jonathan decided to keep her handcuffed. The Culiacán Airport tower confirmed the flight plan of the U.S. pilot, and the government's G-5 moved toward the North runway. The Mexican horizon grew more expansive as the U.S. Gulfstream climbed higher into the sky. Robert rested quietly with two Navy nurses caring for him; he was in good hands. Madeleine Underwood sat in a chair normally reserved for important diplomat. She was dozing off and on. No wonder with handcuffs attached to her wrists behind her.

Franco and Jerry sat with the guys and explained all about the existence and use of white phosphorous.

"Tomorrow, we'll fly to Dallas to pick up Culberson and take him to his son."

"We will make a special trip to Nogales to do something for Arturo Gonzales—maybe take him to New York," Jonathan murmured as he lay his head back on the soft headrest. "You'll love him, and he'll love New York." Jonathan closed his eyes and fell asleep.

—◆◆◆—

The next morning, a black SUV pulled into Arturo's driveway. Arturo sat up in his chair as he gazed through the front window. For a moment, his heart and head pounded in fear from what was to come. He called to Sofia to take her mother and Carmella to the back room. Then…

There was a knock on the door. Everything, every event, every day, every emotion came rushing to the forefront of his memory. He stood and moved hesitantly to the front door. Arturo took a deep breath and opened it. Jonathan, Franco, and Dan Rondell stood smiling at him.

"Good morning, Arturo," Jonathan said. "Can we come in?" Arturo swung open the door and backed away. "We're here to pick up you and your family. You are all going to Washington, D.C., to meet the president of the United States. The FBI's plane is waiting at Nogales Airport."

Laughing, Arturo fell back into his chair. It was difficult to call to his family—he could hardly speak.